A Tyrannosaurus rex tooth made entirely of fire opal?

Opalized fossils were Raine's professional specialty—and her personal obsession.

"Let's throw a little light on this." Cade produced a penlight from an inner pocket and flicked it on.

Coruscating with green and pink flames, then glimmers of coppery gold, the tooth flamed as Cade played the light over it.

Lia held the tooth up, the gently curved fang nearly twice as long as her hand. "Would you like to buy this?"

Cade, Raine's professional rival, laughed under his breath, then glanced ironically at Raine—and held her gaze.

You against me!

Dear Reader,

June marks the end of the first full year of Silhouette Bombshell, and we're proud to tell you our lineup is strong, suspenseful and hotter than ever! As the summer takes hold, grab your gear and some Bombshell books and head out for some R & R. Let us entertain you!

Meet Captain Katherine Kane. When she uncovers a weapons cache and a dangerous criminal thought to be behind bars, this intrepid heroine gets the help she needs from an unlikely source, in beloved military-thriller author Vicki Hinze's riveting new novel in the WAR GAMES miniseries, *Double Vision*.

Don't miss the incredible finale to our popular ATHENA FORCE continuity series. A legal attaché is trapped when insurgents take over a foreign capitol building—and she'll go head to head with the canny rebel leader to rescue hostages, stop the rebel troops and avert disaster, in *Checkmate* by Doranna Durgin.

Silhouette Intimate Moments author Maggie Price brings her exciting miniseries LINE OF DUTY to Bombshell with *Trigger Effect*, in which a forensic statement analyst brings criminals down by their words alone—much to the dismay of one know-it-all homicide detective.

And you'll love author Peggy Nicholson's feisty heroine, Raine Ashaway, in *An Angel in Stone*, the first in THE BONE HUNTERS miniseries. Raine's after a priceless opal dinosaur fossil—and to get it, she'll have to outwit and outrun not just her sexy competition but a cunning killer!

Enjoy all four fabulous reads and when you're done, please send your comments to my attention, c/o Silhouette Books, 233 Broadway, Ste. 1001, New York, NY 10279.

Best wishes

Natashya Wilson
Associate Senior Editor, Silhouette Bombshell

Please address questions and book requests to:
Silhouette Reader Service
U.S.: 3010 Walden Ave., P.O. Box 1325, Buffalo, NY 14269
Canadian: P.O. Box 609, Fort Erie, Ont. L2A 5X3

PEGGY NICHOLSON

An Angel in Stone

Published by Silhouette Books

America's Publisher of Contemporary Romance

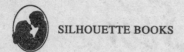 SILHOUETTE BOOKS

ISBN 0-373-51362-3

AN ANGEL IN STONE

Copyright © 2005 by Peggy Nicholson

This edition published by arrangement with Harlequin Books S.A.

® and TM are trademarks of Harlequin Books S.A., used under license.
Trademarks indicated with ® are registered in the United States Patent
and Trademark Office, the Canadian Trade Marks Office and in other
countries.

www.SilhouetteBombshell.com

Printed in U.S.A.

Books by Peggy Nicholson

Silhouette Bombshell

*An Angel in Stone #48

Harlequin Superromance

Soft Lies, Summer Light #193
Child's Play #237
The Light Fantastic #290
You Again #698
The Twenty-Third Man #740
The Scent of a Woman #770
Don't Mess with Texans #834
Her Bodyguard #874
The Baby Bargain #929
True Heart #1025
The Wildcatter #1067
Kelton's Rules #1119
More than a Cowboy #1217

Harlequin Presents

The Darling Jade #732
Run So Far #741
Dolphins for Luck #764

Mills & Boon Romance

Tender Offer #3009
Burning Dreams #3100
Checkmate #3172
Pure and Simple #3250
The Truth About George #3322

Harlequin Special Projects

My Valentine #1991
"Hartz & Flowers"

*The Bone Hunters

PEGGY NICHOLSON

grew up in Texas with plans to be an astronaut, a jockey or a wild animal collector. Instead she majored in art at Brown University in Rhode Island then restored and lived aboard a 1920s wooden sailboat for ten years. She has worked as a high school art teacher, a chef to the country's crankiest nonagenarian millionaire, a waitress in an oyster bar and a full-time author. Her interests include antique rose gardening, Korat cats, ethnic cooking, offshore sailing and—but naturally!—reading romances. She says, "The best thing about writing is that, in the midst of life's worst pratfalls and disasters, I can always say, 'Wow, what a story this'll make!'" You can write to Peggy at P.O. Box 675, Newport, RI 02840.

This one's for Jimmy, James Grimes, little brother grown big—King of the Dinos back then; King of the Road now. All the hugs in the world!

And with infinite gratitude to Paula Eykelhof, for much wisdom, forbearance as needed and many a smile.

Prologue

Police horses ought to come equipped with sirens. Galloping up West 79th Street in Manhattan, Raine found the heavy
evening traffic was slowing her down. In the taxi ahead, the
passengers turned around to gape and point at the horse and
rider. Okay, so she wasn't wearing much more than a swathe
of red silk, a red thong bikini and red wedge-heel sandals.
Next time I dress for a black-tie gala, I'll choose jodhpurs,
she promised them grimly. *Now will you for Pete's sake get
outta our way? This is an emergency!*

They were too busy staring. Now the cabbie had turned,
as well. His brake lights stuttered.

"Blasted rubberneckers!" She reined the bay onto the sidewalk and kept going.

Up ahead, an awning stretched from the raised entrance of
a swank co-op to the curb. A uniformed doorman ambled

down its crimson carpet. *"Coming through!"* Raine cried, ducking to lay her cheek alongside the bay's hot neck.

"Hey!" The doorman stumbled backward and sat down hard on the co-op steps. "What the *hell* d'you think you're—"

"Call the cops! Over on 80th Street! Need 'em *NOW!*"

"You better believe I'll call 'em, blondie! And when they catch up with *you*—"

But Raine was peering ahead to the next awning. "Look out! Coming through!"

Not exactly the way she'd envisioned this evening. Cocktails, they'd said. Then dinner, after which she'd make a short speech—that was the worst ordeal she'd figured on facing tonight. Then they'd hold the auction, and her half of the bargain would be fulfilled. To celebrate, she'd planned on taking a nice walk home from the museum by moonlight.

As they neared the intersection with Amsterdam, she slowed the horse. "Easy, sweetie." No sense wiping out, turning the corner.

Hooves clattering on concrete, they wheeled right—and bore down on a woman, who stood, peering intently into a shop window. A leash stretched from her lax hand all the way across the sidewalk to the curb, where a Scottie dog was equally absorbed in anointing a lamppost. "Drop it!" Raine called, waving the pistol she held at the leash. "Drop it *now!*"

The woman whirled, shrieked, and raised both her hands in surrender.

"What? No, I don't mean— Oh, never mind! Call the police, would you?" Holding her horse to a controlled canter, Raine swept past the packed tables of a sidewalk café. Forks froze halfway to rounding mouths.

But at last, there ahead lay the crossing of West 80th and Amsterdam. The bay shied violently as a man came staggering around the corner building. "Gun! Gun! *He's gotta gun!*"

Well, that sure wasn't firecrackers she could hear popping now, above the traffic noise. Sidestepping and snorting, the bay danced around the corner as Raine surveyed the scene.

A third of the way down the block, an SUV had been abandoned. Its back bumper was crumpled against the flank of a parked car; its passenger door swung wide.

Then beyond that—she gasped in relief. Trenton was still alive! Kneeling midstreet, the big man swayed with exhaustion, while his captor ranted and raved above him. Spinning to face the curb, the gunman took aim at the nearest parked car—or somebody sheltered behind it?

Bullets flew, smashing glass, punching through sheet metal. She couldn't see Kincade, but he must be the shooter's target. So he was still in the game, hanging tough.

"Distract him for me just a *minute* longer?" Raine prayed, as she tucked her gun into the NYPD saddlebag. No way could she hope to make a precision shot at a full-tilt gallop, and she sure didn't want to accidentally shoot Trenton.

Raine crouched over the bay's withers and tapped his ribs with her heels. "Sweetie, let's take him down."

Chapter 1

Framed by the murderous claws of the *Allosaurus,* the man stood. Looking at her.

Whoa. The hairs stirred at the nape of Raine Ashaway's neck. Here was something…different. His impeccable black dinner suit fit in with this glitzy Manhattan crowd, but his utter stillness…

"See somebody you know?" inquired Joel Whittaker. An assistant fund-raiser for the Manhattan Museum of Natural History, he'd been assigned to smooth her path through the evening's gala. It was Joel's job to see she met the right people and stroked the right egos.

"No-o. But who is that guy? He sure seems to know *me.*"

Joel scanned the drifting guests on the far side of the museum's most famous dinosaur exhibit. "Which one, that oh-so-distinguished blond to the left of that *fabulous* diamond choker?"

"No, no. Mr. Tall, Dark and Forgot-how-to-smile. See the woman with the ruby earrings? Just to her—arrr, he's turned away."

Which was just as well. They were neglecting their current prospect. Raine smothered a sigh. God, did she hate fund-raising! But the deal she'd cut with the museum had included her coming to New York to help make this event a success.

Judging by the sapphire necklace that draped Mrs. Lowell's ample bosom and matched her blue hair, the old girl could afford to bid in the benefit auction tonight. Minimum opening bid was a million dollars.

"Now Raine," said Mrs. Lowell, waving a plump little hand at the rearing dinosaur skeleton beneath which they stood. "Could a *Brontosaurus* really stand up on her hind legs like that?"

The MMNH's most spectacular exhibit featured a five-story-tall mother *Barosaurus* rearing to defend her baby from the attack of an *Allosaurus.* The tableau was heart-stoppingly dramatic. It was the first thing a museumgoer saw, after pushing through the big bronze revolving entrance doors and into the echoing rotunda. The fossil castings stood on a knee-high dais that filled the middle of a hall the size of a basketball court. Raine adored the display.

"Well," she said diplomatically, "if a circus elephant can stand on its hind legs with only a rope of a tail for balance, then why couldn't she, with a forty-foot caboose for a cantilever?" Raine was more troubled by the fact that the baby dino, huddled behind his defending dam, stood astride her massive tail. In the coming battle, mama would surely whip her tail around, and her horse-size baby would go flying.

"And who do you think won the fight?" Mrs. Lowell worried.

Knowing what she did about *Tyrannosaurus rex's* older, nimbler cousin, Raine hadn't a doubt who'd triumphed. "Hard to say. She'd outweigh him four to one. If she lands a punch…"

"And what are *you* going to name our new dino, Mrs. Lowell, if you win the bidding tonight?" Joel broke in with a twinkle as he squeezed Raine's elbow.

Mrs. Lowell chuckled. "I'll name him Erwin Elwood, of course, after my dear papa. He was the fossil hunter in our family. My sister and I collected ostrich eggs, and my brother…"

Once Joel had eased them off through the crowd, Raine muttered, "Your patrons are bidding tonight for the right to name the *specimen*—this particular dinosaur that I gave you guys. You've got to make sure there's no confusion." She nodded at her distant find, the object of tonight's auction.

In the far corner of the gallery, they'd stacked the six-foot-square wooden crates in which she'd packed the fossil bones, months ago in Patagonia, into a pleasing jumble. A giant child's fallen tower of building blocks. Out of the top box thrust the massive skull of the beast—all that the museum's preparators had had time to clean so far. He was as fearsome as his carnivorous cousin across the room, and more exotic with his horns. Couples stood below him, gazing up as they gestured earnestly with their champagne flutes.

"Somebody's buying the right to name the *museum's* example of the already named species—*Carnotaurus.* There're going to be some hurt feelings if you don't make the difference clear."

"We will, we will, Raine. Now here's someone you absolutely *have* to meet. Mr. Fish? Have you met Raine Ashaway of Ashaway All?"

"You're the little lady that collected that ol' boy there?" demanded Mr. Fish, in a West Texas drawl.

Little lady? He barely came up to her chest! And he'd made his fortune in oil, Raine remembered.

"I picture me a bone hunter tromping around Patagonia, I see some kinda Indiana Jones. I don't see a leggy blond filly," Mr. Fish assured her.

"Picture it." Raine showed her teeth as she reclaimed her

hand. "And when I meet a Texas oil tycoon, I expect a ten-gallon hat—if not a twelve."

Fish hooted as he rubbed his age-spotted dome. "My girl's been workin' on me. Alice says boots and a Stetson just don't cut it with a tux. That if I want to step out on the town with *her,* then I better look sharp."

"You name my dinosaur after Alice, and I bet she'll let you wear whatever you like, Mr. Fish."

"Might be worth a try," the oilman allowed, his shrewd eyes crinkling.

"That's the most complete *Carnotaurus* skeleton ever discovered," Raine assured him. "Once she's prepared and mounted, she'll stand two-stories high. People will come from all over the world to *ooh* and *ah* over her."

"Alice'd like that, all right."

"There's only one to compare her with," Joel chimed in. "The *T. rex* Sue, at Chicago's Field Museum. And when Sue was auctioned off at Sotheby's, she went for almost eight and a half million."

"That was to buy the entire *dino,* not the right to name it!" Raine hissed as they moved on, stopping to shake a hand here, or make a pitch there.

"True. But that was ten years ago. Think about inflation."

Raine was thinking about what time it was. Half an hour max for cocktails, they'd told her, before they went in to a sit-down dinner, served in the Hall of African Mammals. The museum was charging twenty-five thousand a table. Then, after that pricey meal and before the auction, she'd promised to rev up the crowd. A short speech on My Adventures in Patagonia, more or less. She'd give the patrons more on the genuine thrill of making a major fossil find—and less on the choking dust, the constant gales, the scorpions that kept snuggling into everybody's boots.

"Getting tired?" Joel asked.

"Hanging in there."

She assured a prince of Wall Street that his brokerage

could buy no finer marketing image for itself than a *Carno-taurus*. "That's Latin for 'meat-eating bull,'" she told him. "Your firm could style itself the top predator of the next bull market."

"Dynamite pitch, but why'd you duck his invitation to dinner?" Joel grumbled as they drifted on. "His eyes just give me the shivers. So masterful!"

"I promised my sister Jaye that I'd check out her dig this weekend. She's struck a major vein of amber in southern New Jersey, can you believe it? Besides…" If there was one thing Raine demanded in a man, it was competence in the natural world. Forget how he handled the bulls and bears of the stock exchange. She wanted a man who could deal with a water buffalo, or face down a grizzly. Her father had spoiled her for indoortypes forever.

"Well, *I'd* have dated him if he'd asked."

"Then go back and chat him up. I'm doing fine on my own."

"I…really shouldn't. I'm supposed to take care of you."

"So be a sweetheart and get me another drink. And take the looong way round, okay?"

Circling the island of battling dinos, Raine stopped for some girl talk. A fashion designer wanted to know where she'd gotten her *stunning* gown?

"Like it?" Raine smoothed her palms down the clinging sheath of red silk, with its intricate gold-thread patterns and its delicately gathered bodice. A split between the two halves of the front showed a slice of skin almost to her navel; it couldn't be worn with a brassiere. But actually it was quite modest—all promise and wild surmise.

"It's made from an antique sari. I managed a dig a few years back, in southern India. There'd been a drought there for years. We could give the men work, but I wanted to do something for the women of the village. I hired a young widow to do the camp mending, and it turned out she was a genius with a needle. I bought some silk and did a sketch and asked if she could sew me a simple dress? And she whipped up something I could have worn in Paris. So the other expedition women got envious and asked for clothes, and the next thing you knew, we realized—hey, this is a viable business."

Raine had loaned Shoba and her two sisters the money to buy three sewing machines, her initial stock of fabric and a satellite-linked laptop. She'd connected her with a sharp marketing student at Parsons School of Design back in the States, plus a wonderful Web site designer. "This is Shoba's latest design, which she'll customize, of course, to size and material. She's fast, utterly dependable and she can deliver in quantity. Here's her e-mail address."

As she drew the business card from a hidden pocket, Raine brushed the sheath of the knife strapped to her thigh. Weapons-grade plastic, so the museum's metal detector had missed it. She'd been silly to wear it, she supposed. But the moon would be full tonight and she never got enough exercise, when she came to the city. After the fund-raiser, she meant to walk back to the firm's apartment in the upper West Eighties. And if John Ashaway had taught his children anything, it was to be prepared. Always. For anything.

"Carpe diem!" was his credo. *"Seize the day. Seize the moment. Seize the opportunity. Seize the damn carp. Live by your wits or die stupid."*

Smiling with the memory, Raine came back to the present—to find her gaze snagged by the same dark watcher. He must have circled the room as she had done; now they contemplated each other from reverse sides of the battling dinosaurs. Where *had* she seen him before?

And then the memory surfaced. That time in Wyoming when she was—what—twelve? She'd skipped out on her father's dig, dreaming she'd top his discovery with one of her own. Up into the foothills she'd hiked, through a stand of trembling aspen.

The wind and the leafy commotion must have masked her steps as she rounded the bend in the trail. Hard to say who'd been more surprised, Raine or the young mountain lion coming down the path. He'd frozen with a big forepaw midair. Ye-es, that was what reminded her now. Here was that same coiled stillness—force interrupted, yet instantly available.

And the man's amber eyes were just like the cat's. Here it was again, total attention. She remembered the moment when attention had turned to *intention.* She'd been small for her age at twelve. She'd looked like lunch.

But being an Ashaway, she had pockets full of fossils. As the lion stalked closer, she'd lobbed a trilobite off his flank. He'd snarled, swerved—and kept on coming.

She'd had to sacrifice the best ammonite she'd ever found. Just as he gathered himself to spring, it struck him square on the nose. He'd shot straight up into the leaves in outraged astonishment. That gave her a moment to grab a fallen limb and charge *him,* shrieking like a banshee.

Her bluff would never have worked on a seasoned hunter. Wouldn't work on this one, something told her. She gave him a slow smile. *So here I am. What's your intention?*

He didn't respond. A hand tipped in long red nails landed on his sleeve. With their eyes locked, Raine couldn't see more of the woman. But he glanced down at those fingers, smiled wryly to himself—then turned aside.

Raine drew a breath, her first in a minute. *What was that about?*

So that...was Raine Ashaway.

Kincade supposed he'd seen photos before. The Ashaway All Web site contained expedition shots featuring various members of the family, as well as pictures of the dinosaur specimens they offered for sale. But he'd never seen this Ashaway without a wide-brimmed hat shading her vivid face. He hadn't expected a huntress, with hair like moonbeams rippling on troubled water.

"Did you hear one word I said, Cade?" Amanda whatever-her-name-was fingered his lapel, as she pouted prettily.

"Nope." Not that he'd have missed much. She'd latched on

to him as soon as he'd arrived. He'd tolerated her prattling, because she made good cover. She let him appear to be mingling, while he studied his quarry.

"You're almost…scary, when you look like that. What on earth are you thinking?" she teased.

He was thinking that vengeance might turn out to be more than a sworn duty. Taking Raine Ashaway down? That might also be a pleasure.

Chapter 2

"Raine-baby!"

Spinning, Raine found herself nose to nose with a ruby tie tack, and an expanse of white satin dinner jacket too wide to hug. "Trenton! What are *you* doing here?" She planted a kiss on his dimpled chin, which was as high as she could reach.

The sports world and his adoring fans knew him as Ten-ton Browne of the Pittsburgh Steelers. "There you are just strolling down the sidewalk—and *WHAM!* It's like a big ol' ten-ton safe falling out of the sky," a sacked quarterback had once described their first encounter.

"Hey, that dig last year? I still dream about it. Stars so big I thought they gotta be flying saucers, and finding that *Stegosaurus? What* a kick! I've been collecting ever since."

While recuperating from a knee injury, Trenton had signed up as a volunteer documentation assistant on an Ashaway dig in Montana. He'd caught the dinosaur-hunting bug, for which there was treatment, if no cure. But along with the bone-fever, he'd caught something much worse.

"I heard you were talking tonight 'bout Patagonia," he rumbled in her ear as they strolled arm in arm toward the boxed *Carnotaurus*. "But I didn't know if any of the rest of your family were..."

"Nobody else is coming tonight," she said gently. "Jaye's digging down in New Jersey, Gianna's doing prep work back at headquarters. Ash is cursing and swearing and suffering through his paleontology doctorate at Stanford. And Dana?" Dana was all he wanted to hear about. "Dana's excavating a fossil whale in Peru."

"I see." He heaved a gusty sigh. "Didn't know she was out of the country. Guess that's why she never returns my messages."

"Mmmm." That wasn't why, but it wasn't Raine's place to tell him so.

"Well." He sighed again and nodded up at the *Carnotaurus*. "That's surely something you found there, Rainy. What d'you think? If I beat out all these fat cats and win the auction tonight, then I name your dino after Dana?"

Raine shook her head. "Don't do it for that reason. The museum would love your contribution, but as for Dana..."

"Yeah... Yeah, I sorta thought not." He pulled his lilac brocade tie through the enormous fingers of one hand, then the other. "Then I guess I oughta ask you this. Nothing's worse than not knowing. Is it because I'm..." He made an oddly graceful gesture, taking in his massive black body.

"*No*. It is absolutely *not* that. You are prime husband and brother-in-law material—and considering your feather touch with a pickax? Dad would clasp you to his bosom, believe me." Why couldn't he have fallen for gentle Gianna? Another year or two and surely she'd be over Jack's death. Ready to love again.

But Dana? It would be disloyal to tell him that Dana kept a tray of ice cubes, where other people stashed their hearts. "Dana doesn't get...involved. Not with anyone." From the day they'd found her at roughly age five, she'd been like that. Friendly—but friendly like a stray cat who'd move on if the food ran out. It was Raine's guess that she wanted nobody irreplaceable in her life.

Raine left Trenton gazing glumly up at the *Carnotaurus,* and prowled on.

She hooked another flute of bubbly off a caterer's tray, stopped to let a woman exclaim over her opal necklace.

"That is absolutely *fabulous!* Do you mind if I ask where you got it? I own a shop down in the Village, and I'm always on the lookout for—" She paused with a look of disappointment as Raine shook her head.

"It's one of a kind, I'm afraid. I made it myself, over a period of years." She touched the rough opals, strung together into a wide ragged sunburst, with bits of beach glass woven in for contrast. "Every time I find a new stone, I find someplace to fit it in." Since precious and semiprecious stones were often uncovered during excavations, Ashaway All sold uncut gems as well as fossils. John Ashaway had encouraged each of his children to specialize in a particular mineral. Opals were Raine's professional—and private—passion.

Circling toward the front of the gallery, Raine didn't spot any opals. Still in this crowd there were plenty of other gems to admire. She saw a pair of tourmaline earrings she'd have to describe to Ash; that was his stone. Pearls galore, though Ashaway All didn't deal in pearls. A man's signet ring with a square-cut emerald that'd be the envy of a rajah.

"Raine, there you are!"

With an inward groan and an outer smile, she turned as Alden Eames, curator of vertebrate paleontology, caught her arm.

"Sorry to neglect you, darling, but I had to smooth some ruffled feathers. The security guard running the metal detector is an ass. Can you believe he was refusing entry to a cousin of the Kennedys? Some sort of steel plate in his leg from a skiing accident, I understand. But if these morons can't distinguish between an honored guest and a mugger wandered in from the Park, then *I* say…"

He said it at length while Raine struggled not to yawn. To think that when she was seventeen Eames had bruised, if not broken, her heart! She'd met the rising young curator that summer when Ashaway All had shared a salvage dig with the Manhattan Museum of Natural History. They'd been granted three months to rescue as many bones as they could from a mass grave of hadrosaurs, discovered during construction of a dam in Venezuela. When the waters rose, the site would be submerged forever. During those months of fevered camaraderie, Raine had fallen hard for the bronzed and pith-helmeted young Ivy Leaguer. Though he was twelve years her senior, she'd taken him for her first lover.

With a teenager's rosy optimism, she'd pictured them together forever, sharing bones, bliss and world-shaking scientific discoveries. But her dreams had shattered at expedition's end, when she'd learned that—all the while—Eames had been engaged to a rich young socialite. His fiancée had stayed back in the States to plan their September wedding.

Still Raine had limped away from the experience with some valuable lessons. She'd learned to withhold her trust till a man had earned it. Learned also that polished charm was often the mask of selfishness, not a caring heart.

She startled now as Eames brushed a finger along her bare shoulder. "God, Raine. Have I told you yet that you're twice as lovely as you were at seventeen? To think that we—"

"Let's *not,* thank you. Let's think about Ethiopia. I'll be taking my usual crew, but I'll scout for a site first, just me and a guide. Do you have any local connections you'd recommend?"

Raine hated to give up her *Carnotaurus,* but she was on the track of even bigger game. A richer prize.

The MMNH held a licence to dig in Ethiopia, but with the wars of the past decade, hadn't dared exercise that right. But now there'd been another truce in the fighting, and Raine was ready to gamble this one would hold.

Apparently Eames was not.

So they'd traded, exchanging Raine's sure thing—her neatly boxed *Carnotaurus,* perfect for a fund-raiser—for the museum's wild card: the right to dig, with no guarantee that there'd be bones for the finding.

But, oh, if there were! Four years ago the shoulder blade of a gigantic new dinosaur had been unearthed in the Sudan, in the same geological stratum that was exposed in the gorge of the Blue Nile. Raine meant to be the first one in the world to bring home an entire specimen of *Paralititan.*

Given the right international auction, Ashaway All could sell a complete fossil skeleton for an easy five-million-dollar profit. Aside from the scientific notoriety, which was valuable in itself, the company could use a cash windfall. They'd taken some unexpected hits this past year. Lost three long-standing licenses to dig out West, that they never should have lost. Been outbid with several of their independent finders for specimens that once would have been theirs without question. Then Jaye had mounted an expensive amber-collecting expedition to Haiti that had come home empty-handed, when cholera broke out in the region. Add all those losses on to the breathtaking medical expenses of her father's accident, and his attempts to recover... With an absent frown, Raine glanced beyond *Eames's* shoulder—and blinked.

There he was yet again—Amber Eyes. Still keeping his distance. Still unsmiling. And still...attentive. *So what do you want?* If he was flirting, he'd get nowhere with her without showing some humor and warmth.

And if he wasn't? Standing there like a tiger, peering through the bushes? Then—

"Miss Ashaway? Miss Raine Ashaway?"

One of the caterer's tuxedoed staff loomed before her. He swung a silver tray of drinks under her nose.

"No, thanks. I'm all set." She showed him her flute, still filled with icy bubbles.

"No, no, no, no. It is this! I was told to give you—"

She cocked her head as he pressed the small white envelope into her hand. An Indian accent, with its iambic inflection and hints of Britannia? "But who gave you this to—?"

He bowed, nodded emphatically and darted off through the crowd.

"What's that about?" Eames murmured at her ear.

With a mystified shrug, Raine looked from the envelope— to her watcher across the room. *From you?*

His dark head dipped an inch in the barest of nods, the salute of a fencer at the first kiss of steel. He smiled at last—a white slash of teeth in a sun-darkened face—and turned away.

You, Raine concluded, ripping into the envelope.

On a square of folded paper, his message was penned in bold block letters.

> I have a fossil of great rarity and interest for sale. If this beguiles you, then meet me in the middle of the Brooklyn Bridge at midnight.

So. This was business instead of pleasure. Or, at least, before pleasure, Raine told herself. But why the weird rendezvous? Why not discuss it now?

On the other hand, the museum was Eames's home court, and she certainly didn't need the curator drooling over her shoulder, while she tried to cut a deal. A fossil of great interest was, by definition, a bone of contention. Careers as well as fortunes rose and fell with paleontology's great discoveries.

Consider me beguiled. She looked up to send that silent reply, but Amber Eyes was speaking to the same Indian with the tray. Something passed between their hands—a tip for the man's trouble, no doubt.

"You would be Mr. Ken…Cade?" the waiter asked with a nervous gulp.

"Kincade. Who wants to know?"

"I was told to give you…this." He thrust a small white rectangle into Kincade's hand, then retreated through the crush.

Odd. Kincade inspected both front and back of the envelope, but there wasn't a mark on it. Who knew he'd be here tonight? There'd been a guest list published in the museum's newsletter, he supposed, and possibly in the *Times,* but—

"Who's that from?" Amanda wondered at his elbow.

"That's a lovely nose, sweetheart." Likely the best that money could buy. "But as for sticking it in my business?" Cade dropped the unread note in his pocket as he took her by the arm. "Let's find you another drink." And somebody else to play with. He'd blown his cover back there anyway; Raine had noticed his interest.

But then, she must be used to men staring.

Even so, maybe it was time to take it up a notch. He hadn't meant to meet her tonight, but he had a sudden urge to learn if her voice matched the rest of her. He'd ditch Amanda, and then—

Raine chanced to be looking up at the *Allosaurus,* when its head exploded.

Chapter 3

The shot ricocheted off the stone wall with a vicious whine. A woman screamed, then stunned silence spread in widening ripples.

"Ladies and gentleman, touch a cell phone and you're dead! I mean *you*, sir!" The gun cracked again. A man yelled and clutched at his shoulder. His phone clattered on the marble terrazzo.

"*Hands on your head. Everybody! Now!*"

By the metal detector, the guard lay in a boneless heap. In a beautifully tailored suit, the shooter stood before him. A Halloween mask concealed his face—ex–President Clinton, with a rubbery *aw, shucks* grin that didn't match his commands.

He'd come in as a guest with the mask in his pocket, Raine assumed, then used either a knife or a Taser to secure the guard's gun. Clinton blocked the main—eastern—entrance, the revolving doors that gave onto Central Park West.

Balancing her champagne flute on her head with both

hands, she swung casually to the south. There was an exit in the center of each wall of this rectangular gallery.

But for this event each had been closed with its own set of pocket doors. These were cast bronze fit for a cathedral, each half of which had to weigh tons. Nothing to be hastily dived through at the best of times, and with a rubber-faced "Jimmy Carter" holding a pistol at the south exit, well, forget that line of retreat.

Jimmy had taken out a second security guard. This one was conscious, wriggling futilely against the nylon ties that cuffed his hands behind his back.

"All of you, move! Thataway, move! Take your hands off your head and you die. *Move* it!"

Amazing how quickly a self-satisfied crowd could be reduced to a docile herd. With shaky whispers, they shuffled in the direction their captors indicated with waving guns, till a smirking "George Bush" shunted them away from the northern doors.

At last everyone converged, trapped against an inner corner of the room.

A glass of perfectly good champagne on her head, and her mouth had gone dry as a stone. *Relax,* Raine warned herself. *Focus.* Danger either numbed the senses—or it sharpened them.

So…two Democrats, one Republican. She counted three gunmen in all. Bush stood fairly close to her left; Carter far off on the right. Clinton was clearly the boss. He stepped up onto the central dais and strode across it till he stopped by the baby *Barosaurus.* His roving gaze cowed the last terrified whispers to silence.

Could this be her watcher? If he had golden eyes, the mask's exaggerated brow ridge shadowed their color. Raine studied the man's shoulders. They didn't seem quite as deliciously wide as she remembered. But how else to account for that aura of leashed danger she'd sensed, each time she'd met Amber Eyes's gaze? At some instinctive level she'd known the man was a predator.

"Keep your hands on your head and kneel," Clinton rasped. "*You* there." He aimed his gun to Raine's right—at Trenton. The linebacker towered over Mrs. Lowell, who looked as if she'd erupt any second. "Help the old bag down. Yeah, like that—now hands *up!* Move it, folks. A little cooperation and we'll be out of here in no time. Just sit tight till the taxman gets to you, then give him everything you've got—your wallet, your jewels, your phone. And meanwhile, *shut up over there!*"

A hysterical sobbing was instantly hushed.

Jerk. Bully. Raine studied the distance from herself to the dais. Her knife was balanced for throwing, but Clinton stood beyond her outer limit of accuracy. Besides, kneeling on the hem of her ankle-length gown, she couldn't reach her weapon discreetly. *Make a note for Shoba. Next dress needs a side zipper for instant access.*

But as for now… Could she really let these creeps take her opals? The necklace wasn't worth a tenth of Mrs. Lowell's sapphires, but Raine's mother had helped her dig up its first stone when she was eight. It was one of the last things her mother had ever touched on this earth. *How can I give it up?*

Her eyes ranged over the crowd. *Who else feels the same?* Trenton? But no, the big man dropped his ruby tie tack in the bag he'd been handed, while Jimmy Carter covered him with his gun. Next he helped Mrs. Lowell unhook her necklace. Trenton might be deadly on the five-yard line, but he played games; he didn't play for keeps.

Eames? The curator's shoulders were hunched high around his ears. His elbows trembled like a fledgling's bony wings. No help there.

A woman somewhere behind Raine pleaded that she couldn't get it off! She *couldn't!* A squeal of pain and Bush's coarse chuckle ended the dispute.

"If you can't remove your rings, ladies and gentlemen, that's no problem," soothed the man on the dais. "Jimmy Carter has the bolt cutters, if you need assistance."

Joke, Raine told herself desperately. Maybe.

All right, if she couldn't reach her knife, what did she have? John Ashaway had taught all his children self defense. Then when Trey had joined the firm, he'd honed their combat skills to an ex-SEAL's satisfaction. *Think.* What would Trey do? The envelope she still gripped between two fingers was too small to roll into a weapon. She wore high wedge sandals, easy to run in, but without stilletto heels.

To her right came a muffled groan. Raine turned in time to see a blood-soaked man wobble, sag—his eyes rolled back in his head. His neighbor cursed and caught him—lowered him gently to the floor, to lie in a spreading, dark puddle.

The wounded one was the man who'd tried to phone for help, and his Samaritan— "Oh!" Raine cried aloud. Amber Eyes! So he wasn't one of these brutes—wasn't Clinton. *Sorry!* she apologized mentally.

He glared past her at the man on the dais. "This guy's bleeding to death. Better let me take him out to the—"

"Shut up!" Clinton took aim on his forehead. "Hands *back on your head!*"

"Look, you don't want him dead, either. At least let me—"

Clinton swung—blew the head off the baby *Barosaurus*—then turned his gun back on Amber Eyes. "Want the same? Keep talking."

O-kay, that was the last straw. Though the *Barosaurus* was a casting whose head could be replaced, Raine doubted that Clinton knew it. For all this thug knew, he'd just smashed an irreplaceable fossil. A creature that had survived a hundred and forty million years to whisper its tale of mystery and awe: *Behold! Dragons once walked this earth!*

Any eight-year-old dinosaur expert could appreciate what a fabulous thing we've got here! But as for you, you know-nothing, money-grubbing Visigoth? That's it. You and your sadistic buddies are going down.

And if she had an ally in the room, it was Amber Eyes.

Trading glare for glare with the gunman, he knelt, blood-stained hands clasped on his head. The muscles in his craggy jaw jumped as he gritted his teeth. Even at a distance Raine could see his eyes darkening, like the lion's as it readies to spring.

But wait for me. Jimmy Carter would reach Amber Eyes in another minute, and Bush was just now collecting Eames's gold Rolex with an appreciative chuckle. *Wait!* Raine turned to beam her message.

And somehow Amber Eyes felt her gaze. As their eyes connected, his brows twitched. His scowl eased to a rueful grimace—he shaped her a kiss.

Got it! She ran the tip of her tongue along her upper lip, saw his grin start to flash—she turned to find George Bush looming above her.

"Hey, sweetcakes! Nice necklace." His masked eyes oozed over her. "Nice…*everything.* Wanna hop in my sack?"

"Best weapon you've got is you're a woman. They'll always underestimate you," Trey whispered down the years. *"Use what you've got."*

And *"carpe diem!"* added her father. *"Seize the day, the instant, seize the carp."*

Gut him.

Raine's wineglass wobbled in her trembling hands—tipped. Champagne splashed over the opals; it poured down the front of her dress.

"OH!" she cried, in a stricken baby-doll voice. She wiped frantically at the drenched silk. "Oh, would you just *look* at—!" Her hand froze. She'd brushed the center slit aside. Her right breast thrust impudently through the gap, its nipple taut with adrenaline, flesh moistly glistening.

"Oh, *baby!*" chortled George, lurching closer. He stuffed his jewel bag under the elbow of his gun hand, to free up the other.

"Wuh oh!" she said in a ditzy half whisper. Tipping her head back, Raine shook her hair out on her bare shoulders.

She rounded her lips to a carnal *"oh"*, then circled them with her tongue. "You wouldn't. You couldn't…" She heaved a shuddering breath, almost a shimmy. "D-don't you *dare*—"

In a graceful half swoon, she collapsed backward to the floor. The hand holding her flute hit the marble above her head. Glass tinkled as its fragile bowl shattered. "Don't—" she whimpered *"—touch…me."* She swung her legs to one side, then down, so she lay helplessly at full length, open and inviting. "Oh, *don't!*"

Tell a man what to do and he'll do the opposite every time. With a crude guffaw, Bush dropped to one knee beside her.

"Leave her alone!" shouted someone. It sounded like Amber Eyes.

"You put your filthy lips on me and I…I *swear* I'll just die!" Raine drawled, southern belle in distress. *Come on, George, lift your mask.*

"Oh-ho, sugarbabe!" At her subliminal dare, his reaching fingers paused—then swerved to peel the rubber up and hook it above his big nose. Leaving only his greedy eyes masked.

"Picture every move before you make it," whispered Trey at the back of her mind.

"Bush, get your ass back to business!" yelled Clinton from the dais.

"I'll give *you* the biz, cupcake!" George swore, reaching for her with a blissful grin.

He had flaring hairy nostrils, and—thank God—he'd worn a tie. Raine half sat to meet him. "Ohhhh," she moaned, her skin crawling as he palmed her breast.

Her left fingers hooked over his tie to pull their bodies closer, while with her right—she slipped the broken stem of her wineglass up his left nostril. An inch.

Then a second inch, gently. Deftly.

"Awgggh!" George gurgled. He'd gone stiff as a board. Behind his mask, his eyes showed a frantic ring of watering white.

"Now that I've got your attention?" crooned Raine against

his cheek. "Make another sound, and I'll shove this halfway through your tiny brain."

"Get off her, you asshole!" Clinton yelled. "Save it for later!" From his vantage point, he was witnessing an assault, not a counterattack. Like most of his sex, he assumed a man on top was a man in control.

"For *shame!*" scolded a nearby woman.

"Somebody *stop* him!' cried another.

Here came the hard part. "Now *ni-ice and eaaasy,* George, give me the gun," Raine purred. Crunching her stomach muscles to stay in a half sit, she let go his tie. To discourage any bright ideas—she twiddled her glass spear, a quarter turn.

He let out a piggy squeal.

"Shhhh… Hush. Don't move." Her left hand walked up his right wrist. "Good. We don't want me to slip, *do* we? No…there…thank you, I've got it."

Pity she wasn't a better shot, left-handed. *Go for the trunk,* she reminded herself as she aimed under George's arm and squeezed the trigger.

Clinton yelled, clapped a hand to his thigh—and stumbled backward over the baby *Barosaurus.* Bones crackled and flew. A gun barked across the room. A hundred people surged to their feet and stampeded screaming for the exits.

"G'night, George." Raine tapped the gun across his skull, precisely where Trey had taught her. Sweet dreams, minimal damage, he'd promised, and Raine could testify at least to the first half. She barely had time to withdraw her glass dagger as George collapsed with a weary moan.

"Offa me, loser!" As she wriggled out from under, she looked for Clinton. His gun, had he dropped it? But people were crawling across the dais, falling over each other and scrambling to their feet; she couldn't spot him. Somebody blundered into a hind leg of the mama *Barosaurus* and Raine cringed, arms wrapped around her skull. If five stories of fossil came tumbling down!

The dino creaked overhead. Its forty-foot neck swayed

perilously—then held. Raine's heart settled back into her chest as she turned. *Clinton, Clinton, come on!* Surely somebody had nabbed him?

There was old Mrs. Lowell—walking, mind you, toward the exit, her back stiff with outrage. And there, Joel was all right; he stood astride the wounded man, protecting him from a trampling, yelling for a doctor. And—

Ah! The relief she felt made her hum in surprise. Amber Eyes rose lithely from a crouch; he'd been hog-tying Jimmy. Using both their ties, apparently. And why *was* it that a sexy man always became instantly twice as sexy when he stripped off his tie? Plus now his dark hair was irresistibly tousled. And that fiery *okay, who's next?* glint in his eyes as he scanned the room. And the way he held Jimmy's gun with a casual readiness along his thigh as he turned… Add up the whole package and you got just, *"Rrrrowrrr,"* Raine growled happily to herself—as their eyes connected.

With a slow sinful smile, he gave her a thumb's-up. Then his gaze dropped—his grin widened. He stroked a forefinger down his chest.

What did he—? She glanced down. Oh! The blood boiling to her face, Raine rearranged her bodice. She looked up again with a laughing shrug. *Hey, it worked, didn't it?*

"Rainy!" called a voice with aching urgency.

Chapter 4

Raine whirled—to see that someone had opened the western doors. Framed in the gap, a couple staggered. That was Trenton in the lead, and behind him, jabbing him in the kidney with a gun—

"Oh, *rats!*" If only she'd aimed higher! Clinton's pantleg clung wetly to his skin. His right shoe had tracked a trail of bloody prints across the hall. *"Stop or I'll—!"*

He glanced back with a rubbery grin. "Sure, bitch, go ahead! You get two for one!" Shoving Trenton around the corner, he limped into the darkness.

"*Bas*tard!" she swore, stalking after him. From this angle her bullets would punch right through him and into his hostage.

Weaving around couples too stunned to run, stepping over a downed body, Raine reached the doorway—then yelped as an arm hooked around her waist. It yanked her back against muscled resilience, a delectable fragrance of bay rum and overheated male. She jabbed an elbow into a stomach soft as a chunk of granite. "Le'go, dammit, that's a friend of mine!"

"Not so fast, Ashaway. You spoiled Clinton's party. The man may hold a grudge." Amber Eyes released her and sank to a crouch. He reached for an elegant red Prada pump that some woman had lost, held it around the corner—a shot sang out of the dark. He stood and showed her the sole, neatly drilled. "And he can shoot. Any idea where they're headed?"

"The terrace!" she guessed. "Twenty yards to the right down this corridor, then he'll turn left."

"Give him a minute to limp to the corner. And then?"

"About eighty yards down another hallway, they'll come to the northwest entrance." Then out across a raised terrace, down some steps to the level of the park that surrounded the museum—and then whoever knew? Could a getaway car be waiting at the rear of the building?

"You winged him good. If we don't push him, he might just bleed himself stupid and sleepy. Lie down for a nap."

"Or he might keep moving, then shoot Trenton out of spite! Or keep him for a consolation prize." The linebacker earned millions every year. If Clinton held him for ransom… "No way I'm risking that." Raine gathered her gown up to midthigh and knotted the silk to keep it there.

"Umm…no?" Amber Eyes looked up from her legs. "Then give them thirty seconds more." He switched his gun to his left hand and held out his right. "Meanwhile, it's Kincade. Or Cade if you like things simple."

"Who doesn't?" She ducked under his arm and out, darting across the darkened hallway. If he thought owning a penis automatically put him in charge, he'd better think again. Flattened against the opposite wall, she peered toward the distant corner. "Damn, they're moving fast!" she muttered as Cade flattened himself gallantly in front of her. "And *don't* block my gun hand!"

"Wouldn't dream of it," he laughed, as they jogged shoulder to shoulder for the turn. They charged around it together— two targets halved the risk—just as a gun roared. Glass shattered somewhere ahead. "Guess the exit was locked."

At the far end of this cross corridor, the plate-glass doors burst open. By the time they reached them, Trenton and his captor were staggering across the terrace, disappearing down the first set of stairs that led to the park. Clinton was using his hostage for support; he'd yanked the tails of the line-backer's tie over his shoulders, then wrapped them around a forearm. No wonder they were making such time; Trenton moved like a runaway freight train, towing his tormentor toward an unseen goalpost.

"Dammit, he'll wreck his poor knee again!" she panted as they clattered down stairs, across a stone landing, then more stairs. Down another flight. Sirens wailed and whooped through the night; the lights in the penthouses on West 81st Street gleamed above the swaying treetops.

"Least of his worries and—hey—'bout time. Here comes the cavalry!" With a thunder of hooves across the grass, a mounted policeman came riding, circling around from the front of the museum.

"Gun!" Raine cried. " He's got a—!"

Locked on his fleeing target, the rider wasn't listening. *"Police!"* he yelled. "Halt or I'll—"

The fugitives stopped, swung obediently toward the command. Clinton raised his arm.

Blam!

As his rider yanked on the reins, the horse reared—then settled back to earth, snorting and sidestepping. With a befuddled frown, the cop slipped gradually from his saddle. Just as Raine reached him, he hit the ground.

"Put some pressure on that," Cade growled, jogging past.

"Jeez, you're bossy!" Raine glared after him, then beyond, where Trenton and the gunman were staggering out through the park's iron fence onto Columbus Avenue. Traffic screeched to a halt as they lumbered across.

"What happened? What happened? Is he all right?" Dragged by a leashed and yapping poodle, an elderly couple hurried across the park.

"Put pressure on anything that bleeds! You'll find an ambulance out front." Raine rose and walked toward the snorting horse, fingers outstretched. "Good fella, good boy. *Come* here, sweetheart."

The bay rolled his eyes and leaned back on his haunches, but he'd been trained to stand when the reins were dropped. He shook his black mane as she rubbed his neck.

"Easy, sweetie." Raine gathered the reins, glanced down at her gown. Ought to just rip some legroom, but this was Shoba's best yet, a keeper. She scrunched its hem up to her crotch, then stepped into the stirrup. "Okay, big boy, wanna collect some payback?"

They plunged through a gap in the avenue traffic, then clattered up onto the far sidewalk. Cade stood, his raised gun by his lean cheek as he peered around the corner of a coffee shop and up West 80th Street. "Where's he headed?" she called.

"Beats me! The subway stop at Broadway?"

"Okay, whatever. Just distract him."

Cade stared after her as she cantered south down the Columbus Ave. sidewalk, indignant yells marking her progress as pedestrians bolted for the doorways or gutter. "*Me*, distract him!" Cade wasn't the one wearing a red silk thong with red high heels. "And where the heck are you off to?" He shrugged, glanced west around the corner—and winced as another bullet smacked the stone just above his head. That was, what, Clinton's fifth shot? But did he have a nine-round automatic like the SIG-Sauer that Cade had taken off Jimmy—or a fifteen?

"Whatever." He dashed for the nearest parked car.

A third of the way up the one-way street, Clinton had stopped an oncoming SUV.

"Great." If he hijacked some wheels they hadn't a prayer of catching— But no; the driver took one look at the gesturing gunman and jammed it into reverse. "Good for you!" Cade sprinted up the sidewalk, then ducked down. Both curbs were lined with parked cars, providing plenty of cover.

Meanwhile, midstreet, Clinton was losing his cool. "You gas-guzzling son of a *bitch,* get back here!" he screamed, wasting a shot that blew out a headlight.

The SUV sideswiped a van—screeched and scraped along the car behind it, then crunched to a glass-tinkling halt. Its far door slammed open and the driver bolted west.

Ripping his mask off, Clinton drew down on the runner, but Ten-ton dropped to his knees—which yanked on the tails of the tie the gunman had wrapped around his forearm. He staggered; the shot struck sparks off a brownstone, half a block away.

"Son of a bitch, you want me to shoot *you?*" Clinton jammed the bore of his pistol in the player's ear. "Get *up!*"

"I've had enough, thanks," the linebacker said in a soothing baritone. "So how 'bout we all just *settle* down and take a deep breath?"

"How 'bout I blow your brains out? On your feet! *NOW!*"

Peering around the front end of a Toyota, Cade lined up his sight. Okay, he could cap Clinton from here, but should he? If the creep squeezed his trigger as he died— Better to draw the heat instead, Cade decided. He shaved a bullet past Clinton's cheek. "Drop your gun, bozo!"

A hail of bullets slammed into the Toyota. Cade retreated to the curb, then crab-walked along the car. A shot punched through its back window, then the side glass above his head. The guy packed a fifteen-round automatic as well as a temper!

"I'm doing this why?" Cade asked the stars above, then startled as a movement down the street drew his gaze. A horse, turning the far corner. Damned if Lady Godiva hadn't ridden clear around the block! And here she came, riding hell-for-leather down the middle of the road. Distract him *now!*

He popped up, bounced a shot off the pavement at Clinton's feet, then dived for the next car under withering fire. He popped up again, squeezed the trigger, and—

And—dammit all—Clinton had seen him try. So much for bluffing. Cade threw the gun at his head.

Clinton dodged it, then straightened with an ugly grin. "All out, hero? Well, ain't that a pity, 'cause I sure saved one for you!"

Sirens whooped, blue lights flashed down at the Columbus Ave. end of the block. Finally, somebody had clued in the cops.

Too late. Clinton tossed the ends of his hostage's tie aside. He took loving aim on Cade, savoring the moment—then paused. His grin faded to frustration. "I really am gonna shoot you."

"Got that. You want me to cry about it?" *Hold his gaze.* Hold him while the hoofbeats hammered louder and louder, or was that Cade's own heart?

"Suit yourself. You can always cry aft—" Clinton spun. Froze before the oncoming apparition: flash of long bare legs and red silk, horse big as a truck and growing bigger by the second. His jaw dropped, his gun drooped from nerveless fingers.

He'd let go of Trenton, so maybe she didn't need her knife. Jamming it back in its sheath, Raine braced her weight in her right stirrup as she leaned down. Reached. Her target's eyes grew wide...wider...his mouth a rounding O of horror. *Just love a man with a tie!* She grabbed it at the knot—"Ooof!"— and kept on riding.

"Aaaaagh! *Urrkkk!*" He tripped—somehow found his feet as she yanked him up—to bound, stumbling and shrieking, alongside the thundering bay.

Thirty feet down the block, she flung him to the pavement and galloped on.

"Hey, cowgirl!"

Once she'd reined her mount to a snorting, curvetting trot, she glanced behind.

Cade sat midstreet on Clinton's back. Making himself

quite comfortable, it looked like. "Where d'you think you're going?"

Sticking around here answering police questions all night would be a total bore. They had plenty of witnesses without her. And Trenton had stumbled to his feet, looking shaken, but fine. She'd call him tomorrow, but as for now— "Got a hot date at midnight, remember?" she called, brushing her tangled hair back from a wicked smile.

Intent on the downed shooter, a wave of cops stormed past her on either side. Raine walked her horse docilely to the corner and peered uptown. Here came a cab, miraculously with its light on. *"Taxi!"*

When it pulled into the curb, she swung down and tied the bay to a lamppost. "I owe you a bushel of apples, sweetie." She slid in behind the goggle-eyed cabbie. "Brooklyn Bridge, please."

Hot date? Oh, yeah, we've got a date. Ignoring the shouted questions as New York City's finest bent over him, Cade stared after the taxi. *And if you think make-up sex is fun, try almost-got-shot sex,* was the thought dancing round his mind.

Even if she was the enemy.

Chapter 5

"How did Cade know that I love the Brooklyn Bridge?" Raine wondered as she approached its first tower. Or was this simply another sign that their minds marched in step?

Whenever Raine passed through New York, she walked the bridge. She hadn't done so yet, this trip. And always before she'd come at dawn or sunset. Now she shivered with anticipation as its massive suspension cables curved upward to either side of the boardwalk. "Don't look back," she encouraged herself. "No-ot yet. You can do it."

Already she'd walked almost a quarter mile up the gradually rising ramp from street level. She was out over the East River itself—must be at least ten stories up in the air and still climbing. Beyond the bridge's first tower, Brooklyn was a molten glow on the opposite shore, while Raine could *feel* Manhattan, looming at her back.

On the roadway some twenty feet below the pedestrian walk, a car rushed past, fleeing the city. Tires growled on concrete, a radio wailed. A cool glissando of sax and trumpet drifted back on the salty air and Raine shuddered with pleasure. Rubbing the goose bumps on her bare arms, she took a deep breath—and turned. *"Sha-zamm!"*

Palisades of light scraped a buttermilk sky—a jagged dazzle of gold and silver, blinking red and strobing white. Diamond rivers of headlights; streaming ruby taillights. While serene in its own beauty, a fat saffron moon smiled above this electric city of neon-crazed cliff dwellers.

The shout of *"Hey!* Bike on your *right!"* brought Raine back to her senses. The rider whizzed past, helmeted head tucked to his handlebars, massive calves pumping. "Damn tourists!"

"Sorry!" Raine laughed after him.

On she strolled, swinging occasionally to drift backward like a child leaving the movie theater, shaking her head with incredulous delight. Born and raised in the wide-open West, she'd never make a city girl. Yet at times like this she could see why New Yorkers thought the sun revolved around their own special little island.

Like the rough granite face of a cathedral, the bridge's first tower reared into the dark. The boardwalk split and flowed to either side of the central stone column, then rejoined on its far side. Rounding it, Raine almost bumped into a desperately kissing couple.

Her thighs tightened in reflex. Her nipples brushed against the silk of her dress. Aftermath of adrenaline, she admitted ruefully as she skirted the *clinch*—that and the knowledge that she should meet Kincade anytime now. "If he could get away from the police," she muttered to herself. They might keep him half the night.

But Raine didn't believe it. He'd come. Something about the man told her that for better or worse he kept his promises. "A fossil of great rarity and interest," she repeated, her blood surging with the thought. If he really had one to sell, she meant to acquire it!

Ashaway All wasn't a nonprofit museum that could throw its money around, but a business, with a business's constant need to score. But would the attraction she'd felt for Cade survive a half–hour of hard-nosed negotiations? He didn't look as though he'd be a pushover, when it came to bargaining. She was no cream puff herself, while cutting a deal. "Whatever." If it came to a choice, rare fossils were in shorter supply than sexy men.

Yet nobody waited on the boardwalk ahead. "Still time," Raine comforted herself.

Beyond the first tower, the view of the East River opened out to either side—a black velvet shawl crinkled with moonlight, spangled with gliding navigation lights. A tug trudged upstream against the monstrous outgoing tide. Nimble as a water bug, an airfoil ferry spun out from a pier below Wall Street. It rumbled off toward the outer harbor, trailing a widening wake of creamy foam.

"Whoa—*baby!* Check it *out!*"

Raine bobbled a stride, then walked grimly on. Up ahead on her right, three young men had balanced their way out one of the iron beams that stretched above the traffic lanes on the deck beneath. This idiot feat took them out to the actual edge of the bridge, where they could look straight down to the water, some hundred and fifty feet below—or jump, if they were so inclined.

They looked more the type to push somebody else, than to jump. "Hey, bitch! Want some company?"

"Sure she does! She dressed up just for me!"

Without a word, Raine walked on, passing the point where their beam intersected the waist-high side rail of the footbridge.

They weren't the type to take a hint. Here they came, catcalling and clowning as they wobbled back along the girder with their arms outstretched.

Not a bicycle cop in sight, nor anybody else. Raine sighed as she stopped to skim her gown up to midthigh. *Definitely a side zipper next time.*

Behind her the chorus rose to gleeful hoots—then missed a couple of beats as she unsheathed her knife.

The heavy silk slithered back to her ankles. Holding the dagger up by its point, Raine turned—and tipped her head inquiringly. *You're sure this is a good idea?*

"*Sometimes a warning works,*" Trey had told her more than once. "*And sometimes it gives away your best advantage—the element of surprise.*"

Holding the stupefied gaze of the leading punk, Raine flipped the knife straight up in the air. Without seeming to watch its whirling rise, she caught it as it spun back to earth. Blade first.

Her audience stood on the beam, uneasily silent.

She tossed the knife again—caught it casually. Their size had misled her. They were younger than she'd thought, still in their teens, which if anything, made them more dangerous. Overdosed on testosterone, and probably they'd yet to learn how to shift into reverse. Still, the second one in line was actually shuffling his feet. The third had developed a sudden interest in the cars passing below. Raine gave their leader a confiding smile; it was best not to challenge. *You're prowlers of the night—but so am I. And it's a big bridge. Who needs trouble?*

She turned and strolled on, her ears tuned for overtaking footsteps. All she heard was a buzz of earnest mutters.

Then there, up ahead, sauntering to meet her from the Brooklyn shore, came Kincade! Raine laughed aloud. He must have driven over to the far side, where parking was better. She gave the knife a final jaunty flip, sheathed it, then met him at the halfway point.

He scowled over her shoulder. "Did they bother you?"

"No more than I could handle."

"Ah." Amusement softened that look of glinting danger. "Then I guess I'll let 'em live."

They turned as one to rest their forearms on the railing, and gaze southeast toward the outer harbor. Miles away, the twinkling spikes and curves of the Verrazano Bridge marked the start of the beckoning ocean.

"Trenton was all right?" she asked as the sea breeze rippled her hair.

"Seemed to be," Cade agreed without turning. "They tried to whisk him off in an ambulance, but he wasn't having any. By the time I ducked out, he was busy buying your police horse. Claimed he and a couple of teammates own a racing stable in Maryland, and any horse that saves *his* life, belongs in high clover, not breathing traffic fumes."

"And as for you?" Cade laughed under his breath. "Ten-ton said if it takes his last nickel, he's naming your *Carnotaurus* 'Rainy.'"

"Oh, *please!*" Raine swung around with a comic groan.

"And as for me…" Cade's smile faded to intention.

Her lips parted in surprise—she turned her head aside as his mouth descended.

Another guy who couldn't take a hint. He smelled of bay rum, tasted of champagne. Easy and slow, his kiss teased the quivering corner of her mouth, till she smiled in spite of herself. Warm lips brushed her cheekbone, then trailed deliciously away. "That's…for saving my neck, there at the end."

"After I'd gotten you into the fix," she reminded him, swearing inwardly at the way her voice had gone all fuzzy— all of her had gone hot and fuzzy. "He was my friend, not yours."

"Well, yeah," Cade allowed with a glimmer of mischief. "But still—"

She flattened a hand on his chest and locked her elbow, holding off a second demonstration of gratitude. "How about we get to business? What's this fossil that you want to sell me?"

"*I* want to—" Cade's brows flew together. "Then you didn't send me—" from an inner pocket of his suit, he fished a familiar white envelope "—this? You said you had a date at midnight. Once I read this, I assumed—"

Raine shook her head. "I got an invitation, too, delivered at the party." She'd dropped hers somewhere in all the excitement.

"Then—" Cade snapped a glance left, then right. No one approached from either direction. "Hmm."

He really hadn't sent it, Raine concluded, noting his wariness. "It's clear why somebody would offer to sell me a fossil—they do it all the time. But why would someone think you'd be interested in buying bones?"

"Ever heard of an outfit called SauroStar?" Suddenly Cade's smile wasn't all that friendly.

Raine's hand twitched toward her mouth, then she fisted it. Too late to wipe that kiss away. "You're connected to SauroStar?" The company had materialized out of nowhere last year. If it even had a headquarters, so far Trey and Ash hadn't been able to find it. SauroStar seemed to be simply a Web site backed by a very deep pocket. But it had been competing with Ashaway All in a way that was increasingly disturbing.

Sure, there were half-a-dozen commercial fossil-collecting and supply houses like her family's around the world. They vied fiercely for significant discoveries with each other—and also with the staffs of museums and academic teams fielded by the paleontology departments of numerous universities.

But though feuds did arise from time to time, generally the competition was nothing personal. Advances in science made by a rival were to be applauded, as well as envied; they were comrades in the same exhilarating quest for knowledge. And considering that one commercial firm might dig up the back end of a *Stegosaurus*—while another found a front—well, in the long run, cooperation simply made sense.

But SauroStar didn't seem to be hunting bones, so much as hunting Ashaway bones. At least it was starting to feel that way, the family had agreed in a cross-country conference call only last month. This summer alone they'd lost three licenses to dig on private property out West, productive and profitable quarry sites that the firm had worked for two generations. And oddest of all, once SauroStar outbid them for these collecting rights, it hadn't bothered to dig. *Dog in the manger tactics,* Ash had labeled that.

Trey with his military background had offered a more ominous term. *Scorched earth.* Where one army burns or steals everything in its path, so the pursuing army can't survive. "You're with SauroStar?" she repeated. "We've been trying to talk to you guys!" Messages to the company had been met so far with stony silence. The only contact given on the Web site was—she winced as it hit her—"You're *OAKincade@tiac.net?*"

"Yes. And I'm not *with* SauroStar—I own it."

"Well, you've got a funny way of doing business, Kincade."

"Really?" His amber eyes mocked her. "Up till now, it's been an amusing hobby. But now that I've got time to give it my full attention…"

Raine bristled. Behind that sardonic smile, he was threatening her. Threatening Ashaway All. But why? And with what—financial ruin? Her family's firm was the biggest, best-known fossil supply house in the world. He wouldn't find it easy to knock them off the top of the hill. But, he looked cool, confident, dangerously capable. A man who accomplished his goals.

"Excuse, please. You are Miss Ashaway? And Mr. Kincade?"

They spun at the softly accented words—to find a slender young woman standing before them. Bundled in a tightly belted trench coat, she hugged a cardboard box to her stomach. A box that was either heavy or precious, judging from the way her gloved fingers gripped it.

"I'm Kincade." Offering his hand, Cade smiled warmly. "You have a fossil you'd like to sell me?"

Hey, not so fast! "And I'm Raine Ashaway of Ashaway All. My company is always in the market for fine fossils." Stepping up beside Cade, she gave him a subtle hip check, then added in Tagalog, "And what is your name?"

The girl's almond eyes narrowed for an instant, then widened as she tossed her head prettily. "That is not my language."

And you're not saying what is, Raine noted. "Sorry. My mistake." But she wasn't far off. The girl came from somewhere south of the Philippines. Quite possibly, like Raine's own sister Dana, she was of mixed race; the southeast Pacific was the crossroads of the world. Well, whatever had gone into this one's genes, the results were certainly pleasing.

And clearly she knew it, the way she batted her lashes at Cade when he asked her name. *"You*...may call me Lia."

Yeah, but who are you at home? There was something about her, a certain watchfulness, a certain smugness in the way the corners of her plump little mouth curled, that scratched at Raine's nerves. Also, what was with those gloves, on a balmy September night? And if her tropic blood was really thin enough to need them, then why choose gloves that had been chopped off at the first knuckles? Pickpocket gloves. *Is that what she's come to do, pick our pockets?*

"Lia, what a pretty name. And how did you find us tonight?" Cade asked smoothly. He'd turned on the charm full blast, but was he as smitten as he appeared—or flattering for his own ends?

"Oh, that was easy. I learn on the Internet that you both have interest in this sort of thing." Lia's fingers caressed the box. "Then I look up your names on LexisNexis to see where I find you."

Now there might be a clue. LexisNexis was a specialized search engine, for tracking citations in print. The browser was much too expensive for the average user, but newspapers subscribed to the service, as did some colleges. Raine studied the girl's honey-colored face. A student from abroad? New York was full of them, many sent here on scholarship.

The cleverest girl from a very small pond. That might account for her air of self-congratulation.

"The *New York Times* say that you will be here in the city, tonight. At the natural history museum how-do-you-call-it? Gala? And so I invite you both to come and bid on something *much* more special than a Carno—" Lia wrinkled her nose and laughed "—a big ugly lizard."

That was my ugly lizard and I bet you know it. Wherever Lia came from, it must be one of those cultures where the women knife each other in the back, when a good-looking guy comes around. But oh, so daintily.

Well, more fool she. Though Raine would have to give her credit. Lia was an enterprising kid, to set up her own auction in the middle of the Brooklyn Bridge. "So, could we see what you have?" she asked briskly.

"But most certainly," Lia agreed, directing her answer at Cade. She led the way to one of the benches that were spaced at intervals along the edge of the walkway. Cade promptly sat beside her, with an arm stretched along the backrest behind the girl's shoulders. Raine gritted her teeth and hovered above them. She almost hoped it was some trashy little dime-a-dozen trilobite! In which case she'd leave Cade to win his auction of one—and bid on whatever else he wanted—and she'd head on home. To a nice hot bath, she promised herself, rubbing her arms.

Cade glanced up at her; his brows knit together as their eyes met. A private awareness skated between them. He started to speak—then turned back to the box, where Lia was lifting away wads of crumpled newspaper.

"Here, let me take those." Raine grabbed a double handful of paper as the breeze snatched at the packing.

"Those are nothing," Lia muttered, intent on a bundle the size of a football that she was unwrapping. "It is *this...*"

As the last paper peeled away, Raine smothered a gasp. A dino tooth! The gently curved fang was nearly twice as long as Lia's hand. Rounded like a lethal punch, it came from a member of the theropod family, for sure; quite possibly a *T. rex.* "Careful!" she murmured. Sixty-five million years after he'd shed it, you could cut yourself on the serrated edge of a *Tyrannosaurus's* tooth.

"Let's throw a little light on this." Cade produced a penlight from an inner pocket, flicked it on.

And Raine grabbed for the railing as her knees went weak.

Oh, my God! "Where did you—!" Where on *earth* could Lia have found this?

Coruscating with green-and-pink flames, then glimmers of coppery gold, the tooth flamed as Cade played the light over it. Chain lightning and rainbows, trapped inside bone!

Or replacing bone, actually. By some happy chance, mineralized water had trickled into the pores of the buried tooth over a million years or more, to create an opalized fossil.

Lia laughed on a shrill note of triumph. She turned the tooth in Cade's light, setting off another explosion of fireworks. "You like?"

A T. rex tooth made entirely of fire opal? "It's...pretty," Raine admitted in a shaken voice. And if she fainted, would they hold up the auction till she'd revived?

Opalized fossils were Raine's professional specialty—and her personal obsession. The circumstances that allowed them to form were so vanishingly rare. With two staggering exceptions, all the opalized fossils that had been discovered so far were invertebrates—small snails and shells, unremarkable except for their composition.

Then, rarest of the rare, came the only known opalized dinosaurs in all the world. Both of them had been discovered in the opal mines of western Australia. The larger specimen was a humdrum little pliosaur. It was fourteen feet long.

But a ten-inch tooth from the bottom jaw meant that Lia's entire outrageous, unbelievable beast had to be close to...*fifty feet!*

And if by some miracle its entire skeleton was made of fire opal? *Where, oh, where, oh, where did you find this?* Raine fought an urge to grab the girl by her shoulders, try to shake the answer out of her.

The largest *T. rex* ever unearthed was Sue—just a plain vanilla fossil, forty-five feet long, eighty percent complete. But collectors adored *T. rexes*. They were scarce. They were sexy. At a Sotheby auction, Sue had brought nearly eight and a half million dollars.

Compared with Sue, what would a fifty-foot, fire opal dragon bring? Enough gold to sink a battleship? A ransom for Bill Gates? Could you trade it for the Great Pyramid at Giza?

Who could possibly say? A fire opal *T. rex* would be priceless. A wonder of the world. You'd just have to put it up for auction and see what bid was hammered down.

Lia held the tooth close enough for Cade to kiss. "Would you like to buy this?"

"Oh, yeah," Cade admitted, his voice husky with desire.

"And you?" Lia challenged, deigning at last to notice Raine. "What would you give me for this?"

Off the top of my head? Raine's stomach whirled. Valuing a unique object, with no sales history, she could only guess at its worth. Ashaway All could raise two million easily— three, scraping the barrel, but that was their total acquisitions fund for the entire year.

If they had time to broker the deal to a private collector, act as a go-between, they could raise much more than that. Or they might put together a consortium of civic-minded dino lovers, who'd pool their funds, then donate the prize to a museum, as had been done with Sue. "Well, that depends."

On so many things. Like for starters, was Lia the real owner of the tooth? And did she have control of the rest of the skeleton—or even know where it was?

Lia made a clicking sound of impatience. "That is no answer!" She turned back to Cade. "And you? What will you give me?"

He laughed under his breath, then glanced ironically up at Raine—and held her gaze. *You and me.* Awareness sizzled between them.

You against me! The breeze caught a skein of her hair, rippled it across her mouth. But still Raine wouldn't blink. Not before he did.

"How much?" Lia cried, swinging around on the bench to intrude between them.

"A lot." Cade shifted casually to one side, and looked up

at Raine with a duelist's smile—a white glove slapped across her face. "Put it this way, Lia. Whatever Ms. Ashaway offers you? I'll give you more."

Chapter 6

Yet neither of them was ready to name a price, Raine realized. Though Lia was doing her utmost to start a bidding war between them, they refused to be stampeded.

Each insisted on examining the tooth, since the first issue was: could it possibly be a fake?

But when—ladies coming decidedly second—Raine was allowed to take the tooth from Cade and turn it in the light, her hands trembled with excitement. By God, it *was* the real thing! She could think of no way to fake its eerie opalescence. Like the northern lights dancing on polar snow. Sunrise shining through a turquoise glacier. *I've got to have it! Simply got to.* Here was glory and fame, as well as a fortune. This was the find of the century! "Nice," she murmured, carefully neutral.

"Then how much you give me for it?" Lia cried, almost stamping her foot with impatience.

"I'd have to talk with the other members of my firm. Come up with a suitable offer—a very generous offer," Raine added as Lia scowled.

One reason to stall was that, given a day or two, Trey should be able to profile Kincade, now that they knew he owned SauroStar. If they could learn how much the man was worth, where his money came from, then they might estimate his top bid. Figure an offer that would knock him out of the game, without blindly overbidding.

"And you're sure you can't tell us where the rest of this dinosaur is located?" Cade coaxed. "I'd like to bid on the whole specimen, if you've got it."

Lia snapped her fingers. "I told you and *told* you! You buy this first, *then* we talk about that."

Raine exchanged a wry glance with her rival. Lia's steadfast refusal to say might mean that she hoped to establish a value for one tooth—then sell the rest of the dino, bone by bone, at the same price.

But a *T. rex* had sixty-four teeth and a couple of hundred other bones in its body… *If I offer her a hundred thou for this tooth, then it turns out she wants to multiply that by 264 for the rest of the dinosaur!*

And try to explain to the kid that the sixty-fourth tooth wouldn't be as valuable as the first tooth, since supply inevitably decreases demand. But would Lia understand and accept economic realities—or simply feel she was being cheated?

And then there were other reasons Lia might refuse to discuss the rest of the dino's skeleton. The tooth might be stolen.

Or Raine's pulse rocketted with the thought—*What if she doesn't know where the rest of it is? What if the skeleton's still in the ground? Up for grabs?* In which case, Raine was on her way to…somewhere. Gone yesterday! *But I've got to learn where.*

"Maybe the Internet was wrong, your Web sites lie! Maybe neither of you have the money to buy such a treasure," Lia cried. She must have imagined herself going home tonight with a fortune in her pocket. Probably she'd picked out the car she meant to buy tomorrow. She was beginning to seem even younger than Raine's first guess of twenty. Hissing with displeasure, she bent over her box and began to rewrap the tooth.

"Lia, calm down," Raine pleaded. "I do have enough money and I do want to buy your fossil. I'll call you tomorrow afternoon and we'll discuss a price, okay?" That was rushing negotiations more than she liked, but she needed to nail the prize down, before Miss Show-Me-The-Money offered it elsewhere. "Do you have a phone number where I can reach you?"

Lia sniffed without raising her face. "Give me a number and I call you. Be by your phone tomorrow at *precisely* three o'clock. This is your last chance, you understand?"

Raine grimaced. "I do." She drew a business card from her gown's pocket, and handed it over. "Oh, and here's your packing," she added, dropping an armload of paper into the box. "Wrap it up nice and safe."

Lia snorted her contempt. "And you, Kincade? Will you bid tomorrow—or lose this amazing fossil?"

Her threat simply made him chuckle. "Let me take you out to dinner tomorrow night, someplace very special. After that, I'll make you an offer you can't refuse."

Blast the man! Raine could have cheerfully tossed him off the bridge. He'd soften up the girl with a drink or two, then ask what Raine had bid—he could trump that by a few thou. Plus he'd sweetened the pot with a promise of romance, a bonus that Raine had no way of matching. Lia looked up from her package, her pout melting to a starry-eyed simper.

"I'll pick you up in a stretch limousine," Cade added shamelessly. "Do you prefer white limos—or black?"

Lia might be young, naive and off her home court—but she wasn't a fool. Her smile widened, catlike, triumphant. "Give me your number and I call *you* tomorrow—precisely at three-thirty. Then you say where I meet you. You can pay for my cab."

"Fair enough," Cade agreed, accepting defeat with a smile.

Lia stood. "Now I go."

Cade rose and touched her elbow. "It's late. Let me drive you home."

Raine clenched her teeth. Knowing where to find the girl would give Cade an edge, as would doing her favors.

Lia tossed her hair. "No, thank you. I have other plans."

In that case, Raine resolved to follow her home. No way was she letting that box out of sight, till it was safely off the city streets. But first. "Lia, I had one other question. Do you have anything else to sell? Anything that was found with this tooth?"

Fossils were often discovered in a narrow geologic stratum, tangled together. If the kid had any other old bones, even if they weren't significant in themselves, their age and species might prove a clue to the *T. rex*'s location.

Lia frowned in thought, then set the box down on the bench. "There is…one thing." Her gloved hand dipped into a pocket of the trench coat.

"It was found with the tooth?"

"I…yes. Of course," she agreed, wide-eyed.

She's lying, Raine guessed. Or possibly uncertain?

"I have another buyer for this, but if you like to bid…" Lia's fingers opened, to show a circular object resting on her palm.

A snail of some sort, Raine guessed, just as Cade switched on his light.

Gold gleamed in its rays. Lia held a closed pocket watch, with a broken bit of chain dangling from its fob. "You found *this* with the tooth?" Raine bent closer. There was a name ornately engraved on its convex case.

Lia's thumb snapped down, hiding the scrolled letters. "I told you, yes."

"But—" Raine glanced helplessly at Cade. Surely the kid realized the two objects were separated chronologically by some sixty-five million years?

"It belong to an American soldier," Lia added proudly. "His family will give much money for it."

A soldier! *Are we talking Vietnam?* Or for that matter, Burma in World War II? Or the Spanish-American War in the Philippines. Or a guerilla clash in any one of a dozen different nations.

"But we're bone hunters," Cade prodded mildly. "Why would we want to buy a watch?"

"Because…" Lia opened the case, then covered a portion of its inner side with her thumb. "You see?"

Cade squinted down at the case. "It's a… Is that a map?"

"Yessss!" She whisked the watch from under his nose. "You like to buy?"

"May *I* see it?" Raine asked, careful to quell her eagerness.

Lia shrugged, checked again that her thumb blocked part of the inner case, then showed it to Raine.

Below the girl's long red thumbnail, lines had been scratched into polished gold. Raine made out a shape that looked like a lopsided butterfly, then angled below that, a range of upside down Vs—denoting mountains? *"Wait!"* she cried as Lia snapped the lid shut.

"You want to see the whole thing, then you must buy. How much you give me?"

For a map that possibly showed the way to where the tooth had been found? Where perhaps the rest of the dinosaur still waited?

Possibly.

But at a minimum, once she learned the name of the soldier, Trey with his connections could find out the man's war. That might give Raine a starting point if it came to a search. "I'll give you five hundred dollars for it."

"It's a nice watch," Cade said carelessly. "I could go a thousand."

Raine shrugged. "I suppose I could go two."

"Three," Cade snapped.

Lia laughed softly, and with that malicious little sound, both bidders paused, eyeing each other. The thought hung in the air between them. *Are we being hustled?*

Still, the tooth was no scam. "Three thousand-five," Raine said at last.

"Five thousand."

As she glared at Cade, Raine brushed a skein of wind-blown hair back from her eyes. *How much money do you have, wise guy? And where does it come from?* Did he have a stopping point—or was he a bottomless pocket? "Six thousand." This was idiotic. The map, if map it really was, could lead to anything, not necessarily to ancient bones. It might be a sentimental picture of the soldier's hometown. "You *will* take a check, right?" Not that she'd brought one. She carried a folded fifty for emergencies, and that was that.

"No!" Lia shook her sooty hair till it fanned around her face. "No way, *Jose!* Cash or no deal!"

Cade threw back his head and laughed. "And I take it you don't accept MasterCard?"

"Absolutely not." Lia failed to see the joke.

"Then I'm out of the running for tonight," Raine admitted. "Let's talk about a price tomorrow at three."

"And whatever she offers? I'll give you even more at dinner," Cade assured the girl.

Lia sniffed as she picked up her box. "The soldier's family is most desperate to buy this. They give me ten thousand, cash. You must do better than that. So goodbye, and I call you tomorrow." Chin high, she marched off toward the Manhattan shore.

Elbows brushing, they watched her go, then glanced ruefully at each other. "We're gonna be pretty obvious, if we both follow her," noted Cade. "I don't suppose you'd let me—"

"*Jose?*" Raine showed her teeth. "No way at all."

"Then if that's the way it's gotta be, why don't we—"

But his proposal was cut short by the puttering sound of a two-stroke engine. An old Vespa motorscooter purred out of the shadows below the Manhattan tower. Stopping beside Lia, the rider wheeled it smartly around. "Why, the crafty minx!" Cade swore as she settled onto its pillion. With a taunting wave, she rolled off toward the city.

"Other plans," Raine echoed, looking after her. A woman of ambition and forethought. It wouldn't pay to underestimate the kid.

"Well, meantime…" Cade swung to face her. "It's even later. Could I drive *you* home?"

As second choice to little Lia?

His amber eyes had darkened. When they rose from her lips, they promised any sort of ride she might want. To any destination she desired. A tongue of summer lightning licked up her spine; still Raine shook her head. "No, thanks."

Mixing pleasure with business was risky. But mixing pleasure with a feud, when only one of them knew the terms or limits of the grudge? That might prove fatal. What *did* he have against the Ashaways?

"Pity. But in that case—" Cade shrugged out of his jacket, and swooped it around her bare shoulders.

His body heat settled deliciously upon her. The soft wool smelled of active, clean male, with a hint of his cologne. Raine started to wriggle free of the jacket, but he'd gripped both lapels. Slip out of it and she'd step straight into his arms. She stiffened for a moment—then shrugged. There was no sense fighting, when it felt so good. The weight of his knuckles resting on her collarbones was seductive as a drug. "I…don't know where to return it."

"No problem. You'll be seeing me around."

But is that a promise—or a threat? she wondered, walking west without a glance behind. And which would be harder to handle?

Whatever. She'd always choose interesting, over safe.

Right now, nothing interested her more in the world than a *T. rex* made of fire opal. As she passed into the tower's shadow, Raine slipped her fisted hand into a pocket of Cade's jacket—she let go a wad of crumpled newspaper.

Chapter 7

When they reached their building, Lia hopped off the back of the Vespa. Leaning against the front door to hold it open, she tapped her foot with impatience while Ravi wrestled his motorbike up the steep steps from the sidewalk. If he didn't chain it in the rear of the dirty hallway, it would be stolen by morning.

Watching her roommate grunt and groan and swear at the machine, she thought of Kincade, so smooth and good smelling. Lia had to giggle at the difference. Such a man would own a car, not a beat-up old motorbike. He'd drive a Jaguar, and he'd have a garage in which to park it. Maybe he even had a chauffeur!

When she was rich, *she* would have a chauffeur—a blond one in a blue uniform, who would carry her shopping bags and open doors for her. *Soon, yes!* She bent to kiss the box she held, then forgot about helping Ravi. She almost danced up to their apartment.

Six flights of badly lit stairs that smelled of cat piss and cabbage dampened her gaity, but hardened her resolve. The sooner she had money, the sooner she could move away from this dump and the losers who lived here.

Placing her box on the shelf above her desk, she took the letter from its top drawer. She paced the room, her lips shaping the words as she reread them.

Like I explained when you phoned me last week, that pocket watch has got to belong to my grandfather, Private Amos Szabo, of the 11th Airborne. He always carried just such a watch. But please, please believe me, miss, it isn't worth beans. I'm sorry if I sounded harsh, and that I yelled at you. You surprised me is all, calling out of the blue like that. And wanting all that money.

But believe me, its only value is sentimental. You see, my grandmother never knew what happened to my grandfather (her dear beloved husband). Only that he and his squad parachuted into the island of Borneo, during WWII. Except for that one letter she got, he was never heard from again—none of them came back. He's gotta be dead by now, but the family would sure like to know where he died and how. You can understand that, can't you?

I'd be happy to pay you fifty dollars as a reward for return of the watch. You went to a lot of trouble to find me, and you must be real clever to have tracked me down on the Internet. Lucky for me, I guess, that my name isn't a common one.

I'd be glad to pay the postage if you want to mail the watch C.O.D. And maybe I could give you a bit more than fifty, if you really feel you deserve it. Maybe if you wrote down all the details you know about where and when he died, that ought to be worth something, I guess, shouldn't it? Fair's fair, I always say.

So why don't you call me again—real soon—and let's talk it over? I swear I'll make it worth your while.

Yours truly,
Amos Szabo the third

As she punched in Szabo's number, Ravi tried the door-
knob, then knocked. "Lia?"

"I'm busy! Use your key." But she'd lost track of the numbers. She swore and started over as he shambled into the living room.

"Who can you be calling at this time of night? So late, it's
not polite. It isn't done."

"Oh? But you see me doing it, don't you?" She gave him
a teasing smile. He was so easy to handle. "Anyway, this man
wants to hear from me, most desperately."

"It is not polite," he muttered with a weary shrug. "And this
time you really must repay me the charges, okay?" He went
on into the bathroom. "Yes, Lia?"

"Most certainly," she called, knowing he'd have forgotten
by the time the bill came. Or if he didn't, why, by then she'd
be rich; her debts would be nothing. She let the phone ring
four times, then five, as she drummed her fingers on the
desktop.

When the man answered, she brightened. "Hello. It is me
again," she began—then frowned as the voice kept on speaking. Ah, an answering machine!

"It is me again," she repeated, after the signal. "Lia, who
has your—"

"Hello!" broke in a man's voice, rusty with sleep. "Missy,
is that you? Hang on. I'm here. Just let me—" He seemed to
fumble with something, then said, "Well, you're sure some
night owl."

An owl? What was that? "It is night," she agreed. "And you
ask me to call, so here I am. I need to know. Do you want to
buy the watch?"

He cleared his throat. "You got my letter? I mailed it to that
post office box number you gave me. Did you read it yet?"

"Yes, I'm reading it now, tonight. And I need to know."

"Well, if you got the letter, then now you do know. That watch isn't even real gold, just gold-plated brass. But like I said, if you could tell me a bit about where my grand-daddy died, then I could pay you maybe a hundred bucks, all told."

"I say to you last time we speak. My price is ten thousand dollars, for your ancestor's watch."

"Now *look,* you little island monk—!" He paused, muttered something under his breath, then laughed. But the laugh had sharp edges. "Look, Missy, maybe I could give you a hundred-fifty for your trouble, if you—"

Lia snorted. "I have two other bidders who will give me more than that."

"*What?* You showed it to somebody else? *Shit!* Now what would you go and do that for? Nobody'd want it but my family!"

"Ohhh, you think so?" Smiling, she wound a lock of hair round and round her gloved forefinger. "One lady, she will give me ten thousand for this watch. And there is a man—a very rich and handsome man—who will give me twelve." At least Kincade surely would tomorrow night, once he'd seen how she looked in her blue model's dress that she'd found at the consignment store.

"So my price must go up, if you wish to bid. The price is now…fifteen thousand dollars." Her face went all hot; her eyes went misty, as she thought of so much money. Picturing what she'd do with all those excellent dollars, she waited till he'd finished cursing. "You like to buy?" she said when he'd wound down to hard-breathing silence.

"*Shit,*" he said softly. "Well…it wouldn't be easy, raising that kind of nut. You said there's some sort of map drawn on the inside of the cover?"

Her smile widened. He was like a little bird that had hopped to her palm for sugar. If the fingers were quick… "Yes, it has a map. But if you are a poor man, without much money to buy the watch of your ancestor, well, I can sell the map to one of these others. I will make a copy of the map and sell it. Then I will scratch out the map on the watch, and you may buy it without, most reasonably."

"No!"

She clapped a palm to her mouth to smother the giggles. *Oh, little bird, you are in my cage now!* "No?" she said innocently. "You want the map?"

"Uh, err, I don't want you messing with that watch. However my granddaddy fixed it, that's the way I want it. Shit, girl, it's an heirloom! His souvenir of the war."

Oh, little lying bird. How you sing! They all wanted the map most desperately. Lia couldn't hide the laughter in her voice, but now there was no need to. He was caged. "So. You want the watch—*and* you want the map."

"That's right. That's exactly right. But at a reasonable price. No more dickin' around."

Whatever that meant. "Very reasonable," she purred. "My price has gone up. Watch with no map is fifteen thousand dollars. Watch *with* map is eighteen thousand."

He roared like a gored water buffalo. Like a lovely silver jet taking off from the Singapore airport. When she was rich, she'd fly on a jet to Paris. First-class ticket.

But now this fool had given her an idea that would make her even richer. Before she sold the watch to Szabo, she would copy its map—and sell one copy to the pale-haired lady who was much too old for Kincade. Why, that one must be almost thirty!

And Lia would sell a second copy of the map to Kincade. Or perhaps she'd give him his copy as a wedding gift, if he offered to marry her. Once he saw her in her blue dress…

"Look," Szabo growled. "You still there?"

"I sit here, waiting most patiently."

"Yeah, right. Well, listen, you can be patient for another day or two, can't you? Don't be in such a rush. I'll raise the eighteen thousand, but it'll take me a couple of days. Meantime, don't you sell it to anybody else—and don't you show it to anybody. Do that for me, then in two days, I promise. You'll get what's comin' to you."

Yes! That was precisely what she wanted. Just what she deserved. After all her dreams, all her hard work to make them happen, at last it was coming.

Szabo cradled the phone, then leaned across the bed to look at the caller *id* on his new answering machine. "Gotcha." Area code 212. That was New York City.

He stood, stretched, then hauled his old army duffel bag out of the closet; he'd packed it days ago. Figure a two-hour drive to Raleigh, then catch the morning flight.

When he got to New York, he'd go to a library, find a backward directory, which showed the address when you looked up the phone number. Dropping by a drugstore for a roll of duct tape and a pack of single-edge razorblades wouldn't take but a few minutes.

By early evening latest, he'd be knocking on the bitch's door.

"One of these days you're going to tell me you were a guy in your last life," Raine murmured drowsily, her fingers ruffling through silky-soft fur. Otto, the portly orange tomcat from the apartment below, had a suspicious fondness for jumping her, every time he caught her in bed. Stretched out full length on her chest, with his nose snuggled under her chin, he rumbled in unabashed contentment. He'd tiptoed up the fire escape, then in through her open window this morning and she'd woken to a familiar twenty-two pounds settling into place. "You know, I've had maybe four hours sleep. Surely a cat can appreciate that that's not *quite*—"

She broke off as the bedside phone rang. Managing to reach it without dislodging her passenger, she yawned and said, "That…was fast."

She'd phoned, then faxed Trey at headquarters when she got in last night. Out in Grand Junction, Colorado, the rising sun would have yet to clear the Rockies. Knowing Trey, he hadn't slept since she roused him.

"I've just scratched the surface so far." Trey's gravelly voice echoed the cat's rumble—about two octaves lower. "But I've got a few things of interest."

Trey was the Expediter of Ashaway All. The still and ingenious center around which Raine and her siblings whirled. The man who arranged, and the man who obtained. He was an ex-SEAL—and maybe ex-merc, though he'd never admit it—with useful connections in the weirdest backwaters of the world.

A dozen years ago he'd come limping into their lives on his one good leg plus a whole lot of attitude, and he'd soon made himself indispensable to the firm and to the family. There wasn't one of the Ashaway women who hadn't sworn at one point or another that she'd die if he didn't love her—and there wasn't one who could claim she'd ever been properly kissed by the man.

But they all would have gone to the wall for Trey, and he for them. He was big brother and stand-in father, since John Ashaway's accident. Keeper of their darkest secrets and their most excruciating bloopers. Teaser and mentor and coach. And he got them whatever they needed, whenever they needed it; he was their expediter. "Whatcha...got?" she asked on another yawn.

"The language on that newspaper you faxed me is Indonesian."

"Darn, I was afraid of that." Indonesia was a sprawling archipelagic nation, covering a swath of the Pacific about the size of Europe. The country encompassed a few monster-size islands to the northwest of Australia, and hundreds of small ones. If Lia was Indonesian, then she and her tooth might hail from Bali, or New Guinea, or Java, or— "It's not from Sumatra, where the tsunami hit?"

"No, from about a thousand miles east," Trey assured her. "The name of that paper translates as the *Morning Star.* It's the local daily for the city of Pontianak, Kalimantan."

"As in Borneo?" Raine rolled to one side, then unhooked Otto's claws from her T-shirt. He scrambled to his feet and stalked to the foot of the bed, tail lashing his vexation.

"Yep. Borneo is the third-largest island in the world. It's divided between three countries. Kalimantan in the south is a province of Indonesia. Sarawak and Sabah in the northeast and northwest are states of Malaysia. Then tucked in between them is the Kingdom of Brunei."

"A lot of ground to cover. What's the date on the newspaper?"

"Mid-August of this year."

"Six weeks ago—that sounds about right. The way the tooth was wrapped, I'm betting somebody mailed it to Lia. If she'd carried it as hand luggage on a plane or ship, she wouldn't have needed so much cushioning—and it was too valuable to risk checking it with her bags."

"Plus you said her English is fairly fluent, which might mean she's been in New York awhile."

"Mmm," Raine mused. "So six weeks ago somebody packs up this tooth and mails it to Lia. Somebody who can only afford to send it surface mail. Somebody who trusts her to find out what it's worth and to cut a deal."

"A relative…a friend…maybe a classmate?" Trey hazarded.

"Somebody who sees Lia as the smart one in the family? The big-city college girl who should know how to tap the American money machine?"

"Sounds about right. And here's another thing. The city of Pontianak is on the coast, at the mouth of the Kapuas River. But that tooth can't have come from there. Geology's wrong for finding fossils—nothing but swamps and mangrove. But more than that, the area's too populated, with an entrenched power structure whose prime law is 'Top Dog eats first.' A priceless find along the coast would have been impossible to hide. It would've been snapped up by the head honchos.

"And when they went to sell it, the boss-guys wouldn't

trust it to a twenty-year-old girl, with no credentials or standing."

"Amateur hour is what we're talking here," Raine muttered.

"Gotta be. So if not from the coast, the tooth came from somewhere in the wilds of the interior. That's the deepest, darkest rainforest remaining in the world. No cities, no roads. Transportation strictly by jungle footpath or by longboat up the river. You've got rice-farming tribes settled along the waterways, and nomad hunters up in the mountains. It's not even a money economy yet in the interior—it's barter. Boar fat and birds and wild honey brought down to the river towns to be traded for shotgun shells and salt."

The back of Raine's neck was tingling. This was why she was a bone hunter! Not just for fossils, but for the crazy adventures in finding them. The new, the strange and the wild were what called her. "That's where it came from!" she said with conviction. "Somebody found it up there, somewhere in the mountains. An innocent who hadn't a clue what it would bring in a city."

"Probably traded it for something practical, like a case of dried beef or a pair of used eyeglasses," Trey agreed. "So it passed into a slightly savvier somebody's hands, who passed it on to Lia to get what she could for it—where the money grows on trees, and the streets are paved with gold."

Raine sighed. "Yep. She was flashing dollar signs on every wavelength."

"Have you thought about an offer price?"

"That depends on what will beat Kincade. What have you found on him?"

"Nothing you're going to like. Turns out he owns half of Okab Oil."

Oil! She winced. "A drilling company out West? He sounds like a Westerner, with a bit of polish."

"No such luck. We're talking offshore oil, the Red Sea. His partner is the nephew-in-law of the emir of Kurat."

"Oh, joy! Dad always says you can judge a person by his enemies. But we have to piss off an Arabian oil tycoon?"

"You're sure he's carrying a grudge? Did he threaten you?"

Raine smiled to herself. She could almost hear Trey flexing, two thousand miles to the west. "Not in so many words. He said something about SauroStar being just a hobby so far, but now that he's got time to give us his undivided attention…"

"Hmm. Is there any chance, considering this is the find of a lifetime and considering you've been known to be a trifle, well…intense…when it comes to getting your dino, that you're mistaking plain old bone hunter's lust for something stronger and more personal?"

Slowly she shook her head at the cat, who'd rolled onto his side to gaze at her with a pair of simmering amber eyes. "No." Cade had looked at her last night the way Otto must contemplate a mouse creeping along the baseboards. As something to be toyed with, then tasted, and finally devoured—and every last bite would be personal. "No, he's got something against us, Trey. Something big and bad."

"Then it's got to be findable. I'll keep on digging."

"Thanks." She stretched to rub her foot along the cat's belly—a dangerous caress, but hard to resist. "Anything else?"

"One last thing. You mentioned the girl's gloves? Are you sure they were gloves—and not tattoos?"

Raine laughed in surprise. "No, the light was hardly the best, but I'm fairly certain. Thin blue gloves, chopped off at the first knuckle. Why?"

"Just something I stumbled across, once in my travels. You know Borneo's head-hunting country?"

"Yikes!" Raine sat upright, then scooted back against the mounded pillows. "But that's got to be…way back in their dark and evil past, right?"

"Well, yeah, if you call 2001 the Bad Ol' Days."

"Oh, *stop!* You're not serious."

"'Fraid I am, though I s'pose you could write off that latest episode of head-taking as a nasty little hiccup. Just a minor backslide during an intertribal tiff about land rights."

"I thought Lia seemed a bit…intense, herself," Raine murmured, smoothing her palm thoughtfully down her neck.

"If she's a Dayak, then, yeah, the women were as warlike as the men. But what you've got to understand is that head-hunting was a matter of prestige. To prove your daring and skill. If a guy wanted to score with a girl, he darned sure better bring a few heads when he came courting."

"Beats a bouquet of roses any ol' day," Raine observed dryly.

"On an island with ten thousand flowers for the picking, I reckon it did. Anyway, to take a head meant you were a great achiever. And to advertise that you were a head-lopping Bravo, you had your hands tattooed blue—from the wrist to the first knuckle."

Goose bumps stampeded up her arms. Raine shuddered as she rubbed them. "Oh, come *on!* This is a thoroughly twenty-first century kid. Uses the Internet and nail polish, for Pete's sake."

"Yeah, but it never fails to amaze me how people hang on to what works for them from their own culture, like polygamy or camel racing, then they graft MTV and cell phones on top of it. All I'm saying is that maybe Lia's given herself blue hands to show she's a high achiever. That she's fearless and she'll stop at nothing."

"Or that she means to score big," Raine murmured.

"All of the above. So my one bit of advice to you is, whatever you do, just don't…lose your—"

Raine groaned. "Don't you *dare* say it!"

"Okay, I won't," he agreed, chuckling. "I'll call you when I've got more." And just like that Trey was gone.

Raine sighed, hung up the phone and oozed back down to mattress level. "Nap?" she suggested, rubbing Otto's belly with her toes.

Like a fuzzy orange bear trap, his paws snapped around her.

Chapter 8

It was 3:08! "Come on, Ms. Precisely, pick up that phone!" Raine prayed, wincing as another helicopter juddered overhead, then roared off over the Brooklyn Bridge.

Betting that Lia would have set their original rendezvous not too far from wherever she lived, Raine had returned to the neighborhood. The bridge breached like a gray whale over her northern horizon. Beneath its belly the blue river teemed with barges and boats. The lunchtime flood of brokers from Wall Street had gone back to their moneymaking, though foot-weary tourists still shuffled along the pier's decks and stopped at its railings to ogle the view.

Raine's laptop lay ready on the table before her, already opened to a Web site that boasted the best backward phone directory online. If Lia called from a landline, Raine could ID her number, then trace it from there.

"Dammit, call me!" Could Cade have gotten to the kid somehow? Outbid her already?

"Nice day. Feel like some company?" A straggler from the

stock exchange touched the back of the chair opposite Raine's and gave her a winsome smile.

"Sorry, but I'm expecting a business—*yes!*" Raine cried as her phone chimed. The suit shrugged and retreated while she said crisply, "Raine Ashaway speaking."

"How much will you bid?" demanded Lia, cutting straight to the chase.

Raine rolled her eyes. "Hello, Lia. How are you?" That drew no response, so she continued. "I do have an offer I think you'll like, but it's a bit complicated. I'd rather show you the figures on paper. Could I invite you over to Pier 17 for a drink and a chat?"

"Not today. How much will you give for this amazing, most beguiling fossil?"

Raine smacked her forehead, then sighed. "Okay. Do you know what I mean by percent? A share of something?"

"Huh! You think I'm stupid? I study math, science, many difficult subjects here in New York City."

"Good, then here's what Ashaway All proposes. It wouldn't be fair to offer you just a flat price for the tooth, because nobody knows what it's worth. Nothing like it has ever been seen or sold before. So here's what I suggest: We pay you a certain amount up front. An advance on what you'll finally realize." Enough cash to keep the kid happy, and let her embark on a shopping spree. Raine was hoping that by the time the real payoff arrived, she'd have calmed down enough to bank some of it. It would be a shame to see her blow her fortune overnight.

"How much?"

"That depends on what you sell me." Much as she wanted the tooth, Raine wanted the rest of the *T. rex* more. Whatever Lia knew about the dino's location, that had to be part of their deal. "But first, here's what Ashaway All would do to earn our cut of the final sales price."

Damn, but she hated to negotiate over the phone, unable to watch Lia's face. Still Raine forged cheerily on, outlining how her firm, with its sterling reputation and worldwide connections, was best suited to vouch for the tooth's authenticity and provenance.

In addition to that, they were uniquely qualified to promote publicity and boost desire. They'd create a buzz through scientific channels by writing scholarly articles for paleontology mags.

They'd alert relevant museums and the most avid collectors to this extraordinary opportunity. And best of all, Raine hoped to form a consortium of buyers to acquire, then donate Lia's tooth to a world-class museum, where dinosaur-lovers from everywhere could come to—

"But how much do I get and when do I get it?" Lia cut in.

"I could give you your advance tomorrow," Raine assured her.

"Then the rest of the money?"

Raine drew a deep breath and crossed her fingers. "Six months, maybe." Maybe much longer if she could find the rest of the dino. If they brought the whole beast to auction at once, at least minimally cleaned so that bidders could see its opaline fire, it would take longer.

But then the sky would be the limit on what they could get. No, forget all limits; they'd shoot the moon. Lia would be set for life. "I know it's hard, but it would really pay to be patient."

"But how much would it pay? Why won't you say this?"

"Because I don't know," Raine said, hanging on hard to her temper. "And anybody who claims to know what your tooth is worth—" *Even if he's tall, dark and toe-curlingly sexy* "—would be lying. That's why I'm recommending that we work on a percentage, rather than a flat fee."

"How much would you pay me flat? Right here, right now?"

Raine ground her teeth. *Okay, you want to be stupid?* "I suppose…something in the range of a hundred thousand." She could up that price if Cade matched it—but not by much, not for a single tooth.

"Hmm," Lia hedged, for once at a loss for words.

"And I'll buy your watch, as well," Raine added. "Say an extra ten thou for that? What do you say, Lia?"

"I say…" Lia's voice held a smirk. "That I have to think, most seriously."

"That offer is good only for today, Lia."

"Ohhh, you think so?" she crooned. "I bet you pay me that tomorrow, if I want it." If Kincade didn't offer her more tonight, is what she meant.

"You think so?" Raine echoed, extra dry. "Well, maybe— and maybe not. I guess we'll just have to see, won't we?" She grabbed the loose braid hanging on her shoulder and yanked it. Temper! If getting her dino required that she swallow her pride, then— "Look, there's other options we could discuss. Why don't I come over and—"

"No, thank you. I have other plans. I must call Kincade."

"Well, what about after that? By the time I catch a cab—"

"No, because then I go shopping. To Victory's Secret, do you know this store? I buy something *special* to wear tonight."

She was turning the knife, and doing it with such childlike glee—some headhunter genes in her pedigree, for sure. Raine bit her tongue. *Honey, if you think I'm sitting here whining with envy, then think again. Sell me the damned tooth and I'll dance polkas at your and Cade's wedding.* "Then would you call me when you get back from shopping?"

"Maybe—or maybe not."

O-okay, that was enough for this round. "Whatever," Raine murmured. "But before you sell that tooth, if you're as smart as you think you are, you'll talk to me again. Bye now." She hung up just as Lia started speaking.

Always bargain from a position of strength, was another of her father's rules. She'd come close to breaking it.

"Time to get tough." Raine consulted the caller ID readout on her phone, then turned to her laptop and typed in the numbers.

* * *

Fifty dollars restored the restaurateur's memory and loosened his tongue. "Ravi Singh?" he repeated, pocketing Cade's bill. "Yeah, I guess he works here. You sure you're nothing to do with Immigration?"

"Positive. Where is he, back in the kitchen?"

Cade had spent most of his day tracking the Indian waiter who'd delivered Lia's message last night at the museum. He'd chased down the caterer who'd served the fund-raising fiasco, locating her finally at a friend's apartment, where she was nursing a sprained ankle. In the stampede out of the museum, she'd tripped and rolled all the way down its high entry steps.

He'd learned from her that the mystery messenger wasn't one of her regular crew. Singh had applied for a job only the day before the gala. Asked for his experience, he'd claimed to have waited tables for two years at a well-known Italian restaurant in the East Nineties.

As far as his boss was concerned, he still did. "Ravi's out of town," said the man, as Cade made a move toward the kitchen. "Took off yesterday and today, to visit a sick sister down in Baltimore." When Cade raised an eyebrow, he turned up his palms. "So who knows if he's got a sister—and who cares? Guy's neat, always on time, never forgets an order or drops a dish. If he wants to take a few days off without pay, who am I to bitch?"

"Got an address for him?"

"Now giving that out *would* make me sorta uneasy."

Cade pulled another fifty from his wallet. "Would this make it any easier?"

When the parking valet returned with his Jag, Cade stayed at the curb while he called his personal assistant. "What have you got for me?" He'd assigned Marc the task of selecting a five-star restaurant for that night, emphasis on decor to dazzle a kid with Hollywood fantasies, not on fine food and impeccable but unobtrusive service, the sort of place Cade preferred.

The sort of place he'd have chosen for Raine Ashaway.

He scowled at the errant thought. His plans for Ashaway didn't include wining and dining her. Bed, maybe yes. No, bed inevitably yes. But when they got to it, it would be a mating, not a date. Tigers rolled in the grass, they didn't unfold napkins.

"I've got you down for the best table at Cafe Gray," Marc reported. "For eight o'clock. But to get a reservation before Christmas, I had to promise 'em your firstborn."

"They want to wait that long?"

"In lieu of a brat, the hostess graciously accepted two hundred. I've greased her already, so don't do it again."

"Right. Good going." Marc was a man to be counted on. When Cade stepped down from managing partner at Okab Oil, he'd hired the PA to oversee his home office. Because though Cade no longer worried about day-to-day operations, he still handled a large chunk of the company's oil exploration.

Marc took care of the details, everything from commissioning satellite surveys to obtaining deep-sea core samples. When they weren't scouting for virgin oil fields, he still had plenty to do, keeping track of Cade's previous drilling royalties and advising on where to bank the ungodly stream of cash.

He'd been somewhat surprised this past year when Cade started investing heavily in dinosaurs. Given his M.B.A. from Wharton, probably Marc didn't approve. But a PA's discretion was his stock-in-trade; he knew when to question and when to hold his tongue. Meanwhile Marc's skills in obtaining drilling rights served him just as well when Cade set him to snapping up licenses to excavate.

Wherever the Ashaways hoped to dig.

"Did the girl call yet?" Cade continued, glancing at his watch.

"She did, at three-forty-five. As you suggested, I told her I was the butler. I thought she'd swoon, for a minute there. Then once she recovered, she started treating me like a flunky."

"Watched too much *Lifestyles of the Rich and Famous* at an impressionable age," Cade agreed. "Did you capture a traceable phone number?"

"I did. She was talking on a landline, and its address is a few blocks east of Chinatown, a rough neighborhood."

Cade grimaced while Marc read off the same address that he held in his hand. He might as well have slept in. But Lia could have called from an untraceable cell phone. He'd learned years ago to never leave anything to chance, if more effort would nail it down.

"Okay," he decided. "Then I'm heading home. Find me a stretch limo—black—and lay on all the frills. Champagne, roses, etc. Tell the driver I'll want to collect Lia at her place at…say…six-thirty."

"Umm, did I misunderstand? I gave her directions to meet you at _____."

"You didn't. But now we've got her address, I'll use it. A simple demo that she's not calling all the shots. I'd say with this kid, the only thing she'll respect is a show of power."

"Ah. The type that confuses a gentleman with a wimp?"

"The type that confuses a gentleman with a sucker."

Chapter 9

"Can you talk right now?" asked Trey, when Raine answered her cell phone.

"Love to. I'm bored out of my mind." Standing in the sixth-floor stairwell of a seedy tenement, with her elbows propped on a windowsill, Raine peered across the narrow street. At the windows of Lia's apartment.

She'd taken up her spy post a couple of hours ago, after inspecting the mailboxes in the unlocked foyer of the building opposite. One box belonged to Ravi Singh, the name corresponding to the phone number Lia had used. Its card showed that he lived in apartment 6A, the unit facing the street. Lia wasn't listed as a resident, but another male name, Ivan Bogdanovich, was scrawled in below Ravi's. Two roommates plus a live-in girlfriend, was Raine's best guess.

"What's up?" Trey inquired.

Tersely she outlined the situation. Since the downstairs buzzer was broken and the inner door unlocked, she'd climbed six flights of stairs to knock on 6A's door. "But nobody was home, so I figure I've got two options here.

"First, assuming that Lia returns to dress for her date, I follow her to the restaurant where she'll meet Kincade. No way does she want to deal further with me, till she knows what he's willing to pay, so why fight it? Let her hear him out. Then I'll drop by their table along with dessert, ask what he bid—and offer more."

"One tiny problem with that," Trey observed. "My latest research shows that Kincade can buy and sell Ashaway All a dozen times over. If he wants the tooth, you can't outspend him."

Raine winced. "O-okay, that brings me to Option Two. I've had a nasty feeling all afternoon that I wouldn't be winning this auction. The chemistry between me and Lia isn't good—in fact, it's rotten. And if Kincade's got more money... But on the other hand, a *T. rex* has sixty-four teeth. So let him score that one—and I go after the other sixty-three, plus the rest of the dino."

"Why am I not surprised?"

Raine smiled to herself. "I figure if I can learn Lia's last name—and verify her first—then I can find her family when I reach her hometown. Once I meet her family, and her neighbors, and the postman, I bet I can bluff or charm or bribe my way to the next link in the chain—whoever sent Lia the package. And then pay that person to tell me where the tooth was obtained, and backtrack it from there."

"Sounds like a plan. And so you're lurking in a stairwell because?"

"Because I need to meet one of her roomies. I suppose I could buttonhole everybody who enters the building and ask 'em if they live in 6A, but this seemed more discreet. From up here I'll see when somebody comes home, then I can zip across. Knock on the door, chat 'em up."

"Ask if they'd like to rat out their roommate?"

"Well, I'm gambling that Lia may have worn out her welcome. We're talking a Borneo Princess here. If she does her share of the dishes or the housecleaning or even pays her portion of the rent, I'd be amazed."

"You'd be amazed what guys can forgive, if the rest of the package is right. And willing to be unwrapped."

"Which is why we women rule the world, but still you'd think—*oops,* here she comes!" Raine stood on tiptoe and craned close to the glass. "Complete with shopping bags from Victory's Secret, as she calls it."

"They'll forgive her," Trey predicted. "*I'd* forgive her."

Raine gave him a pitying sigh, then checked her watch as Lia disappeared into the building. Six-oh-five. "So…did you learn anything else about Kincade, besides that he's rolling in oil bucks?"

"Still digging into it. You were right—he's from our part of the world. Montana. According to a profile a few years back in *Forbes* magazine, he was raised in a boys' home for delinquents. Kincade refused to discuss it—the reporter got that fact from another source. Apparently the home wasn't a junior country club—anything but. Most of its inmates graduate from there, then take an advanced degree at the state prison."

"But Kincade didn't?" Raine rubbed the back of her hand slowly across her lips. No wonder the man had an edge; in a place like that he'd have had to toughen—or go under.

"Not him. Guess he was smart enough to learn his lesson. On release at age seventeen, he was hired as a roughneck by a drilling company—some sort of state-sponsored apprenticeship. He worked with them for two years, and I guess he must have been a standout—they paid his way through five years at Colorado School of Mines.

He got his MS in geology, then went back to work for the same company. They sent him to Saudi Arabia, then Kurat. For five years he gives them their money's worth—he set some kind of record for finding wildcat wells. Then the next thing you know, he's gone into business for himself, partnering with the nephew-in-law of the emir of Kurat. Nobody can figure out how he swung an introduction to the royal family, much less an exec-level buy-in."

Across the street, a lamp blinked on in Lia's apartment. Raine glanced at her watch. Nearly eight minutes to climb all those stairs. She couldn't see 6A's entrance door from her vantage point, but this must be the living room. Strictly student decor. The floor lamp stood beside a desk that was piled high with books. On the opposite side of the room, a sagging couch faced a TV set. Lia flitted past the window, then vanished. A light went on in the next window to the left, but Raine couldn't look in from this angle. A bedroom or bathroom? "Go back to the home for delinquents a minute. What was he in for?"

"Beats me. Juvenile records are sealed. Sometimes they're even erased, if you can obtain a pardon. Maybe if I fly up there…"

"Yeah, right," Raine teased. Trey would seize any excuse to fly. He owned a home-built ultralight, a glider, plus a WWII-vintage Cessna. "Maybe you should focus on getting me off to Borneo first?"

"You're reserved already, on a direct flight, three days from now, New York to Singapore," Trey assured her. "And I'm working on connections from there to Kalimantan. There's nothing direct to Pontianak City."

Two expeditious steps ahead of her as usual. "And a visa?"

"Working on it. If there isn't time to get it legal, anything's obtainable over there with a bribe. You're up to date on your tropical shots, of course. Tomorrow morning let's plan your field kit."

"Oh-ho!" Raine interrupted, peering down the street. "Now here's a development. Here comes Kincade, dressed to kill, and he's carrying…yep…I'd say he's brought the champagne." She glared at the long paper bag tucked under the elbow of his conservative black dinner suit. "Damn the man! If this means he's already sewn up the deal and now they're celebrating—!"

"Just as likely it means he's trying to soften her up," Trey consoled her, while she watched Cade vanish beyond the foyer. "Look, would it make any sense to send Ash in to negotiate with the kid, if the chemistry's wrong between you two?"

"Might work," Raine muttered glumly. "He's nearer her age than Kincade, and he's certainly prettier." Though Cade seemed by far the sexier. But then how could a sister judge? "If Ash could take time off and get here *pronto...*"

But if her older brother outmaneuvered or outcharmed Kincade for the tooth, then it wouldn't be her kill. And the way Ashaway All was structured, that mattered. The top moneymaker in the company each year commanded the most funds the following, to finance the expedition of his or her choice. "Let me think about it.

"But for now...I'd better start paying attention," she added as Lia passed the window, apparently hurrying to answer a knock at her door. Cade must have taken those stairs two at a time. "Talk t'you, Trey." She tucked her phone in a pocket...as Lia flew backward into view, arms flailing, hair flying. The girl's hip hit the corner of the desk—she clawed at the floor lamp and it toppled with her. The lightbulb flared and blew out.

"Jeez!" Raine pressed her forehead to the glass as somebody followed the girl in a rush. Black clothes and big in the dusky room—Kincade, it had to be! "You *bastard!* Leave her alone!"

As he swooped down on the girl, he vanished from sight. Then, limp as a broken doll, Lia was hoisted to her feet. Her body blocked Raine's view of her attacker—all but those big hands gripping the girl's naked arms—shaking her.

Calling 911 would take too long. By the time the cops arrived—Raine spun, grabbed the brass banister, and took the first flight in two bounds. *Go! Move!* She wheeled around the landing, grabbed the rail and leaped again. *Hang on, Lia, I'm coming!*

Another flight down: images cascading past in an adrenaline rush. Red-brown stains on a step; a broken window lit this landing; was this the third floor or still the fourth? And— oh God!—was that somebody climbing to meet her? *"Coming through!"* Raine yelled, as she hit the next landing, wheeled around it—

To slam head-on into a bearded man with a bag of groceries. "Ooof! *Sorry!*" Cans rolled down the steps; a bottle smashed. "Excuse me! Emergency!" She ducked under his elbow, grabbed the rail again—a hand as big and rough as a pineapple clamped on her wrist. "Can't...stop!" she panted, whirling back to face him.

"Oh, yeah? Then who's going to pay for all—"

"I will! But later!"

"Yeah, right, babe. Let's see some money now."

"Le'*go!*" Her fingers found the nerve just above his funny bone. He roared and released her—then swung a backhand that would have decked her if it landed square. She swerved her head and it raked her cheekbone.

That would hurt later, and plenty, but for now—Raine let the blow spin her the way she was going. She leaped, missed a can of tomatoes by an inch—kept on descending. His threats echoed down the stairwell behind her.

Bursting out through the front doors, she vaulted the steps to the sidewalk, dodged between a row of empty garbage cans, staggered out into the street. Gulping for air, she looked up at Lia's window.

Its upper sash shivered as something dark pressed against it from within. A pane shattered. *"No!"* Throwing her hands up to shield her face, Raine shied out from under—and stumbled backward over a can. Her feet flew up, her head cracked against the curb.

Flat on her back, she stared dazedly up. Beyond the dark rooftops, the sky was infinitely clear, a heart-piercing shade of lilac.

Glass tinkled and chimed on the pavement, then...

Whump!

She'd never heard the sound before, but there was no mistaking it. Raine's fingers crept toward each other...wove together...squeezed till they ached. A gull wheeled overhead, its wings flaming red-gold with the setting sun—it sheered away in a wide lovely turn and soared off toward the sea. *Oh, Lia, I'm sorry!*

Raine rolled wearily to hands and knees. No hurry now. Somebody was screaming and pointing as she hung out a window of the next building down. The silly fool would fall herself, if she wasn't careful. Onlookers came running to look, made gagging sounds, then scuttled away. Not the kind of neighborhood where people stayed to chat with the cops. Raine stumbled to her feet and limped over. No way could Lia have survived that drop, but still...

She crouched beside the girl—less blood than she would have thought. Raine put two fingers to the pulse point in her neck.

Nothing... Not a beat, not a flicker of hope. Just Lia's unblinking eyes, staring blindly at forever. All that ambition and pride and drive and desire just...stopped. *Poor little blue-handed dreamer.* Raine hadn't liked her, yet she'd had to admire her. The kid had been a fighter.

And the man she'd fought? As the thought rammed home, Raine spun and looked up.

To lock eyes with Kincade. Six lethal stories above, Lia's killer leaned out the open window, gazing bleakly down. "You *bastard!*" Raine whispered, her hands clenched to fists.

Echoing through the concrete canyons, a siren whooped louder and louder.

Sometime around midnight, the police finished with Raine. She signed the typed transcript of her statement, then dragged herself to her feet. "There. May I go now?"

Tipped back in his desk chair, Detective Henderson clasped his stubby hands behind his stubby neck. "Long as you're sure you've got nothing else to tell me. You're absolutely *certain* you didn't take something offa the body?"

"I told you. I checked her pulse—that's all." He'd grilled her on this point till she was ready to scream. What were they looking for?

"If you say so. But if you happen to think of anything else... Something you forgot or left out or want to change your mind about—"

"There's *nothing* else. That's what I saw and how I saw it. Now when do you think you'll make an arrest? It's an open-and-shut case, isn't it?" When he gave her a smirk and a patronizing shrug, she scowled and turned away. "G'night, Detective." She headed for the door to the corridor, half expecting him to object.

Instead he ambled behind to yell at a uniform who'd just emerged from the bathroom. "Jekyll. Lady here needs a ride."

She glanced back. "No, thanks. I'll catch a cab."

Henderson snorted. "After midnight? You want to get mugged, do it on your own time. And not on my turf. Take her home, Jekyll."

Too tired to argue, Raine stalked out the front doors of the station, with Jekyll tagging at her heels. Several patrol cars were parked illegally along the curb. Behind the last of these stretched half a block of black limo.

With a tall, too-familiar figure lounging against its glossy flank.

"You!" Raine stopped short. "What are *you* doing here?"

"Waiting for you." In the harsh glare of a streetlight, Kincade's face looked like a rough stretch of the Badlands. Shadows hooded his deep-set eyes; still they seemed to glow in their sockets like a hunting cat's.

She spun so fast that Jekyll retreated two steps. "Why isn't this man in jail? For murder!"

"Because I didn't do it." Cade opened the limo's back door. "Let's go."

"I mean it! He pushes a girl out a window and you let him walk?"

"Umm, you'll have t'ask Henderson," mumbled the young officer, not meeting her eyes. "I just do what he tells me." He jerked a thumb at a squad car. "So if you'd like that ride…"

"I'll save you the trouble. She's headed my way." Cade gestured at the limo's interior. "Raine, if you want an explanation, get in."

"Like I'm going anywhere with you!" She glanced back at Jekyll. "I'll take that ride, but hang on a minute. And keep an eye on me, will you?" She stalked to the rear of the limo, and as she'd expected, Kincade followed.

She swung to confront him. "If you've anything you want to say to me, then say it now." *With a witness.* Lia's neck had been snapped before she was tossed out the window, Raine had heard one detective tell another. Her gaze swerved to his big hands—she flinched as one of them rose toward her throat.

He touched her chin. "Where'd you get that?" Cade scowled at the bruise blossoming on her cheekbone. "Somebody *hit* you?"

How could they have not arrested him? He certainly looked murderous enough at the moment. "It's nothing." Compared with what he'd done to Lia? "So why didn't they throw you in jail? Fancy lawyer?"

Cade crossed his arms and shrugged. "Only a fool talks to the cops without one."

"Money talks and bullshit walks—or rides home in a limo. Why did you *do* it? Wouldn't it have been simpler just to buy the damned thing?"

"When I got to her door it was locked," Cade said heavily. "I could hear her screaming. Might have been curses, could have been pleading, who knows? It wasn't English. And I heard a man laugh. Things were falling and smashing, clearly a fight going on. So I broke the door in." He rubbed his left bicep reflectively. "That took a while. It wasn't hollow core, and the locks were…well, what you'd want for this neighborhood. By the time I got through it, she was…gone."

He was smooth, she'd give him that, but Raine didn't buy it. "And Lia's *mysterious* attacker?"

"Went out the kitchen window, which overlooks the fire escape on the side of the building. Screen was kicked out. Curtains still flapping."

"How convenient! And original! The Soddit defense—some other dude musta dunnit." It would have taken Cade less than a minute to set that scene. "Well, thanks for nothing." She started past him, then jolted to a halt as he caught her wrist.

"Look, it's late. If you're afraid to ride with me, take my limo and I'll catch a cab."

"Afraid!" With his fingers encircling her bones—overlapping them with inches to spare—she had a sudden, body-deep awareness of the contrast in their sizes. It sent a shock wave pulsing down her veins. With one twist he could shatter her wrist as easily as he'd snapped Lia's neck. "It's a question of taste."

"Have it your way." He gave a rueful grimace and released her. "But before you go, Raine, one question."

"What?" she growled, backing away toward Jekyll.

"When you searched her body, did you find her watch?"

Chapter 10

"Eight!" Raine exhaled as she lifted the weights sideways to shoulder height, then held them for a count of five. She inhaled as she lowered the ten-pound dumbbells in triple-slow motion. Sweat darkened the midline of her T-shirt, beaded on her brow. *"Nine!"*

Balancing her workout with his own version of feline Zen, Otto sat on the counter that divided living room from galley kitchen. Eyes half-closed in ecstasy, the tom was eating one of the yellow roses Raine had found outside her door last night, with a thank-you card from Trenton.

The football player had sent white and pink and salmon roses, as well—she'd lost count around fifty dozen. Raine had given all but this arrangement to Otto's parents, James and Eric, one floor below. *"Ten*-and-you're-going-to-be-sick," she warned the cat, who naturally ignored her.

Her cell phone rang as she started her eleventh rep. She growled and walked across to it with weights on high, brought them down, then answered, "Raine Ashaway. Hang on a sec.

Twelve!" she said through her teeth, which completed her final set. "Yes?"

"Me," Trey announced. "I finally caught up with Mac-Pherson."

Trey had a friend of a friend in the NYPD; Raine had expected no less. "What I mainly want to know is why they won't arrest Kincade?" she said, moving the remains of her bouquet to a cat-proof shelf.

"Well, for starters, their only witness said she never saw the killer's face."

"I didn't, but given the timing, who else could it have been?"

"You told them that he climbed six flights of stairs in maybe three minutes."

"We were talking, remember? I wasn't paying precise attention." She blew out a frustrated breath. "I guess I said it seemed sort of fast." But with the shape Kincade was in, he could have run six flights of stairs without breaking a sweat. "But I did tell 'em that Lia's attacker was wearing black, the same color as Kincade's suit."

"Last time I passed through the city, nine out of ten New Yorkers wore black. Place looks like a standing-room-only funeral."

"When was that?" she asked quickly. Trey steadfastly refused to say where he went on his vacations.

"A while back," he drawled with the barest hint of a smile in his voice.

She rolled her eyes—then bent straight over, forehead to knees, stretching her hamstrings. "Still, if not Kincade, who else could they suspect?"

"They like her roommate, Ravi Singh. Seems they picked up Lia's other roomie, an Ivan Bogdanovich, who works night-shift at Bellevue Hospital. He wandered home to change to his uniform round about 9:00 p.m. and they grabbed him. He claims he ran across Singh in the corner bar at roughly seven-thirty."

According to Bogdanovich, Singh was crazy in love with

Lia, but his affections were unrequited. The girl traded on his hopes without mercy. Yesterday Lia had taunted Ravi, telling him she had a date with a man who needed no green card—a rich and handsome American. "Bogdanovich says Ravi was stinking drunk when he met him. He figures, and the cops figure, that Ravi offed the girl, then went out the kitchen window and down the fire escape, when Kincade knocked at the door. They figure his binge last night was murderer's remorse."

"What does Singh say?"

"He'd left the bar by the time they hit it. Two uniforms staked out the apartment overnight, but he never showed. Which makes him look guiltier."

"Or he's guilty of nothing but bad taste in women. Lia snubbed him, so he drowned his hurt feelings in booze, then passed out somewhere and slept it off. They've got no more on him than on Kincade—less, since I can place Kincade at the scene of the crime. And Kincade had motivation—he wanted Lia's tooth."

"'Fraid from the cops' point of view, a jealous boyfriend seems a more likely killer than a millionaire. A millionaire whose thousand-dollar-per-hour defense lawyer is breathing down their necks."

"That's *so* unfair. And if it was jealousy that killed Lia, then why would Singh steal the tooth? How do they explain that it's missing?"

"They don't seem to be too worried about that. My guess is they're having a problem wrapping their minds around a *Tyrannosaurus rex* tooth in the middle of their nice, normal case of domestic violence. If they do believe it really exists, then they're thinking you've got no proof that she kept it in that apartment. Maybe she hid it at NYU, where she went to school? Or how about a safety deposit box?"

"Or how 'bout Cade—Kincade—removed it?" Raine snapped, whipping upright. "He wanted it, he went for it, and—hey!—now it's gone."

"And he stashed it where? If Kincade can pocket a ten-inch dino tooth without a bag or a bulge, I want to meet his tailor."

It took Raine a moment to wrap *her* mind around the concept of Trey in a suit instead of his usual T-shirt and faded jeans, then she said, "That's easy. After he killed her, Kincade found the tooth and its box. He hid it someplace in the apartment, planning to collect it later, then he strolled downstairs just as the cops arrived."

"If there's one thing the police know how to do, it's how to search. And I understand they looked, so you can scratch that idea."

Raine wasn't so sure; Cade wasn't some burnt-out druggie hiding his stash in the freezer. The man had brains and imagination. Given a few minutes, he might have devised an unassailable cache. "Or-r-r, he took it with him, out of Lia's apartment," she said, thinking aloud. "He walked down a flight or two, knocked on somebody's door, handed whoever answered the box, and wrote him or her a check for ten thousand dollars. He promised this person that if he'd meet Kincade tomorrow—i.e. this morning—somewhere, say at the arch in Washington Square, and bring the box with him—"

"Kincade would redeem it for ten thou in cash?" Trey finished skeptically. "What if the receiver hands the tooth to the cops instead?"

"Believe me, the Boy Scouts cleared out of that neighborhood a long time ago. And anybody with street smarts would know that if he turns in the tooth to the cops, they'll give him a pat on the head—maybe—and *zip* reward. If he brings it to Kincade, he's paid and paid well."

"I s'pose it could have happened that way," Trey conceded, "but me, I like things simple. I'm leaning to the roommate theory. Even if Singh killed her for love, he had to know the tooth was valuable. He's the guy who helped Lia arrange her auction. So why not grab it on his way out the window?"

"And the watch?" She hadn't mentioned Cade's question of the night before.

"The watch is easy. If the girl had two things of value that came from the same place, it's likely she stored them together. Whoever grabbed the box, got them both."

"Mmm, maybe." Raine wandered to the sliding-glass doors and stared out over her own tiny balcony, at a green and cluttered oasis. Tiers and rows of similar balconies jutted out from the backsides of the brownstones that faced on the next block—the hanging gardens of Upper Westside cliff dwellers. Walled-off from the rumbling streets, the balconies formed a precious and secret refuge, all the wilderness most of her neighbors would ever explore. She made a face. The city was starting to get to her, right on schedule.

She peered up at the rectangle of hazy blue enclosed by the rooftops. It was hours yet till dark, when she could go prowling. Try to find some facts to replace all these theories. Surely the cops wouldn't stake out Lia's apartment two nights in a row?

"Speaking of the watch, was that sketch I faxed you of any use?" she asked idly. To the best of her memory, she'd drawn the butterfly-shaped lake—if it was a lake—with the range of mountains below it. If Trey could locate this spot within Borneo, perhaps she'd start her search there.

"Not so far. Maps of the interior are mostly vintage World War Two, and they come with polite little disclaimers that say in effect 'nobody's ever been here or seen this, but rumor has it that maybe, just possibly, within a couple of hundred miles of hereabouts, you *might* find…'"

"Hmm. I'll see what I can find at this end. Now about my field kit. Should I take a folding kayak?"

The e-mail message from the B-frog opened with its usual warning:

You have fifteen seconds to hit the print key!

Cade executed the command. While the hard copy slid out of his printer, he watched the digital words melt into rain and drizzle down to make a puddle at the bottom of his computer screen. A frog stuck his head up from the pool. Out shot its tongue to nail a letter *k* that had turned into a frantic butterfly. With a gulp and a rude belch, the bullfrog sank from view. Then came the sound of a flushing toilet; the water drained away.

Most e-mail messages were recoverable even after their receiver had deleted them, the B-frog had warned Cade at the start of their association. But not his. Cade reached across his desk for the hacker's hard copy, from which all origination info had been omitted. If this paper ever fell into enemy hands, it would incriminate only himself.

Latest activity on the Ashaway credit cards. First: Raine Ashaway is ticketed Raffles class, seat C-1, on flight 143, Singapore Airlines, leaving Newark Airport, September 28 at 11 p.m. Booked nonstop to Singapore. No connecting reservations so far. I note that there's still space on this bird, in case you're interested.

Second: someone just purchased a folding kayak in NYC.

All for now. You can wire my usual fee to:

Never the same bank twice, Cade noted as he read the routing instructions. And he doubted the money would stop there. Wherever and whoever the B-frog was, he didn't mean to be gigged for the services he provided.

Cade jotted a note for Marc, who'd gone out to lunch.

I need a folding kayak, and reservation on this flight, this date.

He smiled grimly to himself. His private assistant drew the line at dealing with hackers, but Cade had no such qualms. He'd use whomever or whatever it took to bring the Ashaways down.

Funny. He'd always expected to feel a savage satisfaction

at the end of his quest. A bleak closure on the day he finally stamped their debt Paid in Full. But in all his years of planning toward that goal, he'd never dreamed he'd feel such pleasure in the task itself. This eagerness that lifted him and carried him along from hour to hour.

He shrugged, then bent his head to the note to add a final linc.

And Marc, I want the seat next to C-1. Make it happen.

Chapter 11

He didn't dare go back that same night, but the next, Szabo spotted only one cop on stakeout. The stupid shitheel was parked down the street, where he could look up from the comfort of his unmarked car at the windows of Lia's apartment. Slurping coffee and watching for the lights to come on.

Not a problem. Szabo had brought a flashlight. Hands in his pockets, he sauntered on down the street, cutting his eyes at the spot where she must have hit the ground. By the yellow rays of a streetlight, he made out a stain that might be somebody's oil leak—or might be hers.

The hair stood up on his arms and he laughed under his breath. He'd forgotten how it felt, that funny glow. Hadn't felt it in years. Like a joyride in a rich man's car, only better. Like the end of the joyride, when you pushed the big shiny Cadillac off a cliff, just to hear it go smash.

Silly bitch. If she hadn't bitten him, he'd have let her live. Probably. Leastways long enough to tell him all he needed to know. But she'd clamped down on his arm with those sharp little teeth and he'd…lost it for a second there. The ol' Ranger training had kicked in, and next thing you knew, her ear was resting on her skinny shoulder. Haste makes waste, as Gran always said.

Then somebody had started kicking down her door. He'd tossed her out the window, hoping they'd think she'd jumped. He'd turned and bingo! there was the box, on a shelf above her desk.

But once he'd had time to look through it, he had more questions than ever. So here he was, back where he'd started. She'd shared her place with a couple of guys, he'd noticed when he scouted the place. If he could lay hold of one of them, maybe the roomie would know something useful. Women never could keep their traps shut.

Szabo strolled on around the block, then cut through a backyard and over a fence. Went in through the broken basement window, same as he had the last time. Up all those damn stairs to her door, which had been patched back together with epoxy and ring nails. A yellow tape marked it as a crime scene. *Mine,* he thought with a twinge of pride as he knocked. "Hey, anybody home?" he called cheerfully, with one rawboned fist cocked and waiting.

When nobody answered, Szabo stood and pondered. He could kick it in, sure, but if somebody heard? Or if the cop stirred his lard ass, and came up to check things out?

Better to go in the same way he'd gone out.

The cop in the unmarked car had a clear view of the front door to Lia's building. He might not recognize her from the night before, but Raine was taking no chances. She circled the block and walked down the alley at the right side of the tenement. The hinged ladder to the fire escape was folded up. If she stood on the Dumpster beneath it and leaped from there, then maybe… She wrinkled her nose at the smell of rotten fish wafting up from the bin. *Gotta be a more elegant approach.*

Twenty minutes later she stepped out on the roof of the building to the left of Lia's. Padding across its tarred gravel, she stopped to consult a gray cat that approached with its tail in vertical "greetings" position. "All clear?" she inquired as it performed the obligatory circle and strop.

Rubbing its cheek along the haft of her knife—she wore it strapped to her ankle beneath her climbing pants—the cat seemed unworried. Politely it accompanied her to the edge of the building. They sat together on the low perimeter wall, peering down.

A gap of some three feet separated this building from Lia's. An easy downward jump of about six feet, since the roof of Lia's building was slightly lower. Coming back would be nastier. "Must be nice not to have an imagination," she groused to the cat. The thought of slipping down that black slot between... Raine shuddered, then put it firmly from her mind. "Why go to the carnival, if you're not gonna ride the roller coaster?" She crouched—and leaped— teetered for an instant along the brink with arms outstretched, then stepped briskly to the rooftop. "Piece of cake," she assured the cat.

Who gave her a look of mild astonishment—then rolled back on its haunches to hoist a hind leg at the sky. Dipping its head, it licked its inner thigh, then paused, lost in thought.

At the far side of Lia's building, Raine looked down at the fire escape which ended one story below. She could have made the jump—reluctantly—but that would be foolish. The iron framework would vibrate and groan. Apartment dwellers in the city tended to notice strange sounds on the fire escapes.

She pulled a length of climbing rope from her backpack, and tied it to a vent pipe. Knotting in a half dozen foot loops for the return trip, she eased it over the drop-off, wrapped it around shoulder and hips, then followed, walking slowly down the bricks.

Stealthy as the cat, she picked her way down two flights

of quaking iron to the sixth-floor landing. Nobody had bothered to reinsert the window screen, or close the window. She
crouched near the square of darkness and listened. Bogdanovich should be working his graveyard shift at the hospital,
and Ravi? By now he must surely have learned he was a
murder suspect. If he had any sense, he'd caught a bus for
Toronto.

Shifting closer along the ironwork, she bumped something
with her knee—she winced as it clinked. What the heck? Her
fingers explored the open grid of…ah, a milk crate! Of course.
Lia and her friends had expanded their limited storage space
beyond their apartment. Raine's fingertips played over the
mouths of empty bottles. This must be the recycling bin.

As her eyes adjusted to the gloom, she made out other
shapes shoved up alongside the building. Her pulse quickened
with a thought. Sure, the police had searched the apartment,
but had they checked the fire escape? If Lia had hidden her
tooth out here…

Exploring by Braille, she found more bottles, an open box
containing parts of a bicycle? Something stringy and damp
and disgusting that at best interpretation was the head of a
mop. She made a face and reached again—*"Youch!"*

Swearing silently, she yanked her hand back. Who would
have thought that Lia would have a green thumb? Or go in
for cacti? This was one of those big floppy octopus types with
an attitude.

Raine sat for a moment, picking out needles, then decided:
Enough of this. She was stalling. Time to enter the cave. If
Lia was now an angry and frustrated ghost, her main grudge
shouldn't be with Raine.

Flattening one hand on the sill, she reached past it with the
other, to trace the smooth border of a metal sink. That would
be fun to climb over. She shifted her weight forward—then
froze. *Jeez, was that a light?*

For an instant the doorway on the far side of the kitchen
seemed to glow, as if a faint light had been switched on be-

yond. *Holy, holy, ohmigod!* She duckwalked back from the window, then peeked with one eye around its frame, ready to bolt.

Cool, be cool, stay cool, she chided herself. Maybe it was just a headlight, reflecting off something below? Or the police around in front, shining a spotlight up at the windows?

From somewhere beyond the kitchen, a voice spoke—one muffled note of inquiry. The light went out.

"Gran?" said Szabo, when his grandmother finally answered her phone.

"Godalmighty, boy, do you know what *time* it is?" She launched straight into a tirade, ripping a strip off him while he propped one hip on the desk and switched off his flashlight. The old bat had no reason to bitch; she never went to bed till after Letterman. But she'd spent her whole life bitching, so why quit now?

Szabo waited till she ran out of steam; the emphysema sort of limited her scope, these days. Then he answered her last question. "I didn't call you before, 'cause there's no phone in my hotel room." And he didn't feel like dropping quarters in the lobby pay phone, while the whores lined up behind him to check in with their pimps.

He'd figured there wasn't much risk in calling his Gran from Lia's apartment. Lia had phoned him twice from this number already. If the cops ever checked, which he sincerely doubted they would, he had his story worked out: Her grandma had met his granddaddy back in Borneo, during WWII. *Met him and showed him a jumping good time,* he amended with a private grin. *Better than Gran ever gave him.*

When she got to the States, Lia had presumed on this long-gone connection to hit him up for a loan. He'd told her what she could do to herself, but she'd kept right on phoning. And can you believe it, now her roommates had taken up the cause. Like he'd give a gook a nickel, but hey, hope springs eternal as the preacher said.

"Hmmph!" Gran wheezed for a minute, then got down to business. "Did you get your granddad's watch?"

"I got it." Now here came the hard part. "And she had more than that."

"The treasure! Don't tell me she had the treasure!"

"Now, Gran, think a minute. In Granddad's letter, did he ever say 'treasure'?" Szabo knew he didn't. Same as she'd done with his daddy before him, she'd raised him on that one letter that made it out of Borneo, two years after the war ended. Some kids got bedtime stories, he'd been tucked in with her reading him that raggedy old scrap of paper. He could recite it line by line. "He said he and his buddies were digging up something of great value and someday, after the war, we were gonna be rich as kings. Richer than King Midas. That's what he said, do you remember?"

"But what else can you dig up that's worth a king's fortune? It had to be buried treasure!"

"I always figured it for a gold mine, myself," Szabo confessed. "Or maybe a diamond mine." That time he'd gone to Borneo to try and claim the family fortune, he'd heard tell about lost diamond mines, way up in the mountains. Though try to find anybody who'd ever been there.

"A gold mine would be good," Gran allowed, though she sounded pissed. "I guess gold would do."

"Gran, you're not *listening*. I never said it was gold, I said I used t'figure—oh, shit." He paused, frustrated. "Look, it wasn't gold. It's something much better." At least he hoped. "I mailed it to you, 'long with Granddad's watch, so look for it 'bout day after tomorrow. And don't you go showing it to anybody, once it gets there."

"What ever is it then?"

He squirmed on the desk. "Well, first I thought it must be a whale tooth. But then I ask myself, what's a whale doing smack-dab in the middle of Borneo?" He'd made a careful drawing of it, and taken it back to that pretty reference librarian at the New York Public Library. The same babe who'd helped him track down Lia's address. "So I asked somebody who oughta know, and she says it must be a dinosaur tooth."

A thunderous silence echoed down the phone line.

"And it's not just any old dinosaur tooth," he hurried to say before she could find her tongue. "It's made out of precious stone. Opal, like that ring Grandaddy gave you for your engagement. But not just an itty-bitty chip. It's a great whacking chunk of opal."

"I *told* that silly fool that opal's bad luck," she muttered. "I said he ought to return it and buy me a proper diamond, but would he? Oh, no, he went all mulish."

Bet he won it in a poker game, Szabo thought with a smirk. No returns.

"But look who got the bad luck in the end?" she said with brooding satisfaction. "Dropped into some godforsaken jungle... Probably eaten by leeches or those piranha fish."

All the nature shows she watched, she ought to know piranhas only lived in the Amazon, but Szabo knew better than to correct her.

She heaved a grudging sigh. "Well...I suppose it's better than nothing. So when are you coming home?"

Try never. Since they'd released him from Leavenworth a couple of years back, he'd been moping around the home place. Grieving his lost career. Envying his old buddies, who were stationed in Afghanistan these days. They must be having a hot old time of it.

But coming to New York had given him a much-needed kick in the ass. There were still plenty of good times to be found, if a guy sniffed around. Still ways for him to be all he could be.

"Amos?"

Aw, wasn't that sweet; she must be missing him. "Ain't quite finished here, Gran." He'd asked his librarian if she knew anything about dinosaur bones made out of opal, and at first she'd thought he was crazy. But then she'd searched her computer. There were even a couple of Web sites where companies offered to buy opalized fossils. Somebody with the weird name of Raine Ashaway promised to meet you anywhere in the world, if you had opalized dinosaur bones for sale.

"I got to thinking about Granddaddy's letter. He said he and his buddies were digging up something. And you recollect how he said they'd persuaded some of the natives to help them?" She wheezed agreement, so he continued. "Well, the tooth I'm sending you is 'most as big as a loaf of bread. Wouldn't take any time at all to dig it up, and the job sure wouldn't take a whole squad of paratroopers plus a pack of gooks. So I'm thinking—" He tipped back his head and laughed at the ceiling, thinking it. "I'm thinking the *whole dang sucker's* gotta still be out there somewhere! Going by that tooth, it's as big as a firetruck. And my friend says it'd be the rarest thing in the world. A gold mine won't even touch it. I'm thinking that's worth finding."

Or die trying.

Something clinked in the darkness and he jerked around. *"Shit!"* he whispered. He'd been dreaming on the job.

"What did you say? What'd you say to me, boy?"

Without a word, he hung up the phone—then slunk toward Lia's kitchen door.

Chapter 12

From where she crouched, Raine couldn't make out the words but she was fairly certain it was a man speaking; the timbre was baritone.

And who's he talking to? Occasional pauses suggested a conversation, yet strain as she would, she could hear only one voice.

After a while it hit her—she laughed under her breath. *A clock radio on a timer, what do you bet?* It must be back in one of the bedrooms. *Well, if that's all it is…* She caught the window frame and leaned into the dark—yet something made her hesitate. Her nerves were jumping. Then she sucked in a breath as she realized: The fire escape was vibrating beneath her!

Yikes! She rose, glanced downward, saw shadowy motion a couple of floors below. *Outa here, now!* She glided toward the open stairway leading up to the next floor, padded up it. *Who the hell is this?*

If she fled to the roof she'd be safe—but she'd never know. Trey had warned her more than once that curiosity would be the death of her, but still… Sinking to her knees on the seventh-floor landing, Raine stretched out flat on her face, to peer between the iron bars. If whoever-it-was looked up, then she was simply a ratty old rug that 7A had spread out on his landing to please his cat. Projecting rug thoughts on all wavelengths, she slowed her breathing and widened her eyes.

Given the gloom of the alley and her foreshortened angle, there wasn't much to see. Her fellow prowler was a man, dark haired, or wearing a dark watch cap. *Kincade?* she asked herself, then decided not. The shoulders weren't broad enough. He seemed altogether smaller, maybe medium height.

He squatted by the window—and something tinkled. He'd bumped the crate of bottles. He paused for a full minute, then spread his hands on the sill. His head and shoulders ducked carefully below the raised sash—

A startled shriek ended in a meaty *WHACK!*

"Wh-what? No, wait! *Don't!*" the prowler cried in a lilting accent that Raine recognized. His body was jerked forward, then—

Whang! Th-*THUNK!*

Heart hammering, Raine flew down the steps as the sound came again.

Thunk!

Somebody was banging Ravi's head in the sink! Bashing his brains out, it sounded like! She lunged across the landing, then froze as the sounds died away. Ravi lay limp and unmoving. *Jeez, he's dead! Is he dead?*

"Ohhh-ah-h," Ravi groaned, starting to stir.

"Huh," someone grunted within the kitchen, on a low note of amusement.

Something about that sound—her hair stood on end.

Big hands reached out from the dark, clamped on Ravi's upper arms—and pulled. Moaning and resisting feebly, he slid a foot into the darkness.

Oh, no. Absolutely NOT! Raine straddled Ravi's body, grabbed his belt—and tugged. "Ooof!" He was heavier than he looked; still she dragged him a foot back toward safety.

"Huh?" The hands shot out, fumbling for a better grasp on the victim. She caught a glimpse of black sleeves up to the elbow. He grunted—and Ravi was drawn inward a foot, like a mouse down the jaws of a snake.

"Let him *go,* Kincade!" she snarled, almost sitting as she hauled back on Ravi's dead weight. Had to be Kincade, who else could it be?

"Whuh?" The exclamation ended in a coarse guffaw.

Oh, what, now you know it's a woman, you think it'll be easy? And damned if he didn't grab hold of Ravi *again!* "I said let him *go!*" Hanging on to Ravi's belt with one hand, Raine groped desperately with the other, found a flowerpot— she lobbed it into the dark. Heard it thump home.

With a wordless roar, he wrenched Ravi inward, sending her staggering.

Stubborn bastard, would you give it a rest? Raine threw the bicycle parts, box and all—and was rewarded with a yell as they whacked into his skull, then clattered into the sink. She seized the moment to regain a foot on the prize, who was squeaking and wriggling, not helping her at all.

The hands shot out, hooked over Ravi's belt—and pulled.

No way could she match the strength in those big bony wrists. "Shit, shit, oh, *shit!*" And Raine remembered her knife. Yanking it out, she slashed it across the black sleeves. A thick sweater of some sort, the fabric dragging at her blade.

"BITCH!" The hands whipped out of sight.

"You better believe it!" Finding the pot she wanted, she fed him the cactus—rammed it straight where his face must be.

"Yiiiii! Shit!"

While he juggled with that, she used all her strength to hoist Ravi backward. Got him all out—leaned over him to slam the sash down. "Come on, move! *Help* me!"

He moaned and crabbed backward toward the stairs.

Raine grabbed the crate of bottles, swung it over her head. Leaning against the bricks beside the window, she waited, panting. *Come on, come on! You want some more?*

"Is he…is he still there?" Ravi asked behind her after a minute.

"I dunno," she muttered. "Why don't you go on down?"

"And leave you? Don't be absurd!"

He sounded so offended, she found she was weakly laughing, her arms shaking so hard the bottles tinkled like sleigh bells. "Why not? Whole night's been nothing but absurd." *And where the hell is he?* She shuddered at the thought of him, waiting in the darkness just the other side of the wall, like a trap-spider. Like a troll. What had he meant to do with Ravi anyway, eat him?

Kincade, is that really you? Somehow Raine couldn't fit her sense of that man—with…*this.* He might be a killer, but he wasn't…creepy. At least, she hadn't thought so. Her whole body jerked at the sound of a distant thud.

"That was…I do believe that was the front door. He's left my apartment," Ravi said, hauling himself to his feet.

"Or he wants us to think he has." No way was *she* checking it out.

Suddenly Raine pictured the alley below, with all its shadows and crannies between the Dumpster and the lighted street. But they had to go down. Ravi was too wobbly to boost him up her rope to the roof; he might even be concussed. *How long will it take the troll to go out the back way, then around to the alley?* Whoever he was, he wasn't a quitter.

"Let's go," she said crisply. "If somebody heard all the racket out here and called the cops, there's one right around the corner."

"Ah, yes." Ravi explored his nose and cheekbones with the fingertips of both hands. "That would be wise." He leaned closer, squinting at her face through swollen eyes. "It is Ms. Ashaway that I have to thank, is it not?"

"It is." She caught his elbow and urged him toward the stairs. "But don't thank me yet."

They didn't stop moving till they reached the nearest subway and caught an uptown train. As they rumbled into the tunnel, Raine swung around to peer back at the dusky platform. Ever since they'd crept out of the alley, the back of her neck had been prickling. Probably nothing but adrenaline aftershocks. If somebody had followed them through the late-night streets, he was good. She'd never caught a glimpse.

"You see someone?" asked Ravi nervously. "Once or twice I thought I heard...*something* behind us."

"A couple of guys got on farther down the train. I didn't get a clear look." Though neither had moved with Kincade's feral grace. "I think we're okay." She glanced at him critically. "But you...I'm afraid your nose might be broken." His face was a mess, masked in a V-shaped swath of dried blood from the bridge of his nose to his chin. And there was no place to clean him up this time of night. "Maybe you should go to an emergency room?"

He smiled and shook his head. "I'll see you home, then I go to friends."

Just who was rescuing whom here? "You didn't kill her, did you?"

His jolt of laughter said the question was ridiculous; the sound wavered along a sob. "She was a beautiful, greedy child and I would have married her in, how do you say it? In a heartbeat."

Which didn't quite answer the question.

"My parents would never have forgiven me," Ravi mused, barely audible above the screech and roar of the wheels. "At least, not my mother. But, ohhh, I would have married Lia."

You didn't do it, Raine concluded, as a wave of weary anger washed through her. That left only one viable suspect—Kincade.

"But who could that have been, back there?" Ravi worried while the tunnel lights flickered past. "A burglar who knew our apartment was empty?"

A burglar might savage a witness who cornered him while trespassing, Raine supposed. But given a clear route of escape, the average break and enter man wasn't likely to drag a witness *in* to keep him company on his rounds. She shrugged. "What were you after?"

Ravi had returned, hoping to collect his passport, some money and some other personal papers that he kept hidden under a floorboard in his bedroom.

"And what about Lia's dinosaur tooth, did you mean to take that, as well?" Raine prodded, just to be sure.

He started to frown—then winced and pressed a finger between his eyebrows. "But surely the police would have found that? She kept it in a box, on a shelf above my desk."

"Her killer took it, I think."

"Ahhh." He shot her a glance full of wary intelligence. "And if he did, then what were you doing on my fire escape?"

The overhead speakers made a gargling announcement; the train braked into Grand Central Station. "I have to transfer here," Raine said as she rose.

When they stepped out onto the platform, she glanced down the tracks. But this midtown stop was much busier, passengers rushing on and off the cars before their doors slid shut. She spotted no one she recognized. As they joined the outgoing flow, Raine said, "I suppose Lia told you that I wanted to buy her fossil? Well, even though her tooth seems to be stolen, I still hope to find the rest of the skeleton it came from. I was looking for anything, letters from her home, maybe the original wrappings her box was mailed in, that would be a clue to where she got it. Could *you* tell me anything?"

By the time they reached the brownstone that housed the company apartment, he'd recounted what little he knew. As they shook hands at the foot of her stoop, Raine said, "Where will you go now?" She'd learned that Lia had been a freshman at NYU, where Ravi was a grad student, working toward a masters in microbiology. If he fled the country, he could kiss all his hard work, all his dreams of a better life, goodbye.

He sighed. "Truly it's best that I not tell you."

"But if something comes up that clears you of suspicion, wouldn't you want to know? Is there someplace I could leave a message?"

Ravi considered her somberly for a moment, then said, "Professor Sadat in the chemistry department at NYU. He will know how to reach me."

"All right. Then…good luck." *And be careful!* she added as he waited till the inner doors of her foyer had locked safely behind her, before he limped off down the deserted street. They'd both glanced back several times as they walked from the subway. Once or twice Raine had imagined she'd seen a flicker of motion half a block behind, but nothing had ever materialized out of the gloom.

And if it's Kincade, he wouldn't need to follow, she reminded herself. *He already knows where I live.* With a weary shrug, she turned and headed upstairs.

Crouched behind the parked cars that lined the far side of the bitch's street, Szabo noted her address. *Later, babe.*

But for now, her friend was still out in the open, heading east. *Let him be headed for the park,* Szabo prayed, skulking behind. Just let him try to cross Central Park, with all its darkness and bushes, the kind of place where Szabo could find the privacy to get creative. He broke into a lazy lope as his quarry crossed the next intersection, still heading straight on. *Oh, yeah, lookin' good. Lookin' real promising!*

He lurched to a halt as a figure stepped out from the shadows to block his man's path. Shit, was that a—

Of all the bitchin' luck, it was! A cop, no doubt wondering what a guy was doing, wandering around this time of night with a busted face.

Spin the nosy bastard a good yarn, he counseled from afar. *Tell him your girlfriend clocked you.* Instead, the idiot stood tongue-tied for an instant, then spun around to run— and slammed straight into a lamppost.

"Smooth move, pal!" Szabo growled as the cop pounced,

then handcuffed the moron. Well, *this* night was a bust, from first to last.

Or maybe, just maybe…

He prowled back to the bitch's brownstone and tried its outer double doors. Locked. He went to press his nose to one of the fancy etched-glass panels—and yelped as a cactus spine he'd missed bumped the pane.

He yanked it out with a snarl, then looked again. Along the side wall, he could see two rows of shiny brass mailboxes, with the tenants' names printed along their bases. And, *ding-dong,* did that one for the top floor ring a bell?

Ashaway All.

Chapter 13

"**Y**ou sure you've got time to help me?" Raine asked, welcoming Eric through her door.

Although Eric Bradley had started out as Ashaway All's official apartment sitter when none of the family was in residence, several years back he'd fallen for James and Otto, and moved down a floor. But in his career as a freelance magazine writer, Eric still used the top apartment as his office. In exchange for its usage, he collected company mail, paid utilities, ran errands as needed.

"All the time in the world, sweetie, especially when it's to go shopping," Eric assured her, then stopped short as he cleared the doorway. "Good God, Raine! Please tell me the other guy looks worse!"

"Hey, he looked worse to begin with." She brushed a knuckle below her shiner, smiled and shrugged. "Anyway, we're even. I broke his ketchup bottle. Really, stop. I put on sunglasses and it's gone."

"Men are such *brutes!*"

"Yeah, but what's the alternative? Anyway, here's my list. I've got a million things to do before my flight tomorrow night. I'll pick up the prescription antibiotics myself, and the reef walkers, and the maps, and my visa at the Indonesian Consulate. But any of these items that you could knock off would be a tremendous help."

"A dozen secondhand T-shirts?"

"Right. They make perfect tips or trade items. Go to the Salvation Army store and choose whatever you like in hundred percent cotton. Rock bands are best, designer emblems or cartoon characters are good. Medium sizes, I'd say. Trey tells me I'm going to be half a head taller than every guy I meet on Borneo."

"A blonde on stilts? They'll just try harder," Eric predicted. "And what's this, ten dozen tweezers?"

"For when I reach the rainforest. They're not much beyond the Stone Age, where I'm going. Metal's at a premium. But tweezers are light to carry and digging out splinters is a universal problem. And, oh, the needles, Eric? I doubt they have access to real thread, so I suppose they use pig gut or vegetable fiber. So get me *big* needles, with the largest eyes you can find."

"But five *hundred?*"

"Trey says they use blowguns to hunt. I suspect the men will want 'em for darts, as much as their women do for sewing."

"A blonde on stilts playing Santa Claus!"

"More a trader come to town, than Santa. It's one of Dad's basic lessons. If you're packing in to the back-of-beyond, and you want to travel fast and light, then it's impossible to carry all the food you'll need. It's too bulky and heavy. So aside from two weeks of high-nutrient emergency rations, you bring the lightest, most desirable trade goods you can carry. Then as you travel, you exchange them for whatever the locals are eating. Both sides figure they've got the best of the bargain. It's win-win all the way."

"As long as you don't mind snacking on grubs and worse things," Eric agreed with a grimace. "Let's see—a thousand medium-size fishhooks. Five pounds of glass beads in assorted colors—no, really?"

"Sounds disgustingly Victorian, I know, but Trey's research says it's true. I could offer them money and they'd think I was nuts, but beads? The women are mad for 'em. Look at this." She led him to the desk, where she'd picked apart her opal necklace and arranged her favorite stones in a simpler design, with an irregular, cream-colored piece of sandstone as its central pendant. "I'm restringing my necklace, and to jazz it up, I was thinking of alternating the opals with glass beads, in turquoise and lime-green."

"And possibly pinky-gold?" Eric suggested, with a critical tilt of his head. He pocketed one of the gems. "I'll try to match the fire in this one. But why use this?" He nudged the fossil at the center of her design. The impression of a single feather, its pattern was so perfect it might have been imprinted in creamy lake silt an hour ago—not two hundred million years before.

"Trey says the people are animists, where I'm headed."

"I thought Indonesia was Islamic?"

"Largest Muslim population in the world, with a smattering of Christians and Buddhists," Raine agreed, "but that's on the more civilized islands, and along the coasts of the others. In Borneo's deep dark interior, they don't believe in one God. They believe that every object, every creature in the forest, contains a hidden power. Good or bad spirits that inhabit the trees and rivers and birds and animals, even the wind. Trey says they'll find me more *simpatica* if I have my own totem. A spirit to advise and protect me. I considered inviting Otto along, but for a hike of more than a hundred yards?"

"He'll feel more spiritual here on the couch."

"Besides…" Raine traced the fossil's elegant whorls with a fingertip. "If Ashaway All has a mascot, a totem, here's its symbol. *Archaeopteryx ashawayi*."

"That was the fossil bird that John discovered?"

"Except that it's the paleolithic *ancestor* of birds—a lizard-like critter with feathered wings that proves the link be-tween dinos and birds. And Dad didn't find *ashawayensis*. That was his twin brother, my Uncle Joe."

"Ah, the legendary Joe. I never had the pleasure."

And never would, since Joe Ashaway had died two years ago, in the same cave-in that killed his son, and crippled Raine's father when he rushed to the rescue. They'd been tun-neling into a cliff, excavating a *Triceratops,* when the entire face of the overburden collapsed. "Joe wasn't everyone's cup of tea," Raine said now with a rueful smile.

For that matter, he wouldn't have approved of Eric and James. "He was hard as nails. A real driver when he was hot on the trail of a fossil. But when he found the first specimen of *Archaeopteryx* in the Americas—" She touched the feather again. "He put Ashaway All on the map.

"Before that we were just another struggling little rock-hounds' supply company. But with the recognition we gained from discovering the first fossil bird in the New World—to say nothing of its half-a-million-dollar sale to the Pittsburgh Museum... After *Archaeopteryx,* we were on our way to the top." The fossil's sale had financed a dozen expeditions, which led to more finds, which ultimately earned the scien tific and popular attention that made Ashaway All known to collectors and museums worldwide.

Eric picked up the feather and turned it in the light. "Not only a pretty totem, but a powerful one! Where did Joe find it?"

"On a ranch in eastern Montana."

"Topographic maps of central Borneo?" repeated the clerk in the map shop. "I don't believe we have those in stock, Ms. Ashaway, but let me check."

Standing one aisle away with his back turned, pretending to study a travel book on sex tours to Thailand, Szabo swore under his breath. So the Ashaway bitch was after the di-nosaur, too!

All morning he'd been wondering what the blonde was up to, while he dogged her around the city. He knew women lived to shop, but this had been ridiculous—he was beat, just from watching her. She'd bought hiking boots and reef walkers, batteries and Swiss army knives. She'd cleared out whole shelves in a drugstore. *She was setting up a first aid kit,* he realized now.

"We have maps for the coasts, of course, but the interior?" said the clerk, returning. "It's hardly been mapped at all. The first *claimed* crossing of the island by an American was made less than twenty years ago, and I understand he was lost most of the way. Lucky to come out alive. He certainly wasn't surveying as he went.

"Now I can special-order the World War Two British maps, and another RAF series that was done in the late fifties, but I'd have to warn you that their accuracy leaves…ummm… much to be desired. Most of the mapping was done from the air, and considering that the geographic contours are hidden by the thickest, tallest rainforest canopy in the world…"

"Well, I'll take whatever you can give me. But unless your special order comes in by, say, three o'clock tomorrow, I'll have to travel without. Find something when I get there," said the blonde regretfully.

Szabo almost fell over backward, craning his ears to catch the conversation. She had a low sort of growly-soft voice, like she'd laughed herself silly, sipping bourbon in some man's bed. He could get a hard-on just listening to her, though she wasn't his type. Too tall, too sure of herself, the way she cut through the crowded streets—reminded him of a tigress he'd seen once in Bangladesh, slipping through high cane.

Too much attitude and too light on the tits, he told himself.

"By three o'clock?" The clerk shook his head. "I couldn't guarantee it, coming from London. But definitely by nine o'clock, the morning after."

Ashaway sighed. "I'm afraid that wouldn't do. I'm flying to Singapore tomorrow night."

Damn! She was going after the dino hard and fast. Szabo flipped blindly past pictures of tiny Thai girls, dancing naked on a bar top. What should he do? Knock her on the head before she left town? For that matter, with the streets as busy as they were he could stroll up behind her. Slip an ice pick between her left-side ribs, then fade away, before the bitch hit the ground.

Onnnn the other hand, he reminded himself, her company was one of two he knew of, that offered to buy opalized fossils. And he damn sure didn't mean to keep the dino once he found it. Might be smart not to whack an interested buyer.

Though if she beat him to the prize, she wouldn't give him a nickel.

Yeah, either way, this was going to take some pondering. He swung around and—son of a bitch!—she was gone. Szabo found only the clerk looking at him, with his eyebrows raised and his mouth pruned up.

"Did you wish to purchase that, sir?"

"Nah, I've already licked the best pages." He tore it neatly down the spine, then handed both halves to the clerk as he swaggered out the door.

Chapter 14

Trey had reserved her a window seat on the left-hand side of the jet, in Raffles Class, Singapore Airlines' luxurious compromise between business class and first. Raine dumped her overnight bag on her seat, along with her parasol, then straightened to unsling her backpack, which contained a folding kayak, her clothes and trade goods.

"Hey now, little lady. Looks like you could use a hand," drawled a man behind her as the weight lifted off her shoulders.

"Oh, thanks, but—" But he'd already jammed her pack into her overhead compartment with none of the care she'd have taken. "Thanks."

"My pleasure."

Her smile turned cool as his washed-out blue gaze made a leisurely tour from the V of her blouse to her toes, then back again, without once lifting to her eyes. A big, rangy, ugly customer, with a sprinkle of pox marks on his cheeks and a nasty case of razor burn. And a self-satisfied, oddly confiding smirk. As if he knew her—or knew what color thong she was wearing. Roughly her own age. *Not my seatmate,* she prayed, sliding on into her row. Not for the longest nonstop flight in the world! Eighteen hours of Mr. Smirky and she'd be ready for a parachute.

As he glanced at his ticket, then ducked into the row directly ahead of her, she breathed a sigh of relief. Another bullet dodged. She tucked the rest of her luggage under his spacious seat, then settled back in her own and closed her eyes. *Whew!*

The last two days had been a rat race, culminating in her running a wreck-strewn, nail-biting obstacle course down the Jersey turnpike with a speed-crazed Bulgarian cabbie, who'd sworn he knew the way to Newark Airport, and who demonstrably had not. But somehow she'd made it. Now she was ready to kick back and let the flight crew waft her up and away, into the midnight stars.

Mr. Smirky in the seat ahead must feel much the same. He slumped against his window and commenced a gentle, but insistent snoring.

Lovely.

Beyond her eyelids Raine sensed the loom of a large body. Something thumped into the overhead bin, a weight settled into the aisle seat beside her. *Whoever you are, please don't be a chatterbox.* She opened her eyes to welcome the newcomer—and let out a yelp.

"Good evening to you, too," Kincade said equably, as he buckled his seat belt.

"What are *you* doing here?"

"Take a guess."

"Excuse me, sir?" A flight attendant stood in the aisle, looking down at Raine's helper. Accompanying her was an elegant elderly Chinese woman, none too pleased. "Excuse me, sir, but I believe you're in the wrong seat?"

The snores *missed* a beat, then resumed their rumbling rhythm.

"Please, sir... *Sir?*" The attendant leaned across to tap the man's arm. Incoming passengers were stacking up in the blocked aisle. The sleeper snored on.

"Be a gentleman twice over," Raine suggested under her breath to Kincade. "Give the lady your seat, and *everybody* will be happy."

"No, thanks, I prefer the scenery where I am." Cade inspected the personal video screen built into the seat before him. "So what's our choice for movies?"

Quite possibly *Murder, She Wrote,* if he didn't stop looking so damned pleased with himself. So…so coolly competent and put together. This was the first time Raine had seen him dressed down and if anything, it suited him better than formal wear. Striving for calm, she drew a deep breath—and felt her pulse wobble at a spicy whiff of bay rum. Damn, she'd forgotten his cologne.

In the embarrassment ahead, the flight attendant had apparently located Mr. Smirky's ticket. "Ah, yes, ma'am," she said distractedly as she studied it. "He does belong in Raffles class. In fact, *his* seat might even be preferable to this one. It's farther away from the passenger lounge, which sometimes can be rather noisy if you're hoping for a restful…" Soothing and cajoling, she led the indignant woman away, toward the far side of the plane.

Watching them go, Cade noted lazily, "He's a long way from home."

"And pooped—he fell asleep in record time," added Raine to a medley of snores. *Are we really going to sit here chatting like two civilized strangers?* As if three nights ago, they hadn't played tug-of-war with a half-conscious man? Played dirty and for keeps, she was fairly certain.

"In that case, he's a doctor," Cade declared. "I've never met one who couldn't go lights-out in thirty seconds or less."

Mr. Snores and Smirks looked more the type to inflict wounds, than one who stitched them, Raine thought privately. And knowing Trey, she knew another sort who could sleep at will; it was a soldier's trick.

* * *

Once they'd leveled off in their flight, and the attendant came to take their order, Raine curled her fingers around Cade's forearm. "Join me in a drink?"

His eyes flicked down to her hand resting on his blue shirt-sleeve, then up to her face. His dark brows drew together. "Great minds think alike. The champagne?"

"Of course," she said absently, her attention focused on the tactile. She smoothed her palm along the hot hard swell of his muscle, squeezed gently, then retreated under his ironic smile.

Cheeks glowing at her own nerve, she frowned into space while he asked for two glasses of Piper Heidsieck. No bandage. She'd slashed him across the forearms, back there at Ravi's window. Not deeply, since his sweater had snagged her blade and she'd been afraid of slicing Ravi, but still… She met his gaze as he handed her a flute. *Could you heal that quickly?*

Cade lifted his glass to her and in reflex she echoed the gesture. "To…" He cocked his dark head. "To Borneo?" The crystal chimed above the drone of the engines.

"Oh," she said sweetly. "Is that where you're headed?"

"You tell me. Whither thou goest…" It sounded ominously like a vow.

Her palm was still tingling from the feel of him. She'd always liked her opals rough, and her men with an edge. But this one was *all* edges. *No bandage,* she mused, at least not on his left arm. But then Kincade was a tough guy; maybe he'd opted to do without? And he was no fool. If there was anything for her to see, he'd never roll up his sleeves the entire trip.

All I want is to be sure, one way or another, she told herself as she sipped burning bubbles. Her brain insisted that her troll and Kincade had to be one and the same. Who else could it be? There was nobody else in the picture.

Yet her instincts kept balking at the logical conclusion. Demanding that before she condemned a man with forearms that felt like that, attached to a body that sang to hers…to say nothing of his mouth…and his eyes…and his—

"Yes?" Cade inquired on a warm note of mockery.

Proof, she reminded herself, holding his gaze as they drank, not bothering to respond. If Kincade was a murderous troll, she'd better know it. If he could switch on and off—turn from killer to charmer and back again in the blink of an eye— she needed to know it before she could deal with him. Beat him.

Survive him, where they were headed. Racing a two-faced killer through the world's deepest jungles for the find of a lifetime? Sleeping within inches of Kincade, would be ordeal enough!

If he'd had any sense, Cade would have searched her bag while she went to the restroom. Beyond Singapore, she'd made no reservations with a credit card. Not according to the B-frog. *Which means she's stopping there for a while. Plans to buy her ticket onward when she's ready to fly?*

Or she'd made other plans. Borneo was roughly three hundred miles southeast of Singapore. She could catch a connecting ferry or steamer, though those would be slower.

There was nothing slow and easygoing about Raine Ashaway. *Which means?*

It meant he ought to search her bag—check for tickets, or directions to the ferry dock, or whatever clues he could find. He'd done plenty worse, stalking the Ashaways, but somehow, just for this moment, it stuck in his craw. He could still feel the blood pulsing, where she'd touched him.

And when she returned a short while later with her hair the color of moonbeams and raindrops brushed out on her shoulders… Plus she'd changed to a loose silk T-shirt that failed to conceal the fact that she'd removed her brassiere for the night… Cade was just as happy he hadn't bothered. When the time came, he'd do what he had to do, but for tonight? *Call it a truce.*

She tipped back her seat to horizontal, so he did the same. All the better to fantasize.

Raine sniffed and pulled the privacy screen out between their seats. But that was hardly more than symbolic, blocking only their faces from each other.

"Sweet dreams," he murmured, and his voice had gone too husky by half. But then she knew what he was thinking. Tonight, they rode the same clouds.

She growled something wordless and sat up again. Found the airline's complimentary sleep mask and pulled it down over her eyes—then lay back on her pillow.

Somehow that mask only made her sexier. More vulnerable. A stranger could come down out of her darkness...savor those luscious lips...and if she sighed, then stretched and opened to him? He lay for a long time, propped up on one elbow, eyes on her mouth, imagining from there.

Szabo hadn't been this beat since the rock pile at Leavenworth. He'd had to hump it, raking enough cash together for this flight. They called him a robber, but look at this airline; they oughta be ashamed, what they were charging!

It had taken nearly half the wad in his money belt to buy a first-class ticket, after Ashaway picked up hers. He'd been expecting she'd go for the best and had come prepared to match her; still it had been a hard pill to swallow.

And the counter agent had gone all big eyed and doubtful, when he laid down the cash. Like it wasn't as good as a credit card. Like only terrorists and drug dealers paid with Uncle Sam's own dollars. What was this country ever coming to? "Don't worry," he'd felt like saying. "It's been laundered with care."

She could trust him not to use the same bills he'd taken off the rich bitch with the baby in the stroller. He'd waited till they rolled out of the ATM booth, then he'd picked up her kid, jiggled it and grinned. Promised he wouldn't bounce little Jake or Gabriella or whatever-it-was on its head, while she dashed back in to clean out her accounts.

Silly bitch had dropped her card three times, she'd been blubbering so hard. While he stood there cooing and sweating, fearful a patrol car would cruise by before they'd finished their business. Or the baby would do his.

He'd had to pull variations of that gig twice more, each time in a different part of the city, before he'd put together his traveling kitty. Then the laundry man had taken twenty percent to change dirty bills for clean, and his necessary purchases had taken a chunk more. Now these airline thieves had taken another bite; he was down to his last five thousand.

But he sure didn't plan to rob any banks where they were headed; it was a take-him-out-and-whack-his-hand-off part of the world. No notion of the Bill of Rights. No, from here on out, if he needed any more spending money, he'd just have to take it off a tourist, then make sure there were no complaints.

Right then Ashaway drifted past, bound for beddy-bye. He couldn't help leering, but she was too stuck-up to notice.

Just as well. Even when tempted, a deer hunter should never wave at the deer.

Unlacing his boots, he tipped back his seat till it became a bed. What he got for that extra thou or so; the poor bastards back in cargo class would have to sleep sitting up. With a luxurious sigh, he pulled his blanket to his chin and turned on his side—then grimaced and rolled back again. The cuts on his forearms were halfway to healed, but Lia's souvenir? That was something else. Her bite was starting to smart some.

Chapter 15

Blame it on the champagne, but Raine's sleep had been plagued by vivid dreams: a migrating dinosaur herd—thousands of *Centrosaurs*—drowning at a river crossing. Then jump ahead seventy million years, and she and Kincade were digging up their tangled bones. Ravi stood over their trench with a gold watch, scolding, asking truly, what could they be thinking? Did they want to be late for Lia's funeral?

She'd rolled over and reached out to touch warmth—Otto in bed with her? She'd stroked his marmalade fur and he'd morphed into the hot, delicious contours of a man, who'd caught her hand and held it against his beating heart.

She tugged free and rolled away—off into a nighttime jungle, torrents of monsoon rain, with a *Tyrannosaurus rex* crashing through the trees, hard on her pounding heels. A *T. rex* that shimmered and glowed in the dark like a forty-ton fire opal. When he caught her, she'd let out a cry, and the *T. rex* had stroked her hair and whispered, *"Hush... You're safe, it's all right... I'm here."*

So she'd sighed and drifted off, but she'd woken the next morning, distinctly surly. With a seatmate to match. Kincade looked as grouchy as a hungover pirate, in piratical need of a shave. Then she'd stumbled over his long legs, getting out into the aisle—and he'd grabbed for her and caught her round the hips. Three cups of coffee and a superb breakfast later, she could still feel *precisely* where his thumbs had pressed into her bottom.

When the trays were taken away, she buried her mortified face in the inch-thick packet that Trey had faxed her at the last minute. Her in-country briefing, plus any other research or advice the expediter had put together.

"Gender Issues," was the topic on page one. "Not a problem inland," he'd written. "But both sexes are modest, so go easy on the bare skin."

Raine snorted. She'd been taught that rule for Third World countries before she could skip rope.

Women are first-class citizens in the interior. Goddess and women warrior legends abound. Sex is enjoyed— no Puritans here—but rape is unknown. Family is crucial and children are treasured. No such thing as a bastard child.

However, the coast cities are another matter. The usual chaos of colliding cultures, with all the social norms and safeguards chucked aside. Watch out for American and Aussie oilies, (oilmen)—hard-drinking cowboys who see Borneo as their playpen. Also beware displaced and disgruntled island males who've watched too many Hollywood movies, and have yet to sort out fact from fiction. Unattached American women are fondly believed to be sex-starved nymphos, looking for help. Plus, in a short, dark-skinned culture, tall blondes are every guy's fantasy. Stay out of bars, don't wander alone after sunset—get inland pronto.

"Ye-es, Mother," Raine muttered.

"Mmm?" Cade glanced up from the guidebook he'd been perusing.

"Nothing." Raine flipped several pages. Snakes. "One hundred eighteen poisonous species in Borneo," Trey had noted. "But many of these are sea snakes. In the jungle, only four are a real concern. Kraits, coral snakes, vipers and—"

"Eighteen-foot hamadryads!" Raine sat up with a shudder. A cobra that size would pack a wallop.

"Thirty-foot pythons," Cade retorted, from his own reading, "but I'm more worried about leeches."

"So turn around and go home—and leave this to the professionals."

Just like that, the gloves came off. "And let you reap a windfall from Lia's murder?" he growled. "I don't think so."

"You think I— Are you *blind,* as well as crazy? You saw me out on the street—you know you did! Not a minute after you dumped her out the window!"

"Yeah, you were down there—establishing your alibi. But who'd you hire to do your dirty work?" While she sputtered with outrage, Cade added in a voice that caressed as it carved, "Oh, I'll give you the benefit of the doubt. You wanted the tooth, not her death. But once you start strong-arming people, taking what's theirs..."

His eyes gazed beyond her for a moment, at something faraway and unspeakable, then locked on again. "Once you go that route, you can't control where it'll end. The final sum of the damage. So you hired a thug to take what you wanted— what you couldn't afford to buy—and Lia ends up smashed on the pavement like a china doll. Just one more little guy that got in your way."

Could he honestly believe this? "Why didn't you tell the cops, if you think I hired her killer?"

"Why?" The rage in his face froze like lava cooling— crystallizing to granite resolve, and bitter derision. "Because I'd rather settle my own score."

They stared at each other, breathing as if they'd raced three times round the plane, then she jerked her head, and whispered, *"Why? Why do you hate us?"*

"I don't. I gave up hatred years ago. It corrodes the hater more than the hated, and I'd promised myself I'd...thrive. You don't have to hate a nest of cockroaches to want 'em stamped out."

"But—" A shudder crawled along her skin; she barely contained it. "What did we ever *do* to you?"

His smile twisted to savage satisfaction. "That's for me to know, Ashaway. And you to learn, on the day I—" His hands curled into fists. He looked down at them, blinked, then knocked them lightly together. "Soon," he swore, barely audible. "Soon as I can manage."

On the day you finish us, Raine realized bleakly as he rose and strode off to the lounge. As if he couldn't sit still another instant. Or feared what he'd do if he stayed.

She blew out a shaking breath. *That settles it.* Now she *had* to beat him to the dino. Whatever his reason, Kincade with his millions meant to ruin them, wreck them. And money would be his crowbar and sledgehammer.

Trey had said Cade could outspend them a dozen times over. Then Ashaway All would need millions to survive his malice. The kind of fortune a fire opal *T. rex* would bring, when she brought it to auction. *I need a big score.* The biggest. A fire opal payday.

Too shaken to read, Raine pulled down her seat's table and set to assembling her necklace, alternating glass beads with fiery opals. Knotting and stringing and inwardly worrying.

By the time she came to the fossil feather's place in her design, she'd calmed enough for the thought to arise: When Cade charged her with Lia's death, his words held a passionate conviction. No way could he have faked that!

Which meant...Raine rubbed her thumb gently across the stone feather, the Ashaways' ancient luck. Which meant that if Cade truly believed *she* had killed Lia—hired the muscle that murdered the girl… *Then whatever he is, he's not a killer!*

As he still meant to ruin them, she couldn't say why that mattered.

But…it did. She touched the feather to her lips.

In the lounge, Cade sat for a long time, staring blindly down at the hazy blue curve of the Pacific. He hadn't meant to lose his temper like that. But something about Raine Ashaway made him forget himself.

Something? He grimaced. Like being roused before dawn to find a slender feminine hand sliding up his stomach, exploring his pectorals—then to realize she was making love to him, all in her sleep? He'd bit back his groans and submitted to her dream, certain she'd wake any minute—find him ready and willing to join her in the Mile High Club. The cabin lights had been dimmed and everyone around them was fast asleep.

Then just when he'd decided to lift her over onto his bed— she'd rolled away, and off into a nightmare. Total change of mood; he wished he'd struck while the iron was red-hot.

Which explained his outburst this morning. Sexual frustration jangling him on every wavelength. All he had to do was look at her and his imagination rioted. Scene after scene superimposed itself on reality—overlapping, writhing phantoms of delight: Raine straddling his legs, ripping his shirt open while he filled his hands with her rolling hips. Raine reaching down to—

Cade sat up, grabbed the book he'd brought along, and opened it on his lap. He glared quickly around the cabin, found nobody smirking, then leaned back with a scowl. Dammit! If anyone deserved the lash of his temper, it was himself. To let a woman—an Ashaway!—disarm him with a touch of her hand.

Not that they hadn't been doing that since Delilah gave

Samson a hair trim, but still. A man liked to think he was stronger than…

Sex? He had the grace to smile. *Okay, so convict me. I'm human.* And it changed nothing, he assured himself. He'd have her to his heart's content before they were done—then he'd turn around and ruin her.

He would. He'd have justice at last.

Smile fading, he stared out the window.

Imagine it, Szabo gloated silently to Gran. Sixty-four choices of films and his own little video screen! Right now, he was on his fifth movie of the trip—a Hong Kong kung fu detective was getting his skinny butt kicked up through his screechy tonsils. Any minute now he'd get mad enough to forget his promise to his pacifist sweetheart with the amazing hooters. He'd start fighting back—kill forty-dozen bad guys in all kinds of creative ways.

Szabo adjusted his earphones, then spared a contemptuous glance for his neighbor. A Japanese businessman, heading to Singapore. He'd been plugged into his laptop, crunching numbers the whole dang trip.

At least the jerk was a heavy sleeper. Last night he'd pulled those terry cloth blinders down, and drifted off with a foolish smile. Hadn't stirred once, when, between his second movie and his third, Szabo had stood, stretched, then glanced casually around. Noted that everybody on all sides was sawing wood. Ashaway in particular lay motionless, with her cute little butt in the air, and her know-it-all face buried in her pillow.

The big guy next to her was out, as well, frowning as he dreamed. Not getting a slice of her in his sleep, and pissed off about it, Szabo guessed, as any guy would be.

With a clear field, he'd sat again—and pulled her carry-on forward, then up between his legs. Her wallet and passport weren't in evidence; the sly bitch must be sleeping with 'em. That was too bad for her; in that case, he'd have to do this the hard way. For which he'd come prepared.

But first…Szabo had unzipped her cosmetic bag, and rummaged its contents. Found her perfume bottle, uncapped it—then wrinkled his nose. Reminded him of nothing but the early-morning ocean. Sand between his toes, and seagulls yelping. She paid good money for this?

A scalded-cat screech brought his mind back to the present. The kung fu detective was sneering at a guy with a blowtorch.

No sweat.

Once she'd finished the necklace, Raine looped it over her head, and tucked it inside her shirt. Magic was best kept secret, till needed. She turned back to Trey's briefing papers, and flipped idly through.

Then stopped at the topic: "Korupsi=Corruption." Trey had written:

In Indonesia, if it moves, bribe it. If you accidentally break any laws, or annoy anybody in power, or want a seat on the bus, (or want your kid to graduate), offer cash with a humble apology. Think of it the way they do—as just a cost of doing biz. A gift to ensure harmony all round. Note that this applies only to the "civilized" cities and towns. In the jungle there aren't written laws to be broken, so nobody will have his hand out.

That doesn't mean they don't have expectations of good manners, inland. But a bribe won't mend an offense; they punish rudeness mostly by withdrawal. (Reginald Cockburn died of starvation in the jungle, in 1955, when his guides walked out on him.) Supremely bad manners—i.e. violence—would likely be met with same.

"Okay, no violence," Raine agreed cheerfully, flipping on. "American Soldiers in Borneo," was another topic. "If Lia was correct and that watch belonged to a U.S. soldier, here's all I can find on short notice," Trey had written.

During WWII, Borneo was occupied by the Japanese, as was most of the South Pacific.

The Allies didn't fight them there till the very end, but in 1944 some bright boy back at HQ proposed an infiltration behind enemy lines. A single American squad of paratroopers was dropped into the center of the island—a night drop into jungle, for pity's sake—with the notion that they'd recruit the natives. Maybe incite and lead a rebellion from the inside-out. Do a recon of Japanese strength and positions at the very least.

Far as I can learn, that was the last ever heard of the poor bastards. Considering the forest canopy is twenty stories above the ground, they probably snagged in the treetops and dangled there till— Well, you get the picture.

Anyway, here's a list of the missing soldiers. It's always possible that one or more of 'em survived for a while, stumbling around out there. A gold watch would have made a good exchange for food. Over the last sixty years it could have been traded a dozen times, till finally it reached the coast and Lia's hands. But how this links to a dino is beyond me.

"Me, too," Raine murmured, as she scanned the twelve names he'd included. It read like the roll call from a Norman Rockwell Fourth of July picnic—just a bunch of American Joes, a long cruel way from home.

Benally, Carleton, Gonzales, Johansen, Jones, Kennedy, Kopesky, Peckham, Rosenblatt, Szabo, Tilley, Van Den Dries... Shaking her head, she sighed for them, turned the page and read on.

This confirms our phone call of last night. I did catch up with my pal Ohara. He's on leave from his offshore oil

rig off Borneo. Currently visiting his temporary wife in
Malaysia, as opposed to his temporary wife in Cam-
bodia.

Trey and his funky connections! Raine growled to herself.
She'd approve of men taking temporary wives, when women
hired temporary husbands.

She noted Trey's warning:

Do NOT argue women's rights with him. He's incorri-
gible, and an Aussie (I guess I'm repeating myself), but
he comes with a heart of gold, as I reckon his wives
would tell you. He'll collect you at your Blue Moon
Hotel, at 1500 on Thursday. Then he'll fly you in his
Cessna to the city of Pontianak, in the Indonesian
province of West Kalimantan—Borneo.

Once there, he'll introduce you to a pilot of the MAF,
the missionary air service, to take you into the interior.
You need this guy, Raine, so don't get a burr under your
saddle. He may even be able to arrange an oil company
chopper to fly your field crew in, then hook your dino
out of there, once you dig it

Raine made a face. True, this scouting trip was only the
first step. If it ended with a find, then she'd need somebody
with connections for the actual excavation. Preferably somebody who didn't need to be bribed.

Ohara can also be counted on—period. If you run into
trouble, you can run to him. He owes me.

"Everybody and his uncle owes you," she muttered affec-
tionately. And Trey would never say for what. Still, that was
good to know.

Not that she planned on any trouble.

Chapter 16

Cade returned silently to his seat as lunch was served. They'd both ordered the satay, Raine noted. But he was in no mood to talk so she went back to reading, while she nibbled on a skewer of spicy grilled shrimp dipped in peanut sauce.

"Found a bit more on Kincade," Trey reported on the next page without preamble.

> Got a line on a retired guard from the reform school where he did time, and the old guy remembers Kincade, all right. Three escape attempts in his first year, at age fourteen, then he settled down and turned into a model inmate. Reason for incarceration was he assaulted a sheriff.

Raine frowned. So the potential for violence she'd sensed was there—or it had been, twenty-odd years ago.

> Details were fuzzy—but it seems the sheriff had shown up to foreclose on the family ranch, and to escort the kid to a foster home. Kincade took exception.

With a wry smile, she nodded to herself. Whatever Cade was, he was nobody to be pushed around; apparently never had been. She stole a glance his way—then jumped when their eyes locked.

"What?" he growled.

"Ohhh…nothing." His suspicious look said he wasn't buying that, so she added, "Actually, I was wondering. Want to trade me a shrimp-stick for one of my beef?"

He complied without comment, and Raine went back to reading.

I asked about family; visitors? The old guy couldn't remember any. Said he believed there was a grandfather who used to have custody, but that—get this—Granddad was doing time at the Montana state pen! For beating the bejeezus out of somebody, and damn lucky that it wasn't for manslaughter.

So…Raine was no longer amused. A history of violence, ill temper, stretching back generations. Can I really be certain that he didn't kill Lia? Wasn't the troll at the window?

"What are you reading, your own obituary?" Cade reached for her sheaf of papers.

"No way!" She held it off to one side. "Proprietary info, Kincade!"

"Ah." He shrugged and backed off.

She wondered if he would have, in less public surroundings. She returned to her briefing, but there wasn't much more.

That was all the guard knew. I'm trying to get a handle on Kincade's granddad—where he is, what happened to him, name of his victim—but so far, no luck. Prison records that far back aren't computerized, and it's occurring to me that if this guy was a maternal grandfather, then I don't even have a name.

I'll keep on digging, but by the time I find anything

useful, you'll likely be out of touch. Meanwhile, while
we still have no explanation for his grudge against Ashaway All, the facts suggest that Kincade's a hard case
with a dangerous temper. But you knew that already,
right?

How do you do it? she marveled. The famous Trey-nose
for trouble! She'd have sworn she'd said nothing to make the
expediter think she was attracted to Kincade.

Attracted? She sniffed and flipped the page—to find only
two words printed on the next.

Right, Raine?

When the jet halted at the terminal and the passengers
scrambled stiffly to their feet, the big guy removed Ashaway's pack from the overhead bin. He stepped back to let
her go ahead of him up the aisle.

Szabo barged out between them, giving her pal a *gotcha*
wink when he glared. He caught up with Ashaway in the tunnel. "Whew! Talk about a buttbreaker! If I don't sit down for
the next month, that'll be fine by me."

She gave him half an inch of cool sidelong smile and kept
walking. Her pack had to go fifty pounds, but she swung
right along, carry-on hooked over one shoulder and folded-
up parasol in hand.

"How 'bout you? You stopping here in Singapore or flying on?" He'd need to handle things differently, depending.

She glanced up at the signs pointing the way to Customs
in half a dozen languages, turned that direction, then shrugged
and said, "Stopping for a while."

Too snooty to care about what *he* was doing, but he'd tell
her anyway. Couldn't hurt to show his cards now; in a few
minutes she'd be history. "Me, I'm headed for Borneo. Pontianak." That was the return address he'd found on a letter in

Lia's bureau. From her family or boyfriend, he figured. Either way, it oughta be enough to go on.

"Oh?" She glanced at him with a tad more interest. "Ever been there before?"

"Sure thing. I checked it out 'bout five years back, while I was on leave from my unit in the Philippines. My granddaddy got himself lost on the island, way back in the second World War. Thought I'd sniff around, see if I could find any trace of him. But you ain't seen rugged country till you've seen Borneo. Without knowing the place to start looking from, it wasn't nothing but a snipe hunt." *Now* he had her attention. Her shiny lips parted to ask a question as he added, "All I ever caught was a *bitchin'* case of the—"

"Raine," said a man behind them, reaching out to grab her shoulder.

She stopped and swung on her heel.

Szabo glanced back as he kept on walking. The big guy off the plane, making one last play for her. *Go ahead, make a date. See where it gets you.*

He'd decided that he didn't need competition on this particular snipe hunt. Ashaway All was a company, not just the leggy blonde, he'd learned when he studied their Web site. Even with this Ashaway cancelled, the rest of them should still want to buy a fire opal dinosaur.

Meantime, he'd find himself a blind, where he could sit and watch the fun.

"Have supper with me tonight?" Cade suggested.

"What makes you think I'll be in town?" For all he knew, she was flying on. Raine glanced over her shoulder; couldn't let Mr. Smirky get away. Talk about coincidence! Could he really be the grandson of one of the missing paratroopers?

"You'll be here. I'll meet you in the bar at the Blue Moon Hotel."

"You…*snoop!*" Jet lag was definitely setting in; she should have realized before. The seat next to hers on the same flight—and now this? "How did you find out where I'm staying?"

She shook her head and glanced again after Mr. Smirky, but dammit, he'd vanished into the streaming crowd. "This is the best you can do, Kincade?" She turned and stalked on. Sooner she made it through Customs, the sooner she could find her hotel and take a nap. Cade strolled along beside her, taking two strides to every three of hers. "You want to be a bone hunter when you grow up? Fine, be my guest. Go right ahead and do it. But find your own dinos, don't tag after me!"

"Why not? I'd say it's high time a bigger dog came along, to take your bones away."

With a wordless snarl she swerved around an oncoming electric cart, wove on past travelers babbling in a dozen tongues. She'd have to call Trey and tell him to sweep headquarters for bugs. Check the computers for data traps and custom cookies. So this was a sample of what Cade's money could buy. They reached the turnoff to baggage claims and she glanced at him hopefully, but Cade smiled and shook his head. Like her, he travelled light.

When they came to the customs hall, a uniformed guard pointed his white-gloved finger at Raine, then sent her to an inspection line on her left. Kincade started after her, but the triage man wagged his finger sternly, then banished him to a line at the right.

Good riddance! She'd deal with Kincade later, but now it was time to relax. She had to pass inspection; customs agents could smell fear as easily as a Doberman sniffed out a timid postman.

She twirled her furled parasol and did what she always did when she had guilty thoughts to hide. She chose a silly, happy song from her childhood, something from an animated film, a song that brought a smile to mind, and sang it inwardly.

The line moved in fits and starts. Some tourists were passed without a hitch. Others, the agent all but shredded their baggage. Raine could see no rhyme or reason to it. The blushing grandmotherly tourist whose polka-dot panties he was currently unfolding didn't look like a terrorist or a drug mule.

Wonder if smuggling drugs is still a hanging offense in Singapore? She wasn't up-to-date on the latest sentences, but this was a state that outlawed chewing gum and caned grafitti artists—if they were lucky!

Given such an unforgiving outlook, its agent was bound to take a dim view if he found the items hidden in the hollow handle of her parasol. Thirty thousand in tightly rolled U.S. cash, always useful in emergencies. Her trusty throwing knife, stripped down to its component parts. *Wonder if they'd call my curare a drug?* She supposed technically the gum was; anesthetists used it sometimes in surgery. Though for her it was ammunition—a reversible paralytic to coat the darts for her blowgun. Which was what the handle of her parasol became, once you unscrewed it from the silk head, then extended its telescoping sections to their full six feet.

Raine took another deep breath and twirled her weapon. *But what's a girl to do?* She couldn't carry a gun on a plane or across borders. And though she'd love to believe she could handle anything or anybody she encountered with her wits and her bare hands, it wasn't necessarily so. *Blame it on my father,* she declared inwardly, as the agent unzipped her shoulder bag on the table. *It's Dad who taught me always to be prepared.*

"Is this your first trip to Singapore, miss?" asked the agent, fingering her clothes.

"No, I came through here on a boat, when I was eight." Her smile wavered for a moment; that had been the trip where she lost her mother. She rallied and added, "I suppose it has changed a bit?"

He twitched a wry smile, then said crisply, "And the reason for this visit?"

"Just passing through on my way to Borneo—to Kalimantan. But I need to buy some maps, camping gear. Thought I could use a break for a night. I fly on tomorrow."

"Your parasol, please." He opened it, pursed his lips at the bold black-and-orange Chinese tiger prowling a field of sky-blue. "Very...hmm...pretty."

"Thank you." He turned his attention to its spokes and stem, and somehow she kept her cool.

When he handed it back, she let her sigh of relief trickle out. Resting the parasol's handle on her shoulder, she twirled the silk to a stream of colors overhead. "I was born in the Year of the Tiger, you see, and the sun is so fierce out here, what with my complexion... Though actually I'm the kind of blonde who tans."

Her efforts at distraction weren't working. He returned to her cosmetic kit and emptied it out. "Two tubes of toothpaste?"

Only one, she started to correct him—as he pulled the second tube from the depths of her carry-on! Not her brand; it had been tucked in below the blouse she'd worn last night. *Ohhhh.* Was her face going white? Or maybe green. "Yes, umm, two. One for regular use. Then a heavy-duty, industrial-strength brand for when I eat garlic and I'm going out on a date."

Am I babbling? I'm babbling. And jeez, doesn't he see it? The bottom end of the tube had been unrolled at one corner. A scrap of clear plastic stuck out in plain view. Had to be the edge of a small plastic bag. *Dear God, is he blind?* He'd never ever believe her if she claimed she'd never seen it before. *Oh, let him be blind!* She closed her parasol with a snap—thought she'd faint as he grinned at the idiocies of women. And moved on to her backpack.

At least a thousand years oozed past before Raine tottered over to the clerk who inspected her passport, marveled at all the places she'd been, then stamped it. On she walked, mouth dry as cotton, heart racing, eyes fixed on the doors ahead. Freedom just beyond them. *But somebody wants me dead. Hung by the neck till I'm dead. Kincade, you bastard, you!*

She couldn't help herself; she looked back. And there he was, just opening his bag for his own inspection. As if by magic their eyes connected. He smiled, lifted a hand in a "hey, come back here" gesture. Then he spoke to his customs agent—who turned to stare at her.

"You *bastard!*" she whispered, wheeling and walking faster. "You murdering snitch!" If only she could toss the tube, but out here in the middle of the floor... *Gotta play it cool. Hang on till I make the street.*

Szabo couldn't believe his eyes; the agent had missed it! Just went to show you there was no justice anywhere. Watch *him* try to sneak through Customs with a pack of bubble gum—they'd bust his sorry ass in a heartbeat. But a blond bimbo could boost her B cups to double D with Baggies stuffed full of heroin—the worst she'd get was her butt pinched, as she sashayed out the door.

"Well, I'm not takin' *this!*" He cut to the head of the nearest line and caught its startled agent by the sleeve. "Hey, you see that blonde over there? Yeah, that one. I sat beside her on the plane from the States, and she was bragging she'd make a killing. She's got half a pound of heroin hid in her bag. Thought you might like to—"

But the guy shrugged him off and dashed away toward a guard.

Good enough. And now it was time to do a fast fade. Once these guys started asking questions and taking names, no telling where they'd stop. He glanced at his dive watch, then lengthened his stride. Just time to grab a hot dog before he caught the plane to Pontianak.

Ten yards to the doors... Nine... And if she didn't have a heart attack first, then maybe her guardian angel had somehow managed to—

"Miss! Hey! *You,* miss!" a man called somewhere behind. "Please to return here!"

Raine ducked her head and bolted for freedom.

"Now that one," said Raine, with both her hands full. She nodded toward the cross rib that fit into the forward part of her foldable kayak. "No, no, not that. Yes, *that* one. Yes! Thank you."

The child beamed as he brought her the piece. He retreated to the circle of his friends, who crouched on the beach, watching with dark-eyed fascination.

"Would you believe the manufacturer claims this can be done in twenty minutes?" she grumbled, easing the rib into place. They couldn't understand a word she was saying; it was all in her tone. "I've never put one of these together in less than thirty."

And how long did she have, before the police traced the cab she'd caught outside the terminal? Learned that its driver had taken her to the harbor where most of the cruising yachts anchored?

"Now, Bart, if I could have the clips?" She aimed her chin at the cord of expansion clips, and this time the smallest boy—the one she'd given a Bart Simpson T-shirt—brought her the pieces with a glorious smile. The hem of his man-size medium dragged in the sand.

"Thank you. Excellent. Yeah…" she murmured absently as she slotted the first clip into its rod. "Now I know you guys must be thinking that probably I should tough it out. Hunker down somewhere for the night." She was exhausted; the adrenaline rush on top of jet lag had left her shaking.

But how to go to ground? She was a fox without a den. Customs had recorded her passport, which meant she dare not use it. And there wasn't a hotel in all Singapore that would give her a room if she couldn't produce one.

She couldn't see walking the streets all night, dodging the cops. Then hoping to somehow connect with Ohara, when he flew in from Malaysia tomorrow afternoon. Even if she found him, doubtless every branch of Customs was alerted. They'd be guarding all the exits; how could he fly her out?

No, her every instinct cried that she put maximum distance between her neck and any noose ASAP. She hoped Trey could

sort out this mess later, clear her good name, but for now…
Stay calm, stay cool, keep moving.

She nodded at the next piece and a third child delivered it.
"Can you guess what it is yet?" she asked her audience.

Considering this was the only show on the beach, did they
even care? It was intricate, it was mechanical, they were male.

Which meant, of course, that they had all kinds of advice
and they were convinced they could do it better. Still, in spite
of their kibitzing, Raine put the FirstLight together in record
time.

She let them carry it for her to the water's edge—twelve
feet long, it weighed all of eighteen pounds. She loaded it,
then shook each small grubby hand with great solemnity.
"Thank you. Couldn't have done it without you guys. And remember? If anybody in uniform asks, you haven't seen me."

More gap-toothed smiles, nods all around. They yelled
with delight as she dipped one end of her paddle, then the
other—and glided out over the wavelets, paddling off toward
the anchored boats.

A hundred yards out, Raine reached for the tube of toothpaste. She hadn't dared ditch it before; it was a death sentence
to any innocent who found it. She dumped the plastic bag's
white powder, then the tube, where they could do no harm.

With a sigh of heartfelt relief she stroked on, her eyes
scanning the fleet. She needed either somebody who'd already cleared Customs for departure, or somebody with a fine
disregard for the rules.

She found her man at the outer edge of the anchorage, han-
king a jib on the forestay of a big catamaran. "'Hoy, *Duetta!*'"
she called, drifting up alongside. "Heading out?"

"I am." The captain had a lean, wiry build and a deep-
water tan. Blue, sun-crinkled eyes above a flourishing crop
of auburn whiskers. A widening grin as they studied each
other.

"I'm looking to charter a boat." Her eyes flicked over the
double-hulled craft. Unpainted aluminum, shabby at first

glance, but its lines were businesslike. The rig looked solid despite the stem of bananas lashed to the stern rail and a green parrot shuffling back and forth in the ratlines.

"Bit late for a daysail, I'm afraid, and like I said—"

"Not a daysail—a passage. I need to get to Borneo. Quick as I can."

"Might want to hop a plane, in that case."

"Well, actually…" She gave him a look that was equal parts rueful and comic and pleading. "I have this fear of flying." *At least, this week I do.* She stole a glance over her shoulder, but there were no patrol cars on the shore. Not yet.

He hadn't missed that hunted look. He grimaced and said, "Then bring your kayak around to the other side."

Where nobody could see it from land.

"Let's have a cool one while we talk."

Chapter 17

Kincade's suite at the Raffles Hotel came equipped with the latest computer, as well as the traditional Jacuzzi. While his e-mail from the B-frog slid out of the printer, Cade watched without amusement as the hacker's digital namesake gulped three letters turned to butterflies. The frog bugged his eyes in astonishment—no, make that indigestion. He exploded into bits and bytes, which fluttered down; the screen wiped clear.

"Clown." Cade was in no mood for anything but results. He snatched the message from the printer and read:

Still no action. Ashaway hasn't used a credit card anywhere in Singapore—or anywhere else. Likewise there've been no charges to the company accounts out of Colorado. Jaye Ashaway in New Jersey bought two shovels, a pickax and fifteen extralarge pizzas.

She was excavating for amber, Cade recalled, with a pack of interns from Princeton. He'd assigned Marc to acquire the

land on which she held a license to dig. Soon as the deed
changed hands, he'd shut her down. But meantime, "Dammit,
where's Raine?"

No calls placed between Singapore and any of the mon-
itored phone numbers. Your target's e-mail account has
not been opened since she left NYC. Whatever your bird's
up to, she's not cruising the cyber realms. Don't you just
hate it when they drop off the grid?

Cade hoped that was all she'd dropped off of. When Raine
had panicked and bolted yesterday morning, he'd tried to
chase after her. Some basic male instinct demanding that, if
she was in trouble, he needed to intervene.

Which was idiotic, when you considered that he meant
Raine nothing but ill. Planned to take her down himself.

But that's precisely why, he insisted inwardly. This was *his*
payback. Vicarious vengeance just wouldn't do.

The airport security guards had been in no mood to humor
him. Before he'd run ten feet, he'd found himself looking
down the barrel of a gun. And once they'd realized that Raine
had escaped, they'd vented their temper on him. They'd
wanted Raine for smuggling drugs, he'd learned, after his release.

Raine Ashaway? If she could figure a way to trade heroin
for dinosaurs, then, well, possibly. But…Cade shook his head.
Somebody had got it wrong. A case of mistaken identity?

Whatever the mix-up, it screwed up his plans. He'd figured
that the surest way to beat her out of her prize was to stick
with her, like a basketball guard going one-on-one with a forward, driving toward the hoop.

Once they found the *T. rex,* well, fair means or foul. He
was bigger, tougher… His mouth twisted as if he'd tasted
something sour. Richer, if that's what it took.

Whatever it takes, he reminded himself, to see the takers
taken. He was still bound by the oath he'd sworn, that first

terrible night in the boys' school, while he stared out his window at a full moon striped by bars.

The Ashaways had taken everything that mattered? His freedom, his home, his future, his hope. The one person in all the world that he loved.

All right, then. He'd spend the rest of his life, taking whatever they cared about. Simple as that.

But simplicity had an odd way of fracturing around Raine Ashaway. One desire had split into two opposing passions: He wanted her laughing in his arms.

He wanted her miserable. Shattered.

Jet-lagged, that's all you are, Cade told himself. He'd hired a cab last night and prowled the city till dawn, looking for her. Wondering where a woman on the run could hide, in this alien world. Hoping he found her before the police did.

But if the Singapore cops were going to catch her, surely they'd have done so by now?

He sat down heavily at the computer and thought for a moment. *What do I know about you, Raine? What would you do on the run?*

She'd keep right on running after what she wanted.

His pulse quickened as it hit him. Her dino wasn't here on Singapore—it was three hundred-some miles to the southeast! If Raine hadn't been knocked on the head in the slums of the city last night, sold off into white slavery or worse... If she was still free and alive, then— He blew out a breath and put his fingers to the keyboard.

Marc, get me a flight to Pontianak, Kalimantan, soonest possible, by whatever means necessary.

Cade sat, fingers poised, frowning into space. He had the name and address of Lia's mother in Pontianak. His PA had obtained that info from the admissions office at NYU. If she was free, that would be where Raine was headed—tracing the next link on a chain that led to a fortune in bones. With any luck he'd cross her trail there.

"Just tell 'em the truth," Zack advised two days later, as he helped Raine put her kayak over the side, two miles off the western coast of Borneo. "You intended to fly from Singapore to Kalimantan, but you met this incredibly sexy man, who invited you to sail there instead."

"Sounds vaguely plausible." Raine laughed as she slid down into the craft, to sit with her legs stretched before her, bobbing in the long Pacific swells. She reached up for her backpack, then her parasol. Stowing them in the aft compartment, she battened down its cover, then adjusted her spray skirt.

"Entirely plausible. You had a mad, passionate, high-seas affair…"

"Or would have, if his parrot had liked me. But, alas…"

"That's why you—?" Zack stopped, realizing she was teasing, and shrugged. "Ah, well. Some other time, in some alternate reality?"

Raine held his rueful gaze—and smiled. *Anything's possible.* She couldn't say why she hadn't responded to his advances. Too obsessed with her coming search? She'd been dreaming of *T. rexes* every night.

Or, maybe stung by Cade's betrayal. Her confidence had taken a knock, once she realized the she'd misjudged the man entirely. If Cade could blithely frame her for a capital offense, then he surely must have murdered Lia.

And, if I can fall for a calculating killer, then maybe I shouldn't be let out alone—much less choose my own lovers!

Besides which, Elsa the parrot didn't want her aboard. "Silly slut!" she screeched now, hanging upside down from the boom. "G'wan, you cow!"

Zack smacked his forehead as Raine laughed aloud. "I did *not* teach her that."

"It's like five-year-olds and curse words. If it gets a good reaction, they repeat it. My sister Jaye has a gray parrot who's just as possessive. I could show you the scars…"

"I'd like to see them."

She smiled and held up her left hand. "Little finger."

He kissed the triangular scar, then leaned down, gave her a swift kiss on the mouth. They squeezed hands and let go. "Well," he said huskily. "You've got my e-mail address. Use it, if you need anything. Or if you're ever in the mood for a cruise."

"I'll do that, Zack, and…thank you." She back-paddled from between the hulls, then steered out into the open sea. The swells were darkening to teal, the sky turning to tangerine. She aimed her bow east, toward the first lights blooming in the city of Pontianak, province of West Kalimantan.

She glanced back once. A black form against the bright sky, the captain looked after her, leaning out from one hull, gripping a shroud. He'd yet to raise the sails. She waved her paddle overhead in one last farewell, then turned and stroked on, right…left…right. Some mystery back there, and perhaps that had been another reason for her detachment.

He wasn't who he said he was.

Searching the first night for something to read, after she'd finished her trick at the helm, she'd checked out his well-stocked bookcase. Flipped through a tattered paperback on tropical trees, bound with a rubber band. Its middle pages had been glued together, then hollowed out—to hold two passports. Each with a clean-shaven photo of Zack, but a different name entirely.

And maybe that explained why he'd not been willing to take her all the way to shore. Not welcome in Indonesia? Whoever he was, he'd claimed to be in too much of a hurry. Bound south for the Solomon Islands.

But in the last glimpse Raine got of him, just as she reached the shallows, his catamaran was skimming north. Up the coast toward Sarawak.

Not her business. She shrugged, stepped out into cool, ankle-deep water, sand fine as silk, and stretched. Borneo at last!

"Does she speak English?" Cade asked the nurse. The woman hadn't smiled once as she led him to the ward that Lia's mother, Sebang, shared with five other patients. Now she fluffed Sebang's pillows, then straightened on the far side of the narrow bed, regarding him with dark, indignant eyes. The other women glared from their cots.

With less than twenty-four hours in Pontianak, he already found that unnerving. Smiles were a reflex courtesy here in Borneo, no matter the underlying mood. Cade pulled up a straight-backed chair and sat beside the patient. "Does she—"

The woman burst into rapid *Bahasa Indonesia.* Lia's mother replied in a liquid murmur.

The nurse looked up. Clasped her hands before her. "She say no."

She'd said a lot more than that. Cade nodded amiably as he studied this older version of Lia. Despite the bruises on her face and her blackened eyes, she looked not a day over thirty. A beauty like her daughter, he suspected, from the regal way she sat, propped against her pillows; she was too battered to be certain.

"Then would you tell her, please, that I come from New York City, in America, where I met her daughter Lia. And that I'm very sorry for her loss."

While the nurse translated, he studied Sebang with growing outrage. The neighbors next door to her little guesthouse had said only that she'd had an accident, was now in hospital. But this was no accident! Those were finger marks imprinted on her upper arms. Her lip was split.

"Who did this?" he demanded. He didn't even know that Raine was on the island, but if she was and she'd done this— ordered it done...

Sebang stared up at the ceiling fan revolving above, sighed and spoke softly.

"She says an American man," the nurse snapped. "He come asking questions."

Cade gritted his teeth. "What did he want?"

Sebang's eyes filled slowly with tears. "He wish to know," she said in clear English with an odd echo of Texas, "where I get the package that I mail to my daughter."

Cade drew a harsh breath. Damn all the taking, breaking, Ashaways straight to hell! "I, also, have come to ask about that package, *Ibu* Sebang."

Her bitter smile stopped midcurve with a wince; she nodded. "This, I think."

"But first, I make you this promise. When I find the man that hurt you, I'll break his head."

She covered her swollen mouth with her fingers and giggled. "You like my husban', Frank."

After that, the nurse huffed off on her rounds. While the ceiling fan flickered, and the sun crept from one side of the ward to the other, Cade sat and listened. He heard the whole odyssey: how the prettiest woman in a tiny upriver town, a Dayak widow with a girl child, had married a Chinese trader. A match made for lust on his side, and more practical reasons on hers, Cade suspected. But judging from her wistful smile, it had worked.

She'd followed her man to Pontianak, helped him run his store down by the docks. They'd wanted more children, a son, but none had come. So her husband had taught Lia to keep the accounts; the girl was most amazingly smart. All her teachers said so.

When Lia was twelve, her stepfather made his yearly trip to Djakarta to purchase trade goods. The ferry had capsized; there were no survivors.

Being a practical woman, the pretty widow soon dried her tears and looked around. This time she chose an arrangement with a Texas oilie, Frank.

Frank stayed for four years, till his company transferred him to Kuwait and his stateside wife decided to join him there. But he'd made a promise before he left. That he'd pay for clever Lia to go to college—go to college in America!

Sebang's eyes brimmed over. "How I wish he never keep that promise!" She wiped her cheeks with graceful fingers. Gave that painful smile. "But Lia, she never satisfy. She say this a small town—this, the only one she know. She say she want it all." Her voice dropped to a whisper. "She want to *eat* life."

But life ate her, was the thought hanging between them. Cade nodded heavily. Add it to the score he'd collect from the Ashaways.

"That package, I think it very bad luck," Sebang added matter-of-factly.

The tooth and the watch had been sent down the Kapuas River, from Sebang's hometown of Long Badu. Sent to Lia by her stepcousin, son of the brother of the Chinese trader; his family owned the only store in that town.

The items had been taken in trade, was all Sebang knew. The cousin had hoped that clever Lia, in America, could learn their true worth and make a fine deal. She could keep half, and send him half.

And I bet he'd have whistled for his share, was Cade's private guess.

So Sebang had packed the things and mailed them off to Lia.

Six weeks later, her daughter was dead.

And now this. A man came asking about the tooth, a man she didn't like. Didn't trust. When she refused to tell him anything, he'd beaten the information out of her, squeezed her bottom and walked out into the night, chuckling.

I'll more than break his head, Cade promised himself. "Could you tell me what he looked like, this man?"

He looked like…an American. Apparently to Indonesians, they all looked much the same. Cade came away with a description that could have fit half the men in New York City. Not ugly, not handsome. Not fat. Big and tall.

"Taller than me?" he'd tried. "Or shorter?"

Sebang's smile held a hint of devilment. "*Never* tell a man that he be shorter!"

Cade smothered his laugh. Here was the one who'd eat life. He gave her no more than a year, before she chose her next lucky lover.

"'Bout the same size," Sebang added, with that odd hint of a Texas drawl layered over East Indies tact. "A soldier, I think."

She couldn't say why, when Cade questioned her, but she stuck to that notion. Not a backpacker. Not a businessman. A soldier. "A man who think killing is a joke, I think."

They were sitting roughly a mile south of the equator, but Sebang rubbed the goose bumps on her bruised arms and, meeting her swollen eyes, Cade felt a chill. "But you told him everything he wanted to know?"

"Everything." She nodded sorrowfully.

"Good. That was very wise. Then he won't come back to trouble you."

Cade reached into the pocket of his khaki suit and pulled out his checkbook. Cash might be crass, but it could smooth the jagged edges on a world of hurt. "And now I should tell you, Ibu. The reason I came today, was that I owed your daughter money." He wrote out a figure that would give Marc heartburn, when he balanced the books. The amount he'd intended to offer Lia for her tooth.

No problem. He'd take it out in trade when he met Chuckles, who'd pinch a woman's ass after he beat her.

Chapter 18

Doing people favors just didn't pay. If he'd known he was headed for Putussibau—known the flight schedule—Szabo would have wrung Lia's mama's neck.

But he'd got the information he'd come for, and he'd figured he'd be long gone from Pontianak before the cops could comb the town, and she had a pert little ass; he'd let her live.

Big mistake. Turned out there were only two commercial flights a week to Putussibau, the closest you could fly to the headwaters of the Kapuas. The next one wouldn't leave for three lo-ong days.

So he'd hustled out to the airfield on the edge of town, the strip the Bible thumpers flew out of. Asked politely if he could buy a ride out on a Mission flight. But they'd looked him up and down, then wanted to know if he was carrying any weapons?

Holier-than-thou types always rubbed him wrong. He'd made a crack, saying, "Heck. My whole body is a lethal weapon." Which with Ranger training, it was, though he'd only been kidding.

They'd stiffened up like a couple of goosed nuns and told him their planes were full-up with God's cargo this week; maybe he should try them the next?

Szabo knew a brush-off when he heard it. If it had only been the pilot, he'd have showed him the Indian handgun he'd bought in the marketplace, soon as he got to Pontianak. Stuck it in his sanctimonious ear and hijacked the damn plane.

But there were two of them plus a mechanic, lounging around the hangar. So he'd said, "Up yours, Jacqueline," and walked out.

The upshot was: here he was, leaning on the rail of a river-boat as it pulled away from the dock, out into the mile-wide Kapuas. Five days to Putussibau by water, sleeping on deck with the headhunters and their pigs and chickens and squalling babies. Then one more day by canoe up to Long Badu, the town where the tooth and his granddad's watch had come from.

Really should have wrung her neck. He sighed and scratched his arm, where Lia's bite was still itching him— then straightened with a yelp. Was that—? Holy shit, it was! The dang woman had more lives than a cat!

Here came Raine Ashaway, sitting in one of those tricycle pedicabs, with the driver pumping away on his pedals behind her. In the shade of her parasol, her smile sparkled as she looked all around. She flashed it at Malays and beggars and dirty mutts and the cats that prowled every roof. You'd think she was pedaling through paradise, not a dirty river town.

Just then, as the boat completed its turn out into the current and blasted its horn, her eyes lit on him! She laughed and waved, calling something he couldn't hear over the rumble of the big diesels as they kicked into gear.

He bared his teeth in a wide grin and waved back madly. "Don't know when to quit, do you, babe?"

If she followed him into the jungle, she'd learn soon enough.

It had taken Raine a full day to placate the *Imigrasi,* then the police, then the military commander of Pontianak. Once they'd forgiven her her unorthodox arrival, they had to be convinced that an unaccompanied American woman should be allowed to travel upriver alone. More bribes, more batting of eyelashes—more gritted teeth, but showing frustration was a major faux pas in Indonesia; the worst kind of ill manners.

It would be smartest to leapfrog over the boys in uniform. Get to the jungle as soon as she could. Besides, Kincade had stolen a march on her, with his tube of lethal toothpaste. He must be somewhere up ahead.

Raine's only hope was that finding Lia's mother might have slowed him down. Since Ravi had told her about Lia's cousin in Long Badu—that the tooth had come from there— she could skip a step that presumably Kincade had to complete.

Don't panic, she told herself as the pedicab trundled out of town, toward the airfield. Even if Cade had caught yesterday's flight to Putussibau, she might beat him yet. If she could beg or buy a seat on an MAF plane to Long Badu.

But the missionaries proved to be as conservative and territorial as the soldiers—and much less susceptible to batting lashes. Unmarried blondes—in pants!—who'd never even heard of their sect, much less signed up for it, ought to go directly to Babylon, not jaunting off into the interior. When she gave them her cover story, that she'd come to photograph orchids for a botanical magazine, they simply glowered. Too fun, too frivolous, she supposed.

They demanded to know if she carried tobacco for the natives? Alcohol? Firearms? Pornography? Comic books?

"None of the above," Raine insisted, trying not to laugh. "Please, I have a deadline to meet on this article. And my friend Ohara said you might help me."

Dropping the Aussie's name tightened their lips—and turned the tide. Apparently Trey's friend was their Mission's source of kerosene and plane fuel, at cost, even though they condemned the oilie's freewheeling morals.

Grudgingly they gave her a seat in the rear of the ancient single-engine Piper, jammed in amidst boxes of baby formula and laundry soap, batteries and gumdrops. The pilot handed her the headphones she'd need to wear during the noisy flight, and told her they'd take off as soon as the other passenger arrived.

The mechanic slammed the cargo door, and the humid heat trapped within the little plane rose from sweltering to sauna. Up front the pilot completed his checklist, gave a signal to the mechanic, who spun the propeller. The engine coughed, then roared. Apparently they'd wait no longer for the missing passenger. The mechanic pulled out the rear chocks—just as somebody yelled over the engine racket.

"Sugar!" was the pilot's comment, if Raine read his lips correctly.

The door opened. Cade swung up into the plane, grabbed his backpack, which was jammed in after him. He yelled something to the pilot—and glanced around. Raine showed her teeth. Sugar didn't begin to describe it.

His own shock faded—to a wolfish smile.

The plane trundled over the grass, then hurled itself down the runway, straining toward the sky.

Given the drone of the engine, conversation was impossible—not that Raine meant to converse with the rat. And ripping his ears off wasn't practical, half a mile in the air. She settled for staring out her window while the world rolled beneath them at a pace that felt as slow as walking.

For the first few hours they followed the course of the Kapuas. A wide, dark, busy river in the coastal flatlands. Rafts of timber poled by tiny figures floated down from the distant rainforests. River steamers and sailing praus glided upstream and down. The Dayaks' longboats looked like water bugs, skating in and out of the traffic.

As the Piper droned on, the forest closed in on the rice fields. The river narrowed and showed lacings of white water. Beyond the blur of the plane's propeller, low lush mountains bucked toward the sky.

Behind them the clouds darkened to purple and steel and Raine remembered Trey's briefing on the weather: "Borneo has a wet season—and a hot." October was the tail of the hot season, but storms were still to be expected. She'd been warned that the rivers could rise twelve feet or more when a cloudburst passed through. She tapped the pilot—Roger—on the shoulder and gestured behind when he turned.

Roger grimaced, shrugged and turned ahead. *Trust in the Lord,* Raine supposed; He certainly hadn't provided a place to land a plane. Trees stretched to the horizon in a thousand shades of vibrant green.

Cade swung to peer past her out the rear side glass and his pupils widened like a startled cat's. His eyes swerved to hers and they stared at each other, unsmiling.

Raine felt a hot slide of sensation down her spine. Weird, how she could respond to a man who was her enemy. "You tried to kill me," she said in a level voice.

"What?"

"You tried to plant dope on me, you bastard! Why?" she called, raising her voice, though with headphones on he'd never hear her.

Eyes fixed on her mouth, he shrugged, shook his head.

"Jerk," she said, just for the record.

He laughed, shook his head again—and reached to touch her lips.

Bastard! She snapped at him, but he was too fast. He yanked his fingers out of range, examined them, then grinned as he shook them theatrically.

"Yeah, and that's only a sample," she growled, looking away. A gust of wind buffeted their wings; the plane swooped like dandelion fluff in a gale.

When she turned forward again, Cade's amusement had faded to a bleak appraisal.

Moody devil. Goose bumps rose along her arms. He meant her and hers ill; he'd never tried to deny that. Still, for a while there on the flight to Singapore, she'd thought—hoped?—that they were competing in a contest where the basic tenets of civilization held. Economic ruin was the worst she had to fear from him.

But if that's not where Cade draws the line... They were bound for the jungle. Long Badu marked the edge of it; she'd found no map to show what lay beyond that dot on the river. In Long Badu there would be a headman of the village. But tradition was the only law recognized out here, and how could that apply to a quarrel between two foreigners?

They'd have to settle it among themselves. And Cade was bigger, stronger, faster. A match for her in wits?

Looks like I'm going to find out. The wind smacked the plane again and it dropped—leaving her stomach in free fall.

Once the worst of the storm had rumbled past, the rain continued. Unable to see the ground, Raine dug out Trey's briefing papers.

"Language" was a topic worth reviewing. He'd written:

Bahasa Indonesia is the official tongue, a crazy blend of Malay, Dutch, trading Arabic, Indian, with dashes of Chinese and English. For instance, to say: Drop the Anchor, you say: Lego jangkar! (Try it three times real fast.)

But for this trip don't bother to learn it; it won't serve you past the coast. Once you hit Dayak country, Bahasa Indonesia is just another foreign language. You'll need a guide to speak for you, or you'll have to mime your way.

She flipped to the next page, which dealt with "People."

Indonesia has more races than even America. Its islands were settled in overlapping waves spreading out from Asia, over the past 30,000 years. High on the unmapped central plateau you'll find Borneo's earliest arrivals, the Punan—small, shy, light-skinned nomadic hunters; probably kin to Australia's aborigines.

Lower down the mountains and along the rivers you'll find the land Dayaks—there are at least twelve separate tribes of them, the Iban, the Kenyah, etc., but generally speaking, they're slash-and-burn farmers and ex-headhunters. Good-tempered, tatooed party-hearties mostly, who could drink your average frat boy under the table. If they declare a dance, look out; it'll make Mardi Gras seem like a tea party at the vicarage.

Then down along the coast you've got the sea Dayaks and the Malays, descendants of Indonesia's notorious pirates. Lots of Chinese. Javanese immigrants, plus Dutch and Brit colonial left-behinds.

"Been there, done that," Raine told him and glanced up as the plane banked to the right. They'd turned away from the main river to follow a smaller tributary winding southeast. "*Wait* a minute, I thought—"

Cade must have had a similar notion—that Long Badu was located along the Kapuas, not one of its many branches. He looked away from his window with a frown, swiveled a mike attached to his headset into position and spoke.

Raine got a crackling in her ears, nothing more. "Hey, you got a mike!" Fuming, she watched as they discussed something urgent. Cade unfolded a map, stared at it. Roger reached over to tap it, with an emphatic negative.

"What's going on?" Raine leaned between the front seats, trying to see for herself, but Cade folded the map with a smirk.

The plane buzzed lower, found a clearing in the forest and circled. Raine could see two longhouses built along a rushing creek. Garden patches and palm trees, chickens and dozing dogs. Children running beneath them, looking up and waving their arms with glee.

Roger made a pass at what must be the landing field, rousting pigs, a flock of geese. He climbed sharply upward as they neared a wall of trees, circled again. This time when they made their approach, the pigs were retreating on dainty trotters, shooed by the children. People came hurrying from all sides to stand along the borders of the field, shouting and waving.

The plane set down—bounced so high Cade banged his head on its ceiling—rumbled and bumped over the rough ground. Rattled finally to a halt. "This is a very short stop," Roger announced. "Don't forget any of your gear." He slid out his door, to be swarmed by the people of Long Badu.

"What did he say back there?" Raine demanded. "About the map?"

"Proprietary info, sweetie." Cade swung out his door and shouldered his pack.

"Double rat!" Raine sat, collecting herself; the minute she left the plane she'd lose all privacy. Clearly strangers were a rare and welcome entertainment; Cade stood surrounded by wide-eyed children. "Roger," she said as he opened the cargo compartment and grabbed a box. "What was that business with the map back there?"

"Huh!" Roger grumbled. "Lord save us from tourists. He bought a ride to the wrong place. This is New Long Badu, not Old Long Badu-on-the-Kapuas, which is twenty miles to the north."

Uh-oh. "Umm, I guess I got confused, too. Any chance you could fly us—I mean me—there?"

Roger snorted and tossed another box to a waiting pair of hands. "Not possible. We don't fly to Old Long Badu. Its people are wicked and stubborn. Refuse to see the Light. You'll have to walk if you want to go there, but I don't advise it. And now, please, if I don't make Long Pa by dark…"

"Of course, but—" Quickly Raine drew a folded paper from her pack. She'd meant to ask him about this in transit, but Cade had foiled that plan. "Have you ever seen this lake before, from the air?" She showed him her sketch of the mountain range below a butterfly-shaped lake, all she'd seen of the map in Lia's watch.

Roger barely glanced at it. "No." He dragged a burlap bag toward the door.

"Please, it's important. You're sure?" Beyond the pilot's shoulder, Cade stepped into view, peering into the cargo space. She folded the sketch and tucked it into her trouser pocket.

"*Quite.* We don't have fuel capacity to fly beyond the mountains, and there's no place to land. Now please…"

"Okay, okay." Raine hopped down out of the plane, hauled her pack after her and shrugged into it as she turned to face the crowd.

The laughing and chattering faltered…faded away. Thirty or more honey-colored, dark-eyed faces stared aghast. A girl of perhaps eight pointed and cried "*Bungan!*" Shrieking with fearful laughter, she darted off to a safe distance, then turned to bounce on her toes and point. "*Bungan! Bungan!*"

The adults muttered and drew inward on each other.

"She's not *Bungan!* Don't be ridiculous!" Roger yelled, his face reddening. He burst into fluent speech, in which the word *Bungan* figured large.

"Who do they think I am?" Raine begged, tugging at his sleeve.

"The children think you look like…like *Bungan,* but they *don't* believe in her anymore. She's just a…something from their ignorant, heathen past. A sort of white goddess creature. A she-devil. Fertility and rice harvests and all that garbage."

"At least they got the she-devil part right." Cade was grinning like a crocodile.

"She's. Not. *Bungan!*"

"*Bungan, Bungan!*" shrieked a pack of giggling children.

Roger threw up his hands, slammed the cargo door and snapped to Cade, "Would you give me a spin?" He swung to shake his finger at Raine. "And you—*don't* encourage this nonsense. Don't let them give you any eggs!" He scrambled into the plane and glared at one and all through the windshield.

The plane snarled and bucked down the field, hit a bump and clawed for the air. Everyone watched it out of sight, then a collective sigh passed around the group, and Raine would have sworn it was relief. Somebody made a comment, which won a burst of laughter.

Raine looked around. The headman was unmistakable. An old guy, his bare chest and shoulders were covered in blue-star tattoos. His big wrinkled hands were blue from wrist to first knuckle. He was the only man who hadn't picked up a box of cargo. His smile was serene and complacent as a tomcat's contemplating a cageful of canaries. These were his people; this was his world.

Always give the top man your first respect, her father had taught her, since a child. Eyes modestly lowered, she crossed to stand before him. Putting her palms together, fingers up, she bowed her head over them—then looked him in the face as she gave him a tentative smile.

His eyes were almost black, alive with intelligence. "Bungan?" he inquired with a teasing twinkle.

She smiled wider and shook her head, then tapped her chest. "Raine."

Chapter 19

She might be a she-devil, but Cade couldn't help admiring Raine, as the afternoon slipped swiftly into dusk. She was good with people. With no words in common, she could still make herself liked and understood.

The only point she hadn't been able to get across was that he and she weren't a couple. It was an easy mistake to make, considering they'd dropped out of nowhere together. And that he'd aimed several *back-off* stares at the younger studs of the village, when they tagged along behind her, enthralled by the sway of her hips.

Not that he felt in the least possessive of her charms; it was simply a matter of maintaining his place in the pecking order. The men of the village would figure him for a big white marshmallow, if he allowed other guys to make moves on "his" woman.

So they'd been treated as a twosome, with Raine as the Graceful Facilitator, and Cade playing Strong and Silent. The headman had invited them up into the larger longhouse—a thatched communal dwelling some two hundred feet long by maybe forty wide, standing above the damp tropical ground on carved twelve-foot pilings.

The whole village had gathered to watch the fun. Could the guests pass the test? To enter you walked up a log—a crude, steeply slanting staircase with steps hacked into its mossy trunk at intervals. Raine had laughed, spread her arms and almost danced up the timber, unimpeded by her heavy pack. Determined not to make a fool of himself, Cade had proceeded more cautiously—then he'd looked down at the final step and almost fallen off in surprise. A howling gargoyle face dared him to step over it and onto the veranda.

"He keep bad spirits out of house," explained a young man, following Cade up the tree trunk.

That was their introduction to Ngali, who'd just returned from hunting. Nephew of the headman, he'd spent a year working for the missionaries, down at their school in Sintang. With Ngali's arrival, everyone settled on the broad, covered veranda that served as front porch and favorite living space for the occupants of the longhouse. It was time to "share news." By which they seemed to mean, not, "what's happened in the world?" but, "what have *you* done lately?"

Raine obliged by describing her voyage across the sea in what Ngali translated as a very big longboat. The dolphins she'd seen, the fires from the oil platforms at night, a green bird that spoke its thoughts—all of them bawdy or wicked or wise.

Cade cocked his head at her. *Are you making this up?* Where *had* she sprung from? But he'd have to wait for an explanation; the village wanted his contribution. So he described their flight on the MAF plane, what the river looked like from above, the storm. The way he banged his head when they landed won an appreciative chortle.

Then Ngali stood to act out his hunt of this afternoon. He'd stalked a deer over hill and dale, but his spear had missed—his expression of outrage and woe won a big laugh.

Then he'd met a—he gave the word in Dayak—and of course, that had ended *that*. He had to come home.

Raine asked for a clarification of what he'd met, and Ngali seemed to be miming a caterpillar crossing his path. *Lost in translation,* Cade concluded.

From sharing news the tribe segued straight into grill-the-guests. *Where do you come from? How many days by long-boat is that? Are you very rich and important? How many children do you have? What—none?* Their hosts stared with pity and consternation; skeptical glances were cast at Ngali, as if they figured he'd got it wrong. Judging from the number of toddlers underfoot, breeding was either the favorite pastime in Long Badu, or everyone's civic duty.

After forty-questions, Raine brought out a series of photos. Pictures of herself and other Ashaways standing near dinosaur bones, half encased in the earth. She passed around a picture of Joe and John Ashaway in their youth, posing proudly before the skull of a *T. rex* as big as a Volkswagen bug. Cade clenched his jaws as he passed it on to his neighbor.

"Have you ever seen bones like these?" Raine asked the marveling crowd, with Ngali's help. "I come looking for big bones. Bones in the earth."

No one had ever heard of such things. "Perhaps these monsters only walk in your land?" the headman's wife suggested with sympathy. "Your hunters must be very brave."

After Raine's show-and-tell, the kerosene lanterns were lit along the gallery. The women served big bowls of rice and bananas and soupy stews that were set down for all on the porch's planks. Then out came the rice wine and the rice brandy. It was time for dancing, tall tales, entertaining each other. What people had been doing for thousands of years, before TV came along to wreck the fun.

After a bear dance complete with bearskin and bear mask, the rice wine bottles passed round the circle. Then came a delicately sensual, swivel-hipped line dance of the maidens, while the young men groaned and swooned.

More throat-scorching rice wine, then the headman danced a solo. He reenacted a war raid, complete with blood-curdling yells and exuberant slashes of his *parang,* a short, razor-edged machete. Either this raid happened many years ago, or he was telling a dreadful whopper about how many heads he'd taken. But another slug of Borneo moonshine made it all seem perfectly plausible, wonderfully admirable.

Then Raine was urged to perform. She demurred prettily twice, till Ngali laughed and pulled her to her feet. At which point the sly wench untied her braid and shook her hair out on her shoulders—then produced a kazoo from her pocket. Sounding like a cross between Daisy Duck and Marilyn Monroe, she played the sexiest, silliest "Girl From Ipanema," Cade had ever heard, while she danced a slow, seductive, shuffle-strut aimed entirely at the Headman. The old guy beamed and chortled and ate it up.

As Cade would have done in his place.

She swayed and sauntered back to her seat in the circle— and sat to yells of delight. Then she beckoned to Ngali and whispered in his ear as the rice wine made its rounds.

"Ho!" Ngali announced, straightening. "We have here, the greatest poet in America!" He pointed at Cade. "Very famous man. He say his poems for King of America and Queen Elizabeth and Fidel Castro! He now honor us with his best and longest poem."

When he caught up with her, she was toast! But it was too late to wimp out now, with the eyes of the tribe upon him. Cade took a fortifying slug of rice wine, stood and launched straight into "The Night Before Christmas." And let Ngali translate that!

Whether they got a word of it or not, they applauded his efforts hugely, at which point Cade turned to give Raine a triumphant smirk—and found she was gone.

Cade looked pretty wonderful, Raine had to admit, with his T-shirt clinging to his broad chest and his rugged face gleaming with sweat. Standing in the center of the charmed circle with his legs braced to stop his swaying, he belted out her favorite line, "Now dash away, dash way, dash away all!"

"*Bungan? Bungan!*" Two young women plucked at her sleeves, while they murmured pleadingly in Dayak. They weren't smiling.

"Trouble? Okay. Sure. Let's go." When Western foreigners were urgently wanted, it was generally for medicine, Raine had learned over the years. She stopped by the room the headman had assigned for her and Cade's packs, to grab her first-aid kit.

Two hours later Raine returned from the other longhouse, sobered but hopeful. The child might make it. She'd stepped on something—a fish in the creek, Raine thought they'd said, though maybe she'd misunderstood. Whatever the source of the wound, it had festered. Since the poultice of herbs on the girl's foot didn't seem to be helping, she'd washed it away, then disinfected and drained the wound. Then squeezed on a tube of antibiotic, and bandaged her with a strip of clean cloth.

She'd given her mother three more tubes of the ointment for later. Germs that had never met antibiotics before were often routed by their powers, and tropical people tended to be hardy. And maybe the *Bungan* mystique would turbo-charge her treatment.

Raine glanced down ruefully at her forearm, pressed across her stomach, where three eggs nestled. She hadn't wanted to accept them—the girl's young mother seemed poor—but she hadn't dared refuse. Payment to the goddess might clinch the magic. As her designated pinch hitter, Raine would have to pray this was so.

She balanced up the log to the veranda, where the party rocked on. A frat-house beer bash did come to mind. Weaving her way between snoring, smiling bodies sprawled on the rough planks, and couples joyfully necking, she came to the circle of hard-core survivors.

An old man played a stringed instrument with ferocious,

fumble-fingered intensity while the headman and others droned mournfully along. Cade sat, surrounded by four of the village's younger beauties, who giggled and tried to coax him to drink from a bottle. When he laughed and refused, they poured it over his head, dodging away when he roared and tried to fend them off—then sneaking back to drizzle more down his face and collar.

Bedtime, Raine decided, backpedaling down the porch.

But he'd spotted her. "Hey, you!" Cade hauled himself to his feet with the help of his giggling tormentors and staggered her way. "Where'd you go?"

"A kid with a bad foot. I always bring extra antibiot—*hey!*" she yelped as he scooped her into his arms. Juggling eggs and her first-aid bag, she could only kick her foot and scowl. "Put me down!"

"Nope." He wobbled on toward the room where they'd left their packs. "You gotta help…me out here. Seems honor requires that…I drink myself into a coma. Or I get a pass if…I take somebody t'bed. But I'm not into twelve-year-old virgins, even when they're cute as a basket of puppies, so…I choose you." He nudged through the crude louvered door with one shoulder and into pitch darkness.

"After you tried to kill me back in Singapore? Not a chance, Kincade. Don't make me hurt you." She tossed her med kit to safety.

He laughed, sat with a thump that jarred her teeth. *"Ooof!"*

Yuk, they'd cracked an egg! Raine flung the shell aside, wiped her hand on his sweaty T-shirt. "I mean it now, le'me go!" She kicked her legs over his forearm, but he simply hugged her closer.

"Singapore?" Smelling of rice wine and bay rum, his face loomed over hers; she could feel its heat. "What're you talkin' about?"

"You planted heroin in my bag, you jerk, remember?" She found the other two eggs wedged between their bodies and rescued them.

"Nooo…I don' remember. Zat's why you ran?"

"Zat's exactly why. But don't bother denying it. Who else would have done it?"

"Beats…me." Cade propped his forehead against hers. He sounded as if he were pondering hard. "You…mean it? Heroin?"

She nodded and his arms tightened with the motion. Her arm nearest him was getting crushed. She moved it to encircle his neck—damn, but he was warm as an oven. And she was hotter, with her breast now flattened against his collarbone.

"Weird," he concluded finally. "But serves you right. They shoulda thrown your hot li'l butt in jail. Thrown away the key… You sent your brother t'beat up Mrs. Lia, didn' you?"

"My— *What?* Ash is in San Francisco. What the *hell* are you—"

Cade nodded too many times, his damp hair brushing her cheek. "Finally…figured it out. There's been two of you all long… One t'throw Lia out the window, while one stands down below. Then there musta been two of you on the plane from New York. I keep my eye on the sexy one—the other one beats Lia's mom half to death and when I catch him, he's a goner. Your brother, *gonezo*."

"Lia's mom was— Is she all right?"

"No thanks t'your bro', whose head I'm gonna pers'nlly bust."

Raine cupped her hand to the nape of Cade's neck and reeled him in till their noses touched. "Kincade, *listen* to me. Ash is *not* here on Borneo. Are you listening?"

"Mmm," he purred, like a lion drifting off to sleep.

"And I didn't hire anybody to throw Lia out the window. And *you* say you didn't plant heroin on me—you swear that? By everything you hold dear?"

"All I'm holdin' is you, dear. An aaarmload of she-devil." Holding her tight, Cade sank gradually backward, till he trapped her forearm between his neck and the floor planks. Another egg cracked.

"You're not going to remember this in the morning," Raine said in disgust. She tossed the shell aside, rolled the intact one off into the dark, wiped her hand on his shoulder.

"In my dreams," Cade murmured. He strained upward, his abs crunching, to kiss her ear.

He needed a shave; she needed... He trailed a chain of openmouthed kisses down her neck...nibbled, when he got to her shoulder.

She shuddered with pleasure. *Yeah,* did she need. And by morning, he'd have forgotten everything. It'd be a free ride. *I shouldn't do this.* Should not. She twisted out of his loosening hold to lie full length on top of him. *But, God, you're gorgeous!* She smoothed a hand down his sculpted torso, trailed it on down his muscled thigh. She couldn't help herself. Her hips rocked a slow suggestion.

He gave that rumbling purr again as he cupped her buttocks—and curled his fingers deep into the cleft between. Snugged her close.

His lips moved hungrily against her throat. He sighed soft and slow—his hands relaxed on her bottom.

"Cade?" she almost whimpered, nudging him again. "Kincade?"

"Mmmmmmmmmmm." He had to be smiling in his sleep.

"You...rat. You quitter. You..." *Man.* When they came up with an acceptable substitute, she'd be first in line. Raine rolled off him and flopped over onto her back—and crushed the third egg.

Chapter 20

Somebody had been playing basketball with his head, Cade decided, without opening his eyes. One of those quaint Dayak customs they'd forgotten to mention, till the fifth time the rice wine went round.

Plus the longhouse was doing barrel rolls—was going to flip over on top of him any second now. Carefully he starfished his arms and legs, the better to cling to this heaving world...with a groan he drifted away.

Who knew how much later, morning drove splinters of sunlight under his eyelids. A memory shafted straight to his groin. Raine. He'd held her? Kissed her! From collarbone to crotch, he could feel her body's imprint—*God*—had she really lain on top of him, her wicked long legs wedged between his? His fingers curled in against his palms, seeking curves and softness. Finding only air.

Did we...? He was surely in Hell, if they had and he'd lost the memory! With a groan, he struggled up to one elbow. "Raine?"

Silence nearby. Low murmurs in the distance, a dog barking, children's laughter. He dared to open his eyes. "Raine."

He was alone in their room. He sat up with wincing care—and grunted in surprise. Crackle shirt? His fingers trailed over patches of squish and caked hardness. *What on earth did we do?*

And there were eggshells scattered all around.

Another ten minutes passed before Cade noticed that her pack was gone. Where it had leaned in the corner, a cluster of objects anchored down a sheet of paper torn from a notepad. He picked up the note.

Bet you forgot to bring guest gifts, so do us both a favor? Give Mrs. Headman these beads, with our thanks for a fabulous meal. The Swiss army knife is for the bossman, of course, and the fishing gear's for Ngali. Please tell them it was a lovely party. I'd tell them myself, but everybody's sleeping in, this morning.

And do yourself a favor, Cade. Stay here till Roger flies through again. He said he'd be swinging back this way in a week or two.

Son of a bitch, she'd gone! That's what this note was—sayonara! Cade staggered to his feet. He was dressed; all he needed was his...

He looked down. Must have gone to sleep in his shoes. He still wore yesterday's clothes, which, come to think of it, must mean they hadn't...

But if he'd slept in his hiking boots... He squinted owlishly. Straightened at last to turn in a slow grim circle. Where were they?

"Ashaway, you didn't." She might be crazy, but surely she wasn't suicidal? He returned to the note he held.

Trust me on this. It would be very stupid to follow. Dangerous. Step on a krait and you're history.

She had. The treacherous she-devil had stolen his boots.

* * *

Five miles down the trail to Old Long Badu, Raine aimed her blowgun at an overhanging branch. She blew gently. Her dart flew true, trailing a gossamer thread of fishing line. The dart reached the apex of its flight just beyond the limb, and fell; she caught it midair. Cutting the doubled line off her missile, she tied one end to the laces of Cade's right boot—then pulled on the other end to hoist it.

When his boot dangled twenty feet in the air, she walked her tail of the nylon line over to a wilderness of vines growing up another tree. She stood frozen, scanning carefully for snakes, then reached into the thicket and tied the line off. In the murky green light of the forest, he'd never find it. If Cade wanted his boot, he'd have to get it the hard way—by climbing. That should cost him half an hour at least.

Hope he has the sense to give up, stay in New Long Badu, she thought—then made a rueful face. Funny how she knew him not at all, yet knew him very well. No way would her trick stop him.

By now Cade must have discovered that not a man in the village wore a size twelve, or anything like it. He'd improvise shoes from something—probably buy cloth from the women to wrap his bare feet, like a soldier at Valley Forge. "Sorry, Handsome," she said aloud, smiling as she used a leafy branch to brush out all traces of her endeavors. Shouldering her pack, she glanced up at his boot. He'd never notice it.

She'd meant to leave him a note at mile ten, but her conscience was pricking her, which was ridiculous, considering Cade played for keeps. Still, roughly two miles down the trail, Raine stopped to draw a large bull's-eye with her heel in the moist humus. She pulled out her pocket pad and printed:

OOPS! You've come TOO FAR! Go back roughly two miles and look up—and you'll find your sole desire.

She weighted her note with a branch and left it in the circle. She'd just given herself a four-mile advantage, which she'd better exploit, because if Kincade ever caught her, he'd stick a cobra down her shirt.

And that was before she'd hung his second boot.

They'd lit the lanterns in Old Long Badu by the time Raine reached the river town. She stood for a moment, looking back to where the trail bored a black hole in the jungle. *Hope you had the sense to stop and make camp before the dark closed down.* She hoped he'd brought a hammock, a mosquito net, waterproof matches, a good water filter.

What am I, his mother? Whether Kincade was a killer or not—and after *his* accusations last night, Raine was finding that harder and harder to believe—still, the man meant to ruin her family.

Beating him to the dino was her only way to prevent that. But all the same… *What if he fell, climbing for a boot, and now he's lying back there in the dark with a broken leg?*

What if, God forbid, he'd stepped on a krait?

If he had, it was way too late to worry. "Didn't see one all day," she muttered, turning and trudging toward the town.

One was all it'd take.

"Punan, they come and they go," said Lia's cousin Ah San, as he re-filled Raine's teacup. "Once, twice, each year, two or three of their men come. They bring boar fat, honey, camphor wood, birds of the forest. I take these things and give them salt, rice, pretties for their women."

Raine nodded and sipped. They'd dealt with Lia's death over the first cup. She'd dreaded breaking the news, but without need. He'd known already; days ago the riverboat had brought a letter from Lia's mother. And if the loss of his clever stepcousin grieved him, he was hiding it well. He was still eager to do business. He'd been disappointed to learn from Raine that his tooth and watch had been stolen. But perhaps there were other ways to turn a profit? He had information. If Raine had come all the way from New York City, then clearly she wanted it.

So far he was giving it freely, but at some point, they both understood: there'd be a fee.

"So a Punan you call White Dog brought the tooth and the watch. Brought them both together?" Raine prodded gently.

"Yes." Ah San glanced around the crowded shelves of his small store, shadowy in the lamplight. "I give him forty pounds of rice for the tooth. And twenty pounds salt for the watch."

Robber. Raine nodded gently and sipped. On the other hand, in the jungle, salt would keep a family alive. Time they had in plenty, and with the sun and moon to measure it, who needed a gold-plated watch? "Did White Dog say that he found the tooth and the watch in the same place?"

Ah San lifted his narrow shoulders. "The Punan don't speak. They put a thing on my counter and smile. If I want it, I set my hand on it and nod. Then they point at my shelves, what they like. And so we come to a bargain."

"I see." Raine sipped and thought for a while. Impatience would be rude. It also showed weakness; Too Eager would pay a higher price. "Would you know how a person could find this Punan?" she asked at last.

Ah San sucked his teeth. "This…would not be easy. The Punan follow the wild pigs, the fruit when it ripens. Camp here one day, there the next. Better you wait for them to come to Long Badu, then ask your questions."

Raine sipped, nodded, then said, "And how long would I need to wait?"

The shopkeeper consulted the gecko that crouched upside down on the ceiling. "Five months? Six? No more than ten, I think."

Yeah, right. She'd found a bed at the only guesthouse in town—and a sleepy five-foot python in its communal shower. Six months of that would get old. Besides which, Cade could reach town by morning—not a healthy prospect. "If a person didn't wish to wait. If she wished to go to the forest, find the Punan…would that be possible?"

"This might be possible. But it is not wise. The snakes, the heat. The rivers have danger higher up, how you say it, waterfalling?"

"You are very kind to advise me. But I would like to try. What would be the price to hire a guide? With a boat."

"Ah." Ah San figuratively rolled up his sleeves and settled to what he did best—cutting a deal.

It was well past midnight by the time they'd hammered out an agreement. Cost for two boats, two guides. Provisions and fuel for same. Ah San's finder's fee if she found the Punan; his bonus if she found the rest of the dino. His price for silence; he'd tell no one who came after her any thing at all.

Like I really believe that! was Raine's opinion on this promise; let Cade open his wallet and the trader would talk soon enough.

Still once he'd demanded hush money, she had to give him another hundred just to help him save face. If she failed to find White Dog herself, then six months from now Ah San would be her only connection. Her last hope.

Meanwhile, she'd hiked twenty miles that day in soggy equatorial heat, with a heavy pack; Raine yearned to put her head down on the counter and sleep. And they'd be starting early in the morning, she'd specified; she'd meet her guide here at eight. "Well," she murmured, "if that's all for tonight?"

But now that he'd softened her up, and gotten a better notion of what she could and would pay, Ah San brought out the gem he'd been withholding. "One other thing more." He dragged a battered aluminum cigar case off a shelf then shook out a rectangular shape. "The Punan also trade me this, when he bring me the tooth and watch. It seem of little value, so I don't send it to Lia. Who would want to buy old writing, I'm thinking? But now I'm thinking…"

He was thinking right. It took Raine another hour, and another thousand dollars, to buy the tattered little notebook, filled with faded script.

The note inside its cover read: "if you find this, please return to Private Amos Szabo, 511th PIR, 11th Airborne."

Ngali actually fell down in the dirt, laughing, when they backtracked to the first boot. "That *Bungan,* that Raine, she mad at you! Very mad, I'm thinking. A man drink much and much rice wine, his spear go soft as an old black banana. He not please his woman in the night, she make him pay and pay!"

"Thanks for the advice," Cade snarled, hauling himself up the vines that clung to the tree. He'd have been delighted to dispense with his audience, but when he'd asked for the path to Old Long Badu, Ngali had insisted he was going that way and he'd tagged along.

Strictly for entertainment, Cade suspected, but Kalimantan was a free country; what could he do? Sooner or later the young man would turn back. Children followed the circus only so far from town.

By the time they reached Old Long Badu the next morning, Cade was revising his notion of what "so far" might mean. Ngali still padded merrily at his side.

Though there was no denying the kid could be an asset in the jungle. He'd built a one-man thatch-roofed sleeping platform last night in the time it took Cade to hang his hammock and suspend his pack from a branch. While Cade built a fire, Ngali had strung his bow and disappeared—returning in twenty minutes with a small, skinned mammal that Cade thought it wise not to examine too closely. Whatever it was, once roasted on sticks, it tasted like the inevitable chicken—with undertones of carp. They'd shared a bag of dried peaches for dessert, then gone to bed.

But in Cade's case, hardly to sleep. The sounds in the forest were astounding. He'd heard quieter Saturday nights in Times Square. He reckoned it must have been well past

3:00 a.m. before sheer exhaustion drowned out the hoots, bellows, clicks, ominous rustlings. Sounds of munching—and of munchees. He'd snatched a few hours of desperately needed sleep, only to be roused by Ngali's laughter at dawn.

"See here, Kincade!" He held up one of Cade's hard-won boots, which he should have hung from a branch last night. Ngali turned it upside down—and out dropped a green-and-white snake that looked much like a garter snake.

"Harmless, I suppose?" Cade sat to unzip his mosquito net.

"Oh, no, Kincade. That one kill you dead before breakfast."

For which he'd just lost his stomach. "Does anything ever make you sad, Ngali?"

"Oh, many things. This girl in Old Long Badu, this most beautiful girl, if she don't put out her lamp and have me in, this time, I very, very sad." He sighed, then brightened. "Till I find another girl."

They reached Old Long Badu, home of beautiful girls, about ten. In time to see another beauty departing. "See there!" cried Ngali, pointing in the island way with his thumb. "There go your woman up the river. You make her so mad, she leave you?"

Cade sighed through clenched teeth and stared after two motorized dugout canoes, dwindling into the distance. Even beneath the shade of her tiger parasol, Raine's hair gleamed like sunlight on the water.

For a few heartbeats he wasn't mad; he was very, very sad. And somehow another beautiful girl didn't seem the answer.

His mood shifted quickly enough however, once Lia's cousin Ah San explained that there were only two dugouts with outboards in town this week. And that for some mystifying reason, Raine had rented them both.

But Cade knew why, if the trader didn't. To stop him from following.

A riverboat gives a man time to think. And the more Szabo thought about the blond bone hunter, the antsier he got. Ashaway was a mover and a tryer all right. And for all he knew, she'd sweet-talked those prissy missionaries into flying her to Long Badu. Once the bitch got the jump on him, who knew if he'd ever catch up?

But no way was he letting her snag his granddaddy's treasure out from under his nose. Time to start hustling.

He learned there was an airport, if you could call it that, in Sintang, so he got off the boat there. Lucked into a flight to Putussibau, the last town on the Kapuas you could fly to, then hired a longboat—a canoe carved from a single whopping tree trunk—to take him on upstream.

His boatman was a surly dude, who got even surlier when Szabo made him push his outboard. Kept saying it was old and tired and it liked to go slow, what was the hurry?

"*This* is your hurry," Szabo had said, showing him his gun. "We understand each other?" He'd twirled the pistol around his forefinger and grinned, then sat, facing the scowling Dayak with the weapon in his lap.

After that there'd been no more arguments. No more nosy questions about how many children he had, or what he was doing here? He'd had a nice, peaceful, relaxing ride with the green river gurgling past, while he lounged against his pack in the bottom of the boat.

That night he figured, the way that Dayak kept giving him the Evil Eye, it might be smarter to stick with the boat and make its owner sleep on the beach. Wouldn't be fun to wake up and find himself stranded, halfway between Putussibau and Long Badu.

Or to wake up—and find out the natives hadn't quite sworn off headhunting, the way everybody claimed they had. Sharp as they kept those sawed-off machetes that every man wore, Szabo had his doubts.

"Kincade, come quick!" Ngali cried the following day, on finding him wandering in the marketplace. "There is a boat come in from Putussibau. A good boat to rent!"

Who said prayers were never answered? Long Badu was

a fine town, filled with fine friendly folk. But Cade had just about reached his limit on parties. At last night's, the headman had urged him to marry his eldest daughter, settle down here and grow rice.

Time to move on—past time. Raine had a twenty-four hour lead on him, at this point. But if this boat was fast and they pushed it....

They found the longboat down at the town dock, where its owner was topping up its two fifty-gallon fuel drums with gasoline. The boatman was a middle-aged man with flower tattoos, the first Dayak Cade had seen who didn't smile. After a sidelong glance, he wouldn't even look at them, simply stared off into the distance, while Ngali talked.

"Is he willing to take us upriver?" Cade broke in after a few minutes.

Now Ngali's smile was fading to puzzlement. He waffled one hand. "He say, no, he don't want to rent his boat. His stomach hurt. And the last man he rent to, he not pay him yet. He got to wait here for his money. Once he paid, he go home."

"Tell him I'll pay him very well to take us upriver. Very, very well. But we need to leave now. You think he might be sick?" You couldn't drag a man off into the wilderness, if he was ill.

The man spoke again, darting a glance at Cade, then away.

"He say..." Ngali scratched his head. "He say the last white man he work for was crazy. Crazy and bad. He think you maybe another crazy man."

"Tell him I'm not. Tell him I'm a pussycat."

"A *cat?*" Ngali burst into startled laughter, then voluble speech, finally switching back to English. "I tell him you crazy, but the good kind of crazy. And a friend to *Bungan,* who is more blond and beautiful than the old men say. I say we pay him very good money to find her and he is a most lucky man. He should pay *us* to see *Bungan,* like the moon walking."

That speech won them the boatman's dubious smile and

Cade breathed a sigh of relief. Ngali's freewheeling charm had come through again.

They all swung around at the sound of heavy footsteps. A lanky white man came loping down the dock. Cade recognized trouble, before he remembered the smirk, and where he'd seen it last. On the plane from New York!

"Hey, small world!" drawled the newcomer, reaching into the canvas tote bag that hung from his left shoulder.

Cade barely contained his flinch. With Ngali bumping his arm and this one blocking his way, the end of the narrow dock was too crowded for action. Eyes locked on that concealed hand, he didn't answer.

The freckled fingers came forth—and Cade breathed again. The guy hadn't pulled a weapon, just a black hose with metal fittings at each end.

"Here you go." He tossed it down to the boatman, with gestures to illustrate his words. "Better hook it up."

No wonder the guy had a stomach ache! This bastard had taken the outboard's fuel line, so he couldn't leave. Bad and crazy, all right.

"So what brings *you* to these parts?" The man's smirk didn't reach his pale eyes. His accent was cracker—backwoods Appalachian.

"I'm renting this boat," Cade said evenly. "I understand you're done with it."

"Yeah? Well, somebody told you wrong," drawled the man, scratching his stomach. He adjusted the strap on his canvas tote—

And Cade ducked without thinking as it slashed backhanded at his head.

Ngali's instincts weren't as keen. The bag missed Cade and swung on—to slam the smaller man in the temple, with the gravelly rattle of chain hitting bone. Eyes rolling skyward, the Dayak crumpled into the river.

He'd been offered a clear choice—it was no choice at all.

Cursing himself for a fool, Cade dove after the kid. The outboard roared to life while he was still searching the mud.

By the time he'd hoisted Ngali to the dock and drained half the Kapuas back out of him, the dugout was rounding the upstream bend.

With a wide merry wave, the cracker vanished beyond the tangled green. Whoever the hell he is, that's our killer, Cade told himself, as he hauled Ngali to a sit and thumped his back.

The smirking bastard was going after Raine.

Chapter 21

Three days upstream from Long Badu, they came to their first village. Raine's guides had never ventured this far before, and they didn't speak the local dialect. Apparently these were Kenyah Dayaks, whereas Raine's men were of the Iban tribe.

The language barrier didn't get in the way of a rollicking good party that night. The only sour note was struck when Raine passed round her photos of dinosaur bones. Nobody had ever seen such alarming creatures; the children shrieked and fled—while their mothers studied her with grave suspicion. *Bungan* was supposed to bring better rice and babies, not go chasing after monsters!

But if they had their doubts, she overcame them when she cured an old woman of "blindness." Antibiotic ointment reduced the terrible swelling in her eyelids, and by the time the party broke up, the patient was starting to see again. In the morning when Raine went to put on her boots, she found them filled with eggs.

On leaving the Kenyah village, they also left the second

boat behind, though they took along its fuel and propeller. The river had narrowed till the tops of the trees on either bank wove together, high overhead. They motored through a winding green tunnel—a steadily climbing tunnel, broken by stretches of rapids. So far the outboard was equal to the rush of white water, but if the land kept rising, soon they'd be forced to drag the boat up the cascades. One boat with three to work it, made more sense than two.

Late in the afternoon of the fourth day, they came to a pool, where two branches of the river converged. "Which way?" Raine asked Baitman.

Her senior guide was a short, broad Dayak with a gorgeous smile and a sunny sense of humor. He'd learned his Aussie-flavored English working on the oil platforms off the south coast of Borneo, and he'd also earned his nickname there. For the first few days Raine had thought this had to be "Batman," mispronounced. At last she'd learned that he'd been in charge of catching bait, when the bored oilies fished off the rig.

"To find Punan?" he mocked with a grin. "Raine, I keep saying you this. We not find Punan. The Punan find us."

If and only if they want to. That was the catch in this expedition, a caveat that Ah San had kept to himself when he pocketed her money. The Punan were notoriously shy, as well they might be. A couple of generations back, the Dayaks had hunted their small peaceful neighbors for their heads.

Nowadays a few brave men of the tribe might venture down to the towns for vital trade. But out in the jungle, with their families to protect, the Punan saw scant reason to mingle.

Raine was going to have to give them a reason. Happy as she was to have the support of two woods-wise companions like Baitman and his teenage brother Dibit, she was starting to wonder if she'd stand a better chance of meeting the Punan alone.

"Then which way to the mountains?" Ah San had known nothing of the butterfly-shaped lake north of a mountain range, when she reminded him of the map scratched inside the cover of his watch. But he'd claimed to have some vague notion that the Punan who brought him the watch and the tooth, a hunter he called White Dog, might have come from beyond the mountains.

Or maybe he'd simply been agreeable. Indonesians were famous for giving strangers directions, even when they didn't know the way.

"That way," said Baitman, pointing to the right branch.

"Why do you say that?" After all, he'd never been here before.

"The water move faster. So mountains nearer."

Not a bad answer, she had to admit. "Let's go that way, then."

"Yes, but tomorrow. This a very good place to stop. Good fishing here."

Jam karet was the *bahasa Indonesia* phrase that translated to "rubber time." A concept much like *mañana*. You couldn't hurry these guys. Time was compressed or stretched to fit the mood; it was never exact. Above all, it was to be enjoyed. Raine had found in her travels that most primitive people remembered this, even if Americans had forgotten. And the only way she knew to keep an expedition on track was to keep its members happy. "Fine," she agreed with an inward sigh. She just hoped that Kincade was still stuck in Long Badu, fuming and waiting for another boat to come along.

Once they'd beached the dugout on the right-hand bank, the brothers grabbed their harpoons and took to the river. They reminded her of cormorants, ducking underwater, only to pop up at an unbelievable distance, usually with a fish wriggling on a spear.

Each catch was announced with cries of self-congratulation—and demands that Raine look up from her reading to applaud. "Fish tonight," she murmured wryly and looked down again. It had been fish and sticky rice every night so far. Also for breakfast, lunch and snacks. She was starting to dream of hot dogs and hamburgers and—oh, God—what wouldn't she do for an ice-cream cone?

Meanwhile, she'd made slow progress with the soldier's

journal. Szabo's handwriting was tiny and terrible and it was badly faded. With all the splashing in the boat, she didn't dare read it on the river. Besides, she could hardly tear her eyes away from the passing jungle. More kinds and colors of orchids than she could count, in rafts and swathes and streamers trailing from above. Hornbills and parrots as bright as the flowers; butterflies bigger than birds. Bands of gibbon monkeys whooping through the trees, and yesterday, a heart-stopping glimpse of a clouded leopard draped along a sunny branch.

Given such distractions, she'd left her reading for evenings, before the dark closed down. So far it had been an unrewarding bore. Szabo had spent ten half-decipherable pages on his basic training. Then five on a last hurried leave home to North Carolina, where his new wife was proudly pregnant. He'd boarded a troopship bound for the Pacific in San Diego, after which there'd been a gap of almost two months when he hadn't written. Then he'd devoted another two pages to the good-time girls of Honolulu. Then the lack of such obliging ladies in New Guinea, when his regiment was shipped south to that island.

"I paid a thousand dollars for this?" Raine murmured and flipped a page. And sat up straighter on her rock.

Well, 'bout time! Some action at last! Captain says we've been tapped for a special mission. Pack jungle gear and three weeks' rations, and we fly out at 1800. If he knows where they're dropping us, he ain't saying.

"Borneo!" she whispered, as if she could warn him down the years.

A gap of one ruled line on the page showed another jump in time. Then the next sentence was wildly illegible, staggering from one smeared line down to the next, as if it had been written in the dark? She squinted at it, then blinked as something passed before her eyes. "Oh, drat!" The butterflies were back.

A cloud of blue-and-black swallowtails swirled around her head. Every so often they swarmed, apparently attracted by the salt in human sweat. Short of hysterically swatting, the only solution was a swim and a good soaping. Wearing an Easter bonnet of fluttering iridescent wings and a living blouse to match, she quickly put the journal away. She slipped on her reef walkers, grabbed her shampoo and waded into the river.

Like the modest Dayaks, Raine bathed with her clothes on, washing them along with her skin. Twenty minutes on shore would be enough to dry them—and start her sweating again. To give the butterflies time to escape, she sank into the cool water by inches, then submerged and swam downstream.

She stopped at an eddy below a run of white water, glad for a moment of solitude. When she'd scrubbed herself deliciously clean, she stretched out on a boulder, propped her chin on her palms and gazed lazily back toward camp. They had less than an hour till dark, she figured, and still much to do. Dibit was cleaning fish at the edge of the river. Baitman must have gone to cut poles and thatch for the men's sleeping platform. She needed to hang her hammock, then it was her turn to cook.

Lulled by the rumbling water, she didn't hear the boat till it was almost upon her. Twisting onto one elbow, she saw a dugout aimed at the gap between two boulders where the river surged deep and smooth. A Dayak sat in the bow, peering down at the rocks and directing.

As the stern drew even with her rock, Raine stared at the man who steered the outboard, intent on his route ahead. A crumpled hat protected his face—skin too pale to be native! She bolted upright. "Cade?"

No way could the driver hear her over the rapids, but he glanced aside—his jaw dropped. He turned ahead, shot the rapids to perfection and the boat glided on. Choosing the right-hand fork of the river, he passed close by Dibit.

Baitman came trotting down to the shore. He called something to the man in the bow, who yelled back and frantically waved his tattooed arms. The dugout shot the next run of white water and vanished up the right fork.

Slowly Raine waded toward camp and her friends who stood waiting. *There were two of you on the plane,* Cade had said, and she'd put that down to rice wine ravings. But that…that had been Mr. Smirky. In Singapore he'd told her he was headed for Pontianak and Lia's mother had been beaten soon after. *For information?* What had he said in the airport, that he was looking for his grandfather, a soldier in World War II? Raine glanced quickly at the treetops. Dark in less than an hour. He wouldn't go far.

"Who was that man?" Baitman demanded, and for once he wasn't smiling. "You know that man?"

"No, but I have seen him before. I think…I think he is a bad man." He'd sat in the seat beneath which she'd stowed her carry-on. Come to think of it—he'd snitched the seat from its ticket holder! No accident, that. God, and he'd come from New York—*Lia!* "We should move camp, Baitman. Head up the left fork." If there was one thing her father and Trey both had drilled into her head, it was that you don't go looking for trouble. Soon enough it would come looking for you. Especially in the wild, you minimized your risks. "We should move right now!"

Muscles ticked below the Dayak's broad cheekbones, and his expression turned stubbornly, hopelessly—there was no other word for it—"guy." In any language, it looked just the same. Testosterone kicking in. Prudence flying out the window. "No, Raine, it too dark to move."

She might have bought their expertise, but she hadn't bought *them.* Given more time she might have cajoled or persuaded, but within minutes night dropped like the lid of a box. Raine's one consolation as they moved close around their campfire, cooking and readying for bed, was that Mr. Smirky would also be pinned down by the dark. Only a fool went stumbling through the jungle when the snakes were on the prowl.

We'll leave at dawn, she promised herself, *and not by rubber time.* Still she propped her blowgun by her hammock, and strapped her knife to her ankle. "'Night, guys."

"Don't let the bedbugs chew you," countered Baitman, a phrase she had *not* taught him. He strolled down to the river, and a few minutes later she heard the slow, methodical rasp of metal against a boulder.

He was sharpening his parang.

Sleep proved impossible. Each time Raine drifted toward it, she'd picture the dark rectangle of Ravi's window. Something lurking beyond it, something hungry and heartlessly chortling. Big hands reaching out of the black— She bolted upright, heart pounding, ears straining.

The one thing she'd learned about the troll, that night, was that he kept on trying. *Who's to say he'll wait till morning to make his move?* If he was crazy enough to throw a woman out a sixth-floor window, then he could be crazy enough to brave the snakes.

The question then became: was he lucky?

Was she?

But trusting your life to luck was stupid beyond words. Hiding in her hammock and praying the bogeyman wouldn't come? *"Get up,"* she snarled at herself and reached for her boots. At least she could stand sentry.

As always they'd camped at the edge of the forest, well above the river's flood mark. Raine stood by her hammock for a minute, peering across the burned-out campfire at the guides' sleeping platform. Sometimes she could make out the pale soles of their comically splayed feet, poking out from one end, beneath the steeply pitched little roof. Not tonight.

The only light to tantalize her eyes came from fireflies drifting through the forest. Patches of phosphorescent fungus creeping over downed and rotting logs. The buff-colored sand along the riverbank formed a winding Milky Way. When her eyes had adjusted as best they could, she picked up her blow-gun and padded slowly toward the water, tapping the ground before her like a blind woman. *Beat it, snakes.*

A cluster of boulders formed a little island, upstream of where they'd beached the boat. She picked her way out to it from stone to stepping-stone. Hopeful that she'd left all slithery things back on dry ground, Raine settled there, assuming a huddled shape, just one more rock. *If he comes at all, he'll come by water, not through the woods.*

An hour oozed past. Her eyes ached from probing the shadows, her ears turned every splash and rumble of the river into sea monsters. Still nothing happened.

Nothing was going to happen. *This is just a bad case of the late-night heebie-jeebies,* she scoffed at herself. Sure, she could jam the pieces of her puzzle together to make Mr. Smirky a murderer—black imaginings were easy after midnight.

But just as easily, he could be innocent. Their meeting out here might be the purest coincidence.

She didn't believe it. Too many coincidences strung together became a pattern. A nasty pattern.

Not fair! the sleepier half of her mind argued. *You want him to be the troll.* Because if Smirky was the killer, then that cleared Kincade once and for—

Splashing, somewhere upriver!

Raine drew a slow breath, then collapsed her blowgun to a baton and stuck it in her belt. If she couldn't see to aim a dart, then she'd better rely on her knife.

More splashing, and now a panting that sounded almost like sobbing? Then a low cry as something rose up from midriver and stumbled toward the shore.

The Dayaks cried as easily as they laughed. "Baitman?" she called softly without moving.

"Raine!" The hunched-over shape lunged for her. Patted her shoulders, then groped for a hand. Dibit—tugging her toward the beach. "Quick! He coming. We go! We go!"

"Who? Where's Baitman?"

"He shoot him, the bad man! And *he see in the dark,* Raine. Now he coming!"

"Shhh, hush, calm down. Baitman, does he live?"

"I don' know. He shoot in the chest. He run for the trees, run and hide. But, Raine, *this one see in the dark.* He walk to us where we hide so very well and he *laugh*—then he shoot Baitman!"

Tell me he doesn't have night-vision goggles! Just tell me, please, that you guys aren't the mighty hunters you think you are. That you gave yourselves away—snapped a twig, or— But if what the kid was telling her was true… Night-vision goggles plus a gun trumped a throwing knife any day.

"And he shoot *me,*" Dibit added on a moan. "My arm…"

"Oh, Dibit, I'm sorry!" But he could still walk, and if Smirky was really pursuing, they made perfect targets—dark shapes on light sand. "Go up to the camp and get your things together." No way to launch the dugout without Baitman's strength, and besides, they couldn't leave him. "I'll get the harpoons." And her kayak, which she'd stowed in the boat. "Go now."

If Baitman was trunk-shot, then the first thing was to find him. Stop the bleeding. While Smirky waded down the river, they'd cut around him through the woods.

Snakes were starting to seem like the least of her problems.

Chapter 22

Raine was throwing the little casting net she always packed—catching nothing but minnows—when the mutter of a big outboard slammed her heart into overdrive. Her eyes jerked first upriver, then down.

A long dugout bumped up through the white water, then glided into the pool with—*oh, thank God!* That was Ngali, beaming and calling from the bow!

Back at the stern, Cade steered the boat toward shore, his scowl moving from the burned-out remains of her dugout, to Raine's face and back again. He ran his craft up onto the sand and vaulted out.

Raine threw her net down. "I need—" She walked straight into his open arms—they wrapped hard and safe around her. "Hi." She dropped her forehead on his shoulder, closed her eyes and sighed. Leaning bonelessly against him, she breathed in his welcome scent. Hot strength, seeping into her weary bones. Troubles instantly halved.

"Hi," Cade said huskily, as he rocked her. His chin rested on top of her head. "What happened? The cracker?"

"Mr. Smirky, yeah. He burned the boat last night—holed the fuel drums and lit 'em, while we were out of camp. And Cade—he shot my guys. One of 'em's lung-shot. They've got to get to a doctor."

"*Bastard!*" he said with feeling. His palms smoothed down her back, molding her against him. "But…" His lips brushed her temple. "What the hell were you planning to do, if we hadn't come along?"

"Feed 'em some supper, if I could catch some damn fish— they positively *refuse* to eat my freeze-dried meals. Then head out after Mr. Smirky in my kayak. Take his boat and bring it back here."

"That sounds like a plan," Cade said wryly, rocking her. "Want to show me your friends?"

Half an hour later they shoved Cade's dugout out into the current, pointed downstream. Dibit sat in the bow, pale and fiercely drawn. His left arm was bandaged, but he seemed well enough to play lookout. Baitman lay out of sight, propped and braced midship. And Ngali proudly manned the helm, as he waved a cheery farewell.

The Dayak insisted he could steer them down to smooth water before nightfall; if he could, then the boat could cruise on without stopping. With a favorable current more than doubling their speed, they should make Long Badu in two days. Putussibau with its clinic in less than three. If Baitman survived that far, they could get him emergency treatment there. After that, Raine had given them airfare for the coast. Once they got him to the hospital in Pontianak, Baitman should be all right.

"You should have gone with them," Cade growled.

"No." They'd argued this one out already. And there was little more she could do for her guide. She and Dibit had found him just before dawn, where he'd dragged himself deep into the bushes. She'd put an air valve patch of tape and liquid skin over his sucking wound. His lung had miraculously rein-flated. The Dayak was incredibly tough. If infection didn't set in…"No," she said wearily. "Got a dino to find."

"So what about a swim before dark, then I'll cook *you* supper? We can discuss this in the morning."

He'd try to dissuade her, he meant, but she'd leave that for later. "Sounds wonderful."

Even better was not having to worry about the Dayaks' tender sensibilities. "For once I'm going to get clean all the way," Raine declared. Turning her back on Cade, she stripped, dropped her T-shirt and pants and necklace on a boulder, grabbed her bar of soap and walked into the river.

"Give me a *break*!" Cade launched himself into a hard crawl across the current. He swam several furious laps while she lathered, rinsed, dipped and came up smiling. But no way could they stay apart. Cade paddled over to where she stood chest deep, too tired to swim, just glorying in the current caressing her body. "Can I…borrow your soap?"

It was the best pick-up line she'd heard yet in Borneo, but she could top it. "Sure—if you'll scrub my back."

His answer was a groan—he didn't *quite* lunge for her. She laughed and turned around, and they stood for a moment with his big hands resting on her shoulders. Closing her eyes, Raine drew a tremulous breath and tipped her head back. *So good.* No more wishing and wondering. *Let it begin.*

"The soap?" he demanded on a strangled note.

"Oh." Could he really be a man who believed in foreplay?

He was. He played—seducing her with a bar of soap, then his slippery, sliding hands, while she purred and swayed to his lingering touches. "More."

"Soon enough," he growled, nuzzling her ear. And now that he'd soaped her thoroughly, he caught her around the waist and lifted her back—using *her* as the bar of soap to lather his chest, his hard hot stomach, his—

Wow. "You swim with a *parang?*" she teased, as she

clamped her thighs around him. After that, nobody had any thought of foreplay. They lost the soap, they stampeded the fish; their cries at the end were a jungle sound, exultant and wild.

When at last they could move again, Cade sighed—then walked slowly toward a boulder that split the rushing current.

"Not yet," she murmured dazedly, her legs wrapped around his waist. She'd hooked one arm around his broad neck; her other hand gripped his hair. *Stay in me, oh, stay!*

"Not…yet," he agreed, propping his hips against the rock.

They sat that way for a long time, Cade seemingly in a trance, with his mouth pressed to her shoulder; she with laughter bubbling inside. Shuddering with aftershocks. *Why didn't we just do this the first night we met?* All the precious time they'd wasted!

But if her joy was wholehearted, Cade… "Where are you?" she wondered at last and kissed his ear.

His arms tightened automatically around her. "Right here."

He wasn't. When she leaned back to see his face, his amber eyes were focused somewhere far beyond this glorious present. Men, always making life so damnably complicated! She sighed, traced the crow's wing shape of his eyebrow and slipped gently free.

And he didn't protest.

We're still opponents, Raine realized with a pang. *As much as I trust you, as much as I want you, there's still something between us.*

But she was damned if she'd let his grudge get in the way of…this. She needed answers, then once she understood his problem, why, she'd blow it out of the water. But not yet. *Give him time. Talk about safe things first.*

While Cade built a campfire on the sand, then boiled the water for their meal, she showed him Private Szabo's journal—then had to backtrack and explain Trey's research. The tale of the twelve missing paratroopers. "And that's why Mr. Smirky's out here beating the bushes. He told me back in Singapore that his grandfather was missing in action in Borneo, during WWII. That he'd come to find out what happened to him."

"He's come for more than that," Cade growled, as he dropped a couple of meal bags into the roiling stew pot. "You don't murder and shoot people, just to check out your family roots. When he passed through Long Badu, he pistol-whipped Ah San—made him tell where he'd gotten the watch and the tooth. He's after the dinosaur."

"Lia," Raine agreed, nodding somberly. "If she had the smarts to pinpoint us as likely bone buyers, track us down on the Internet…"

"Then somehow she found this guy—stirred him up. Do you remember, on the bridge, she said she had another bidder for the watch?"

"She did, didn't she? Talk about calling your own fate down on your head!" Raine shivered, then opened the journal. "Anyway, this belonged to one of the twelve. Maybe even Smirky's granddad? I'd just gotten to the point where they were headed out on a night drop, he didn't know where." While the food simmered, she studied the next page. "He wrote this, it looks like, without any light. Or running full tilt." She cleared her throat, then read:

"Christ, what a friggin' disaster! We circled our landing zone twice, a big field way up on a plateau, range of mountains to the south. Middle of nowhere, not a light in sight. I stepped out of the plane last, and with the full moon, I could see 'em floating down to the target. Really pretty, they looked like moonflowers drifting down on a big black butterfly. I wondered why anybody'd clear a field in such a raggedy shape."

"Oh, *God!*" Raine pressed a hand to her throat. The journal continued:

> "Wasn't a field. It was a friggin' lake! Covered in the biggest lily pads in the world, was why you couldn't see reflections. Before I hit, I could hear the guys yelling, tangled and drowning. I tried to steer clear—didn't quite make the bank, but I landed close.
>
> "At least I had a minute before I splashed in, to get my knife out, and start unbuckling my pack. If I hadn't gotten free of that, I'd have been a goner. Sunk under sixty pounds of gear. Those poor bastards. You couldn't stand on the pads, and you couldn't swim through 'em—stems like rope—and I think, God help 'em, there was something out there. Crocs? The screams… Every time I try to sleep, I hear those screams. Yelling for help, then yelling for God, then yelling for their—"

"For their mamas," Raine finished in a husky whisper. She shut the book and set it aside, and wiped a wrist across her lashes. "Oh…"

"Hey…" Cade came and sat in the sand behind her and pulled her back between his knees. "Come here." He folded her in his arms and rested his cheek on the top of her head. "Long time ago, sweetheart."

"Yeah, but…"

"I know." He kissed her temple, then rose to serve her on a tin plate. "But try not to cry in your macaroni and cheese."

They ate in companionable silence, shoulders touching. As her stomach filled with the first meal in a day, good American comfort food, Raine started yawning. "So-orry. Didn't get a wink of sleep, last night."

"Mmm," Cade glanced up at the trees. "Not long till dark. I wonder if I should keep watch tonight? If the Cracker came back…"

"Yes. But he definitely moved on. Once I'd patched up

Baitman, I slipped down to the river to check. Saw his boat head out."

"Guess he's more intent on stopping us, than killing us," Cade allowed.

"Whichever's more convenient," she guessed darkly. "Doubt if it matters much to him, either way."

"Why did your guys sneak up on his camp like that? Looking for...souvenirs?"

Raine shuddered. "Could be. I'm afraid I told Baitman he was a bad man. I suppose I thought he ought to be warned. But also, Dibit told me this morning...Smirky's Dayak yelled for help, when their boat passed us. And I saw why, when I crept down to their camp and watched them leave." She rubbed the goose bumps on her arms. "He'd chained his guide to a tree."

Cade swore softly, viciously, at length. "Well. There's reason enough for following, right there."

After they put out the fire, they hung their hammocks, sneaking glances at each other as they did so. Making love in a bivouac hammock covered in mosquito netting was, if not impossible, at least a contortion for the record books.

"One more swim?" Cade suggested and his voice had roughened as it dropped half an octave.

"Mm-mmm..." she hummed doubtfully—then shot him a look of glinting mischief. "Last one in is a bowlegged kangaroo!"

With a shout, he raced after her—smacked her bottom as he passed.

Cade stood stripped—and very ready—knee deep in the river, by the time she tossed off the last of her clothes and waded to join him.

"Missed you!" he said on a groan, as she rose on tiptoe to meet his kiss. Hooking his arms around her waist, he lifted her and twirled her around and around—they fell with yelps of laughter, tumbling in the rapids.

Otter time. Thoughtless, fearless joy.

* * *

They ended their romp a quarter mile downstream, on a boulder worn smooth by a thousand wet seasons. Stretched out on top of Cade, still hugging him within, Raine pressed her ear to his chest, listening…in vain. The rapids must be drowning him out. "Can't hear a thing," she teased. "Does that mean you're heartless?"

Running his fingers through her damp hair, he murmured blindly, lazily, "Don' know. I've wondered that, from time to time."

She winced—and he slipped free. "Oops, darn!" She wriggled higher upon him, so they lay nose to nose, her breasts flattened to his chest. "Well, nothing good lasts forever."

"Hmm." She could barely see his smile in the dusk. He traced the curves of her mouth, smoothed the long line of her throat till his fingers encountered— "What's this?"

"My necklace. Forgot to take it off."

He followed its stones down to the central pendant. "Isn't the same one you wore the first time I saw you, at the museum."

"It's got some of the same opals, restrung. And then the piece you're holding is extra special—a fossil feather. The Ashaway family totem, I guess you could call it. Have you ever heard of *Archaeopteryx ashawayensis?*"

His body was turning beneath her from hot resilient muscle—to jagged stone. Waves of cold seemed to radiate out from his skin, raising goose bumps on hers. "I've…heard of it." His fingers tightened on the fossil as they drew away from her—the cord bit into her neck.

"Ouch." Cade? What had she said? She went on, hardly knowing what she was saying, simply using her voice to soothe, as she'd have soothed an upset horse. "My uncle, Joe Ashaway, found it—years ago. It was an incredible find. First of its kind in America. It sort of started the family fortune."

"I *know* that!" He rolled to one side—dumping her off.

The boulder rasped her skin, not as smooth as she'd thought. "Cade, what's wrong?"

He sat up abruptly. "Nothing. What could be wrong? I've gotten my rocks off and now I'll sleep like a baby. Who's complaining?"

"I am." To go from such playful tenderness—to this? She slid down the stone and into the river, chilly now.

"Well, that's an Ashaway for you," he drawled, coolly contemptuous. "Never satisfied. Gimme, gimme, gimme, all the way home."

Her throat was hurting, a sure sign she wanted to cry. No way would she. "Would you please just tell me—why are you so *mad?*"

"Who's mad? How often does a man get to settle a score— by scoring?"

She hugged her forearms across her aching breasts. "That's what this was to you?"

"What else?" he asked briskly, vaulting down into the water.

To answer that—what it had felt like to her—would only invite further humiliation. "Never mind." She shook her head in disgust, turned away—then swung back for the last word. "Well, Kincade, for my part? It was nothing but a lapse in good taste." Off she stalked—not easy to do, wading.

"Hey, no need to apologize," he jeered. "You tasted just fine!"

OH! She stooped, found a river pebble, hurled it at his dim shape in the dusk.

It bounced off his ribs. "Ouch!" he called after her, laughing.

Not half as *ouch* as the pain in her heart.

Chapter 23

Raine didn't cry waking, but maybe she cried in her dreams. Her lashes were stuck together when she woke. She rubbed her eyes, turned over and went back to sleep. She'd get up when she damned well pleased.

She roused again as the mists burned off and the day heated. Lay, listening to the birds calling. The river rushing. A gibbon hooting in the distance. But no sound of Kincade, and no smell of campfire or coffee. With any luck, one of those thirty-foot pythons had found him in the night. Swallowed the bastard, hammock and all.

Finally she unzipped, sat up, and glared toward…where his hammock had hung, last night. Oh, no. You didn't…

But he had. What a fool she'd been! Fool in every way, to trust, to give. To care.

To leave her kayak unguarded! When she walked down to the beach, she found that he'd stolen the end frames that held it together. Without the stiffening of its Kevlar skeleton, it would paddle like a sock. Shaking with rage, she nearly shredded the note he'd left on top of her plundered craft, instead of unfolding it.

"Tit for tat, babe—or is it the other way round?" she finally brought herself to read.

"You jerk!" She crumpled the paper, threw it across the sand, kicked the kayak. Sighed—then bent to retrieve the wad and smooth it out. His note continued:

> I'll give you the same advice you gave me. STAY
> HERE. Ngali said he'd bring the boat back here in two
> weeks, and you can depend on that. Then he'll camp at
> this spot till I return. Meanwhile, I've left you a week
> of my rations, and checked your supply. You won't
> starve. Just stay put—and wish me luck, in finding the
> find of a lifetime.

"Yeah, hope you choke on it!" she muttered.

No. On second thought... Even to choke on, Kincade couldn't have it.

He could steal her pride. Borrow her heart. Amuse himself with her body—but an opal *T. rex? No way.* That was *her* dino.

She'd find a way to beat him yet.

On the afternoon of the second day since she and Kincade had parted company, Raine came to another message stick. Her third since that morning.

The waist-high branch had been stabbed into the earth beside the trail. At its top, the bark had been stripped back from the wood, to hang in delicate scrolls and spikes. A series of chips had been cut away along its length, making an intricate pattern of light Vs on a dark ground.

Trey had included a page on Punan message sticks in his briefing—but not how to read them. To those in the know, this stick could mean anything from, *Look out! There's a stranger in the forest!* to *We're hungry and have gone off hunting pig.* To *No trespassing! Go back!*

To Raine's uneducated eye, each stick had seemed more "talkative" than the last. This one fairly bristled with intention—but to what end?

Just beyond the stick, a slab of pink sandstone thrust up through the jungle ferns. She inspected it for creepy-crawlies, then sat with a weary groan. Eased out of her pack and set it beside her, murmuring, "Or maybe you guys are just trying to tell me, 'Party at Pete's tonight. BYOB. And oh, by the way, who does your hair?'" she comforted herself. Whatever. Welcome or not, she wasn't about to turn back now.

That first dreadful day she'd tried following Kincade and Smirky—only to find that the river quickly turned too deep and swift for wading, with piles of driftwood blocking its banks. So she'd forded across and cut away inland. After some fearsome bushwhacking, she'd come to a trail that seemed to vaguely follow the water.

It was a path beaten by whimsical and wandering feet, whose owners were more interested in the nearest stand of fruit trees, or a tinkling brook with a spot to kneel and drink, or a good source for palm fronds, than they were in tramping a straight line from A to B. Still, by her compass it was gradually trending northeast. And it certainly was rising. Toward the mountains?

"Sure would be nice to ask some directions," she told the surrounding forest. Drawing in a full breath, she let out a series of loud hoots—her best approximation of a gibbon's call—except hers ended in a fit of helpless giggles.

Trey had warned that it was bad manners to speak loudly in the rainforest—human voices scared the game. Long-distance communication among hunters would be by bird or animal calls.

She'd been hearing more and more gibbons, these past two days. Raine sucked air and hooted again, then muttered, "Yeah, you're too busy holding your sides and rolling around in hysterics, to answer me back."

While she waited for a reply, derisive or friendly, she made her usual response to a message stick. She pulled out a film can full of beads from her pack. Strung ten red-and-yellow glass beads on a loop of fishing line to make a bright, simple necklace. Hung this peace offering on top of the message stick.

Perching again on the rock, she pulled out a bag of trail gorp, and ate a handful. She hadn't had much appetite since her fight with Cade at the river. *For such sweetness to go so sour...* She kept trying to boost her regrets into rage—anger energized, while the blues just dragged her down.

She sighed and made herself eat another handful. This nut mix was part of the week of extra rations that Cade had left her, no doubt to soothe his guilty conscience. "And how're *your* supplies holding out?" she wondered morosely. He was bigger than she. Would burn more calories, especially kayaking his way up a staircase of white water. If he'd miscalculated what he needed...

So what? "Hope you starve!" she swore aloud.

No, she didn't. If he starved to death out here, then she'd never get to see him on his knees, groveling for forgiveness. With a wry smile she swung around to put the gorp away—and turned to stone.

A snake longer than she was tall wound its way up her pack. Its dark head jerked erect at her movement, and now it hung poised, a foot in the air. And about that far from her forearm.

Oh, God. Her throat dried to ashes in an instant—but if she swallowed?

His tongue flickered, seeking her body scent. Whatever he was, he had the triangular head and extra wide jaws of a viper. Plenty of room for poison sacs there at the hinges. And he wasn't shy. Without moving his head, with perfect control and horrid grace, he dragged a coil of his thick body up—that would give him a longer strike range.

Shit, shit, oh, please... She could roll away off the rock—but not fast enough. He'd nail her in the butt. What a way to go.

An arm bite would be better. Possibly survivable. *Tourniquet in the first-aid kit,* she reminded herself, *then all the vitamin C you can swallow.*

Meanwhile, God help her, she had to blink.

Die if you do, she told herself. *Kincade, you jerk, I wish you'd at least told me why you hate me so.*

I wish we'd made love about a thousand times, before you saw my necklace.

Sure as sneezes and death, the blink was coming. What was God *thinking* of, when He invented snakes? Tears burned as she fought the reflex.

From the far side of the boulder, a feathery shape wafted—to float down by the snake's tail. His head swerved fluidly toward the motion.

A second tiny missile sailed straight toward the serpent. Mouth agape, he struck to meet it—as Raine whirled away. She hit the ground running—stumbled, rolled—let out a shriek as she realized she was probably rolling over dozens of snakes! Ending in a heap in the ferns, some ten yards away, she burst into tears and hysterical laughter. *"Wow! OH!"*

The dart took the viper straight in the tonsils. Gagging as he reared, he cracked himself like a bullwhip—convulsed, coils rippling. Collapsed…twitched…rolled dazedly to show his white belly. And lay still.

Raine wiped her wet cheeks. Tried to rise, then fell back again. No matter how many snakes she might be sitting on, her knees wouldn't work. She drew up her legs and hugged them. "Th-th-thanks!"

Silence. Not a leaf trembled in the surrounding bushes.

"That…was…s-some really sweet…shooting," she added in a softer voice. "I would really, really…*really* like to shake your hand. You're the Lone Ranger. The Top Gun. My hero." She made it halfway to her shaking feet—and fell on her butt.

Far off through the trees, came the sound of hooting laughter.

* * *

On the third day, Cade came to Smirky's abandoned dugout.

He'd been expecting this. The river was flowing faster and faster down the rising hills. It dropped in great ragged steps— a stretch of smooth jade water rushing to meet his battered kayak, next a merciless down-escalator of foaming white ripped by stony fangs. Then there'd be another stretch of smooth to sucker him ever onward and ever upward, panting and digging in his paddle to gain every muscle-cracking inch.

Twice, yesterday, he'd simply picked up the damn kayak and carried it, staggering from rock to slimy rock up the cascades. He'd been amazed that Smirky and his guide could flog their much heavier boat up these rapids, even with the help of a big outboard. Unless the river soon leveled out and ran smooth, they'd grind themselves to exhaustion.

And then, when he doesn't need a boatman? That was the question that kept Cade slogging onward, when all he wanted to do was spin around and go flying back to Raine.

Late in the afternoon of the third day, he jinked out of the current and into the swirling eddy behind a fallen tree—and there on shore lay the dugout. Shit! He froze, ready to wheel and retreat. If Smirky was drawing down on him from the cover of the boat...

But if he was...he didn't shoot. *No smoke,* Cade realized as his heartbeat settled. And no fire. His eyes lit on a blackened circle near the tree line. Yesterday's campfire. He blew out a breath he hadn't realized he was holding, then squirmed out of the kayak and stepped into the shallows.

End of the road, he realized, peering upstream. *They've gone on, on foot.* Beyond this point, the river's banks rose higher and higher, till a quarter mile on, they formed a narrow gorge. With white water bursting endlessly from its shadowy mouth, it looked like the nozzle on a giant's fire hose.

Cade hauled his kayak up onto the sand. He prowled around the stern of the dugout—and stopped short.

The boatman crouched on the ground, with a sharp rock upraised, ready to throw. His face was a mask of hatred—and desperate hope. A galvanized chain stretched from his bloody ankle, to encircle the trunk of the nearest tree. Rugged padlocks secured the links at each end.

When Cade ran short of curses, he went back to his kayak. He dug out his water bottle, a packet of jerky, some dried fruit—and the little hand ax that he'd brought along for firewood. He fingered its fragile cutting edge, meant for kindling; it would never cut chain. And if he broke the tool on the lock's steel shank... With a grimace, he glanced toward a gap in the trees.

The clouds were mounding to the west like purple mountains. If it stormed tonight, with these slopes to funnel the rainfall? By morning this stony little beach could be twenty feet under the raging river.

He returned to the Dayak, set the food within his reach, then walked warily around him. The guy was half-crazed with fear, and if he did know any English, by now he must figure it for the language of lunatics and liars. Cade's acts would have to do the talking.

He stood for a moment, sizing up the trunk—massive—and the way the tree would probably fall. He drew a deep breath, rolled his shoulders and started chopping.

With every muscle aching from her snake-evasion acrobatics, Raine took to her hammock early that evening. In the dim light filtering through her mosquito net, she propped Szabo's journal on her bent knees. She'd barely had the heart to look at his writing since the night she read aloud to Cade. And what she'd learned hadn't been pretty.

Five of the twelve paratroopers had crawled out of the butterfly lake. Muddy and miserable, they'd huddled together, hands clapped over their ears to block out the terrible screams. At dawn, they gone looking for more survivors, but their friends had vanished beneath the lily pads.

Among the lost were both officers—along with the squad's field radio, the compasses and maps that the top men had carried. Also sunk was most everyone's gear and food. Only Szabo and Peckham had managed to drag their heavy packs to shore. They had perhaps a week of rations left, to feed five.

And Tilley had kicked off his jungle boots as he swam for his life. "He's a goner," Szabo noted privately, "but what can we do? Can't carry him piggyback through the jungle for five hundred miles."

That was their calculation; they were that far from any coast—and if they ever got there, they'd face a Japanese prisoner-of-war camp. Without a radio to signal for a nighttime extraction, they were marooned.

Yet not entirely leaderless. The "old man" of the unit was a thirty-year-old Texan who'd worked as an oilfield geologist before he volunteered for the army. Nicknamed "Professor," Peckham had seemed a quiet, bookish loner till now. But it was he who rallied the shattered little band, got them on their feet and moving north.

During their flight they'd been told that their destination was Borneo. Their mission was to contact the natives of the interior, befriend them with gifts of beads and tobacco. If the Americans could inspire the islanders to rise up against their Japanese occupiers, by all means they should lead a revolt.

If that proved impractical, then the squad should recruit guides to take them down one of Borneo's mighty rivers to the sea. They were to map and gather data about the enemy's locations, airfields and troop strength as they proceeded, in preparation for a future invasion.

Once they'd gained the coast, the plan was to find a deserted beach, signal for a nighttime pickup by PT boat. They should be back at base, eating steak and fries and ice cream, within three weeks.

"I'd give my right nut to have whoever dreamed up this SNAFU along with us now. See how he'd like the jam he got us into," Szabo had written wistfully in his tiny script. "Better yet, wish he'd dropped dead-center in that friggin' lake. Be nothing left of him, by now, but his belt buckle and a crocodile's fart."

Resuming the story at that point, Raine read, with the page almost touching her nose.

Professor figures if we can climb that saddleback mountain to the north, maybe we can spot a river. He says the middle of this island is highest, so any river takes you to a coast. Seems like as good a plan as any.

But the going was brutal. And on the second day, Tilley stepped on a snake. Szabo had written:

Just a little gray thing, no bigger than a hognose. But he swoll up something terrible and started screaming.

Professor had applied a tourniquet. He'd slashed the wound, then as he bent to suck it, several small brown men rushed out of the bushes, along with their hunting dogs.

Their leader grabbed Prof and wouldn't let him suck Tilley's foot. Prof argued some, but I reckon he got the picture. Anyway, Tilley was having fits by then. And damned if those ignorant heathen didn't sit right down in a circle around him and cry—sobbing like a bunch of sissies—till he was gone.
    So we buried poor Tilley.

Then the Punan—at least Raine would bet they were Punan—had led the soldiers off through the forest.

After we'd gone a ways, the headman's dog went on point. A big ugly white brute, but the leader took his word for gospel. Off those two went, and we went on.

When they caught up with us, the headman was carting
a deer on his back that was near as big as he was.

The evening concert of wails and whoops, insect creaking
and buzzing, was tuning up. Raine squinted to make out the
last lines on the page. The hunters had taken their strays to a
camp, or "if this is their idea of a village, then they're in trouble," Szabo had noted scornfully. "Nothing but some little-
bitty huts on stilts, and a fire."

But their women, now there's something! Bare tits and
big smiles, that's what a man calls a warm welcome.
And can they cook—roasted up that deer pretty as you
please and fed us till we near to burst.

Then the exhausted waifs were led to the huts. Each family made room on its tiny sleeping platform for one over-
grown, dirty, homesick stranger, and the starless night drew
in.

Raine closed the journal and lay, blinking drowsily at a
firefly that had landed on her mosquito mesh. "A white dog,"
she mused aloud.

Ah San had called the Punan who brought him the tooth
and the watch White Dog, hadn't he?

In all the time she'd been in Borneo, she'd yet to see a dog
of that color. "But it can't be the same guy. This happened,
what—sixty-some years ago?"

Coincidence. Had to be. Or maybe the Punan simply ran
with a different breed of dog from the Dayaks?

"You tell me," she said to the deepening dark. And slept.

Chapter 24

When she awakened next morning, Raine found a gift waiting—four eggs. Each one was enclosed in a tiny rattan basket fixed to the end of a stick. The egg-sticks had been planted like a clump of four white flowers, near the head of her hammock. "I'm not *Bungan*," she told the surrounding trees with a laugh. And nobody had ever explained what the goddess was supposed to do with her offerings, anyway.

Boiled, they made a nice change from beef jerky.

When she set out up the rising path, she found yesterday's melancholy had vanished. But if she was happy again, she still could use some company. As the path rose gently mile after mile and she passed no more message sticks, Raine began to fear that she'd committed a gaffe, by eating the Punans' eggs. A fertility goddess probably should have hatched them.

By late afternoon she'd climbed from rainforest up into moss forest. The air was noticeably cooler and dryer. Now that the jungle creepers and bushes had given way to low-growing temperate flora, she could make out the bones of the earth. In the lowlands it had been granite. But now it was sedimentary rock, folded and faulted and broken. Rock that had been formed by layers of silt and mud—the only kind of rock that held fossils. "I'm getting closer," she murmured aloud. "It'll be terrain like—"

Far down the slope, a dog yelped. Another joined in, then another, and another, in a high-pitched hunting song.

Hunting me? Raine shrugged off her pack, then pulled out her blowgun. Extended and locked its sections. She'd seen dogs at every village she'd come to, big rangy hunting hounds. But did they also run wild, like the spotted packs of India that could take down a tiger? She dipped the point of a dart in her sack of gum, pushed it up the tube. Running with hunters or running wild, they were fast approaching, yelling hysterically on a scent.

A glance to all sides showed no climbable tree; on this slope there were only pines, without a limb near the ground. She chose a wide one and put her back against it. Gummed up two more darts, to hold ready between the fingers of her left hand. Unsnapped the sheath on her ankle knife.

Feral dogs could be the worst. They were damnably swift and they knew how to team up on their quarry.

She could make out their separate voices now, the soprano bitches and the roar of the males, and below that a desperate panting, a lumbering beat. So it wasn't she they were chasing, but if she looked like easier game? She aimed the pipe down the trail, drew in a slow, deep breath.

Like a boulder rolling uphill, the boar burst into view. Hounds raced at his shaggy shoulders, nipped at his flying heels. With a wrenching squeal, the pig whirled around. Dipped his wicked tusks and heaved—a dog shrieked and went flying.

As he wheeled, the wooden spear that dragged from his shoulders tripped a second dog. The boar squealed and went for him as he fell, but a white dog flew in, caught his ear, was flung aside.

The pig turned to flee uphill—and saw Raine. Its massive head lowered.

Down the hill came a yell of warning, but it was too late to pass on this fight. To the boar, she was just one more hateful spear maker. Raine moved the pipe from her lips, blew her spent breath out, sucked in…

He lowered his gory tusks and charged.

Looking down the length of her pipe, she would have sworn she had hours, years, a lifetime to choose her shot. The cold shaking sweats would come later, but for now, with adrenaline zinging through her veins, no fear, only serene calculation… His oncoming head was armored with bone. *Not there.* The right shoulder then, since the white dog was lunging in on his left. Raine blew gently…steadily. *Pft!*

The dart flew true—bloomed where his neck met his shoulder—the pig was *here!* She smelled its reeking breath, the coppery blood; she pivoted around the tree as the beast slammed it head-on, shaking it to its roots.

Shoving her second dart up the pipe, Raine peered around the trunk.

The boar lay like a slab of mountain, dropped from the sky. The dogs snarled as they worried its bristly coat—then they skulked away as their masters arrived, yelling commands.

The Punan.

"Hi," said Raine shakily, averting her blowgun. "Pleased to meet you."

There were half a dozen hunters—small, stocky men, panting from their chase. Barefoot and clad only in breechclouts, not a one of them stood high as her chin.

The leader patted the white dog that hurried to lick his hand. He walked to the boar, gazed down at it—then let out a yell. He swung to give her an accusing glare, pointing down at the boar as he made a loud, disgusted pronouncement.

Raine turned her hands palm up. "I'm sorry. I know he's yours. Believe me, I'd have left him for you, but he was about to rip me to—"

More yells, more accusations. Whatever she'd done, it wasn't good.

"You know, I'm sorry. But we need to talk, and we need to talk *now*. Listen up, guys! I use *curare*. It's a paralytic. Mr. Pig could wake up any second now and when he does—"

The white dog's owner stamped his bare foot in frustration. He grabbed Raine's hand and led her to the boar. Made her touch the tail of her dart. He scowled at her and shook a scolding finger.

"Ohhh. You think I used poison? Now we can't eat it? Well, I've got good news—and bad." With a reassuring smile, she took *his* hand, and drew it down till... "Uh, just where would a pig's heart be?" She pressed his palm to the boar's larded rib cage.

He gave her a look that in any culture meant, "Lady, are you a few darts shy of a full quiver?"

"Heart, *you* know." She released him and patted her own, which had finally realized how close they'd come to being pig fodder; it was merrily galloping. She pat-patted the hunter's bare dusky chest, then pointed at the pig. "*Heart!* Find where it is, and you'll find it's still—"

His eyes widened as he got it, but still he didn't believe her. He shrugged indulgently, put his palm to the animal's chest—and let out a yell—just as the boar staggered drunkenly to its feet.

With whoops of startled laughter, the hunters fell back. The dogs roared in. Raine stepped out of the way and turned her head.

Some mountains could fool you. You'd figure for sure that was the top, there, just over that next rise. You'd hump yourself up that bump—and find you'd been suckered again. So Szabo didn't get his hopes up, this time, as he topped the rise.

He dug in his heels and stopped short. "Whoa-*baby!*" The ridge fell away in a sand-colored cliff, like Godzilla had taken a bite out of this side.

At its foot, half a mile below, the jungle was broken by a green, smooth field, mowed in the shape of an enormous, lopsided butterfly. He rubbed a sweaty wrist across his eyes. "Somehow…that don't seem precisely right," he told Gran. He'd been talking to her for a couple of days now, since he didn't have the Dayak to bounce his thoughts off of, anymore.

"Looks like one of those fancy courses, designed by some washed-up pansy pro who shoulda stuck to his wood irons. But if that's what it is…where's the golf carts?"

A white bird sailed below, some kind of stork, gliding in over the grass. It landed on tiptoe with wings spread wide, pretty as you please, on about the eighth hole.

Like a bass hitting a june bug, something black and *big* slashed up out of the earth. A frantic flurry—and the bird was gone. Nothing but a puff of feathers, drifting on the breeze.

"Holy *shit!*" What was that, some sort of giant killer mole?

A ring formed on the grass… Expanded like a slow greasy shadow. No, hang on there! He was looking at *ripples*. A lake, covered in some sort of duckweed or something.

"If that was a bass ate that bird, it was big as a couch." He sat abruptly.

"Must be getting jungle rot in the brains," he muttered, unslinging his pack. This was the lake he'd been looking for! The lake beyond the mountains, like the Chinaman back in Long Badu had said Ashaway asked him about.

Szabo pulled a folded paper out of the top section of his pack. He'd made a sketch of the map inside his granddaddy's watch, before he'd mailed it on back to Gran. "Yeah!" He hadn't noticed when he drew it, but it did look like a raggedy swallowtail. "*Now* we're getting some place."

All he had to do was get across to the lake's far side. From there you looked for a creek, draining out of the lake, headed northeast, and you followed that till you came to…he squinted northeast and laughed aloud. "Bingo!"

Out on the misty horizon stood a two-tit mountain, looking not much bigger than the picture that his granddaddy had scratched inside his watch cover. A couple of green D cups, joined by a low saddle between. "That's gotta be what I'm looking for," he told Gran.

To reach it, he had to get past this lake. "And forget swimming." So go left—or go right?

To the left, the ridge sloped away to low land. Maybe low enough to be swampy? Lot of smooth duckweed-green showing between the trees. Whatever was cruising the lake, might be paddling around in there, as well.

On the other hand, to the right, the cliffs continued for miles. Could be a hell of a scrabble.

He fingered his left arm reflectively, where Lia's bite still hadn't healed. Itched him like crazy, and it was weeping some. "Whichever way I go, what happens if Ashaway comes traipsing along? Takes the other route and beats me to it?"

He should have finished her off when he had the chance. But he'd gotten to worrying, while he was torching her boat. What if the bitch was upstream, burning his? So he'd waded on back to camp, telling himself that without a dugout, she was out of the contest. She'd have no way to follow him.

But there was something about her, kept him fretting. Who'd have believed a girl would make it this far? "Stubborn. Like the alligator snapping turtle that won't let go till it thunders."

Or maybe it was Gran, the blonde put him in mind of. Hanging on to her hope of treasure all these livelong years. Never taking "no" for an answer. Pushing first his daddy, then him, to go find it for her. A man didn't like to admit it, but sometimes women could be downright…scary.

"Aw, hogwash." He hauled himself to his aching feet, and struggled into his pack. If Ashaway *was* still sniffing up his trail, well, when she came to his boatman's body, that should scare her off, for once and for all.

"'Less he's still alive," Szabo muttered, turning right along the cliff.

In that case, if the Girl Scout hadn't packed a saw or a hatchet… "She's probably back there, gnawing that trunk with her teeth."

He glanced back the way he'd come and grinned. "And sugar, you better gnaw fast." 'Cause it sure looked like rain.

"No, thank you. I'm really not hungry," Raine assured the chief, when he offered her a strip of smoked pig.

She just might swear off bacon for life. The first night's feast after the boar hunt, she'd matched her hosts bite for succulent bite. After the Dayaks' boiled fish and rice, then her own freeze-dried trail food, pork roasted with herbs in banana leaves had been heaven.

Then the next day featured pork served in ant sauce. Not bad, actually, with the insects' formic acid giving it a mouth-puckering lemony flavor. But that dish had been breakfast, lunch and dinner while the women busied themselves, rendering the boar's fat in an ancient iron kettle. They'd stored the precious lard in bamboo tubes for trade or future use, while their men smoke-dried the rest of the carcass, cut into long strips.

Late on the second day—yesterday—the rain had drifted across the forest in a silvery curtain. They'd bundled the half-dried jerky into their tiny sleep platforms—and insisted that Raine crawl in with them, too.

Frankly she'd have preferred the quiet and privacy of her own hammock, with its overarching rain flap. But it could be bad manners to reject hospitality, especially the headman's invitation. So she'd spent the night with White Dog's family, wedged between his two squirmy toddlers—with the increasingly smelly strips of boar dangling from the rafters, a few feet above her nose. At least they didn't have to reach far for breakfast.

Now, after a nap, apparently it was snack time. "No, really, I couldn't," she repeated, when White Dog's wife Abat offered again. She patted her stomach, smiled and groaned with repletion. In bad weather, eating must be the main amusement.

Other than sex, judging from the giggles coming from the nearest shelters. So far, thank heavens, Raine's presence was putting a damper on that pastime at White Dog's house.

Still she supposed she owed them some sort of distraction. Careful not to bump the jerky, she sat up and reached for her pack. "Let's see... What have we got here?"

Not the photographs. She'd made several attempts to question everyone already. But all the photos proved was how far from the twenty-first century she'd traveled in space and time. Shown the pictures of Ashaway family members with various dinosaur skeletons, the Punan had all reacted the same way. They'd study the images for several minutes with polite frowns—then they'd reverse each photo, looking for the backside of the scene.

She'd watched Otto the cat do much the same, once, back in the city. He'd poked his nose *behind* a TV set, searching for the birds that were being shown on a *National Geographic* special.

Seeing in two dimensions didn't come naturally to humans, any more than it did to cats. It was a learned skill that the Punan had never needed in the forest. Some of the tribe were intrigued by these peepholes into a place where strangers had no bottoms or backsides. Others glanced at her uneasily, then hurried off to tend the fire or snatch up a child, as if they needed the reassurance of their normal, well-rounded world.

But nobody drew the least connection between Raine's photos of dinosaurs—and anything they'd ever seen in their own life.

"So no more photos." And for the same reason she couldn't draw sketches or maps of what she was seeking. Too abstract.

She'd tried showing White Dog her opals, hoping the shiny stones might remind him of the opalized fossil he'd traded to Ah San. If he really was that same Punan, with the same white hunting dog.

But if he was the man she was looking for, he'd failed to recognize a link between her small fiery stones and the big iridescent dinosaur tooth. He'd admired her necklace, especially the fossil feather. Then he'd proudly showed her his own totem: two enormous, curving boar's tusks, flanked by two tiny burned-out lightbulbs, all strung on a leather cord with some gorgeous blue feathers.

"So you've been to Long Badu or some town at least once," Raine had concluded. But if she couldn't find a way to ask him what he'd traded and where he'd found it? Had she come all this way for nothing?

"Meanwhile…" she rummaged deeper into her pack, while the headman's family watched with avid attention. "Could I play you the kazoo?"

But she'd done that already, when it had fallen her turn to entertain at the pig roast. She'd gone "on stage" directly after the tribe's best mimic. He'd given a blow-by-blow, wickedly comical rendition of Raine's encounter with the snake at the boulder, which had set the whole group to weeping with laughter.

They'd liked it so much, they'd insisted he do an encore— complete with popping eyes and knocking knees and silly feminine shrieks—then yet another, where a second hunter played the snake, and White Dog came forward to reenact how he'd aimed his darts.

Finally Raine had jumped up to steal the show out of sheer self-defense. "No…enough with the kazoo." Her fingers brushed the little notebook. "Then…how about a bedtime story?" She needed to read the rest of Szabo's journal. And the Punan seemed to like listening to her voice, even though it carried less meaning for them than a birdcall. A rainy day in the jungle, she supposed any novelty would do.

She pulled it out, then remembered. "You brought this to Ah San, also. Right?" She handed it to White Dog. "Yes? Seem familiar?"

He touched it gingerly, then looked up at her, smiling but perplexed.

"You're wondering how I would have gotten it, when you took it to Long Badu? Or you're asking yourself, do strangers all carry one of these things?" With a sigh, she took the book back from him, flipped to the right page, and commenced reading:

"We stayed in camp a couple of days, till the venison ran out. Professor is trying to learn their lingo, but the rest of us are getting along fine without it. We just open our mouths and point and grunt, when we're hungry. Then last night, Carleton grabbed one of the girls and pointed at his privates. She just giggled and scooted off into the bushes. Professor got mad and said we shouldn't mess with their women. Sez who knows how they feel about that?

But we'll never know if we don't ask 'em, is the way I see it."

"And you're the guy with a pregnant wife back home," Raine muttered, looking up. Seeing she had everyone's rapt attention, she continued.

"Then today we hit the road. Can't just sit on our cans till the food runs out, sez Professor, and I guess he's right. But danged if things aren't looking up. White Dog and his people are tagging along. Guess they're as curious about us, as Prof is about them. Me, I don't mind saving 'em from boredom, as long as they keep feeding us. Monkey for supper tonight—a great big red ape."

Raine winced. They'd eaten an *orangutan,* with those soulful eyes? She'd been yearning all this trip to see one of those rare gentle giants!

The mismatched band of soldiers and natives had wandered on for a couple of days, following a stream that flowed northeast toward the twin-peaked mountain. "'Professor's a real rock hound,' noted Szabo.

"He got all excited this morning. Found a fossil he sez is the same kind you can see in Texas. Just a crummy little snail, was all it was. He sez that means we're walking in the same time as the land west of San Antonio, whatever that means."

Raine laughed with soft excitement and glanced up at her audience. "It means he thought he'd found the same geologic layer! Sediments laid down in the same period that similar beds were created in Texas, when that snail was common." In parts of West Texas, wind and water had eroded away millions of years of sediments, stripping the land back down to the layers deposited in the Cretaceous Period. When *T. rex* stalked the earth. "Bless you, Professor!"

At last the soldiers had come to the base of the mountain they hoped to climb—and the Punan, the cheeriest and most compliant of companions to this point, had dug in their heels. "'After all this bushwhacking to get here, they don't want us to climb the dang mountain,' noted Szabo in disgust. 'White Dog keeps saying a word that Professor sez means "bad."'"

"Then he fell all over himself, trying to act out something to make us see. Professor kept trying to guess, like we were playing charades or some such. He thought maybe White Dog was saying monster. Or a great enormous big bird? Or maybe an angel, 'cause the chief kept pointing up, as if it could fly? Then he'd go to patting Professor's rocks, and saying 'bad, bad, bad!'

"'A bad angel in the rocks?' asks the professor.

"Bunch of heathen garbage, if you ask me. These guys are so superstitious, that if a caterpillar crosses their path, they'll start mumbling 'bad' and quit walking for the day. Well, I don't care what anybody sez. Come daylight, I'm headed up that mountain. And if you can see the ocean from the top, ain't nothin' or nobody gonna get in my way. I've had about all the monkey I can stomach."

Chapter 25

Cade wished he'd waited for morning, to start across the swamp.

Too late now. He figured he'd passed the halfway point an hour ago, though there was no way to be certain. Down here in the gloaming, the moss-strangled trees shut out all hope of a horizon. Curtains of orchids and lianas dripped down till they nearly touched the dark water, with its monstrous lily pads.

Should have gone around the other way, by the cliffs, he told himself. But this way had looked shorter, and why lug along a kayak if you weren't going to use it?

Big mistake. He paused between paddle strokes to listen. The silence out here was making him edgy. He'd grown used to bird and monkey sounds, and when you took them away...

SPLA-ASSSH!

He flinched at the sound—glanced to the right. The open lake was somewhere off in that direction. Must have been a fish jumping?

From the impact, he'd have said a moose, taking a high dive off a cliff.

Thoughtfully he touched the kayak's urethane skin. Good for keeping out water, but for anything with…teeth? Balancing the paddle across the deck before him, he found the *parang* that Ngali had insisted he buy back in Long Badu, and tucked it within easy reach, by his right thigh.

Should have brought a gun along. But he hadn't bothered to find a blackmarket weapon once he hit Borneo. He'd been picturing Raine as his opponent, and whatever he feared from her, it wasn't bullets.

He consulted the compass attached to the boat's centerline, then resumed paddling, taking care not to bump any of the floating branches or the bent knees of the cypress trees he glided past. Sooner he was out of here, the better. The thought of spending his night afloat…

And you? Where are you tonight? he wondered. Raine had been much on his mind—hell, constantly on his mind—since the river. If he'd known he'd miss the she-devil this much, he'd have never sabotaged her kayak. At least, if he'd brought her along, he'd have known she was safe.

PLOP!

Cade's mouth curved ruefully as he froze, blade uplifted. Safe, on the other hand, was a relative term. He rested the paddle across the foredeck and drifted, peering behind, around, above and below.

Saw nothing but lily pads and drowned trees. *Okay, let's just sit here a minute, making no noise. See what arises.* Maybe he was hearing beavers?

The minutes crept past and nothing arose and his thoughts circled round again to Raine. He'd realized before he'd gone a mile that disabling her kayak wouldn't stop her.

Still, there'd been the cracker's boatman to worry about, and having failed to help him back in Long Badu, somehow Cade felt responsible. He glanced down with a grimace at his battered hands. *Paid in full.* He'd chopped till he blistered, then bled, then the Dayak—Tong—had spelled him. They'd slipped the loop of chain off the tree's stump at dawn, just as it started to rain.

After Tong was free, Cade had helped him cut smaller logs for rollers, then they'd hauled his dugout well above flood level. Tong had explained in sign that he'd wait till the river rose high enough to float his boat over the rapids. Then he'd go home to Putussibau, where the people were sane, and they had bolt cutters. As Cade had walked off up the gorge, Tong had been busily spearfishing in the shallows. One very tough—

This time there was no sound—just a shock wave—as something *huge* swept under the kayak, lifting it on a bulge of water. Cade sucked in his breath—and hunched forward over the deck as the boat rolled, gunnel to gunnel. *Steady, baby, STEADY there!* Whatever had just passed by, he did NOT want to meet it, hanging upside down from a capsized kayak. Didn't want to meet it *at all*.

Gradually, miraculously, the arc of his roll subsided. Ripples expanded, rustling the lily pads, washing against far-off trees. *A croc swimming beneath me?* Cade guessed, swallowing hard. Or the world's largest python?

But no, to displace a wave like that, it'd have to be bigger, bulkier than the largest snake. He pictured the illustrated dinosaur books of his childhood. Primeval steaming swamps, swarming with *brontosaurus* and toothier monsters.

A twenty-foot tropical croc would be monster enough.

But how do crocs hunt? By sight? By smell? By sound? He was damned if he knew. *And has it homed in on me?*

Pray to God that was a chance encounter. Strangers passing in the night. Because if it wasn't…

Slowly, with exquisite care not to rock the boat, he sat upright. Groped for the *parang* and laid it across his thighs. *If the thing homes in on cold sweat, then I'm done for.*

Moving only his eyes, he probed the lurking shadows. The sun must have sunk below the ridge. Beyond the trunks of the nearest trees, he could make out a downed log floating... *Or is that a log?*

But a croc could submerge to its hungry yellow eyeballs. It could be watching him from the cover of a lily pad. Lurking behind one of those humps of mud and rushes that pocked the surface here and there.

And if it hunts by sound? If it was my paddling that attracted it?

Then he was truly up the creek, if he dared not dip his blade. *Any advice from a she-devil?* he asked the air bitterly.

With the day cooling to dusk, mist drifted up from the murk. Formed out of twilight and desperation, a vision of Raine wavered...retreated...gradually coalesced...till, real as she needed to be, she sat facing him astride his kayak, her long lovely legs dangling in the black water.

Not a good idea, he tried to tell her.

She wasn't worried. With a wicked, teasing smile, she leaned to meet him, till their lips barely brushed...a slow sweet waltz of a kiss in the gathering darkness. *Missed you,* he told her mirage.

She pulled back—sat haughtily erect. Stared at him reproachfully, the way she'd stared, that night on the river, when he'd lashed out at her.

God, if I'm croc bait tonight, then that might be the only time—the last time—I was ever inside you?

She bowed her bright head in sorrowful agreement, then faded the way a dream goes at dawn—a swirl of color here, a haunting taste on the lips... Nothing a man can hold.

The kayak drifted, revolving on unseen currents, the needle on his compass pointing true, while its fixed case spun slowly with the boat... Not lost, but as good as lost.

Get out of here! Cade told himself and lifted the paddle.

Like the night torn in two—a groaning bellow, so low it touched fear more than hearing, came rumbling through the mist.

Croc, he told himself as he laid the paddle down again. God, if he was going to die tonight, he wished he'd made love to her a hundred more times. A thousand. If he hadn't lost it back there at the river...

But when he'd explored her necklace—found himself *holding* the stone feather—he'd lost it. Lashed out. The same damned stone that had started everything...

He might have been looking down the wrong end of a telescope, looking back all those years at his fourteen-year-old self, brushing the dirt off an odd rock. Holding it up to the light. Then comprehension dawning... He held a *fossil*, same as Mr. Joe Ashaway had shown him, at his dig site a few miles to the west! But not a fossil of a dinosaur bone—he'd found a feather turned to stone.

Could there be more?

Using his pocketknife, he'd dug and scraped and scratched at the earth till he uncovered the flattened imprint of the creature itself, embedded in pale stone. Its feathered wings were upraised, its spine arched, its billed head thrown back in a pose of agony—or could it be exaltation?

The nape of his neck prickled as he stared. It reminded him of...what? Something from the Bible? Or an old poem he'd run across somewhere... A fallen angel.

It was too wonderful and strange not to share. He'd show it to his grandfather. Heck, he could show it to Mr. Ashaway, ask the expert about it. What was it? How many millions of years ago had it fallen?

The *Archaeopteryx* was nothing but a thing of wonder and beauty to him as he mounted his pony, and tucked the stone feather into his saddlebag. How was he to know he'd found their ruination...?

Cade's cheeks were wet and he brushed at them savagely. He glanced up and his eyes stung; his lashes beaded with diamonds. A fine drizzle falling.

He flinched at a distant hissing, then realized: rain on the way! Marching across the unseen lake, rattling on lily pads, drumming on the leaves above. The clouds cracked wide in a silvery benediction.

He tipped his head back. Licked his parched lips, drank from the air. *Raine, is this falling on you, wherever you are?*

No answer, but inspiration sizzled out of the streaming sky. If crocodiles hunted by sight, then let them spot him through these torrents!

And if they stalked by sound? A thundering downpour was the best cover he'd get. Cade lifted his paddle and dipped right, right again, pivoting back onto his course.

Then on and on through the night he paddled, every stroke a prayer.

The day had grown so dark with the downpour outside, that Raine could no longer see Szabo's journal to read. She'd stopped for a while, in spite of White Dog's urging her to continue. It hadn't been easy, making him understand that if she couldn't see the funny insect tracks on the paper, they couldn't lead her to the story.

With the rain muttering on the thatch overhead, his wife had served lunch, which was—surprise, surprise—pork jerky. Then she'd fed the toddlers, nursing and cuddling each in turn, while Raine and White Dog lay back for a nap.

Fingers laced behind her head, feigning sleep, Raine replayed Szabo's story behind her closed lids:

In the morning, the paratroopers had left the worried Punan at the base of the double mountain and climbed. Late that day, they'd reached the top of its higher peak—and been crushed to find no river. Only an ocean of jungle, stretching on all sides to an endless green horizon.

Disappointment had slowed their steps coming down the rugged track, and Professor had lagged behind, picking up chunks of what he said was limestone. They'd chosen a different route down from the top and it led them to the sway-backed bench between the peaks. Thirsty and footsore, they'd reached this point at sunset—to find a clear spring at the base of a cliff, where the slope above had sheared away.

Though White Dog had begged Professor not to let night

catch them on the mountain—at least Prof thought that was his warning—they'd agreed that it would be crazy to continue in the dark. They'd camped by the spring.

At sunrise, Carleton had gone off to the bushes on a call of nature—and let out a yell. His friends had come running, and there, leering at them from out of the rock, was the Punans' "bad angel."

"Or maybe they were trying to tell us it was a devil," Szabo guessed. "Or a dragon?"

Professor told them it was a dinosaur, who'd died along a lake or riverbed, millions of years ago, then been buried in its mud. The mud had hardened gradually to limestone. The limestone had been buried under millions of years of such sediments, building up like a giant layer cake. The cake had been covered by rising seas. Ages passed and the great waters receded; the land had been folded and forced up by underlying lava. Wind and rain had worn it away again. The earth never rested—it built itself up; it tore itself down.

Now, sixty million or more years after the death of the dinosaur, the beast was rising from its grave. Or rather, its grave was being washed away from the bones. Countless years of monsoons had stripped off the overburden, and now erosion had exposed the creature itself.

A creature transformed. As the sun's first rays touched the beast's grinning muzzle—it flamed! Rainbows danced in the terrible teeth. Sparks of burning color shot along its monstrous jaws. The eye socket that peered from the stone was a smoldering well of purple and orange and rose.

Professor had never heard of such a thing, a fossil made of fire opal. He surmised that at some point the sediments that encased the bones had fractured. In the same way that a petrified tree is sometimes formed, minerals dissolved in water had trickled down the cracks in the limestone. They'd seeped into the pores of the bones, gradually replacing the organic material, atom by atom, shape for shape, with dissolved opal.

Which had hardened and crystallized over the aeons to make a monster made of fiery gemstone.

It was Szabo who'd asked what a dinosaur made of opal might be worth?

"What's the Great Pyramid at Giza worth?" Prof had responded. "Or the Colossus of Rhodes? You're looking at the eighth wonder of the world. There's nothing like it anywhere!"

"Yeah, but what would it bring if you sold it to some collector? A rich guy who likes rocks and lizards and stuff?" Szabo had prodded. "Thousands?"

"More like millions," Professor had guessed. "But where it belongs is in a museum, for the whole world to see." The pity of it was, he'd gone on to say, that the creature would flame out forever, here on this mountain. A few more years of wet-season rains, and it would weather away like the rock around it.

The soldiers had stared at each other, then Szabo had shaken his head. "Not on my watch, it won't."

Prof had done his best to dissuade the others. He'd pointed out that if they could chip the dinosaur free from its rocks, they couldn't carry it away. The skull alone would weigh tons.

And even if they could have moved it—then to where? Without shelter, it would still be at the mercy of the elements. But the Punan's huts were temporary structures meant to last weeks with constant patching, not years of neglect.

And it went without saying that they were talking years. Even if they could secure their find, they couldn't cash it in during the midst of a world war. The Japanese controlled Borneo's coasts; there'd be no smuggling tons of dinosaur out from under their noses.

And if the paratroopers could have managed that miracle, they'd face yet another obstacle. They'd been sent to gather intelligence, not treasure. The brass would hardly sympathize with four enlisted men taking time out from battle, to make their own fortunes. Show up with a fire opal dinosaur and they'd end up in the brig—while the generals split their hard-earned gains.

"Leave the critter where it is," Prof had insisted. "Maybe there'll be something of it left, after the war. We could always come back."

"If we're maybe still alive," Szabo had jeered. "If maybe the Japs don't find it in the meantime. If maybe some rich collector will still want to buy a dinosaur with its head dissolved away. Well, that's too many if-maybes for me!"

Still, in the end, Prof's logic would have prevailed, Raine told herself. They'd have chipped out as many teeth as they could carry and gone their regretful way.

But Carleton, the kid, had grown bored with the older men's wrangling and had wandered off to explore. Now he returned on the run. He'd traced the spring to its source, among the boulders at the base of the cliff—and found the mouth of a cave!

And that changed everything.

"Ren-Bungan?" Abat patted Raine's arm, then nodded at the platform's triangular end. The rain had stopped and her husband was scrambling out into the open.

"Great idea." Raine pulled on her boots and followed the rest of the family outside. Then the women, to a far clump of bushes.

Returning, she made a face at the single gap in the treetop canopy she could find. "It's going to rain more, isn't it?"

The nearest Punan followed her gaze to the patch of roiling purple and nodded agreeably.

"Please tell me it's not going to rain like this for the next six months," Raine begged. Surely the weather would ramp up to the monsoon, not change overnight? "'Cause swimming or walking, I'm out of here tomorrow." If she could figure no way to ask White Dog about the twin-peaked mountain, then she'd find it without him.

* * *

When the next downpour swept across the forest, they crawled back into White Dog's sleeping platform. Unbelievably, another two men crawled in after them.

"Poker party?" Raine guessed. "Or how many Punan can you fit in a phone booth?" If she hadn't been wedged in the middle, she'd have definitely fled to her hammock.

White Dog tapped the top of her pack and said something, that in any language meant, "Tell us a story."

Well, it was better than trying to make small talk in an unknown language. Raine sighed, took out the notebook and read:

> "So now we've got a safe place to hide the beast. And to sleep dry while we dig it. Prof isn't happy. He sez we have a duty to get on down to the coast and scout the Japs. That once we get there, we'll figure some way to steal a boat and get back to base.
>
> "We'll end up in a POW camp, eating rats for the rest of the war, sez I. How about a vote on it? Who wants to stick around here with a bunch of half-naked dames and dig treasure? And who wants to stumble through five hundred miles of snakes, so they can end up in jail?"

"Let me guess who won," Raine said dryly, and turned the page.

Bowing reluctantly to majority rule, Prof had helped his fellows start their dig. The Texan had gained some field experience in fossil excavation while studying geology in college. Without his expertise, most likely the amateurs would have wrecked the skeleton.

He showed them how to chip away most of the rock, but leave a protective matrix around the skull. Then how to carefully tunnel beneath it, so that the heavy mass stood on narrowing piers of stone. He also engineered the graded ramp from the dig site to the cave, along which they'd eventually drag their find—once they'd built a sledge beneath it, then cut away the piers, to leave the sledge resting on log rollers.

Meanwhile White Dog's people had not forsaken them. The soldiers slept in the cave, but several nights a week they'd hike down the mountain to where the Punan had camped. They'd trade one tiny glass bead for a meal of roasted meat— and a chance to flirt with the unmarried girls of the tribe. Each time they went up the mountain again, the Punan begged them to stay. They should keep away from the bad thing up there! It was very bad luck! It would eat their hearts!

But as time passed and the soldiers weren't devoured by an evil spirit, the Punans' curiosity got the better of them. Day by day, they crept closer to the dig. By the second week, they crouched around the site, watching in fearful fascination. "Like watching a scary movie, waiting and hoping for something bad to jump out," noted Szabo.

Something bad did happen, but it was more subtle than a monster rising from the grave, to slay its impudent defilers. The soldiers' hands had blistered from constant digging with their two folding shovels, plus their improvised picks of jagged stone and bamboo. Szabo got the idea of paying the unmarried girls of the tribe two beads per day, if they'd help in the digging and chipping.

Soon it was only the girls laboring alongside Prof, while the other soldiers lounged around. Or snuck off to go hunting with the Punan men.

"Guys." Raine snorted—and glanced up.

Hopelessly, unapologetically male, her audience beamed back at her. One of the hunters patted the page and made an encouraging noise.

"Yeah, and if you can't go spear something, then you might as well listen to foreign rap music?" But she smiled and continued.

Finally Prof threw down his shovel and declared he'd had enough. "Said he'd signed up to fight a war, and this dinosaur was nothing but a distraction. Big hero!" sneered Szabo. "He said we could do what we liked, but him, he was heading for the coast."

The other three voted to stay. At Prof's suggestion, each of them wrote a letter to his loved ones. The Texan would carry theirs out and mail them if he could, in case they never made it back alive. They'd keep his for the same reason. But since he might be captured and their letters fall to enemy hands, he warned his friends not to give any details that could betray their location.

"So now we split the pie three ways," gloated Szabo as they watched Prof walk off to the east, guided by White Dog and another hunter. "Good riddance to the Eagle Scout. He was nothin' but a pain in the butt, anyway."

"I hope you guys aren't going to insist on a happy ending?" Raine said, closing the notebook. "'Cause something tells me—"

But the Punan were already scrambling for the exit. The rain had stopped again.

This time the gap in the leaves showed blue sky. But it was too late in the day to leave, and Raine still had no directions to follow. She wandered around the camp, turning down offers of jerky, watching Abat weave some of the beads Raine had given her into a strip of bark cloth. The children were playing in a puddle, forming human figures and animals out of—

"Wait a minute!" Raine crouched beside them. "Clay! Where did you get this?"

They took her hands and led her to a bank of it, along the nearby creek. "All *right*, now we're talking!" She gathered pounds of the squishy material onto several elephant ear leaves and carried it back to camp. Commenced modeling alongside the children.

An hour later, when White Dog sauntered over to see what the strange Ren-Bungan was doing now, she showed him her efforts. From the clay and the earth itself, she'd fashioned a three-dimensional map. She'd scooped out a butterfly-shaped lake and filled it with water. Built a range of mountains to its southeast. Mounded up a twin-peaked mountain to the north. "Does this ring any bells?" Raine walked her index and fore-finger around the lake, then toward the double mountain.

The headman squatted beside her and stared at the scene.

"Have you been there before?" she asked urgently.

With a mystified frown, he looked at her.

She tapped the mountain. "Is this where *you* found…" And she swung around to touch the clay model her body had been blocking from his view. "Where you found a dinosaur tooth—like this?" She'd sculpted the tooth life-size. Then to prod his memory, she'd embedded one of her necklace opals in its sticky surface.

He let out a grunt of surprise. Glanced sharply from Raine to the tooth, then back again.

"Yes!" Raine agreed. "That's why I've come. I want that. Where did you find it? Did you find it…" Again she walked her two fingers from the lake to the mountain—then showed them pouncing on the jeweled tooth. "Here? The tooth came from this mountain, yes?"

This time he nodded vigorous agreement—expanded this with a stream of excited comments and gestures.

"Great!" Raine tapped her chest, then tapped the twin-peaked mountain. "I need to *go* there. That is my heart's de-sire. Could you help me?"

Chapter 26

"Look, if you're going to cry about it, I think we should stop," Raine suggested, the following night.

White Dog and two other hunters were escorting her on a trek toward the twin mountain. After they'd made camp at day's end, they'd insisted she read to them by the banked fire. Anything to keep her guides happy, she'd figured.

Except they weren't happy. Though they didn't understand a word of the paratroopers' story, they were exquisitely attuned to her emotions. Watching her face as she read, they'd started silently weeping about a page back.

"We should tell knock-knock jokes. Or go to bed." They'd covered a good twenty miles today at a hunter's fluid pace and Raine was exhausted. But at least they were making excellent time.

And she'd recognized her first landmark from the watch's map, when they'd topped a high ridge around noon. Far off to the south, she'd caught a glimpse of the butterfly lake.

She'd expected they'd head that direction and stop on its

shore. Instead they'd swerved in a wide arc around it; they were camping dry tonight. But though there was no way to wash up, they had plenty to drink. White Dog had shown her how to cut the lianas that grew around camp. Chop the stem and out gushed a clear liquid, purer and tastier than the filtered river water she'd been living on, these past few weeks.

"Really, why don't we go to bed?" she tried again, waving a hand at her waiting hammock.

The tears dried up; the chins stuck out in stubborn disapproval. They wanted their story. "Okay, okay. The Greeks liked their tragedies, so why not you guys?" She stood to stir the coals of their fire. Plenty of damp wood was making a nice smudge that kept the mosquitoes at bay. Sitting in the pungent smoke, she opened the notebook again. "Where were we?"

No place good, was where. With Professor's leaving, the situation had gone rapidly downhill. The Punan girls were growing bored with the drudgery of digging. Working till you blistered was a civilized concept, not the nomads' way.

To encourage them to work longer and faster, Szabo and his friends upped their daily pay to three beads, then four. But the girls quickly learned that sulking and working slower earned them more beads, not less. Besides, with this raise in salary they'd accumulated enough beads to create bands for their foreheads and shapely calves; who needed more?

Frustrated by the girls, Szabo turned to the hunters for help, but the males of the tribe scorned to work for beads. Tobacco might have tempted them, but the soldiers had smoked all the weed they'd saved from the lake.

"'We've gotta do something!' Szabo had fretted in his journal.

"Prof said before he left that the wet season's coming in another month. After that, there'll be no way to get these heathen to dig in the rain. Besides, the game's just about played out around here. I'm betting when White

Dog comes back from the coast, the tribe'll move on to better hunting. We've got to find some way to make 'em help us, and find it now."

"Hoo, boy," Raine muttered as she came to it.

"So we took a good-behavior hostage this morning," Szabo wrote. "White Dog's son." They'd lured the child into the cave. Then they'd leashed him there like a puppy, with Carleton to keep watch so that nobody freed him.

Naturally the boy's mother, then everyone, had protested. In the Punan way, the elders of the tribe had come up the mountain to discuss this grave matter; a consensus must be reached.

"They jabbered and jabbered and nagged at us. I tried to tell 'em to forget it. That all we wanted was some help digging, and soon as we'd dug up the dinosaur, we'd let the boy go. But they kept on fuming and fussing till I couldn't take anymore. So I shot one of their dogs."

It was the first time the soldiers had fired a gun. They only had two, with no more than forty bullets. Prof had counseled from the start that they should save their ammunition for emergencies, learn to hunt the native way.

"'But I figured one bullet and one dead dog would get my point across,' wrote Szabo. 'That if they want to stay healthy and happy, they should do things our way. Just because we've treated 'em fair and friendly, that don't mean we can be disrespected.'"

Astonished and terrified by this needle that flew through the air, the Punan had retreated for the night, their women weeping as they went.

"'But not the men,' said Szabo, 'which seems sort of funny. When Carleton hurt his foot digging last week, they cried more than he did.'"

Raine blew out a gusty sigh, and glanced up—to find her own outrage mirrored in every face. "We really ought to go to bed," she said again, though she wasn't going to sleep easy after this.

But they wanted to know the end of the story—or at least to feel it—and there were only a few more pages to go.

"'Wasn't sure if any of 'em would show up for digging the next day, but by God, they did,' Szabo wrote.

"We set 'em a good example, me and Jonesy swapped time on the shovel, while the one not digging kept look-out with our second gun. Just in case any of the men get any notion to stick a poison dart in somebody."

The excavation proceeded—slowly. Sullenly. The girls no longer flirted or teased, and the soldiers were obviously feeling guilty. They raised the standard salary to five beads per day; their generosity won no smiles or forgiveness.

The only one having a half-passable time was young Carleton in the cave; he was teaching his charge how to play the harmonica. "'But a few days of grin and bear it and it'll all be over,' Szabo wrote.

"I ordered the men to go cut logs for the sledge today, and gather rattan to tie it all together. The ramp's about smoothed out. Three days from now we ought to be able to cut the head loose from its pilings and drag it down to the cave.

"After that, I'm thinking we'll have to call it quits. If it took a month to dig out the skull, I figure it'd take a year to get the rest of the critter. But I figure the head is what a collector would want to buy most of all. When the sun shines on those teeth, well, I get the cold shivers. It's like something you'd see coming for you at the Last Trump. Purely amazing."

Szabo decided that once the bones were safely stored, they'd seal up the cave, then make their way toward the coast.

"Reckon we've about worn out our welcome here anyway," he observed.

"Oh, no. Really?" Raine jeered and White Dog growled agreement. His dog pricked his ears, sat up, and added his growl to the chorus—then scratched his neck thoroughly and flopped down again.

"'Reckon we'll find us some other tribe,' continued Szabo.

"See if they'd like some company till the war winds down. Once we've got a prayer of shipping our treasure home, we'll come on back and collect it. I've been scratching a map in my watch, of what it'd would look like from the air, in case we can hire a float plane, returning. That would sure beat walking."

Raine shut the book. "I've got to stop, guys. If it gets any worse, I won't be able to sleep."

They complained, then coaxed, turning on the Punan charm. Laughing, she shook her head. "No, honestly. I'm beat. But I'll tell you one thing." She leaned to rub the white dog's ears. "This is your story," she told his master.

She cocked her head, considering how she could sign that, then gave it up. "At least, I bet it is. White Dog's son that they took hostage? I'm guessing he was either your father, or—" Since they seemed to start their families in their teens out here… "Or your grandfather. Your tribe has moved on some, since then, but that's no surprise. But you're the only man I've met out here who runs with a white dog." She scratched the hound's ears again. "So I bet this guy's great-great-who-knows-how-many-great-grandfather is in this story, too. Wish I could tell you that."

The next day didn't start well.

Raine spent the night tossing and turning, plagued by nightmares, just as she'd feared. The worst came at dawn, when a *T. rex* lunged out of her dig site. Flaming teeth clamped down on Cade, ripping him from her arms, dragging him down into the pit. She woke screaming and flailing, fighting her mosquito nets.

She'd scared the Punan more than she scared herself. They poked their heads out of their sleeping platform—stared at her appalled, as she unzipped and sat up, panting and swearing. Without a word, they vanished again.

A nightmare wasn't a mere nasty nuisance, in some parts of the world, Raine reflected, while she caught her breath. It could be an omen. A warning. Give another silly performance like that one, and her guides might decide they wanted no part of this expedition.

She'd be smarter not to sleep again. But if she rose and stumbled around the camp, she'd disturb the guys, who'd apparently gone back to bed. She reached for her pack, which she'd hung, as always, alongside the hammock, then fished out Szabo's notebook. If he was going to trouble her dreams, he might as well entertain her, waking.

"Moving day went smooth as silk," he'd written.

Have to hand it to Professor. He knew his stuff. It took a couple dozen of the tribe, ladies and gents, plus Jonesy, pulling and pushing, to get the skull moving. But after that, the sledge rolled right along. Downhill all the way, past the pool, into the cave. I stood back, supervising, and holding the gun, just to keep everybody's mind on business.

But the Punan had business of their own. During the excitement, one of the laborers must have tossed a stone blade to the captive, who'd been tethered at the back of the cavern. The next time the soldiers looked his way, the boy was gone.

"Which was sort of a shame," noted Szabo. "I figured on getting one more day's use out of him." The following day, he meant to wall up the mouth of the cave. He'd counted on the Punans' help, lugging stone for the job. "I figured we'd let the kid go, after that.

"But I reckon since we've lost our little bargaining chip, we'll have to finish the job ourselves." The soldiers had worked hard all the rest of that day, gathering rocks. "Felt really strange, with none of them hanging around. Even when they were mad at us, they were company. It's so damn quiet up here now, it makes me jumpy." Szabo had kept his gun at hand.

Then at twilight, Carleton had glanced up, let out a cry and pointed. The others had spun around—to see nothing but bushes.

He claimed White Dog was back. Said he'd seen the chief, over by the edge of the trees. Standing there with one hand on his son's shoulder, just looking at us. Me and Jonesy figured it was nothing but nerves and shadows.

All the same, Szabo had been wary enough to post a guard inside the mouth of the cave that night. Jones had taken the first watch while the others slept. When a rock rattled down the cliff, then another… "The damn fool grabbed his gun and ran outside, I guess to see what was going on."

He was instantly buried, as tons of rock came crashing and rumbling down the cliff face.

Once the dust had settled, the two survivors stared at each other in horror. They'd always kept a fire burning in the cave, for fear of its smothering darkness. Now the flames showed them a wall of rubble, blocking the entrance. The only exit.

"Those fucking heathen!" Szabo had written in a staggering hand. "They fixed us but good! When I dig my way out of here…"

So he'd reached the twin peaks—and now what? If the original map in the watch had shown an X to mark the spot where he'd find the treasure, then Lia had snatched it away too quickly. Cade had missed that crucial detail.

You could hide a thousand T. rexes up there, he estimated grimly. The mountain massif must be twenty miles or more around its base. Its lower terraces were covered in head-high thickets that would cloak any fossil. Outcrops of pale, crumbling limestone jutted up from the bushes, like a giant child's tumbled blocks. Higher up reared the weathered cliffs, with their feet buried in slopes of shattered scree.

All Cade could think to do was start climbing. A well-defined trail wound up the right-hand peak, spiraling gradually around the ragged cone. He followed it cautiously, squeezing between clefts in the rock, edging his way along narrow ledges. Stopping often to listen. The cracker might be somewhere ahead, or he could be days behind.

Or he'd fallen prey to any number of woes in the jungle.

And, you, Raine? Cade wondered, as he stopped on a bare ledge, about a thousand feet above the treetops. *Are you somewhere out there? Headed this way?* His blood quickened with the image.

He couldn't imagine she'd turned back. Turned tail. She was coming. *So bring it on! Come help me find this thing, then I'll wrestle you for who gets to take it home.* He could hear the blood striding in his ears, an eagle shrieking on the winds above. Somewhere a rock rattled down through the scree. He turned and kept climbing.

Maybe she'd set the tone for the day, with her conniptions at dawn. The Punan had been skittish all morning. They'd slept late, then dawdled in camp, showing no inclination to leave. Finally Raine had shouldered her pack, and asked White Dog to point the way toward the twin peaks. When he'd done so, she'd set off in that direction.

Minutes later the men had bustled up the trail, to pass her and take the lead. After that, they'd made good time, padding along in their tireless, splayfooted walk.

But Raine felt like running. *Cade, where are you?* He might be days behind her—or days ahead. No way would she ever forgive him, if he beat her to the dino. Still, she'd have felt happier if she'd known he was... *Not eaten by a T. rex?* she scoffed, recalling her dream.

If she wanted to worry, she should worry about Szabo. Mr. Smirky could be the grandson of any one of the original dino finders, Raine supposed, kin to Carleton or Jones or even Peckham. But given his blithe way with tossing women out of windows? *He's gotta be a Szabo. He's got those same carefree genes.*

If that one was someplace up ahead... She reached over her shoulder to fondle her blowpipe—and bumped into the man she followed. "Oof! Sorry." He caught her arm when she tried to step around him. "What's up?"

Ahead on the trail, White Dog and the other hunter teetered frantically on tiptoe, as if they'd come out at the edge of a mile-high cliff. Raine edged up to peer past them—the headman swept out his arm to block her way. With an urgent word, he pointed at the trail.

Where a red caterpillar, about the length of her little finger, paraded deliberately across their path from right to left.

"Well, for pity's sake! Does he jump? We can't just step over the sucker?"

No, no, no, no! Absolutely not! White Dog hustled her back a dozen feet to safety, where everyone regrouped and stared uneasily toward the monster.

Who'd paused in his journey to munch on a fallen leaf. One of the hunters groaned.

Raine blew out a breath. "Okaaay. Could we go around?" She tried to demonstrate a detour—and was instantly reprimanded.

"No, huh?" She wanted to laugh, she wanted to tear her hair. "But I'm in a hurry here, guys." Something kept telling her, she needed to move, run, *fly* toward the mountain. Time was running out. "You're sure this isn't just some silly superstition?" she coaxed. "I mean, I'm the first person to toss salt over my shoulder when I spill it. And I try not to stroll under ladders. But when there's no other way around and it's an emergency…"

Their grim faces didn't relax. That caterpillar was a drop-dead nonnegotiable.

"Right," she muttered, clenching her teeth. Half of her ached to elbow White Dog aside. To heck with this voodoo nonsense. She'd go on alone.

The other half of her was John Ashaway's daughter. She'd been taught since her first field trip to respect local knowledge. *"The people who live here are the experts. You wouldn't try to tell a New Yorker that it's okay to jog naked in Central Park after midnight, would you?"* she remembered him snorting to an intern on one early trip. *"So whatever they tell you, even if it doesn't seem to make any sense—listen up!"*

"Okay. Then how 'bout a lunch break?" she suggested. People tended to be more flexible on full stomachs than empty.

They brightened immediately when she unslung her pack to pull out her bag of trail mix, the only provision she'd brought that they found remotely edible. Crouching in the path, they shared that around, along with the ripening jerky. White Dog went to check on the caterpillar—and came back looking grim.

Raine stifled a moan. "So what's the plan? Are we going to just sit here till Mr. Wiggles spins his cocoon and changes himself to a cabbage moth?"

White Dog said something stern but soothing, that sounded like, "Well, of course. If necessary." And hunkered down again.

If she didn't find a way to distract herself, she'd snap! Start screaming and stamping her feet—all over their fuzzy road-block. Raine pulled out Szabo's notebook and dived into its last few pages, reading them aloud:

"'When I dig my way out of here…'" There was a gap of

several lines after that blustering threat. When the writing continued, it was sloppier. Larger, as if Szabo could barely see to write.

"Morning was about ten years in coming, but when it came, well, Carleton started crying again, and me, I got religion. The natives did their usual half-assed job. There's a gap at the top of the landslide. You can see a patch of daylight showing. Room enough to squeeze through, if the rest of the pile don't collapse."

Weeping with relief, Carleton had lunged for it, and Szabo had slapped him back to his senses. "If I was trying to bury a man, I wouldn't just drop some rocks on him and stroll away," he'd observed.

"I'd stick around. Make sure nobody crawled out from under. I said if there was one thing we knew about the Punan, they might be lazy, but they were patient as cats at a rat hole. They could be just squatting out there, back in the trees, with their blowguns loaded."

He'd told the younger man that they should play possum.

"Put the fire out so they don't smell any smoke. Then lie low for a day or two or maybe a week. Let 'em be satisfied we're dead and done for. We have water, so that's no problem."

The spring that fed the pool outside started deep within the mountain. Instead of drowning the cave, it seemed to have found a way to seep past the fallen boulders.

"So our only problem is rations, which were getting low before this SNAFU. And what we've got, we'll need for hiking to the coast, once we get out of here. I'd figured we'd shoot game as we go, but now we're down to one gun and nineteen bullets."

"Oh, boy," Raine murmured. She could see where this logic was leading.

"And Carleton's still limping. Dumbass broke some toes when he was digging. Once we get out of here, he ain't gonna be able to move fast. And with those heathen sniffing down our trail, moving slow's as good as dead."

So Szabo had helped the boy on his way. "He didn't suffer none. I did it while he was sleeping." And then there was only one, to eat those dwindling rations.

But if he was stunningly short on conscience, he had plenty of nerve. Szabo toughed it out in the damp semidarkness for another three days, with nothing but his journal for company.

He managed to work one tooth loose from the dinosaur's jaws. "Might as well take something to show what all the fuss was about," he noted wryly. "And if the whole dang skull's worth a million, what's a fire opal fang worth?"

He'd cleaned his gun, packed his gear, then waited till half an hour, he estimated, before sundown. Enough light to find his way through the gap, but with darkness soon coming, in case they were waiting for him and he needed to hide. "So if this is the last thing I ever write and only the palm rats are gonna read it, what should I say?" he asked himself. "When they warn you about a bad angel in the stones, then…"

The rest of the sentence had been scratched out.

"That's…" Raine squinted at it, shook her head. Flipped the last few pages and found nothing more. "That's the last thing he wrote."

The Punan wiped the tears from their faces, and gave her brave, satisfied smiles. White Dog grunted and heaved himself to his feet and went to check on their problem and let out a happy yell.

When they crowded up beside him, there was the caterpillar. Or maybe this was a different but similar caterpillar—trundling left to right across their path.

Apparently that made all the difference. Though Raine did notice that when each Punan came to the fatal spot, he leaped high over the critter, like a goosed jackrabbit.

"When in Rome," she murmured—and did the same.

Chapter 27

A few hours before dark, Cade reached the bald summit. Turning in place, he found nothing but a view of infinite tree-tops, like the tops of clouds seen from a plane. Out at the edges of the rumpled green horizon, thunderheads towered, purple and gold with the setting sun.

Not a soul in sight anywhere. Not a mark on this desolate world that would prove he lived in an age of men, not dinosaurs. If a *pterodactyl* had soared past this peak, Cade wouldn't have been surprised. This feeling grinding in the pit of his stomach was…what? Homesickness?

Except where was home these days? He'd had plenty of mailing addresses, but nothing like a home, for years and years. Not since his grandfather's ranch was lost.

And that's why you're here, he reminded himself. *To take anything the Ashaways want. Everything they need.*

But he felt no satisfaction, picturing Raine's defeat. He'd rather see her laughing, the way she'd laughed when he spun her around in the river till they'd toppled, dizzy with want-ing. And nothing in the way of their having.

I want that again. This wasn't homesickness. He was miss-ing *her,* dammit. *Witch. She-devil.* In a world full of willing beauties, how could he have been so feckless—to fall for the woman he'd meant to destroy?

"This is nothing but empty-stomach blues," he said aloud. He needed food, a place to camp before dark-fall. *Get moving.*

He followed the same route descending till he came to a fork. A faint path led off through a split in the rock, so he took that way down. In the last of the light, winded and footsore, he arrived at the broad bench that connected the two peaks.

And was he in luck! He found trees tall enough to support his hammock, growing near a pool of clear water.

"What now?" Raine wondered, when her guides huddled on the trail in front of her. "You're *not* stopping for the night, are you?" All afternoon, shivers of dread had been rippling down her spine. Maybe the air pressure was falling, a big storm looming up behind?

The men crowded around a message stick, planted at a fork in the trail. Muttering and scowling, they turned from the stick's fronds and notches to the surrounding jungle. Their dark eyes showed rings of wary white. Rising up on the balls of their feet, they touched the *parangs* hanging at their sides, while the white dog bristled and whined.

"What is it?" Raine asked in an undertone.

Holding her gaze, the headman slashed his forefinger sav-agely across his throat. Then held it up between them.

"A headhunter? One man?" Echoing "one" with her own raised finger, she grimaced to show she realized this was serious.

He nodded a vigorous "yes," then gestured widely at the forest.

"Beware of one headhunter, somewhere nearby?" But did the stick literally signify a headhunter—a Dayak, since the

Punan didn't take heads? Or had the word generalized to mean "a dangerous man"? Possibly a killer?

"Szabo?" she wondered aloud. Kincade had mixed easily and amiably with the islanders, she'd noticed. It was doubtful he'd have frightened or threatened anyone he encountered. But Szabo, on the other hand, spreading joy and good times wherever he went...

"And who left us this message?" But just because she'd seen nobody, didn't mean the woods were deserted. The Punan let you see them if and only if they chose.

Meanwhile, her friends were arguing. One hunter wanted to turn back the way they'd come. The second had drawn his *parang* and was jabbing it toward the right-hand fork—proposing they go hunt the headhunter? But that would mean a turn to the southwest, back toward the butterfly lake, when they'd been walking eastward for the past two days.

White Dog gestured to the other fork that continued east, but clearly his heart wasn't in it.

Raine knelt in the middle of the eastward path—raked up dirt to make a crude, double-coned symbol. She tapped herself on the chest, then walked two fingers toward the peaks. "I've got to *go* there." She tapped herself on the chest again, pointed down the eastern fork, gave White Dog a look of pleading and inquiry. "If I keep following this trail, will it take me there?"

His troubled expression said, *yes, but...*

Meanwhile the hunter who'd wanted to go home, had changed his mind. He'd joined the tough guy, and now both stood a few feet down the southwest fork, shuffling from foot to foot, urging Raine and White Dog to join them.

Raine paced five feet to the east, then turned around. The Punan decided issues by reaching a consensus. It wasn't a matter of majority rule as in the West, one side outvoting the other. Here everybody must agree, even if it took days to convert and convince the other side. "But, guys, I haven't *got* days. So I hate to be rude, but you're either with me, or I'm outa here."

White Dog made a mournful face, and drifted a few steps backward toward his friends. "Ren-Bungan?" he pleaded, beckoning her to follow.

"I can't. I wish I could, but I can't. Oh, *please* don't be sad." Unslinging her pack, she pulled out the gift she'd meant to give him for farewell. A bright red, multipurpose Swiss army knife. "You're the guy who saved my life. I won't forget you." She showed him how its blades opened and closed, the miniature tweezers slipped out and slipped in. "Lord knows what you'll do with the bottle opener, but you'll think of something." His tears dried to a dazzling smile. She touched the knife to her heart, to her lips, then put it in his broad, brown palm. "Take care of yourself, okay?"

Raine turned and walked east, a bit tearful herself—then glanced back for one last wave goodbye.

Not a leaf waved, not a twig stirred. The Punan had faded into the forest.

Something woke Cade just before dawn. He lay listening, but if it had been a sound that aroused him, it didn't come again. He wriggled into his worn and sweaty clothes, checked his boots for surprises, pulled them on and slipped out of the hammock. He walked down to the pool. Stood, gazing up at the peaks, dark against a brightening sky.

"And if I don't find the dino today?" he wondered aloud. To have come all this way for nothing? Talk about a snipe hunt!

Something stirred at the edge of his vision, and he swung toward the left-hand peak. This side of it had sheared off in a ragged cliff. A pile of scree sloped from near the top of the cliff into the pool, marking the site of some long-ago rockslide. At the top of this heap of rubble, a cloud of smoke swirled and billowed. He squinted, staring.

The smoke sucked inward, eddied…blew outward and dispersed. "Bees!" he realized. Flying out at dawn. There must be an entrance to a cave up there, a big cave, to hold such a swarm.

Cade rubbed the bristles on his jaw and considered. Fossils were most often found where the land was breached by erosion or by digging. You needed to look below the skin of the Earth, search a cross section of sediments, the layered millennia. A cavern, cutting down through the mountain strata would give you that. He grimaced. He wasn't fond of tight places.

Maybe he'd explore the left-hand peak first.

By noon, a tropic sun hammered down on the sparsely shaded peaks. The pale limestone bounced back the heat in shimmering waves, a white glare to stab the eyes and stun the brain. Cade's explorations of the outer slopes had proved a fruitless endeavor; he was thinking more kindly now about cool, damp, shady spaces, no matter how claustrophobic. He fished his flashlight from his pack, which he'd hidden at his camp near the pond, then he started up the scree.

The pile of rocks creaked as his weight shifted, but it didn't slither. An old slide, he figured, the stones had found their resting points. Mindful of snakes in the crevices, he climbed deliberately, checking every handhold. Halfway up, he paused to look down at the pool. Not a killing height if he fell, but a broken leg out here was just a slower, nastier way to the same ending.

He climbed another ten feet, then paused again. He turned to gaze out over miles of jungle lowlands. *She should have showed by now.* If she didn't come by tomorrow, he'd have to give up hunting dinosaurs and start hunting Raine. The thought of her out there, lost somewhere in all that endless green, running low on food by now, maybe hobbling along on a twisted ankle?

"You should have thought about that sooner," he told himself bitterly. It was one thing to dream of revenge; quite another, he was learning, to achieve it.

When he reached the hole at the top of the slide, it was smaller than he'd thought. Barely wider than his shoulders and about that high again. *You don't have to do this,* he reminded himself.

But he did. You didn't chase a dino halfway around the world, then wimp out just because you hated dark, tight spaces. Turning onto his stomach at the lip, he eased his legs gingerly into the shadows, felt for a toehold. "Okaaay." Like a diver preparing to submerge, he sucked in a breath, a deeper second one. He held the third—and slithered out of the sunlight, into dusk.

Stood there paralyzed for a moment—then blew out his breath. And kept on climbing down the inner face of the rockslide. God, if the rocks tumbled now, maybe covered the hole?

As he descended, his eyes adjusted to the gloom. No need, so far, for his flashlight. Pausing halfway to the floor, he found the hole let in enough light to show him an irregular cavern, at least thirty feet wide and who knew how deep? Here and there, stalactites and stalagmites had dripped, joined, built themselves into voluptuous, hourglass columns of glistening stone. They blocked much of his view of the inner reaches, but it seemed the cave didn't drive straight in. It twisted off to the right, sloping gently, dreadfully down.

Somewhere far off, water dripped and tinkled. He could hear the bees humming, but searching the ceiling, he couldn't see the hive. Maybe it hung near the—

He made the mistake of glancing up toward the hole. *"Shit!"* Bright as a spotlight, the glare dazzled him, robbing him of vision as his pupils contracted. "Smart move." But he couldn't stop here; he kept on descending toward the floor he'd seen. As his feet found level ground, he sighed with relief, backed away from the wall of rubble—and stumbled over something.

He fell, twisting to one side, one hand flying backward to catch his weight. His right palm landed on a jagged stone and he bit back a yelp. Broke something? Wrenched the hell out of it, anyway. He sat for a minute, absorbing the pain in wrist and thumb, then realized his ankles were hooked over the bundle that had tripped him. Branches, he guessed, from the dry rustling sound as he disengaged himself. He rolled to his knees and crabbed closer to see.

"Oof!" A body sprawled facedown at the base of the slide.

For a stomach-twisting instant he thought it was Raine. *God, no, I never wanted this!* If he could stop time, turn it back, do it again, he'd never—

Then he saw the white showing, where a hand rested by the head. The delicate fan of bones. All that remained of splayed fingers.

"Oh, *Christ!*" *Thank you!* Anyone but her!

Guilty at his rush of relief, he fumbled for the flashlight in his belt, found his right hand wasn't working, dragged it out awkwardly with his left. Switched it on and to hell with his night vision.

Bones gleamed whitely through tattered cloth. Once upon a time, the body had worn camouflage pants and shirt. Jungle boots. The deflated shape on his back must have been a pack? "A soldier," Cade muttered, wearing clothes like that. Judging from the length of his legs and the breadth of his shoulders, he'd been too big for a native. "One of the paratroopers from Raine's journal?" Lying here some sixty-odd years. Plenty of time for the bugs to pick him clean.

Cade moved his circle of light over the ruined pack. Anything in there to identify the guy? He could make out nothing but bits of rusty junk and shredded material. He aimed his beam at the neck vertebrae rising above the pack, but if the soldier had worn a dog tag, it was gone. The head was turned to one side, as if it gazed at something in the back of the cave. And in the skull's shadowed eye socket—

Cade gagged—sat back on his heels. The thing blooming out of the eyehole was a blow dart!

"Poor bastard!" He'd climbed up there, stuck his head out the gap in the rocks toward freedom... Probably been dead before he tumbled to the floor.

Cade stood and played his light around. Shouldn't waste the batteries, but he didn't feel like blundering along half-blind, after this special treat. The beam swept over pale sta-lactites and stalagmites like a great beast's dripping fangs. At one end of the rockfall, a pool of water gleamed, opaque in his light.

There wasn't much else here in this front gallery; just the blackened remains of an ancient campfire. A stack of mold-ering wood piled against a nearby wall.

He steeled himself and walked deeper. Farther in, colon-nades of glistening limestone divided the depths of the cav-ern into alcoves. Some of these were dead-end rooms in the rock; others seemed to be passages, extending endlessly into the black. Odd how you could feel the weight of the moun-tain pressing down, making it harder to draw a full breath. Cade hated the way the floor slanted. He could imagine the pitch suddenly steepening, his feet flying out from under. Could picture himself sliding down into narrower, deeper, darker chutes, bloody fingers scrabbling at slimy stone.

But there's no use pretending this isn't the place, he had to admit. Not with that bag of bones standing sentry.

Prowling deeper, he probed each dusky pocket with his light. He came to a column wide and thick enough to be a load bearer for the whole damn mountain overhead, the king of all columns. To its left, the main passage swept clockwise around its massive, baggy curves, then out of sight. On its right a smaller opening, about the size of a garage door, cut past it to a deep alcove.

He'd search this one last space, then he'd have to recon-sider. His batteries were working fine so far, but after weeks in the tropics, how long could they last? Or think if he slipped—dropped the flash, broke the bulb… "Get a torch or three or twelve and come back," he decided reluctantly. But first, this last alcove… He turned, aimed the light—

Fireworks!

"Ho-o-ly—!" Flames danced in stone—a dragon's snarl-

ing mask. The monster leered at him from the shadows—
seemed to lunge—fangs burning, eyes glowing with hellfire.
A skull as big as the hood of a speeding Mack truck, coming
right at him, grinning its gemmed, carnivorous grin... A predator's joke.

Not really moving, it was just the light made it leap. His
knees trembled; the beam danced as his hand shook, setting
off more sparks and showers and fountains of light. *"God..."*

Hypnotized, snake charmed, moth to the flame, he drifted
past the king column, into the lair. The *T. rex* skull rested on
a crude altar made of logs. *Devil worship!*

Or no—the platform was a sledge. Which balanced on log
rollers. "Good ol' yankee know-how," he marveled.

"The can-do boys," agreed a man's drawling voice to his
right.

The hair shot straight up on Cade's neck as he froze.

"Smart boy. Come on in and join the party."

From the corner of his right eye he saw the sweep of the
gun, motioning him in toward the beast. Should have jumped
back at the first sound, but with his senses on overload— Too
late to try it now?

"Don't even think it. Move straight ahead," said the
Cracker. "Keep moving. Yeah... That'll do."

Cade stopped when his knees bumped the front fangs.

"Look at him, Gran. It's the big guy off the plane."

"The name's Kincade. Who the hell's Gran?" He skated
his eyes left, toward a gap on the far side of the column. That
should lead back to the main passage. Through there, then
turn right and he'd be running deeper into the mountain.
Dodge left around the column and he could cut back toward
the mouth of the cave. Or he could spin on his heel and bolt
back the way he'd come in. But the guy was fast as a snake;
remember how he'd moved on the dock?

"Gran? She's the ol' bag who sent me. *Allll* those years of
bedtime stories, readin' me my granddaddy's letter from Borneo, treasure and stuff, when all I ever wanted was Goldie and

the Three Bears like the other kids got. But hey, you gotta admit, Gran knew best. Just look at this sucker. He beats the bears hollow."

"He sure does." *Let's be agreeable here. Is he drunk? Crazy? And what's he got for a gun?*

"And m'granddad? Reckon you've already had the pleasure. That's him out there with a dart in the brain. Dang gooks and their blowpipes. Guess I was collecting some family payback, back there by the lake. Something told me I oughta blow him away. You figure that something was Granddad?"

"Might have been. You mean you shot somebody?" Damn, no, he shouldn't have asked. Too late now.

"Little brown guy with some *mighty* fine tattoos. But not polite. He had him this blowgun and he kept on lookin' at me funny. I figured the minute I turned my back it was pincushion time, so-o-o..."

Bang!

Cade jumped in his tracks as the gun barked. Rock shattered overhead; chunks of limestone rained down; echoes rumbled way back in the mountain.

"Bang, just like that."

A twenty-two, Cade figured. But how many rounds? "Nice shooting." And it was, fast and straight. The odds increased that his friend was not drunk. Which left crazy. "So I'm Kincade, and I didn't catch your name?" Hostage negotiators maintained that a gunman found it harder to kill somebody he'd connected to, than a stranger. *So let's get friendly here.* Pals forever. Moving slow and easy, Cade turned just his head.

Shoulders pillowed on his pack, pistol propped on his bent knees, the Cracker lounged in the shadows along the wall. Unshaven cheeks, mad-dog grin, eyes fever bright. He groped awkwardly with his free hand, to lift a metal rectangle hanging at his throat. "Amos Szabo, same as it says here on Grandad's dog tag."

"Pleased to meet you."

"Oh, yeah, pleased as punch. I can surely see that." His wolf smile wavered. "Hey…you bring any antibiotics?"

Ahhh. That explained his left arm. The sleeve had been torn entirely away, and though the light wasn't good over there where he sat, his limb seemed all wrong. Grotesquely swollen except for that odd, deep dent along the bicep. Or maybe that was a trick of the light—a shadow, not a hole?

"Sure," Cade lied easily. "I've got ointment and pills in my pack."

He didn't; he'd used the last of his meds on the boatman from Putussibau. The lacerations on his chained ankle had been infected. *Your doing, you crazy bastard.*

"And where might your pack be?"

"I hid it outside, the other side of the mountain." *No place you'll ever find by yourself,* was the implicit message. *But don't sell it too hard.* Let Szabo come to his own conclusion that he'd need Cade alive, if he wanted relief. "Got yourself a touch of jungle rot?"

"Huh! That Dayak bitch back in the States. She bit me, is why I wrung her scrawny neck. 'Fore I found out how high she'd bounce."

Shit. Szabo intended to kill him. He was talking to Cade the way you pour out your heart to a stranger on the plane. Knowing you'll never see him again, you can confess the damnedest things. Revel in the telling, then walk away clean.

"It keeps on *itchin'!*" His voice rose to an anguished snarl.

"Little penicillin should fix that."

"Yeah…that'd be nice." He shifted restlessly, but the gun's round eye didn't blink. "So…here we are, and who'da figured? Here I've been frettin' all along 'bout the blond bitch, Ashaway, but then it's you shows up. Or maybe…" His smirk faded, his eyes narrowed. "Ya'll working together?"

"With that she-devil? Not a chance."

"Hmm." Szabo tilted his head, trying to scratch his left

shoulder with his left ear. Gave it up and straightened. "So where is she, Gran? We 'specting more company?"

Stone crazy or delirious, it hardly mattered which while he still could aim a gun. Cade answered for Gran. "I left Ashaway back at the headwaters of the Kapuas. Wrecked her kayak. You won't be seeing her."

"Now ain't that a shame? I figured on asking the expert could I pull a few teeth off ol' Brutus, here, without ruining his value. Funny how all along I've been picturing this sucker, but I never really believed he'd be so…dang…*big!* Looks like I'm gonna have to rent me a cargo chopper and some coolies. Come back for the rest of him."

"That's a plan." Sooner or later Szabo would have to scratch with his gun hand, and when he did— *Spring straight back—twist around and dive,* Cade told himself. *Keep rolling till I'm out of the room.*

"Yeah…pull some teeth. Sell one in Singapore and I can rent the chopper. I was counting on Ashaway, when I heard you scufflin' around out there. Figured she'd make me a nice little pack mule. Oughta be able to carry half a dozen teeth or so, if I whip her along."

You're dead. Dog meat. Shuddering with rage, Cade waited till he could trust his voice, then said evenly, "Instead you've got me. I can carry more than that." *Till I get a chance to waste you.*

"Reckon you could, but looks like I'll have t'shoot you first." Szabo tipped his head again, craning to reach the wound without looking away. He failed, grimaced.

"Antibiotics would stop that itching. Save your arm. But shoot me and you'll never find my pack."

"Yeah?" Szabo showed his teeth. "Seems to me you've got the wrong end of the bear trap. Tell me where I can find that pack—or I'll shoot your knee."

"Then it looks like we've got a standoff," Cade allowed, swallowing hard.

"You think? By the time I blow the second kneecap to

Kingdom Come, you won't be precisely *standing. So*...nice
and easy. Turn around t'face me. Good... Now I'm asking one
last time, polite as I can. Where'd you hide that pack?"

Chapter 28

No, no, no—oh, no! Raine could hear the smirking anticipation in Szabo's voice; whatever Cade answered, he'd shoot him anyway. *If only I'd gotten here sooner!*

Fingers shaking, she rubbed the dart's point in her bag of gum—no time to measure the dose, and if the curare smothered him, so what? She jammed the missile up the butt of the pipe, rolled around another column on the far side of the passageway—nearly groaned aloud.

Still no view of the gunman! From this new angle, she could finally see Cade's back. Infinitely precious, horrifyingly vulnerable, his big body blocked whatever lay beyond.

"Not gonna tell me?" Szabo chortled. "Then where d'you want it first? Left knee or—"

No choice, then. Raine inhaled, aimed… *Pfft!*

The dart struck Cade in the right bicep. "*Ow!* What the *hell?*" He clawed at the pain, his knees already buckling.

Szabo yelled—erupted to his feet.

Bang! A bullet slapped the column by her head. Raine

whirled off down the passage, sprinting deeper into the cavern. She dodged around another column just as a bullet sang past to—smack stone somewhere ahead. Echoes cracked and rumbled. *Damn,* but he was fast!

"*Fucking gooks!*" he screamed after her. "Heathen fucking *headhunter!* You're *dead!* Nobody ever told you the cowboys beat the Injuns?"

Not this time they don't! Raine gummed another dart, rammed it into place. Dropped to a crouch with her hips pressed to the column. She could hear him shuffling deeper into the darkness, mumbling curses. *Come on, come on, bring it on!* He'd be looking for her high; she'd attack low. She drew a slow breath, put the pipe to her lips—pivoted gracefully on one bent leg around the column, her other leg stretched sideways to support her.

"*Hey!*" His gun dipped as her pipe rose…centered on his looming silhouette…

Flinching in every atom of her body, she held her ground. Puffed—

Blam! Fire kissed the inside of her arm—she fell on her butt—scrambled backward, then rolled for cover. Sparks flew as another bullet hit by her heel. *Shit, shit, shit, how did I miss?*

"*Fuck!* You hit my Granddaddy's dog tag! You think you can kill me? Not with luck like that!" he yelled after her. "Angels are on *my* side, you tattooed murdering moron—*my side!* So come on out with your hands up!"

Leaning against the column, she tipped back her head and laughed half-hysterically. *He thinks I'm a Punan!* His eyes hadn't adapted to the dark yet. He was shooting at shadows.

She groped for her blowgun, gummed another dart. He'd gone utterly silent; what was he doing out there? And Cade—oh, God, what was she thinking? She had to get to Cade!

Not with Szabo standing between them. *Then I won't miss again.*

She shoved—frowned. The dart wasn't sliding easily up

the pipe; it rebounded softly, compressed air pushing back. *What?* Raine slid her fingers up the pipe—her heart stood still in her breast. *Oh, nooo!* Two-thirds of the way up its length, the metal tube was smashed flat. His last bullet must have struck it.

Grimly she set the pipe aside, drew the knife from her ankle sheath. She'd have to get close. Couldn't risk a throw, because if she missed and the blade sailed off into the black? She'd never find it. So up close and *very* personal. She sidled around the backsidc of thc column, eyes so wide she feared he'd see their whites… *Where the hell are you?*

And Cade, if he regained consciousness, crawled out into Szabo's path?

Get him, get him, end this! She crept closer to the passage-way, then startled at a distant sound. Coming from the far front of the cavern! *Oh, Cade, if it's you, be still! Let me handle this!*

The sound came again—a rock rolling, rattling other loose rocks. *Szabo's at the hole!* She took to her heels, flying through the dark, knife tipped up and ready.

She staggered to a halt at the edge of thc outer cavern. Light flickered. There he was, up at the hole, shoving his pack though the gap! Szabo swung around—shc ducked aside—

Blam! Rock chips flew, stinging her face.

"And don't think you beat me!" he yelled. "I'll be back!"

Daylight flickered again as he squirmed through the hole. What a shot if she'd only had her blowgun! Raine stood, panting and frustrated. Her right hand smoothed absently up her left arm, till she found warm wetness—then pain to make her wince. Seemed to be just a graze, but when had he hit her?

Deal with that later, she told herself. First there was Cade.

He lay where he'd fallen, facedown. "Oh, *Cade!*" She yanked the dart out of his arm and threw it away. Hauled his dead weight over, lay her cheek to his mouth, felt no breath. "*Oh,* love…" She ripped his shirt open, smoothed her palms down his sweaty, sculpted torso. "*Breathe,* sweetie!"

Under her hands, his rib cage jerked, spasming the tiniest bit. "Yes! Oh, *yes!*"

Curare paralyzes the voluntary muscles. Give the appropriate dose and the target faints for lack of air, then revives. For all she knew, she'd given him enough to drop a five-hundred-pound boar. There'd been no time to calculate or measure. Raine cupped his chin and started breathing for him, murmuring wordless pleas between breaths, stopping every three to compress his chest. *Come on, come on, we can do this! Don't leave me! Breathe, dammit, Kincade, don't you dare give up on me! Breathe!*

Breathe!

Breathe!

The cave closed down, the darkness closed in, or maybe *she* was fainting? How long could she suck air for two? If she couldn't keep this up and he couldn't breathe without her and Szabo was coming back… Her tears dripped, she sat back on her heels, swearing and gasping, "*Dammit,* you lazy bum, if you'd *just*—" She stooped to kiss her life into him again.

His mouth curved beneath her lips.

"*Oh!* How long have you—"

Cade wasn't wasting his wind on speech. His eyes gleamed faintly in the twilight. Sobbing and laughing, she kissed his nose, his brow, his lean, bristly cheeks. "Can you breathe without me?"

No answer, but a faint labored exhalation puffed against her ear. "I'm going to keep pressing your chest to help you, okay? We'll do it together."

She kept on helping, praising each breath as Cade made it, stooping to feed him more air, to kiss him and coax the effort out of him. Suddenly his hand jerked across the dirt to touch her knee. "*Yes!*"

Oh, he'd make it now. She hadn't killed him! Weeping with relief, she lay down beside him and stroked him all over. "You're going to live!" She felt as if she'd made him herself—

birthed him or carved him, like Michelangelo dragging his David out of the stone. "You really are going to live!"

At least he would till Szabo returned.

Stretched on the cold hard ground, wrapped in each other's arms, Raine told Cade about her skirmish with Szabo. "He didn't realize he'd smashed my blowpipe, so I guess when that last dart hit him, he lost his nerve and ran."

"Took a penicillin break," suggested Cade. He told her about Szabo's infected arm, a memento from Lia. "Bet he's out there, tearing the landscape apart, hunting for my pack. And he just may find it. I hid it down near the pool. When he realizes I was lying, that there's no antibiotics, he'll *really* be ready to shoot me."

"Except he thinks you're dead," Raine pointed out, smoothing her hand up to his beating heart. She'd brought her own pack into the cave; hidden it when she heard the men talking. "But I used the last of my antibiotics on White Dog's people."

"White Dog?"

"A friend of mine. The Punan who took the tooth, the watch and the notebook from the pack on the body out there—Szabo-the-paratrooper's pack. At least that's my best guess of how things happened. I think he found this cave while exploring the mountain early this summer. He traded the stuff to Ah San and so on, till here we are."

"Here we are," Cade agreed wryly. "Wonder how long we have before Szabo starts Round Two?"

"I'm betting we've got till tonight. He's afraid of the Punans' poison darts, and so he ought to be. But once the sun goes down and this cave goes pitch-black? Then it's totally his advantage. Remember what my guide Dibit said, back at the Kapuas? Szabo's got some kind of night-vision gear. He walked right up to the Dayaks and shot Baitman. "So tonight, I imagine he's coming back for me."

"Can't have you." Cade's arm tightened fiercely around her waist.

That's easy to say, but how do we stop him? Effectively blind, no long-range weapons. *And you, love, after that over-dose?* Cade moved as if he'd been injected all over with Novocain, clumsy and slow; who knew how long that would last? They lay, staring grimly at the cave ceiling, a half shade lighter than black in the faint glow reflecting from the distant hole. "Maybe he won't come back," she said without conviction.

"He will. He's figuring on taking some of the teeth. And the creep's persistent, I'll give him that."

"The teeth." She swung her head on Cade's shoulder to stare at him. "Szabo found the *T. rex?* You've seen it?"

Cade laughed softly. "Now *that's* what I call a tight focus. Turn around."

"No!" She'd had a vague impression of a massive boulder at her back, while she worked on Cade. Almost dreading to look, Raine rolled in the circle of his arms. Stared up at a dark forest of intermeshing fangs, the overhanging snout— "Oh...my...*God.* Would you *look* at you, sweetheart!"

Her body shuddered, a near-orgasmic convulsion of delight. She swung back to demand, "Are her head bones made of fire opal, as well as the teeth?" Without a direct source of light, there was no way to tell. The skull was a merciless shadow, lunging brutally out of the dark.

"She?"

"Well, come on, Kincade, even in this light I can tell she's the *robust* form of *T. rex,* not the *gracile!* Female dinosaurs are generally larger and heftier than males." She scrambled to her feet. "You had a flashlight, didn't you?"

She found it where it had rolled beneath the sledge when Cade dropped it, but its bulb was smashed. "Umm. Well, no problem. Stay here and I'll go get mine."

Raine returned with her pack, her delight somewhat tempered. In the outer cavern, the light was turning pink, up in the westward-facing hole. How long after sunset would Szabo wait to attack?

Later, she told herself firmly. Fishing out her flashlight, she aimed it, warning, "Watch your eyes," as she touched the button. *"Ohhhhhhh!"*

Her knees gave out; she sat in a boneless heap. *"Oh. My. GOD!* Oh, *my!* Oh, *Cade!* Oh, you gorgeous *thing,* you!" She crawled across to the dino. Tears streaming over a double-wide smile, she played her light over bones made of shimmering fire.

Too shaken to stand, she crawled around the beast, worshipping it on her hands and knees from every angle, crooning to it softly. "Aren't you just *beautiful?* The only one in the whole wide *world!* Fifty feet at least, with a head this size, oh, you've *got* to go to a museum! *Everybody's* got to see you! Can you believe it, Cade, *sixty-five million years old,* and yet…here she *is!"*

Raine brushed her wet lashes, shook her head in amazement. "And you know, I think the rest of her may have survived, too, or at least most of her. I stumbled on the cliff they dug her out of, the far side of the pond, on my way to the cave. I think most of her bones are still buried, protected from the rain. If half a dozen feet of neck vertebrae have weathered away, well, when they mount her Ash and my father can—" She stopped, her smile fading.

"If I've got a prior claim," Cade said dryly, "then Szabo's got even a better one. But if we don't figure a way out of this trap, then the question of ownership may be moot."

"You're right." Raine tore herself away and came back to sit beside Cade. "Time to make a plan."

Making a plan that will save or forfeit your life isn't easy at the best of times. But when the planners are two opinionated, strong-willed people, each more accustomed to leading than following… And when each is determined to take care of the other, well, agreement isn't exactly a given.

"Look, hiding's the only sensible alternative," Cade argued. "Szabo's got a gun and night vision. We've got two knives, a failing flashlight—"

They'd turned it off as soon as its light dimmed; there was no telling when the batteries would be drained entirely—and it took a different size than those in Cade's broken light. Besides, using a flash would only give Szabo a target to shoot for.

"And I've got one-and-a-half useful hands, which makes punching him out somewhat iffy, and my knife work not much better." Cade had hurt his right hand in a fall on entering the cave. Raine was fairly certain his thumb was dislocated, and that the spasming muscles had locked to keep it out of joint. Later, maybe she could relax him with morphine and reduce it, but for now, she didn't dare try. He'd have to muddle through.

"I'm trained in hand-to-hand combat," she reminded him crisply. "If it comes to that—"

"It'll come to that over my dead body! Szabo's been a soldier of some sort, you can see that at a glance, and I'd bet Special Forces. He's snake-mean, crazy with pain, and even injured, he's too big and too quick for you."

"Don't be so sure of that!"

"Don't make me knock you on the head and drag you out of harm's way, because I will!"

She burst out laughing. That was precisely what she'd been considering, with him! "Look, if we start fighting between us, we'll solve Szabo's problem for him. We've *got* to agree, and we've got, what, an hour till dark?"

"If I was him, I'd wait till after midnight. Let my quarry decide I wasn't coming, so he'd lose his edge, maybe even fall asleep. That means—*right now*—we should go as deep into the mountain as we dare. Find a hiding place, and wait him out. Maybe it's not heroic, but it's damn-sure prudent. And it puts time on our side. The guy's arm is going septic. Another day and he'll be out of his mind with fever, if he's not dead from blood poisoning. Tomorrow, when we've got daylight to see, we can creep out, handle him however we have to."

"It's smart, it would work, I don't deny it. *But*—" Raine shifted warily out of head-knocking reach. "You said Szabo wanted to take some teeth? If we stay out of his way, then that's just what he'll do. He's got to know time is running out—that his one chance to live is to get back to the clinic in Putussibau ASAP.

"So he'll grab and smash—take as many teeth as he can carry. And he'll wreck her! She's big, but she's relatively fragile. She's survived *millions of years,* Cade. No *way* will I let her be busted to bits in my lifetime!"

"Which could be a very short one."

"I'll risk it. You can go hide if you want to. Face it, you aren't really here for fossils, but for some sort of grudge against my family. So compared with that, maybe she doesn't mean that much to you.

"But me? I'm a bone hunter. I get my dino and I bring it back intact. I *have* to stay and fight."

"That's almost as gallant as it is stupid! And as for my *grudge*—"

"Cade, I want to know about it—every last thing about it. If Ashaway All owes you amends of some sort, I'll see you get them. But if we don't live till morning…" Raine pleaded.

"True." He blew out a harsh breath. "You're right. Okay, Tiger, what's your plan?"

"We take him out. Not in here where she might be damaged, but somewhere out in the corridor."

"How?"

"I…haven't got that far." She groped for her pack, unzipped a pocket, explored its contents by feel. "Let's see what we've got that might be useful. I still have some trade goods."

A hasty inventory showed that they had about five hundred feet of fifty-pound-test nylon fishing line, half a hundred fishhooks, Raine's circular casting net, a few handfuls of glass beads.

"If your fish line was heavier, we could set a snare. But this'll never hold him," Cade observed.

"Ye-es. But think of a clothesline, with a pulley running along it. We could string it up between stalagmites, hang things from it, pull them back and forth along it? The line is so thin, I doubt he'd see it, even with night-vision goggles."

"What do we have worth pulling?"

"Well, there's Carleton." When Raine went for her pack, she'd found the second paratrooper's skeleton.

Chapter 29

Raine woke with a wild start—then relaxed as Cade's arm around her shoulders squeezed reassurance. "Have I been asleep long?" she whispered.

"Maybe twenty minutes." He checked the dial of his luminescent watch, then tucked it out of sight again. "Half past midnight."

They'd completed their preparations, and now they sat waiting, just inside the tunnel that led back to the dino cave. "Maybe Szabo isn't coming." He'd collapsed into septic shock. Or he'd cut and run for civilization, or—

"Listen!"

Somewhere a rock creaked. Raine sucked in a breath as a pebble rattled, up near the hole. They'd placed dozens of small rocks along the larger stones up there, so Szabo couldn't sneak up on them unawares.

They'd debated unbalancing the first few boulders inside the entrance, so that they'd fall away when he stepped on them—send him tumbling all the way to the cavern floor.

But the fear that they might set off a larger rockslide had stopped them.

Another pebble clattered down. *"Showtime!"* Cade whispered.

Stealthily they rose. Raine had tied their guiding line to her belt. She turned and began pulling herself gently along the taut fishing line, coiling it up as she went. Gripping the back of her belt, Cade trailed blindly in her wake. Like Ariadne's thread through the labyrinth, this skein of nylon would lead them straight to the dino cave.

Szabo should be slower in following. She could picture him checking for ambushes before he wriggled warily through the hole. Scanning the front cavern as he descended. Bending over his grandfather's skeleton to make sure it hadn't been replaced by a live enemy, lying in wait.

She'd used night-vision goggles herself once, on an expedition to Africa. A field-worker had brought them along to enjoy nocturnal wildlife. The goggles came equipped with a built-in infrared light source for illuminating targets in total darkness. The IR beam would be pointed wherever Szabo turned his gaze. It worked precisely like a flashlight, lighting everything within its cone of illumination; leaving things beyond the cone in darkness. Like a flashlight, the range of the cone—of Szabo's vision—would be limited by the power of his goggle batteries.

Cade and she wouldn't see the IR beam, of course, since its rays were invisible without the goggles. But to Szabo, they'd stand out clear and helpless as a couple of jacklighted deer. *So it's simple. We make sure his beam never touches us,* she told herself, coiling faster.

The goggles had only one weakness of which she knew. To protect the user's eyes, they were made to shut down *instantly* if a bright light struck their lens. The wearer then had to reach up with his left hand, press a button to switch them back on.

For that moment he'd be not only blind, but distracted.

He'd have the use of only one hand. They meant to capitalize on that weakness.

But for now... *Is he coming?* They were moving along the passage in ghostly silence, as if they drifted through starless space. What if Szabo had scouted the front cavern faster than they'd expected...was even now standing behind them, taking aim, smirking as his finger tightened on his trigger?

Her elbow bumped stone. Here already? Groping left-handed, she found the massive limestone column that framed both entrances to the dinosaur's cave. Cade patted it, also.

The line led past it to the sledge. Arriving there, she crouched to cut the nylon, then tucked the coil into her back pocket. She sheathed her knife and turned on her heels—reached out. Cade knelt before her, ready to sprawl facedown on the ground. Szabo expected to see his dead body—and so he would.

Gripping Cade's shoulders, she leaned close. "Oh, be *careful.*"

Hard warm hands framed her face. He kissed her for answer—hot, deep and slow—as if they had all the time in the world.

I want more of those! she told any angels who might be listening while Cade arranged himself facedown, with their flashlight and half her blowpipe hidden beneath him.

Raine stroked the back of his head, then rose—patted the *T. rex's* snout both to orient herself and for luck. Groping her way to the smaller gap beyond the king column, she hovered at this entrance to the passageway. Goose bumps rose as she listened. If Szabo was closer than they'd calculated—

Don't think, act. Seize the day! She struck out from the gap, angling off to her right. Counted twelve paces to cross the passage—then swept her right arm through the dark. *Oh, God, if I missed it!*

But, no—her fingers brushed stone and she almost hugged the column she'd come to, on the far side of the passage. The left-hand side, as you walked deeper into the mountain.

This column was thick as a hundred-year-old oak. Raine circled it clockwise till her questing fingers found the smear of her lip gloss on its far inner side. Put her right knee to that mark and she could stand, knowing she'd be concealed from Szabo's view as he approached the dino cave—then exited it the same way she had.

Good so far. With her foot, she felt for her casting net. It lay on the ground where she'd left it, spread out and ready to throw.

And now— Raine found the line she'd tied to the column. She took up slack in the gossamer thread till she felt a distant resistance. Paused. *Okay, Carleton, ready for some payback?* His ghost should have no fondness for Szabo.

Water dripped and tinkled somewhere far off, then— A pebble rolled, not much louder than the blood striding through her ears. *There! Here he comes.*

Raine stood motionless, except for her trembling. Listening to a troll stalking closer and closer with murder in mind... *If he thinks to check Cade—feels he's warm!* She gulped, picturing the path she'd race to his rescue.

But if Szabo discovered that Cade was alive, he'd put a bullet through his brain before she could drop her line and turn.

Shouldn't have gambled. Should have done it Cade's way, gone and hidden... She was risking his life for a damn dinosaur? *What's wrong with me? I must be out of my—*

"Hey, Brutus!" Szabo's hoarse whisper came floating. "Where's your headhunter pal?"

He's in the dino cave! Standing over Cade. Too late for second thoughts now. Raine drew in a shaking breath, and lifted her pull string to waist height—reeled in a foot of line for a final test.

Some sixty feet farther down the passage, on her same side, the decoy glided a foot on his clothesline, then stopped again.

Her pull string crossed the corridor at a steep angle, till some thirty feet farther on, it reached a stalagmite on the right-hand side. This smoothly rounded spike served as a rough pulley. Turning counterclockwise around this column in a wide-mouthed U, the pulling line angled *back* across the corridor, leading deeper into the mountain, till it reached its attachment point. It was tied to Carleton's skull, which hung from its own "clothesline."

This clothesline was stretched tightly from the back of the passage, left, to the pulley stalagmite at near right.

Raine had only to rapidly reel in her pull line and Carleton would come flying along his clothesline, angling gradually from left to right as he approached.

"Come out, come out, wherever you are!" Szabo sang under his breath.

He must be circling the dino on its sledge in there. Making sure nobody hid in back of it, to creep up behind him, after he'd hunted on.

Trust a woman to make it too damn complicated, Cade fumed, lying with his cheek in the dust. *I should just grab the crazy bastard's ankle. Yank him down, pound him to mush.*

If he could see Szabo's ankle.

But he couldn't. Not ten feet away, the Cracker seemed to be circling the dino skull. Cade stole another peek.

And saw—nothing! A darkness to confound the eye. His optic nerve frantically served up expanding purple rings and swirls to fill the midnight void.

Shut your eyes, he reminded himself, as Szabo chuckled. *Maybe you can't see, but he sure can.*

Raine's plan was to scare him into shooting his gun. Shooting off his whole round of bullets. Then they'd jump him while he reloaded.

Might work, if we knew how many rounds his gun held, Cade thought acidly. It could be a seven-shot, a nine, or—oh, joy—a fourteen. Though he was to blame for their ignorance. If he'd focused on Szabo's pistol, instead of which way he intended to leap… If he hadn't been so busy imagining what a shattered kneecap would feel like…

"Ain't in here," muttered Szabo. "Maybe we should just leave the little dart man be?"

Only feet away, his boot scraped the dirt. Cade tensed his muscles. To hell with the plan! If he got the chance...

"Naa, you're right, Gran. Can't trust him to stay put. If he sneaks up on me while I'm busy pulling teeth..."

Another scuffling sound, but harder to locate, coming from almost overhead. What the—?

"God *damn,* it itches!" Szabo whimpered. "My arm, Gran, it's allover black streaks. That can't be good." He sighed mournfully. "Yeah... Yeah, I know... Can't quit now. Just get the damn teeth." His voice dropped half a vicious octave. "Then if you want the rest of it, you can come get it yourself, you greedy ol' bag!"

Get him. Here he comes.

"No, ma'am, I'm *sorry!* I didn't mean it!" His voice dipped to a spiteful whisper. "Not *much* I didn't."

Now! Cade told himself—

Just as Szabo's weight came grinding down on his right hand. "*Oops!* Sorry there, big guy," he chortled. "So much for leaving a beautiful corpse."

DON'T yell, don't yell, do not yell! Blackness layered upon blackness layered on throbbing red. If he couldn't yell, he'd faint! *Get the hell offa me!*

The load lifted as Szabo stepped on over him, padding on toward the rear exit.

Eyes streaming, nose running, Cade shuddered with the raw pain. *Broke something for sure.*

Forget the hand. Remember what comes next. Pain bloomed in his brain, crowding out all thoughts but one: Raine, out there alone in the corridor.

Here he came, out from the dino cave, soft-footed as a ferret! The merest shuffle and slide along stone.

Wait for it, Raine warned herself. *Wait till he hits his mark.* When Szabo reached the glass beads they'd strewn across his path, he'd be positioned *precisely* where she wanted him, in the middle of the passageway, on the opposite side of the pillar behind which she lurked.

Meanwhile, Cade should have risen from the dead. He'd be standing barely out of sight in the dino cave, holding their flashlight and half her blowpipe for a club. Waiting for his cue.

Crunch...creak...pop!

"What the fuck?" whispered Szabo as his boots ground the glass beads into the stone.

NOW! Raine yanked on her pull line.

Far down the corridor, Carleton should be lunging out from the left-hand shadows. A white, grinning skull that topped a broad-shouldered body, made by half her blowpipe run through a Save the Whales T-shirt.

When Raine stopped hauling, he'd halt and sway and grin—about ten feet closer to the gunman.

"*What* the—"

Blam!

Raine tugged again—set the skull to flying and swaying nearer, attacking with a toothy smile.

Blam!

Quick, oh, quick, oh—

"God, what the hell *are* you? *Getthefuckawayfromme*—"

Blam!

Tinkle! Plop!

The pull line broke free, lashing Raine in the face as she yanked. *Jeez,* he'd shattered the skull in only three shots!

"Wh-wh-what the hell was *that?*" whinnied Szabo.

He still had four bullets left—maybe more—but there was nothing for it. Stick to the plan. She gave a bat squeak, Cade's signal, a sound hard to trace.

"*Shit!* What the—!"

Szabo should be whirling her direction, staring wildly, and now—

Thunk! That would be Cade, reaching out from the dino cave to drop a rock, draw Szabo's gaze on around.

Squint. Count one and count two and then—

"Yahh!" Szabo screamed as Cade's flashlight snapped on. The beam nailed him square in the eyes—it switched off the goggles strapped to his face. Now they could see and he was the blind man!

Raine stooped, grabbed her net and rose—as Cade charged down his beam of light.

Blam!

Five!

Blam!

Six! Oh, God, Szabo hadn't waited to turn on his goggles—he was shooting blind!

Blam—tinkle—crack! The flashlight exploded—the black slammed down—Cade yelped in pain.

Szabo burst into a mad cackling—hyena in the dark. "Yeah, and who's sorry now?"

Oh, God, where is he? A deliberate shuffling, drawing away from her. Of course, he'd switched his goggles back on; he was going after Cade! With—what?—at least one bullet left? *No, no, no—oh, no, you can't!* Careful of all the hooks she'd added— Raine raised the circular net.

"UNH!" The sickening sound of metal slamming into flesh and bone! The sound of a body falling.

Oh, Cade! Raine edged around her column, head craning back and forth.

"The big guy!" Szabo cried. "You were fuckin' darted! *Dead!* I saw you!"

"Hide," Cade mumbled blearily.

He was talking to *her!* Raine homed in on the sound, turning slightly to her right. There? *Oh, God, let it be there!*

"Too late for hidin', pal. Yeah, *yeah,* Gran, I'm doing it. No problem, yeah, right this minute. He's—"

Raine cast her net through the dark.

"What the—*yieeeeeeoo-o-ow!"*

"Hooks, that's what!" She'd tied fifty fishhooks into her

net, so that they dangled on short lengths of fish line below it. "Try dancing with that, you troll!"

Blam!

His last bullet slammed the rock over her head—last bullet, if his gun was a seven-shot. Raine didn't care. Drawing her knife, she ducked low and slid in toward the squeaks and wails and stomping.

Whirling, squealing, Szabo bumped into her—she slashed at his leg. He shrieked—fell, kept right on rolling. She started grimly after him by sound—kicked something and paused.

Oh, could it be? She knelt, touched…his fallen goggles! *"Yes!"*

She brought them to her eyes—saw nothing. Broken, maybe, or— She tried the switch. Still nothing. Cracked when they fell? "Whatever." She lobbed them off into the dark. Heard the distant, soul-satisfying *crunch* and *tinkle* as they hit stone.

Not far away, Szabo sobbed and gibbered brokenly to himself, but in this sheltering dark, she'd nothing to fear.

Nothing but the loss of Cade. Oh, sweetheart, where are you? Raine took a tentative step—and glass beads crunched underfoot. Ahhh. She stood for a moment, visualizing the passageway, orienting herself. A half turn to her left?

Maybe. She knelt again, stretched full length, swept hands and feet out through the dark…touched nothing. "Cade?" she called softly.

No response.

If Szabo had cracked him in the skull with his pistol. Cracked bone. *Oh, please, no!* No way to fix that out here in a screaming wilderness. She crawled forward a foot, starfished her limbs again—grazed warm flesh. "Oh, *sweetie,* oh, love!" She felt her way up his limp body. Traced the dear shape of his skull, his hair wet and warm with blood. "Cade? Please don't leave me." She caressed his motionless face; sobbing, bent to kiss him.

His lips answered hers.

Chapter 30

They'd strung one last line, an escape line, in case all else failed.

Raine used it now. Supporting Cade with one arm around his waist, she steered them slowly and blindly along the thread. It led down the corridor, then swerved off deep into the mountain.

Trudging along, she could hardly keep her eyes open. They needed a rest. Someplace where she could examine Cade's wounds. Someplace where they wouldn't have to listen to Szabo's mad chuckling and whimpering.

They limped right past him in the dark and he never noticed. Too busy cursing his grandmother, cursing Raine, cursing the dino and Lia and Borneo and his grandfather and "these *hooks*—these *fucking hooks!*"

Deal with him in the morning, she told herself. She couldn't imagine he'd be able to find the *T. rex* in the dark, much less damage it. Right now, Cade was her sole concern.

At last their line turned a right angle around a stone, leading them into the alcove. She walked them to its far end, then stopped where the nylon was anchored to a stalagmite. "We're here. Can you—"

With dazed obedience, Cade sagged toward the floor. She staggered under his solid weight, then eased him on down. "There, love. Lie still and let me do the rest." She'd stowed her pack here earlier in the night. Now Raine found her candle lantern and her matches, positioned it so its light wouldn't reach beyond their hiding hole.

By its homely glow, she could see Cade's face at last. The gash just above his forehead, his blood-matted hair. Ruffling gently through it, she blew out a thankful sigh. If Szabo had hit him square in the temple... But he hadn't. *I can fix this.* She framed his face with her hands and murmured, "Look at me?"

His lids struggled open. His amber eyes glowed in the candlelight. Their pupils were wonderfully, perfectly symmetrical. "Jus' need a little rest," he muttered. "I'll be fine."

"You will be. You are!" She kissed him full on the lips... tasting her own tears. Tasting laughter to come.

Sometime later they woke in each other's arms. For a moment, half dreaming, Raine assumed that they'd been making love, must have drifted off afterward. She stretched blissfully— let out a yelp as every muscle complained—remembered it all.

She lit the pocket lantern and, when Cade's eyes still showed no signs of a concussion, she went ahead and injected him with morphine. Then set and taped his poor battered fingers.

Afterward they curled up again, sharing warmth under her rain poncho. Raine could have slept for a year, but the morphine had made Cade giddy. Talkative.

Might as well take advantage of his mood. Reaching for her necklace, she pulled the stone feather up from between her breasts, put it into his hands. "Tell me about this?"

"The feather. Do you know I'm the one who found it?"

She jolted with surprise. "No, I thought—" Oh, this wasn't going to be good! "Tell me?"

"Well...'bout twenty-two years ago, your uncle opened a

dig site on the next ranch over from my grandfather's—the StarO Ranch in eastern Montana."

Cade lived on the StarO with Matthew Oates, his mother's father. They were all the family each other had in the world. Cade's young parents had died in a car wreck when he was eight, and his grandfather had gladly taken him in.

They ran their modest outfit with the help of a couple of hired hands. Although the work was unending, still it was filled with satisfaction and freedom. To be a cattle rancher under the wide Montana sky was the only life Matthew had ever known or wanted. The only life Cade could imagine at age fourteen. Someday the ranch would be his.

But though Cade was a rancher through and through, he'd still found himself fascinated when Joe Ashaway and his crew began to turn up fossils on the land next to the StarO. He'd ride over when he could, to see what they'd dug up, and to hear tales of the awesome monsters that had been discovered in other parts of the West. "Like a lot of boys, I'd been crazy about dinosaurs when I was a kid. So when your uncle came along, I could see myself being the hero who found some new, amazing critter. He made me welcome around his dig all that summer. I took to bringing him fossils I'd found, trilobites and such, asking him what they were."

Then one day, out on his own land, repairing a fence line, Cade had noticed an outcrop of sandstone similar to the formation Joe Ashaway was excavating. He'd explored the ledge, turned over a fractured layer of rock, and below it... He rubbed the stone against Raine's cheek in the dark. "I found this."

With further digging, he'd discovered the rest of the *Archaeopteryx.*

"Oh, Cade!" Raine murmured helplessly. *Archaeopteryx ashawayi* was the foundation to her family's fortune. Their fame and reputation were built upon it.

"Right," he said bitterly. "I showed it first to my granddad, then we persuaded your uncle to come have a look. He acted pretty cool when he saw it. Said it was nothing too special, but it was a nice, complete specimen."

"He said *that?*" Raine cried. Joe Ashaway had always been the ruthless one, the driven one of the twins, but still—this was unforgivable!

"Yep. And he asked to buy it straight out, there in the ground. He wanted the fossil and he wanted the right to name it." He'd offered five thousand dollars.

Matthew had been staggered by the princely sum. All that money for an old rock with a feathered lizard in it?

It had crossed Cade's mind that if the fossil was worth that much, maybe it could be worth more? But his grandfather was eager to sell. Five thousand would just about bring them up to date on the mortgage they'd taken out on the ranch, a few years back. It had been a bad season, with cattle prices falling and a drought that had cut their production in half.

And Cade liked and trusted Joe Ashaway. So they'd accepted his check for the fossil, signed a bill of sale.

Three months later they'd learned that the *Archaeopteryx ashawayi* had been resold to a museum in Pittsburgh. For five hundred…thousand…dollars!

"The absolute worst of it," Cade mused huskily, "was that Matt felt he'd let *me* down. It wrecked his pride. Here he'd thought he'd cut a fine deal, to take care of me and the ranch—and he'd been rooked. Cheated like a child or an old fool."

Meanwhile the fall cattle sale had been the poorest one in a decade. Matt had already used up the five thousand, paying off their debts. Now he realized that if he'd charged Ashaway what the fossil was really worth, they wouldn't be teetering on the brink of bankruptcy. "It preyed on Matt's pride…and his sense of justice. On his trust in his fellow man. His sense of his own competence in the world."

He'd gone to town and hired a lawyer, who assured him that indeed he'd been cheated. That with a lawsuit—even the threat of a suit—the fossil could surely be recovered.

But Matt had no way to pay the lawyer's stiff retainer fee.

So he'd gone to the bank, signed another note—with the ranch as collateral.

"Oh, *no,* Cade!" Raine buried her face in the hollow of his shoulders as she wrapped her arms tight around him. "Oh, I'm *so* sorry!"

"Yeah, it was sorry all the way around." Cade rested his chin on her hair. "The lawyer lost the suit, of course. We'd signed a sales contract, fair and square. He claimed with some more money, he could appeal. That we still had a chance to win. But the bank was yelling for its payments already—we were falling behind. Matt realized he'd be just shoveling money down the rat hole if he took out another loan.

"So instead, he went to see your uncle. Found him out on some dig."

Cade never knew quite what happened, what was said, but clearly Joe Ashaway offered no relief. Must have showed some fatal disrespect. "Matt was sixty-five. Thirty years older than your uncle. But he was a big man, tough as rawhide from working outdoors all his life. I guess he lost his temper."

He'd beaten Joe Ashaway within an inch of his life. Maybe would have killed him, if Raine's father and other members of the crew hadn't pulled him off and subdued him. "You don't remember any of this?"

Raine shook her head. "I was only—what—seven? I remember visiting my uncle in the hospital. His jaw was wired shut, and he couldn't walk, but I don't think anybody told me what put him there."

"Yeah. Well, your uncle went to hospital for two months. And my granddad went to prison, for aggravated assault, for four years."

All that terrible winter and the following spring, Cade had stayed on the StarO, struggling to hold things together. But with no money to pay the hands to help him, and the school district chasing him for truancy, and the bank for mortgage payments... "Finally the bank foreclosed. The sheriff came to get me, take me to a foster home, and he cornered me in the barn." Like his grandfather, Cade had fought for his freedom—for the sheer outrageous injustice of it all.

He'd ended up in a juvenile lockup. When his grandfather died in his cell of a heart attack... "Or a broken heart?" Cade hadn't been there for Matthew. Hadn't seen him in over a year. "I swore to myself that the Ashaways would pay. That they'd taken everything that mattered to me—*every last thing*—and so I'd do the same to them."

"Oh, I'm *sorry!*" Raine's tears trickled, wetting his skin. "I'm *so* sorry. There's no amends I could make for this!"

"Yeah, not in one lifetime. But come here anyway." Cade's arm tightened around her waist and he rolled, until she lay on top of him.

She wriggled up his body till they fit perfectly together; her face in the warm hollow of his throat, her forearm pillowing his neck, her legs clasped between his. They shuddered at the contact, then lay still. Heart to heart, breathing as one.

"That's what I've been starting to realize," Cade said after a while. He stroked her hair. "No matter how you want to, no matter how you try, you *can't* go back and make it right. It's over. Matt's dead. Your uncle's dead.

"And taking my revenge out on the rest of the Ashaway clan doesn't seem to feel quite as good as I imagined it would, when I was fourteen. Hasn't seemed such a great idea, since the day I met you."

"But still..." Raine protested. *So* much pain—pain dealt out to a man to whom she wished only happiness. And she *had* benefited from her uncle's sleazy deal, even if she hadn't known.

"It wasn't yours to fix," Cade said as she kissed his jaw. "And even if it had been, you've thrown something on the balance tonight. Twice today, in fact. I owe you my knees and I owe you my life. Szabo would have shot me for sure, there at the end, if you hadn't netted him.

"So if one Ashaway stole my life away? Looks like another gave it back."

"But you saved my life, too!"

"Yeah... Who owes who what is getting kind of hard to figure." Raine couldn't see his smile in the dark, but she could hear it. "So...what d'you think? Maybe we oughta just kiss and make up?"

"Or...make out?" She squirmed a few inches higher. Cupped his face with her palms. Her hips rocked a slow, joyful suggestion.

"Both," he agreed instantly.

Though the dark hadn't lifted in their lover's nest, somehow Raine knew it was morning. Cade slept on, his chest rising peacefully and steadily under her palm. She smiled to herself. *Wish we could stay here a week, just send out for pizza.*

At the first thought of food, her stomach grumbled. Other practicalities came to mind. Like what to do about Szabo?

If she was going to drag him back to civilization, hand him over to the authorities, she'd need to bring him back alive. He needed antibiotics and he needed them badly. *Bees,* she reminded herself. Cade had told her about finding the cave by watching the bees. She'd have to locate their hive, stupefy them with smoke, steal some honey. You could treat even gunshot wounds with raw honey; it was a superb antimicrobial.

Tie him up, stick him so full of morphine he doesn't feel a thing, then deal with the hooks, she told herself. *Then pack him full of honey.* That should work.

But to treat her troll, first she had to catch him. Slowly she untangled herself from Cade and slid away. He seemed to have suffered no lasting harm from that knock on the head—at least his lovemaking certainly hadn't suffered for it! Raine paused, smiling dreamily—then recalled her purpose and moved on. If she was lucky, she could deal with Szabo, then slip back for some more bedroll snuggling, before Cade woke to the day.

Once Raine turned the corner out of the alcove, she found the faintest rays of light reached even back here, reflecting from the distant hole. She stood motionless, letting her eyes adapt while she listened—heard nothing. Maybe Szabo was sleeping, too?

Two hours later, Raine dropped by the dino cave. She walked over to the *T. rex* and sat before it, crosslegged. Leaned back on her hands and stared thoughtfully upward for a while.

"Szabo's gone," she reported at last. "I don't know how he did it, but somehow he found his way out of here." She'd discovered his bulletless gun dropped to the ground, not far from where she'd netted him. Found her net, quite a bit worse for wear, in the outer cavern near the hole.

Raine sighed. "Well, it's probably for the best." Three would have certainly been a crowd, heading back.

And she didn't care that much about dragging Szabo back to civilization's version of justice. In the end, there were all kinds of ways to work out one's fate. "What goes around, comes around."

The skull before her seemed to crackle with the faintest jeweled fire for a second, some trick of the light that, still, seemed eerily like agreement.

"And you, you angel." Bad…good…maybe reflecting the spirit of whoever found it? "Can you be patient for one more wet season? We'll come back for you early next year, with a proper team to free you from your stone…escort you off to someplace where the whole world can come admire you. Learn that dragons once walked this Earth."

Can I be patient? Fire sparkled along the fangs like laughter. *After sixty-five million years, what do you think?*

Raine smiled and rose. "I think it's time I went and woke up my guy."

Szabo damn sure set a record, getting back to the lake. Things were chasing him—ghosts or gooks, or God knew what—speeding him on his way. He kept finding weird sticks in his path, curly with peeled bark, carved with strange notches. Once, a dart had nailed a tree trunk only inches above his head. Somebody trying to tell him something, like, *Get the hell out of our jungle!*

"Only too happy to oblige," he told the trees.

He was making good time, staggering along in magic boots. Couldn't see his feet; they seemed to be miles below him, but they kept trucking along, day and night and now day again. And he was careful not to look at his arm. No news was good news.

"But I'm gonna beat that bitch in the end," he told a big red no-tail monkey that hung from one branch, peering down at him. "Beat her back to Pontianak. Get me some medicine, sleep straight on through for a couple of days, then wake up in time to whack her, before she catches her plane. Her and her fuckin' boyfriend, who won't stay dead. But this next time, oh, yeah. Deader 'n doornails."

Then next year, when he was feeling better, he'd come back with a chopper and crew, whip that old lizard out of there. Make a jillion dollars. "You hear that, Gran? Maybe I'll even share it with you."

Or maybe he wouldn't. She sure wasn't helping *him* out, when he needed it most.

But all the same he'd win in the end. The angels were on *his* side. And if he'd had any doubts, Szabo knew it for sure, when he reached the butterfly lake. Somebody had left him a kayak, and a paddle, just pulled up and waiting on the shore. *"Dang!"* Cutting straight across the lake would save him two days of walking around it by the cliffs.

"On the other hand…" he muttered, scratching his arm.

A dart smacked into the kayak by his knee.

"Shit! Now there's a tiebreaker!" He shoved the craft out into the shallows, scrambled in, paddled frantically. Looked back to see what the hell had been hunting him.

With evening drawing nigh the mist was rising. But for a

second there, Szabo could have sworn he saw a little man. Standing there at the edge of the bushes, blowgun propped on his shoulder, one hand resting on the head of a big white dog. And damned if he wasn't grinning like a crocodile.

"So long, *sucker!*" Szabo yelled, baring his teeth.

On he paddled, without another glance behind. He'd seen enough of the jungle to last him quite some time.

Behind and off to the right, a V-shaped ripple broke the dark water, pacing him through the lily pads.

Epilogue

Once the latest storm had rumbled on through, Raine and Cade shifted end for end on their sleep platform. Now they lay, peering lazily out their foot hole at White Dog's camp. Raindrops sifted down through the high green leafy canopy; pattered on the thatch overhead. Somewhere nearby, a woman sang what had to be a lullaby. Soft laughter drifted on the misty air.

"Really ought to move on today," Cade murmured, nuzzling the nape of Raine's neck. "Ngali should be back at the Kapuas by now, wondering what became of us."

"Mmm," Raine agreed drowsily. She lay spooned within his heated length, her cheek pillowed on the hard swell of his bicep. "Could leave this afternoon, if the sun comes out. Or maybe...tomorrow?"

After they'd sealed up the dinosaur cave, they'd slogged for three days through the increasingly sodden jungle. When they'd straggled into the Punans' camp, White Dog had studied his tired, muddy guests, then smiled to himself and set his men to building another sleep platform.

From the jokes the men had made, and the site they'd chosen for the construction—a stone's throw away from the main camp—Raine gathered they'd been given a honeymoon suite.

The past two days had certainly felt like a honeymoon. Nobody had intruded on their bowered bliss, though, whenever they'd crawled out of their cocoon, they'd been cheerfully welcomed into the tribe's easygoing circle.

A shaft of sunshine filtered down through the treetops, setting the colors of leaf and orchid ablaze. Gibbons hooted in the distance. "Green mansions," Raine murmured.

"Hmm?" Cade's fingers trailed the taut curves of her arm, her hip, her thigh, then wandered up again.

"Oh, just the name of an old book about the jungle." But this was more than any mansion. *It's a living cathedral,* she thought, as the sunlight intensified and the forest glowed like stained glass.

Shrieks of childish laughter rose as the children tumbled out of their family's platforms to seize the day. Their parents followed, pausing to stretch and yawn and survey their kingdom with sleepy smiles. Couples who'd passed the storm as Raine and Cade had done touched each other in farewell, then wandered off to hunt or gather.

White Dog's youngest baby staggered across the clearing, hanging on for dear life to the shaggy shoulders of his father's hunting dog. Teaching himself to walk, with the help of a patient friend.

"Glad I got a chance to see this," Cade murmured in her ear. "Guess it's been like this from the dawn of time, but how much longer can it last? Do you remember all those rafts of logs, we saw, floating down the Kapuas? Tropical hardwoods are in demand, the world over. People don't realize what they're destroying, when they buy a mahogany bureau or teak decks for their boat. Another ten years or so, and the bulldozer and chain-saw guys will make it up to here, and then…"

"Yeah…" Raine shivered agreement, then turned in the circle of his arms to rub her nose along his collarbone. "You know, I've been thinking."

"Uh-oh!" he teased as he brushed a lock of hair out of her eyes.

"About that—and about this." She lifted the stone feather that dangled between them. Yesterday, she'd removed it from her own necklace. She'd hung it on a leather cord with a few red beads to set it off, then draped it around his neck with a kiss. It was Cade's family totem, not hers, after all, and among the Punan, a hunter would be naked without some emblem of his prowess.

"I said, back at the cave, that there was no way I could make amends for all the harm the Ashaways did you and your grandfather."

"And I told you to forget it," he reminded her roughly. "We're even now. What's past is past."

That's what he thought, but forgiveness wasn't an effort of will. Raine wanted his feelings healed, too. His heart at peace. "No matter how you want to, you can't go back into the past and fix it," she mused, rubbing the ancient stone along his shoulder. *Can't erase the grief, or soothe the pain. Give you and your grandfather back your lost freedom. Your lost home.*

"But what you can do, sometimes, if you're very very lucky, is you can pay your debt forward, into the future. Pass it on to somebody else who needs it. Saving somebody else's home, now maybe that would bring the world back toward… some kind of balance? Harmony."

Cade laughed softly as he bent to kiss her. "So what've you got in mind, Ren-Bungan?"

The New York Times [Late Edition (East Coast)]. New York, NY

A world record price for a dinosaur fossil was hammered down today at Sotheby's Auction House, when a consortium of twenty-seven philanthropists and non-profit institutions bought the fire opal *T. rex* known as

Lia. A ferocious bidding war amongst private collectors and international institutions for the only known specimen of an opalized *Tyrannosaurus rex* ended with a staggering purchase price of fifty-seven million dollars.

"Lia would have been very proud, I think, to be remembered in this way," said microbiologist Ravi Singh, a friend to the dinosaur's late namesake.

"We all won today!" exulted auctioneer Tom Winslow, executive vice president of Sotheby's. "Lia's buyers plan to donate her to the Smithsonian Institution, where she'll be on permanent exhibit for all the world to see and admire. Then, after the consignors deduct their expenses, her sales price will go to the Indonesian branch of the World Wildlife Fund, to acquire an enormous tract of land in the Borneo highlands as a forever-wild biopreserve."

Discovered jointly by the commercial fossil-collecting firms of Ashaway All and SauroStar, the spectacular fifty-four foot carnivore, a female, is also the largest and most intact specimen of the thirty-nine *T. rexes* found to this date. "We hoped she'd go to a public institution," said collector O.A. Kincade. "She's a world wonder and as such, she belongs to every kid who ever dreamed about dinosaurs. We're delighted that they'll be able to come and visit her whenever they please."

Kincade's partner in this paleontological find of the century is Raine Ashaway of Ashaway All, a third-generation, family-owned, fossil supply house. Ms. Ashaway was not available for comment. She's currently leading an expedition to Ethiopia, in search of the first entire specimen of a Paralititan, the few bones of which, discovered so far, suggest that it will be the world's largest known...

* * * * *

Prologue

French countryside—Location: undisclosed
5:55 am

Sooty, the sunless morning sky. Rain beat upon a dented metal awning that scrolled over the study windows. A yard light mounted on a rusted flagpole sketched a haze of blurry gold across the grassless muddy courtyard.

The limestone facade of the Lazar compound offered a sheer three-story rise facing east. The windows were matte gray, no lights behind them. Raindrops pattered the tin air vents spotting the red-tile roof.

The day always began before dawn. Rachel could not remember a time when it had not. Hop from bed, meditate with Tai Chi, down a protein breakfast, and then run laps, or—if raining like today—go to the gym to lift weights. Routine kept her body hard, her mind sound and her vision focused. Vision—having nothing to do with eyesight and everything to do with the purpose of her life—to follow orders and be nothing less than the best. A machine. Christian Lazar's pretty machine.

Today, a sporting match of blades had been offered—in Christian's usual you-know-better-than-to-refuse tone. Refusal hadn't entered her mind. Rachel enjoyed the rain. The challenge and exhilaration of the weather had spurred on both opponents.

Now Rachel crouched in the center of the courtyard. Cold November rain beat down from the lightening morning sky. Her long black hair, secured tightly in a ponytail with a wrap of thin leather strips, sat heavily upon her right shoulder. Her Doc Martens were slick with mud, as were her black pants. The ultra-thin gabardine and Kevlar jacket she wore as protection against a swift and cocky blade repelled the rain in speedy rivulets.

Propping her elbows on her knees and bowing her head, Rachel closed her eyes. A shiver encompassed her body. She was not chilled, but unsettled.

In the shadows of the timber soffit Christian sat—no, he didn't sit—he had collapsed.

Could he be dead?

Water dribbled off Rachel's nose and in the curve of her upper lip. Splaying one hand over her knee, her fingertips shot out pearls of rain. Concern beat out a reluctant empathy. So difficult to show compassion, yet, the compulsion was there.

Snippets of last night's conversation with Christian eddied inside her skull. He'd quietly entered her small, spare bedroom. Rachel hadn't realized he had settled next to her on the ironwood bench until he'd remarked on the absence of koi in the pond outside her floor-to-ceiling window. The groundsman had removed the three giant fish for the winter.

Levity had softened Christian's tone. A rare occurrence. *Beware.*

After moments of silent reflection, the two of them sitting facing the window, staring at the still pond, he'd cleared his throat. Then, with a slow start, but gaining confidence, he'd actually asked what Rachel had wanted to be when she was a child.

The question had stunned her. But she had learned long ago to simply answer, never argue a query, no matter how conversational it sounded.

"I don't know," Rachel had answered. Had she ever been a child? He had taken so much from her. *You allowed it to be taken.* "Doesn't matter any more. I am...what I have become."

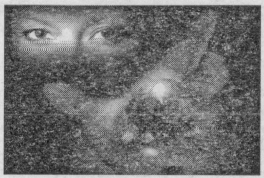

Silhouette®
BOMBSHELL™

COMING NEXT MONTH

#49 ONCE A THIEF by Michele Hauf
International cat burglar Rachel Blu had finally escaped the diabolical man who'd taught her all she knew about thieving. Now all she wanted was to live an honest life—but fate had other plans. When a priceless ruby was stolen, she was blamed. Locating the missing jewel would set things right. Could Rachel grab the gem before the police nabbed her?

#50 HOT PURSUIT by Kathryn Jensen
NASA engineer Kate Foster never thought her job would involve chasing terrorists—until armed intruders invaded her laboratory and hijacked a sophisticated satellite capable of being used as a deadly weapon. Now it was up to Kate, international intelligence experts and counterterrorist expert Daniel Rooker to find the satellite before the terrorists used the weapon for their own gain....

#51 COURTING DANGER by Carol Stephenson
Legal Weapons
When lawyer Kate Rochelle was summoned to Palm Beach to represent a family friend on trial for murder, she hadn't expected to flee gunfire, escape explosions or unearth thirty-year-old clues about her grandparents' mysterious deaths. But someone wanted the past to *stay* in the past—even if they had to kill Kate to keep it there.

#52 THE CONTESTANT by Stephanie Doyle
Talia Mooney's father was in serious danger from loan sharks, and the only way to earn the money fast was for Talia to win a reality-TV survival show. But when a killer was reported missing in the area, she realized that someone in the game wasn't who they claimed to be. And when a cameraman turned up dead, Talia found it was up to her to protect the group from one of their own....